Texas Lily

By Elizabeth Fackler from Tom Doherty Associates

Badlands
Backtrail
Billy the Kid: The Legend of El Chivato
Blood Kin
Texas Lily

Texas Lily

Elizabeth Fackler

A TOM DOHERTY ASSOCIATES BOOK / NEW YORK

TEXAS LILY

Copyright © 1997 by Elizabeth Fackler

A Forge Book
Published by Tom Doherty Associates, Inc.
175 Fifth Avenue
New York, NY 10010

Forge® is a registered trademark of Tom Doherty Associates, Inc.

Library of Congress Cataloging-in-Publication Data

Fackler, Elizabeth.
    Texas Lily / Elizabeth Fackler.—1st ed.
        p.   cm.
    "A Tom Doherty Associates book."
    ISBN 0-312-85912-0
    1. Lincoln County (N.M.)—History—Fiction.
2. Violence—New Mexico—Lincoln County—
History—19th century—Fiction. 3. Frontier and
pioneer life—New Mexico—Lincoln County—
Fiction. I. Title.
PS3556.A28T49   1997
813´.54—dc21   96-54233
                                          CIP

First Edition: July 1997

Printed in the United States of America

0 9 8 7 6 5 4 3 2 1

To the Spotted White Girls—
Jean, Terry, Nancy, and Joan—
because they listened.

.

As the honeycomb is sweet to thy taste, so
shall the knowledge of wisdom be unto thy soul.

Proverbs 24:13

August

1878

1

*A*t midnight, Lily walked through the dark to the graveyard, feeling slightly drunk. The sensation wasn't of lev-
ity but of a heaviness in her limbs as if the yard were flooded with
murky water that dragged at her skirts. An hour earlier the last
guest had finally left, officially ending her father's wake. Now he
was dead forever. Lily had put her mother to bed, then peeked
into her kid brother's room to see Theo sprawled on top of his
quilt, asleep, still fully dressed. She'd gone to the kitchen and
washed the dishes, the glasses and cups and plates and silverware
dirtied by the living to commemorate the dead.

Midway through the dishes, Lily had dried her hands and
poured herself a shot of brandy, drunk it down standing at the
table, then resumed her work. When the last dish had been put
away, she drank another shot, nestled the bottle deep in the
pantry, blew out the lamp, and left the house.

The summer night carried a chill, the stars like fragments of
shattered ice in the black sky. Above Sierra Blanca on the western horizon, the crescent moon reflected a thin ring outlining its
missing part. The mountains yawned to the south. To the east,
the valley opened onto the plains of the Panal. To the north, Deep

River was silent, though along its banks wind rustled in the leaves of the cottonwoods, dry with the advent of autumn. Near the grove of pecan trees planted by her father from seeds he'd brought from Texas in 1866, Lily leaned on the whitewashed rock wall around the graveyard and looked at the lost members of her family: her older sister, whom she couldn't remember though she had been held in her arms; her older brother, whose boots she often wore; two younger brothers who hadn't survived childhood; and now her father, murdered in his prime.

Lily hadn't been allowed to see him dead. The bullet that took his life had stolen his face. Alone, her mother had washed and dressed him for burial. Jack Crawford, the millhand, had lifted him into the coffin and nailed it shut. Now all Lily could see was a mound of fresh earth the length of her father's body. *Ashes to ashes,* she repeated from the prayers, *dust to dust.* Except Robert Cassidy had never before been ashes or dust. He had been strong arms, tall legs, a laughing, wet mouth within a soft, black beard, blue eyes below bushy brows, hair that smelled of wheat or corn depending on what he had been milling that day. On Sundays, it smelled of tonic from a bottle, a sweet smell she could capture on her fingers. A full foot taller than her, he had been so thick her hands had barely met when she hugged him, the smell of his shirt permeating her nose, soap if he was clean, sweat if he'd been working. The metal buckle of his gunbelt hard against her breasts.

She wondered where her mother had put his gun. In their trunk, most likely. The one they'd owned since their wedding and had carried here from Texas. Lily imagined the darkly oiled gunbelt wrapped in cloth to keep it away from the white satin of her mother's wedding dress, folded in tissue paper. White satin and blue-black steel. Old lace and lead bullets. Perfumed sachets and the power of loss. *Murder most foul,* her mind echoed from the eulogy, then added of its own will, *vengeance most just.*

Lily was fifteen years old. She knew she was as homely as a gunnysack, but that had never diminished the high opinion she held of herself. Though she felt humbled now, she didn't often suffer from humility. She could ride, rope, and shoot as well as most men, bake and sew nearly as well as her mother, read and cipher better than most grown-ups, and was also the confidante of Emmett Moss, the biggest rancher and wealthiest man in the territory. Uncle Emmett said she had more common sense than other folks, and she'd struggled all day to use that asset as she'd contemplated the formidable task of achieving vengeance for her father's murder. Knowing if she simply took a gun and shot the culprit she would be as guilty as he was, she searched for a strategy that wouldn't bring retribution on her or her family. In normal circumstances she could rely on the law, but the sheriff of Union County was controlled by the man she wanted to kill.

Lily turned away from the shadowed patch of ground within the low stone wall and walked across the moonlit yard to the barn. Inside she saddled her palomino. The mare had been a gift from Uncle Emmett, who wasn't her blood uncle but she was allowed to call him that because he and her father had been such close friends. Uncle Emmett was out of the territory now, in St. Louis on business, and probably didn't even know what had happened. When he returned, she'd petition him for justice. If he wouldn't give it, she'd find it herself with her father's gun and let retribution fall where it may.

She led the palomino to the mounting block and settled herself in the sidesaddle, then reined her horse up the canyon toward the mountains. The canyon was named Cassidy after her father, who had owned it. Now it belonged to her mother. Eventually Theo would inherit it along with the gristmill and the house their father had bought with sections of land on both sides of the river. As a girl, she was expected to inherit from her husband when someday she, too, was a widow.

The canyon narrowed as she ascended into the mountains. The moonlight was lost above its walls and she traveled a dark path, leaving the wide expanse of grass and entering the first growth of pine. Stubby piñons, twisted by the wind that even now cut with a biting chill as she rode without a jacket or hat. At the top of the canyon, she entered a thick forest of juniper and the beginnings of ponderosa. The path meandered through the trees, an old Indian trail between their stronghold in the mountains and the river below. Not too many years before she was born, this land had belonged solely to Apaches.

They rarely made trouble anymore. When they did, it was only the acts of renegades, warriors unhappy with life on the reservation. Even they left her family alone out of respect for her father. Shortly after arriving here, Robert Cassidy had tracked a band of raiders for the army. They found the Apache camp in the Guadalupe Mountains, but only women and children were there. The men had heard the army coming and escaped to the hills. Enraged, the soldiers began shooting the women until Robert Cassidy stood between the army's guns and the defenseless mothers shielding their children. He stopped the carnage, bellowing with disgust for his own kind. A week later, when he was home again, women from the reservation walked into his yard and knelt in the dust until he came out of the mill. They thanked him for his mercy, bestowing gifts of deerskins and cougar pelts and the promise of their men never to harm his family or steal his stock. That promise was kept. Of all the ranchers in the Deep River Valley, Robert Cassidy alone lived without fear of theft from Apaches. A white man had killed him.

Lily remembered all the people who had come to his funeral. More than she had imagined lived in the county, certainly more Americans than she'd ever seen in one place at one time. The Beckworths—the widower Hugh, his sons, Paul and Adam, and his daughter, Clarissa, and her husband, Ben Reed—had come all the way from their ranch near River's End. An itinerant journalist, Lash Cooper had come; she'd seen him taking notes, probably for the story he'd write for the Vegas *Optic*. Frank Hannigan and Butch Simon, both bachelors like Lash, had come from Siete Rios. So had Mr. and Mrs. Jedediah Stone with their daughter, Elise, and son, Jasper, whom Lily knew well, especially Jasper. Manny Tucker, Uncle Emmett's ramrod, and Shiloh Pook, his top hand, had come from Bosque Grande. Lily guessed they were bachelors, too, though she didn't really know. All those people had traveled thirty miles or more from their homes along the Panal, the big river east of Cassidy's Mill, the one Deep River emptied into.

The lawyer Edgar Homer and his wife had come from Union, the county seat twenty miles west of the mill. Mrs. Homer's sleek black frock made Lily intensely aware of her own plain brown dress. But as she looked around the assembly of people, she realized black was a luxury few could afford. Most of the women wearing black were old enough to have attended enough funerals to warrant the expense of a hot, confining garment that showed every speck of dust in a perpetually dusty land.

Sheriff Red Bond brought his native wife, who wore a mourning frock of shiny black satin, but that was no surprise. Mexican women always had black gowns. It was how they dressed up. Lily found it amusing, though she'd never told anyone except Uncle Emmett. She'd laughed at how the native women wore white peon outfits most days and then dressed up like the *conquistadores* for special occasions. Uncle Emmett had asked where she'd heard of *conquistadores,* and she'd told him about Lash Cooper's lecture on territorial history back when he'd been their teacher at the mill. Way back when she was a child. She'd been a child when she told Uncle Emmett the story. Watching people arrive for her father's funeral, she knew she was no longer a child.

Whit Cantrell had come, though he never did get off his horse. When Jasper Stone walked over and reached up to shake Whit's hand, Lily had admired how handsome Jasper looked with the sun falling on his face beneath the brim of his dark hat. She noticed that Rufus Bond, the sheriff's brother and a no-account troublemaker in Lily's opinion, was also watching Whit and Jasper. Seeing Rufus turn his head and spit tobacco juice in the dust at his feet, Lily quickly looked away and saw Woody Wheeler with the Becerra daughters, all of them somber enough to put her in mind of a funeral if she hadn't already been at one.

Now, hours later, Lily ambled her mare along the crest of the ridge, then stopped on a promontory overlooking the Panal Valley. *Panal* meant "honeycomb" in Spanish, so Lily guessed the Mexicans who named the place thought they'd discovered the Promised Land. *Panal* also meant "hornet's nest," however, and she considered that a more apt description since gunshot wounds were as common as bee stings in the county.

The foothills sloped down to the prairie, which stretched flat to the river, invisible in the starlit dark. Not a flash of a fire or feeble glow from a lantern broke the wilderness with light. Feeling melancholy in her solitude, Lily turned her horse higher into the mountains. She intended to follow the trail a little farther, to where it circled an outcrop of pale rocks embedded with mica that sparkled even on the darkest night. But she started crying, so she rode by the rocks without seeing them, and missed the loop that would have taken her home.

All day she'd kept her face as rigid as granite. She'd smiled and said thanks to the many expressions of sympathy and offers of help that would never be asked for. Now she cried in grief for what she'd lost and fear for what lay ahead. Her family's strength had been cut in half, and Lily didn't think her mother would ever recover. There had been a defeat in her eyes as she drifted to sleep, holding her daughter's hand as she'd held her husband's while he died. Lily's brother couldn't offer much help. When he was three, he'd been kicked in the head by a horse and hadn't regained full use of his right leg. It barely held his weight, so he'd never be able to do a man's work. The fate of the family was Lily's responsibility now, and she cried, too, partly in self-pity that such a burden had been dropped on her fifteen-year-old shoulders.

Neither aware of the path her horse chose nor of the moonless night around her, she wiped so many tears and blew her nose so many times her handkerchief was soaked. Sniffling, she forced her sobs back down her throat, then rode with silent tears falling across her cheeks. She wiped them with the sleeve of her dress until the sleeve, too, was wet. Then her breasts were wet, and her shoulders and back, and finally her skirt, and she realized it was raining. She'd been so lost in herself she hadn't noticed the clouds blowing in to steal the stars, hadn't noticed the gentle, almost mistlike drizzle falling from the sky. She stopped her horse and looked around, shivering with cold as she wondered where she was.

She'd never been so far from home alone. No trace of a trail anywhere. Only the tall pines soughing in the wind, the underbrush dark and wet. Without the moon or stars to guide her, she didn't know north from south, east from west. All the world was a misty forest, black silhouettes against darkness, silence beneath the wind and the dripping of rain.

"Where you going, Nugget?" she asked her mare.

The palomino nickered as if with reassurance, so Lily slackened the reins and let it continue, hoping the horse had a destination in mind. Its sure little hooves carried her through the forest, winding an imperceptible intention toward what turned out to be another horse. When Nugget whinnied, an answer echoed through the mist. Lily peered into the darkness, her eyes searching. She saw nothing, but her nose caught the faint scent of smoke. She kicked her horse to move. The trees were thinning, which meant the forest was being left behind and they were entering the prairie again. Her skirt snagged on the Spanish bayonet of a yucca, telling her she'd ridden so far south she was on the edge of the desert. A few more steps took them around a cliff and she saw a glow ahead. She puzzled over the deflected source of light until she realized it was a fire inside a cave.

The horses exchanged greetings again, so it was no use pretending she wasn't there, though she doubted the caliber of the man inside the cave. Who would camp so far from company if not someone wanting to hide? She touched the stock of the rifle in her scabbard, wondering if she should pull the gun and cock it before announcing herself, thinking she would merely ask the man for directions and that the weapon would ensure he gave only that. Before she could do it, though, she heard a footstep behind her and wheeled her horse around. Seeing Jasper Stone emerge from the forest, she laughed, pleased that of all the people she might have encountered, she had found him.

"Lily!" he whispered in astonishment, coming up on her right. "What're you doing here?"

"I'm lost," she admitted.

"I'll say," he agreed. "What're you doing riding alone at night?"

"I wanted to be alone," she said, "but I got more'n I bargained for."

He stepped closer and caught hold of her reins beneath her

horse's chin. "You ain't even wearing a coat," he said with fresh bafflement. "You best come in by the fire or you'll find your death."

She smiled. "Reckon that's what I was looking for. Not my own, a'course, but some kinda understanding of it."

He gave her a puzzled scrutiny, then ducked under her horse's head to come around on the left, reach up, take hold of her waist, and lift her to the ground. Looking down at her now, he said, "You're drenched clear through." Then suddenly he swept her off her feet and carried her toward the mouth of a cave.

He smelled of the piñon smoke of his fire mingled with sweat off his shirt and the faint fragrance of the oil on his gun. Inside he set her on her feet, then crouched by the fire and added sticks from a pile nearby. She huddled down to watch the light dance across his face, his strong, straight nose and cheeks still as smooth as a girl's, their skin translucent as if they glowed from a fire within. His finely etched lips lay in a noncommittal line as he concentrated on his task, his long brown lashes throwing shadows from the light. When he stood up and looked at her, his eyes were the deep blue of the bottomless lakes on the far side of the Panal.

"You best get them clothes off," he said, then reached to the floor to pick up his blanket. When he shook it out, dust flew around him like a rain of gold. "Wrap yourself in this and call me when you're done." He handed her the blanket, then walked out of the cave and left her alone.

As she unbuttoned her frock, she heard hoofbeats and guessed he was tethering her horse with his, which must be nearby, though she hadn't seen it. Shivering as much from cold as the excitement of being alone with him, she dropped her dress and peeled off her soaked petticoat and shimmy. She hesitated before unlacing her camisole, but finally took it off and dropped it on her other clothes. She kept her drawers on, then wrapped herself in his blanket and called into the dark, "I'm done."

He came back and looked at the pile of her clothes in the dust. She watched him pick them up, using his foot to push a dead tree limb close to the fire, then casually drape them over the twigs on the branch, as if it were nothing new to him to handle women's things. Looking around the vault of the cave, she saw a covered wooden barrel, a *ristra* of chiles suspended from a crag over a rolled quilt tucked neatly against the wall. The cave was twenty feet long, ten feet high at the deepest point, the ceiling slanting upward toward the mouth and stained with the soot of many fires above the flames.

Watching him hang his hat beside her clothes, she asked, "Whose cave is this?"

He moved to stand beneath the *ristra* and pick up the quilt. "Don't know who owns it, if anyone does," he said, unfurling the quilt to lay flat by the fire. "Whit lives here off and on."

She watched him drop to his knees and smooth the quilt over the dirt. "Why're you here?" she asked.

"Came with Whit," he said, "but reckon I wasn't good company so he rode into Union. You best sit here close to the fire and get yourself warm."

She held the blanket tight around her body as she settled cross-legged onto the quilt, then looked up at him kneeling above her. "I've never known you not to be good company, Jasper."

He stood up and moved away. Hunkering on his heels, he added more sticks to the flames. She admired the folded line of his long legs in their snug jeans, the silver rowels of his spurs barely beneath the curve of his butt. "How come you and Whit," she asked softly, "didn't stay for the wake?"

Jasper considered his answer, then said, "Reckon the eulogy turned our stomachs."

"Mine, too," she whispered.

He met her eyes. "Why'd your mother ask Henry Hart to deliver it?"

"She don't know he paid Wilson to kill Father," Lily said.

"How do *you* know he did?"

"I heard Hart and Elkins talking about it. I snuck into the grove just to grab a snitch of peace and they walked by and didn't see me. I heard 'em saying things about helping Wilson escape."

Jasper looked into the fire and muttered, "That ain't gonna happen."

Lily swallowed her tears, not wanting to cry in front of him. "I hope Mama never finds out. She'd feel awful knowing my father's burial was disgraced by that blackguard's speech."

"She'll likely learn the truth sooner or later," Jasper said.

"It'll break her heart," Lily said. "What's left of it, anyway."

"She looked pretty tore up," Jasper agreed. "But Wilson will hang. The army'll make sure there's no hitch."

"I want more'n that," she said. "I'm gonna see to it that Henry Hart pays, too."

"How?" he scoffed.

"I'm gonna tell Uncle Emmett when he gets back."

Jasper spit into the fire. "You may mean a lot to him, Lily, but he won't go against Hart even for you."

"My father was killed 'cause he beat Hart in the election for terr'torial representative!" she cried, fighting fresh tears. "A gov'ment kept in power by paid assassins ain't any kinda democracy. Uncle Emmett'll see the truth of that."

"Seeing it and opposing it," Jasper said, meeting her eyes again, "are two dif'rent things. 'Sides, no man gets as rich as Emmett Moss without being in cahoots with whatever gov'ment's in power. You know that as well as I do."

"I don't know any such thing!"

He studied her a moment, then sat down and pulled her close. "You're shaking all over," he murmured into her hair, "but I don't know if it's 'cause you're more cold or mad."

"I'm both," she answered, soaking in his warmth.

He chuckled, a sound she heard rumbling deep inside him. "Reckon I'm glad you came along," he said, his voice, too, reaching her ear from inside his chest. "I was kicking myself for not going into town with Whit but staying here like an ornery cuss who'd rather wallow in his misery than try'n get out of it."

"Why were you miserable?" she asked, her anger overshadowed by the peace she felt being held in his arms.

"Funerals always make me feel that way," he said.

She thought of how Jasper had only his sister, Elise, left, as she had only Theo, though both of them had been born to large families.

He said, "Sometimes I wonder how Whit can handle being alone in the world."

Knowing Whit was an orphan without any brothers or sisters, she thought about how desolate that would feel, then said, "Least he ain't got nobody to lose."

Jasper snorted. "Reckon that's why he's always on the look-out for a good time. Not like me, who savors his melancholy as if it was some kinda elixir for loneliness."

"Are you lonely, Jasper?" she whispered, raising her face to look up at him.

"I was 'fore you came," he said. Leaning close, he gently kissed her mouth.

Lily had never been kissed by a man who wasn't kin. When Jasper broke the kiss, she licked her lips to catch the sweetness of his lingering taste. He chuckled and kissed her again, this time penetrating her mouth with his tongue, softly wet yet hard as an arrow. With a moan he laid her down beneath him, kissing her even more deeply as he slid his hand inside the blanket and found her breast. His hand was cold, and her breast seemed to stand up straight beneath his touch. He unwrapped the blanket and looked at her body in the firelight, then bent his head and kissed her breast, so pert and proud beneath him, and she felt her loins contract with heat.

Meeting her eyes, he said, "You're prettier'n you look, Lily."

She laughed. "What's that mean?"

He let his gaze wander her body as if savoring its beauty as he'd said he savored melancholy as a cure for loneliness, then he wrapped her up in the blanket again. "I best take you home," he said.

"I don't want to go yet," she said.

He sat up. "You already lost something today you can't ever get back. Wouldn't be right for me to take something else just 'cause we're both feeling lonely."

"Even if I want to give it?" she asked.

He shook his head. "Whit's always told me it's like taking candy from a baby. I didn't believe him till now." He sighed, meeting her eyes where she still lay beneath him. "I've never ruined a good girl, Lily, and I ain't gonna start with one half out of her mind with grief."

He stood up, walked over to lift her clothes off the tree limb, then tossed them across the distance he'd imposed. She caught them and watched him settle his hat low above his eyes as he backed toward the mouth of the cave. "Get dressed while I fetch the horses," he said.

She watched him disappear in the darkness outside. One by one, she held her clothes close to the fire to dry the last damp before she put the garment on. She took her time, hoping he'd come back and stop her, but he didn't. When she was dressed, she took his blanket as she left the cave. Walking across to where he stood holding the reins of both horses, she offered him the blanket.

"Keep it," he said. "The rain's stopped now, but it's likely to start again before you get home."

She looked up at the sky congested with clouds and knew he was right. Taking hold of her waist, he lifted her into the sidesaddle, then turned away and swung onto his own horse as she wrapped herself in his blanket. It and all her clothes carried the fragrance of piñon smoke from his fire, and she followed him into the forest feeling as if she were wrapped in a cocoon of his love. For hours they rode without speaking, her mind a tumult of desire and hope. When they were almost in sight of the mill, he reined his horse to a stop beside hers.

"Reckon you can make it from here," he said, his gaze searching the forest lit now by the gray light before dawn. He met her eyes. "I won't tell nobody I saw you naked, so there's no need for you to mention it either." He hesitated, as if he wanted to say more.

When he didn't, Lily said, "I'm glad, though. I'd never been kissed before, and I'm glad it was you who kissed me first."

"It don't mean nothing, Lily," he said sharply. "Neither my kissing you nor that I saw you with no clothes on. Don't be thinking you've lost anything 'cause that happened."

"I liked it," she whispered.

He frowned. "Don't go making it into more'n it was. We was just lonely, is all. It ain't gonna happen again."

She nodded, fighting tears.

Seeing she was close to crying, Jasper reined his horse

around and galloped away from her. She watched until he disappeared in the shadowed canyon, then she wiped her eyes with his blanket and continued her solitary journey toward home. Snuggled in the smoky scent of his fire, she kept thinking about what had happened and what he had said, trying to arrange it in a way that set well.

Finally she decided he'd shown his honor in not taking advantage of her, and that as hurtful as his words had been, he was telling her he didn't love her so she wasn't to pine for something that could never be. That had shown his honor, too. He would keep their secret, as she must, harboring the memory of his admiration as a joy she would never know again.

2

The rooster sported red and yellow tail feathers, a crimson crown, and shiny black eyes staring at the ax in Lily's hand. She was angling the blade to catch sunlight on its face, not out of any need to blind the cock but from mere curiosity at how he watched the shimmering steel as if mesmerized by its charms.

The cock opened his mouth to crow but didn't. She took a few steps closer, holding the ax hidden in the folds of her skirts now, familiar with its weight and intimate with the precise strength needed to decapitate a chicken. First she had to catch him, though, and this cock was mean. He'd pecked her bare feet more than once when she was throwing grain for the birds. Stupid rooster. As if she'd threaten his flock, when it was hens she valued. Cocks were only good for increasing the brood, and only for that till a younger rooster caught Lily's eye and so was spared being supper while he pranced triumphant around the yard. This particular rooster's prancing days had been numbered since he'd first pecked Lily's bare toes.

Slowly she approached him, holding her arms wide now to make herself bigger. The rooster crowed his last and flapped his wings to rise above the ground in the dust devil created by his commotion. Lily swooped low and grabbed his feet, carrying him upside down to the chopping block. The rooster squawked and flapped his wings against her skirt but Lily wasn't moved to compassion. She laid the cock on the block and whacked his head off, jumping back at the spigot of blood his neck had become and throwing his body a good distance away. The headless cock circled the yard, running erratically as his legs worked in spasms.

Lily drove the ax into the wood, then heard the trotting of a horse on the road. Shading her eyes with the palm of her hand, she squinted against the morning sun of the last day of September. Traffic had been heavy all morning as people traveled to Union to witness the execution of William Wilson for killing her father. Lily had frowned every time she watched someone ride by, not because she disapproved but because she wanted to go and her mother had forbidden it. This time, however, she smiled as she recognized Emmett Moss.

The rooster would need his toughness stewed out of him, and Lily's mother had promised dumplings to go with. That was Uncle Emmett's favorite supper, so the chances were good he'd come back after the hanging and tell them about it. Ignoring the chicken still circling the yard, she walked forward to greet the man the newspapers called the Cattle King of the Panal.

Emmett Moss was fifty years old and had spent most of those years in the weather. He was a tall, wiry man with a shock of gray hair, light blue eyes, and a salt-and-pepper mustache over a mouth that wore a smile as often as not. His suntanned face was pitted with the pale circles of smallpox scars, a disfigurement he sloughed off by joking that he'd lost his good looks but still had his winning ways. He always winked at Lily when he said that, making her laugh. Having nursed three brothers who'd died in that same epidemic, she well knew the suffering dealt by the pox, and she admired Uncle Emmett for being able to joke about it. She considered him the finest man in the county, after her father, of course, though he was dead, and Jasper Stone, though he was barely on the cusp of manhood, and anyway, she tried not to think about *him*.

Uncle Emmett reined his big roan to a stop and smiled at her from beneath the brim of his expensive, gray felt Stetson. "Morning, Lily," he said in his dry, rumbly voice. "Thought I'd take you into town today. We should be back by the time that rooster's ready to be eaten."

Lily felt a surge of excitement but had to say, "Mama don't think it's seemly for young'uns to witness a hanging."

"In most cases I'd agree with her," Emmett said. "In this case I don't. You get your horse and I'll talk to your mother."

Lily thanked him with a smile, then ran for the barn. When she led her palomino toward the house, Uncle Emmett's big roan stood tied to the hitching rail. Theo was dunking the rooster in a pail of scalding water on the block, but Lily didn't give her brother more than a glance, suspecting he'd want to come, too. Though she knew it would be unjust to leave him behind, she hoped he wouldn't be allowed because she wanted the time alone with Uncle Emmett.

The house was a boxcar adobe, four rooms in a row, each having a connecting door and one that opened onto the portal. She went first to her room to change clothes, knowing her mother wouldn't resist Uncle Emmett's appeal for her company. Lifting the skirts of her homespun dress and petticoat, Lily sat on her bed to kick off her shoes and pull on her knee-high boots, the ones that had once belonged to her older brother. She shrugged into a denim jacket that had also been his, took her matchbox of pennies out of her bureau and dropped the box into the breast pocket of her jacket, then carried her gloves and hat as she walked through Theo's room and her mother's before entering the kitchen.

Uncle Emmett sat at the table sipping coffee while her mother stood in front of the black cookstove twisting her apron around her hands. Seeing Lily in the door, Emmett stood up and put on his hat. "Ready, squirt?"

She nodded, looking at her mother.

"S'all right," her mother said. "If Emmett says it's fittin', reckon it is. You mind him, now. I'll expect you home for chicken and dumplin's at suppertime."

Thinking her mother looked especially tired and worn today, Lily dropped her hat and gloves on the table as she crossed the room. She gave her mother a hug and whispered, "Thanks, Mama."

Her mother patted her on the back, then they broke apart and Lily put on her hat and walked out with Emmett while pulling on her gloves. Theo watched from where he plucked the rooster. As Lily climbed the mounting block and settled herself in the sidesaddle, she felt sorry for her brother. He gave her a sad smile, as if being crippled was why he had to stay home, but since he had no trouble sitting a horse she didn't guess that was the reason.

"I'll bring you some peppermint sticks," she called, then wondered if it was proper to buy candy at a hanging, or if the stores would even be open. As soon as she and Emmett were out of the yard, she asked, "How'd you get Mama to let me go and not Theo?"

He smiled beneath his bristly black mustache sprinkled with silver. "I said the oldest child is the right person to witness the retribution of the law, being as she didn't want to do it herself. Way I figure, someone in the family oughta see it happen so there ain't no doubt it was done."

Lily nodded in agreement, reining her horse alongside his as they turned west on the road.

"Your father was the best hope for this county, Lily. I know in your mind that prob'ly don't count for much. You miss him as a father, and that's right, too, but Bob Cassidy would've turned things around for all of us. Now it don't look like it'll happen for years to come. Ain't too many men'll risk assassination to better the world. From here on out, they'll look after their families and keep their noses outta politics, which is what Hart wanted."

Lily took a deep breath. "So you know it was him put Wilson up to it?"

"Stands to reason," Emmett said. "Paul Beckworth saw Wilson eating dinner with your father in the hotel dining room an hour 'fore he shot him. Beckworth didn't see no animosity at that table, so in all likelihood something come along after that meal to change Wilson's feelings. I ain't alone in suspecting that something was a large amount of money."

"If that's true," Lily said, "the man who paid it is as guilty as the man who did the deed."

"Here now!" Emmett said sharply, yanking his horse's teeth away from the muzzle of Lily's palomino. "This roan's green broke," he apologized, "and ain't learned its manners yet."

Neither caring about the training of his horse nor being unable to control her own in rude company, she asked, "What do you think of what I just said, Uncle Emmett?"

"Ain't no proof nobody paid nothing," he said. "The law turns on proof, Lily."

"The law turns on the whim of Henry Hart," she answered.

"Maybe so. But by hanging his pawn, we'll be sending a message that Hart can't protect those who do his dirty work."

"That ain't enough," she said.

"It's what we got, Lily," he replied sternly. "What's gonna happen today is a letter of the law. It's how justice is dealt, letter by letter. 'Cause you can't clean the whole slate don't mean you shouldn't take satisfaction in wiping out the wrongs you can."

Lily tried to think of an effective argument to that, but before she could, he said, "Your mama looks about done in."

"Yes, sir," Lily murmured. "I hear her crying every night."

"It's rough, no two ways about it. She's buried four children in this territory, and now her husband lies beside 'em. Wears a woman down." He looked intently across the space between their horses as they ambled along the dusty road. "You're the mainstay of the family now, Lily. Do you know that?"

"Yes, sir," she said.

"You got a good head on your shoulders, and you'll make out. You aim to keep the mill?"

"It and the store are our only cash income," Lily said. "Though the cash is mighty scant. Theo does all right running the mill long as he's got a man to do the heavy work. Mama used to tend the store but ain't up to it now. I been doing that and keeping the books, too, though I'm having trouble making sense of the business."

"How's that?" Emmett asked.

"Well, for one thing, Father never took money for the grinding, just a toll of the corn 'fore it was milled, and we got a powerful lotta corn I don't know what to do with. When I asked Mama, she seemed scared 'cause she didn't have an answer. 'Bout broke my heart. Most everybody around here grows their own corn, so they ain't looking to buy any. I was hoping you'd know what Father did with what he got."

"He sold most of it to me," Emmett said. "How much you figure's there?"

"That's another stickler," she said. "Father kept his count in fanegas, but what we got is loose in bins. I ain't got no idea how much is there."

"You know how much is in a fanega?"

"No, sir," she said contritely, then brightened when she said, "but I know a fanega's worth six dollars and fifty cents."

"That's right. One and a half bushels make a fanega. You know how many bushels you got in your bins?"

She shook her head.

"Well, we'll measure it out when I send the wagons to fetch it. I'll pay cash, like I've always done. How's that sound?"

"Sounds fine," she said. "I ain't paid Mr. Crawford since Father died. If I don't pay him soon, he ain't gonna stay. Me and Theo can't do the work of a strong man, even 'tween us. But there's something else I need to know, Uncle Emmett."

"What is it?" he asked kindly.

"The farmers keep their own books, you know, and oftentimes Father didn't pay 'em for their grain but gave 'em credit at the store. Now these fellows're showing up asking for what they got coming, but most of 'em can't read or write, so they keep their account with dots, each dot being equal to a fanega. I reckon their method would work if there weren't so many flies in the world."

Emmett laughed.

"You can see my point," she said. "When the farmers show

me their accounts, I can't tell the dif'rence 'tween a dot left by a pencil and one left by a fly!"

"That's what *your* books are for, Lily."

"What if our accounts don't agree?"

"Go by your own. If the farmers don't like it, let 'em take their business elsewhere."

"Ain't no other gristmill in the county."

He smiled. "Then you ain't got a problem."

She nodded thoughtfully. "It's hard to argue, though, with a man who uses his hungry children as a reason why he's right."

"Those are two dif'rent things, Lily. If you want to be feeding hungry children, that's your choice, but it ain't business. Keep 'em separate or you'll never make sense of the accounts."

They took the right fork at the junction of the rivers, crossing the Noisy above where it joined with the Pequeño to become Deep River. As they ambled along the road following the smaller stream toward the township of Union, Lily said, "That sounds right. Since we lost our herd to rustlers, the mill and store are all we got."

Emmett frowned. "When'd you lose your herd?"

"Rustlers run 'em off 'bout two weeks after Father died. Mr. Crawford went after 'em but never found nothing but one steer with its throat slit. Why'd the rustlers kill that steer, Uncle Emmett, if they didn't mean to eat it?"

"Prob'ly it got footsore and couldn't travel further, and prob'ly they did intend to eat it but got interrupted. Any clue as to who the rustlers were or where they took the herd?"

"They drove 'em downriver then cut south, but it rained hard the next day and wiped out the tracks. Mr. Crawford thought the rustlers were Mescaleros since the trail was heading toward the Guadalupes, but I don't agree with him."

"Why not?" Emmett asked.

"The Mescaleros promised my father they'd never steal from him, and I don't believe they'd steal from his family just 'cause he ain't here no more."

"So who do you think the rustlers were?"

"I can't say as to the particular men, but Buck Robbins's cow camp is down that direction. It's a well-known fact he sells stolen stock to Henry Hart to fill his gov'ment contract."

Emmett frowned. "If it'd been Mescaleros, their horses would've been unshod. Did Crawford think to notice that?"

"He didn't mention it," she said. "But he ain't the best tracker in the world."

"Wasn't nobody with him?"

"Marty Turner and Jasper Stone. They'd stopped by to water their horses when we discovered the cattle gone, and they helped Mr. Crawford track 'em."

"Did Marty or Jasper mention whether the rustlers' horses were shod or not?"

"They went on home after the trail was lost."

"How do you know they didn't go down to Buck Robbins's cow camp and split the take?"

She stared at him in amazement.

The crow's-feet around Emmett's blue eyes crinkled as he smiled. "Just 'cause a man offers to help don't mean that's what he's doing."

"I believe in this case it was," she said.

"Uh-huh. And they just happened to stop by to water their mounts?"

"That's what they said," Lily answered, looking away. The cottonwoods crowding the narrow valley were a brilliant gold in the sunlight.

"They could've watered 'em any place on the river," Emmett said.

Keeping her eyes on the trees, she said, "I don't believe they'd follow in the dust of rustlers they were in cahoots with."

"Maybe they came by that day to court you."

She jerked back around to meet his eyes. "Marty Turner's a work-shirking rambler. I wouldn't encourage the likes of him."

Emmett laughed. "What about Jasper Stone?"

She shrugged, looking away again. "He ain't got no int'rest in me."

"You got an int'rest in him?"

She studied his teasing smile. "Why're you asking me that, Uncle Emmett?"

"Seems to me, the situation your family's in, a husband for you might be the answer."

"Maybe so," she said with a flash of anger. "But I thought we was talking 'bout rustlers."

"We are," he said. "Jasper Stone's been pilfering off my herds a few years now. I can overlook a cow here and there, but when stealing from me becomes a man's main sustenance, I gotta ask what I'm getting outta the deal. And the answer in this case is nothing. One of these days I'm gonna come down on him hard."

Softly she said, "You know he's got personal reasons for acting against you."

"I'm sure he does. Just like the farmers who try to trade a speck of fly shit for a fanega's worth of goods think they got a good reason for cheating you. There's no dif'rence, Lily."

"Jasper ain't bad," she said.

"He rides with Marty Turner, who by your own admission is a work-shirking rambler, and he spends even more time with Whit Cantrell." Emmett's blue eyes twinkled with fun. "Ain't your mother ever told you what happens when you lie down with dogs?"

"You get up with fleas," Lily said, fighting a blush. "But I've never lain with any of those boys."

"I'm glad to hear it," Emmett said. " 'Cause none of 'em's gonna be around long enough to make any woman a reliable husband."

"I ain't looking for a husband!" she said tartly. "I wish you'd quit talking 'bout that."

Emmett laughed again. "All right. How's this for a subject of conversation: My brother lost his wife back in Texas last year and has accepted my invitation to live with me at Bosque Grande. He's got two kids, one of 'em a daughter 'bout your age. Think you could ride over and stay awhile to help make her feel welcome?"

Lily felt pleased with the invitation, then remembered her mother. "If I can be spared at home," she said.

"Harvest is over, so there won't be any work at the mill. Don't you think Theo can handle the store while you're gone?"

"Reckon he can," she said.

"My niece's name is Claire. She's been to a proper young ladies' school and comports herself with the grace of high society, but I figure you have enough in common that you can teach each other things worth knowing. I'm hoping you'll be friends."

"I'm sure we will, Uncle Emmett."

"She's got a brother named Andy, but he ain't worth much," Emmett said.

"Why's that?" she asked.

"You'll find out when you meet him," he said.

Although it was the seat of government, Union was a village of half a dozen stores and a few dozen homes. When Lily and Emmett rode in, the town's single street was so crowded it looked as if nearly everyone in the county had come to witness the hanging of William Wilson. Many of the men were boisterous with drink, and families had spread picnic blankets along the river to pass the time pleasantly until the fatal event. Not only were all the stores open, but vendors walked among the crowd hawking candy and tamales.

After leaving their horses in the hotel's corral, Emmett took hold of Lily's elbow to escort her through the throng. Their progress was slow because every few steps a man emerged from the crowd to catch a few words with the Cattle King of the Panal. Even the Americans took their hats off while speaking with him. The Mexicans nearly bowed. All of them complimented his health and bestowed condolences on Lily before they got to their point, which was invariably something they wanted Emmett to do for them. His answer was always the same: "Come see me at Bosque Grande and we'll talk about it."

They backed away as if he'd given them something, but as the crowd was left behind, Emmett said to Lily, "I'll be sure and not be there if any of those fellows show up." Seeing her frown, he added, "I can't please 'em all, Lily. Would you rather I be rude and tell 'em to go to hell right now?"

She shook her head. "That ain't what we're here for."

When he put his arm around her waist and hugged her tight, she saw people notice his affection for her, and she felt so proud that she forgot how uncomfortable she'd felt at hearing him make empty promises.

Halfway through town, he stopped in front of a small adobe house with a whitewashed picket fence and a discreet sign announcing it as the residence of E. A. Homer, Esq. Already leaning to open the gate, Emmett asked, "You mind if we make a call 'fore the festivities begin?"

Though she felt confused by his sarcasm, she shook her head, secretly thrilled to think she was finally visiting the lawyer's wife.

She had met Mrs. Homer on a shopping trip to Union two years ago. Before that chance meeting, Lily had been unaware of her own homeliness. Then, for the first time, she'd seen a woman whose beauty was stunning, whose elegance and grace made Lily want to curtsey in awe. Mrs. Homer's face was delicately proportioned and so pale she obviously never exposed her complexion to sunlight. Her hair was a flounce of auburn curls framing her golden-brown eyes, and her attire was breathtaking. Never before had Lily seen such a gown. Sewn of a blue fabric whose subtle chalky color had come from no native dye, the dress was a grand, sweeping affair draped in scallops falling from her hips over a bustle. Lily had to ask her mother what that bump on Mrs. Homer's behind was, whispering it in the corner of the store because she felt certain it was a physical deformity the lady was gallantly making the best of. Lily felt Uncle Emmett would approve of the gesture and she was anticipating telling him when her mother broke her bubble by saying, "Hush, child, that's a bustle. I've seen 'em in the catalog."

Lily had hushed, blaming her lack of interest in lingerie for her ignorance of feminine wiles. She had never understood exactly what wiles were supposed to be, but she'd assumed they were bad because dishonest. Yet Mrs. Homer was certainly fetching. Lily admired the attention everyone gave her, especially the many men who turned back for another look before going out the door. If wiles they were, Mrs. Homer's were so beautiful nothing else about them mattered. When Lily left with her mother, she had been unable to resist turning around and giving the lady a last look, too. Mrs. Homer had been staring right at them with an odd expression of longing on her face.

Without even raising her voice, though Lily's mother was halfway out the door and could be expected not to hear, Mrs. Homer asked, "Is this your daughter, then, Mrs. Cassidy?"

Her mother proudly led Lily over to the lawyer's wife and introduced them.

"You're not very pretty," Mrs. Homer said. "You'll have to work harder because of that."

"Yes, ma'am," Lily answered, feeling she'd do anything if it helped her look like Mrs. Homer.

The lawyer's wife smiled at Lily's mother, one of the few American women within a day's ride of Union. "Why don't you and Lily come by for tea? I'd so love to have you."

"We'd surely like to, Miz Homer," Lily's mother answered. "I'm ever so pleased you asked. But we gotta get home 'fore dark. Mr. Cassidy's fixin' to leave right now. I jus' popped in for some candy for the boys. They're still at home and will be wanting supper long 'fore we get there as 'tis. I'm awful sorry."

Lily blushed with embarrassment at the crude country talk, then felt a surge of fierce loyalty for her mother.

"Perhaps next time you're in town," Mrs. Homer said, her voice as much breath as tone.

Impulsively, Lily held out her hand. "Powerful glad to've met you, ma'am."

Mrs. Homer laughed and took Lily's small, coarse hand in her own gloved one. "And I, you," she said with delicate precision. "Please call on me next time you're in town."

"We surely will," Lily's mother said. "Now we gotta skedaddle or Mr. Cassidy'll be in a state half the way home."

Mrs. Homer had smiled with understanding as they parted company, and Lily's concept of femininity had been changed forever. That visit, however, never happened. Within a month, smallpox struck the Cassidy home. Before it was spent, the pestilence had taken three of the boys, and the next summer Lily and Theo were forbidden to go anywhere out of fear of contagion. Then their father was killed, not by disease but a bullet.

As she and Uncle Emmett waited for someone to answer his knock on the lawyer's door, Lily remembered that at her father's funeral she'd briefly spoken with Mrs. Homer. After offering her condolences, the lawyer's wife had agreed with Lily that Emmett Moss would see justice done if he were there to know what had happened. Now he was. He'd brought Lily to town to witness the hanging of Henry Hart's pawn, but she expected Mrs. Homer to be her ally in achieving more than the execution of a pawn.

The door was finally opened by a tall, thin, black man. Though Lily had seen them from a distance, she'd never been so close to a Negro before, and she stared with fascination at the hickory tones of his face as he smiled a greeting.

"Mawning, Mr. Moss," he drawled, the syllables falling from his mouth like leaves floating from a tree on a windless day. "Da missus say ya be heah, and she raht, as u-shal."

"Morning, Tolliver," Emmett answered. "This is Miss Cassidy."

"Ah'm pleased to mee' cha," Tolliver said, beaming his smile on her. "Come on in, bof of ya."

When Emmett gestured for Lily to go first, she followed Tolliver through a tiny vestibule to the parlor, where Mrs. Homer had stood up to greet her guests.

She was as beautiful as Lily remembered, today wearing a copper-colored taffeta gown that rustled as she took a step forward. "Emmett! I'm so glad to see you," she said, her face aglow. "And Lily," she added, the glow diminishing. "How kind of you to call on me."

"Couldn't come to Union without paying my respects to the prettiest lady in town," Emmett said.

Lily looked up at him, puzzled by the odd tone in his voice.

Mrs. Homer laughed with pleasure. "Please sit down. Would you like coffee?"

"No," Emmett said, guiding Lily to a purple horsehair settee and sitting beside her, "but I'd take a sip of brandy if you offered it."

"Then I shall, and join you, too. What would you like, Lily?"

"Coffee, I reckon," she said.

Mrs. Homer smiled at Tolliver, who left the room. Moving to a needlepoint bow-backed chair, she fluffed her skirts as she sat down, the taffeta crackling like mice in tissue paper. "Edgar will be sorry he missed you," she said to Emmett.

"Where is he?"

"At the jail. Seeing that his client's rights are preserved."

"What rights can a condemned man have?" Emmett asked dryly.

"Dignity and the utmost decorum allowed by law," she said.

In astonishment, Lily asked, "Mr. Homer's representing William Wilson?"

The lawyer's wife smiled with the condescension of an elder to a child. "Every man is entitled to a defense, Lily. Edgar is the county's only practicing attorney and could not refuse his services."

"I don't see why not!" she retorted. "There ain't no defense for a guilty man."

"Indeed," Mrs. Homer said. "My husband's only duty in this case was to ensure the accused a fair trial and decent treatment up to the time of execution." She glanced at the mantel clock. "Which should occur an hour from now. Then we can all put this odious event behind us."

"That ain't something my family's gonna do," Lily said, "till Henry Hart's brought to justice for his part in my father's murder."

To Lily's further dismay, Mrs. Homer responded by giving Emmett a beseeching look. He took hold of Lily's hand and squeezed it tight, which made Mrs. Homer frown. After a moment, she asked, "Will you do us the pleasure of dining at our table, Emmett? I'm certain my husband will be delighted to have you."

" 'Fraid not," he said. "I promised Lily's mother I'd get her home 'fore dark."

Mrs. Homer's smile was forced. "That's the wisest course with a child," she said.

Emmett laughed, which again puzzled Lily. Looking up at Tolliver entering the room with a laden tray, he said, "Here's my brandy in the nick of time."

Tolliver handed Lily a delicate china saucer holding a cup of creamed coffee. Preferring her coffee black, she kept quiet, wanting only for the refreshments to be finished so they could leave. Beyond her disappointment at Mrs. Homer's lack of allegiance to the sentiment she'd expressed at the funeral, Lily felt uncomfortable being in the home of the man who'd defended her father's killer, and she couldn't understand why Uncle Emmett had brought her here. He took his time, however, sipping his brandy, as did Mrs. Homer. Gradually Lily caught on that the lawyer's wife was flirting with Uncle Emmett, as if her husband had died and she was now a widow on the marriage market.

Uncle Emmett suffered the attention with far more grace than Lily thought the situation warranted. His frequent chuckles and smiles were evidence that he was enjoying himself. When he asked for another glass of brandy and Mrs. Homer rose to pour it, Lily saw his gaze slide over the lady's sumptuously clad body with an appreciation entirely too familiar. If she hadn't known him so well, Lily would have suspected she'd been brought along merely as a ploy to allow him to spend time with another man's wife. But Emmett was too honorable to do such a thing, and anyway, Edgar Homer was his lawyer and he was too wily to want an attorney with an ax to grind against him. Still in all, the visit was unpleasant for Lily. She felt relieved when Emmett refused another brandy and announced his intention to leave.

As they all stood up, he asked, "Ain't you going to the hanging, Suzanne?"

Lily perked up to hear him use Mrs. Homer's first name. That certainly wasn't proper, unless he knew her awfully well.

"I don't consider hangings appropriate entertainment for ladies," Suzanne replied. Glancing at Lily with an unspoken condemnation of her scuffed boots beneath her homespun frock, the faded denim jacket that had once belonged to her brother, and the man's hat held tight with a chin strap, Mrs. Homer said, "Nor for children, even country girls who have grown up without the benefits of culture."

To Lily's surprise, Emmett laughed. "My niece is coming from Texas next month, and Lily's promised to help welcome her to Bosque Grande. Claire's got more culture than any girl needs, so I figure some of it's bound to rub off on Lily."

"She's fortunate," Mrs. Homer said coldly, "that you're taking such an interest in her education."

"Her father was a close friend of mine," Emmett answered, his eyes twinkling with fun, "so I consider it my duty."

Lily didn't get the joke. But apparently Mrs. Homer didn't find it funny either. Only Emmett seemed to be amused. When they had finally made their farewells and left the lawyer's house, Lily said, "I don't like that woman. Why'd you take me there, Uncle Emmett?"

He slid his arm around her waist as they walked along the now deserted street. "You were talking earlier about feeding hungry children, Lily. Mrs. Homer's starving for another kind of sustenance. Her husband's so busy she's nearly always alone. I consider it an act of kindness to share time with her when I get the chance."

"Then that's your choice," Lily replied, using his own words against him, "but it ain't mine."

He chuckled. "Okay. I'll never take you there again. Does that suit you?"

"Yes," she said. "Where'd all the people go?"

"They're down at the scaffold. The hanging's about to commence."

She threw him a worried look. "I don't want to miss it."

"We won't," he said. "The sheriff'll drag it out to please the crowd."

As they rounded the curve in the wide, shady street, she saw the people clustered close to the gallows, their noise subdued to a hum of hushed anticipation. Children sat on their fathers' shoulders to be able to see. Women laughed nervously beneath the brims of their sunbonnets. Men muttered to one another, some of them passing bottles from hand to hand. Lily shivered, thinking the event was already ghoulish though it hadn't even started yet.

Emmett kept his hand on the back of her waist as he guided her up the steps to the courthouse and through the front door. No one challenged her right to be there. Few of the men inside even looked at her; those who did merely shifted their gaze and nodded at Emmett, then turned away. He led her up the stairs and through the hall to the front veranda. Mr. Homer was there, standing next to Judge Houghton and Mr. Ryder, the district attorney. They all nodded at Lily and Emmett, then turned back to watch the scene below with solemn eyes.

At the appointed hour, the condemned man was led from the first floor of the courthouse to the gallows. With his hands shackled behind his back, he was escorted by the burly, redheaded sheriff and four armed deputies. A black-clad priest walked behind them with Henry Hart, who was territorial representative by default of the assassination. His flaxen hair shining on his hatless head, Hart was dapper in a dove-gray suit that Lily bitterly thought must have cost a pretty penny.

As the men climbed the stairs of the scaffold and took their places, she tried to see the face of William Wilson. He kept his head down so she couldn't catch more than a glimpse of his dark form, telling her he was small compared with the loss he'd effected. The crowd fell silent as the priest spoke to him, but even in the quiet, Lily couldn't hear Wilson's mumbled reply. Raising his voice to carry across the crowd, the sheriff asked the condemned man if he had any last words. Wilson shook his head. A black hood was dropped over his face and the noose secured around his neck.

Lily held her breath, watching Henry Hart on the scaffold and remembering what she'd overheard him say at her father's funeral. She didn't see the sheriff's signal, but she heard the trap spring. Jerking her head at the gasp of horror from the crowd, she watched Wilson lurch to the end of the rope, his feet kicking until he was still. Then she raised her gaze to Henry Hart. He quickly descended the stairs, walked into the shadow of the gallows, and held his hand to the throat beneath the black hood before nodding at a deputy, who cut Wilson down. Two other men caught his body as it fell and laid it in a plain pine coffin waiting nearby.

Lily trembled. Emmett pulled her close and tried to turn her face toward his chest, but she resisted, keeping her eyes on Henry Hart. "Reckon it's done," Emmett murmured in her ear. "Let's go home."

"Not yet," she whispered, noticing a Mexican woman draped in a black rebozo who was edging toward the coffin.

The deputies were still on the scaffold, but the sheriff and priest were beneath it now beside Henry Hart. It seemed only Lily was watching the Mexican woman as she leaned over the coffin and peered in. Suddenly she shrieked, then screamed, "He breathes!"

Sheriff Bond hurtled himself across the scant space to the open coffin.

"He is still alive!" the woman insisted.

A cry of outrage erupted from the crowd. Above the excited frenzy of voices, a man shouted, "Do it again!"

Henry Hart held up his hands to quiet the throng. "It's been done," he said. "There's no legal precedent to hang a man twice."

"It ain't done!" a man shouted.

"If you don't get outta our way," another yelled, "we'll hang you, too!"

Hart took a step back. The sheriff strode between him and the men. "I'll hear none of that!" he bellowed.

Lily watched Sheriff Bond turn around and meet the eyes of Henry Hart. She saw the sheriff shrug and Hart slink deeper into the shadow of the gallows. A new rope was given to the sheriff. He leaned into the coffin and secured a loop around the unconscious man's neck, still covered by the black hood. The sheriff threw the tail of the rope through the gaping hole of the trap. A deputy caught the tail, tossed it over the scaffold, and threw it into the crowd. Half a dozen men took hold and hoisted Wilson out of the coffin and up through the trap to dangle from the crossbeam of the gallows. Suddenly Wilson awoke and danced again to the ribald jeering of the people's amusement. The crowd laughed at his comic display until he fell slack, twisting on the rope as the people watched, now silent. This time he hung a full twenty minutes before he was allowed to fall again and drop on the ground with a final thud.

Lily hid her face in the rough wool of Emmett's jacket, feeling his arms encircle her with strength. "He's dead now," Emmett said.

She nodded.

"Ready to go?" he asked.

"Yes," she said, looking up to meet his eyes. They were darker than she'd ever seen them.

He laid his arm on her shoulders and guided her off the porch, along the upstairs hall, down the steps, and out the back door. They took a circuitous route to the hotel's corral, where he paid the hostler, then Emmett lifted her onto her horse and swung onto his own. As they rode through the crowd, it parted to let them pass. "Bob Cassidy's daughter," she heard people murmur. "Emmett Moss," she heard others say. She looked at no one, merely watched the ears of her horse turning this way and that as she concentrated on sitting straight in the saddle.

When they had left the village behind and were once again riding through the cottonwoods golden in the sunlight, she said, "I almost got what I want."

He looked at her sharply. "You mean you didn't?"

"Henry Hart's still alive."

Emmett frowned. "Wilson was hung twice. Ain't that enough to satisfy your bloodlust?"

Tears stung her eyes that he'd attach that word to what she felt. "Wilson was just a dumb fool," she argued, "who died for doing Hart's bidding. All I've heard since my father was killed is that the good men of this county will see justice done. I ain't seen it yet. Maybe the only way I will is take a gun and shoot Hart myself!"

Emmett was quiet a long time. She listened to the muffled cadence of their horses' hooves on the dusty road as she waited for his answer. When he finally spoke, he asked, "You remember when your father stood up to the soldiers in defense of the Apache women?"

She nodded, turning her head so he couldn't see her tears.

"That was the finest act I've ever heard of any man doing," Emmett said. "It wasn't done with a gun, but with the argument against using guns on women and children, no matter what color. He couldn't have made that argument if women were warriors. That's why they ain't. So we can all breed the next generation and let history decide who was the better man by the caliber of his children. It's how we better ourselves, Lily: generation by generation. And it's women's job to raise the children. There's no task more important."

Looking at the bright sky through the canopy of golden leaves, Lily felt desolate.

"It's a man's job," Emmett continued, "to protect and provide for his family in the world as it is. Your father was big enough to extend his protection to all women and children. He was a Texan in the truest sense."

"What's that mean?" Lily mumbled.

"He had the kind of raw courage that makes a man stand his ground at any cost. You're his best child, Lily, and you got that kinda courage, too, but your duty is to help make the world a better place for the children yet to come, not take a hand in the violence."

Lily held on to her sidesaddle as her horse splashed across the Noisy River and clambered onto the south shore. She turned around and watched Emmett coming behind, keeping his seat with his legs, his hands free to handle the reins, use a gun, or do anything he pleased.

He smiled, the crow's-feet in his weathered face reminding her of the lost pleasures of childhood. "What do you say we pick up the pace? I'm hungry for some of your mother's chicken and dumplin's."

Lily didn't feel the least bit hungry, but as she rode beside the mighty Cattle King of the Panal, she couldn't help remembering she'd been the one who killed the cock.

3

*A*ndy Moss was fifteen and hadn't reached his height yet, though he was so skinny if he grew any more he'd stretch thin as a beanpole. He'd heard it said he was simple-minded. He knew what that meant, but he couldn't see anything simple about being confused. If he'd found life puzzling in the east Texas town where he grew up, out here in the territory it was downright bewildering.

The men were different, for one thing. They dressed rougher and worked harder and their play struck Andy like a contest of how much pain they could take and stay on their feet. Sometimes not even staying on their feet mattered as long as they could laugh about being knocked down, usually spitting blood when they got back up. Andy didn't want to fight, certainly not for sport. The men's knuckles were scarred when they weren't scabbed, and their palms were as rough as a slab of prickly pear, their fingers clumsy for any task more delicate than knotting a cinch.

Andy's hands were as soft as a girl's, each of his fingers limber and agile from years of studying piano. Sometimes he thought he missed his piano more than his mother, though she'd so often sat beside him while he played that his memory of her lilac scent and gentle approval was mixed with the pleasure of music in his mind. His father had asked if Andy wanted to bring the piano, saying it would be a mighty chore to wrestle it in a wagon five hundred miles but could be done. Suspecting it would mark him as a sissy on his Uncle Emmett's ranch, Andy said it wouldn't bother him none to leave the piano behind because he'd decided to become a cowboy.

That notion hadn't lasted long. The work hurt from dawn to dusk. Starting with conquering a half-wild horse that objected to being saddled let alone mounted, the men spent all day riding range so rough they were constantly jumping arroyos or skittering up and down banks, dodging prairie-dog holes that could throw a horse, or winding through tornillo thickets with three-inch thorns. A cowboy soaked his feet in freezing water if he crossed a river, or sweated in the sun without a drink if he didn't; burned his hands roping an ornery cow; wrenched his shoulder when his horse and the thousand-pound steer went different directions; moved at a butt-breaking trot more often than not; twisted his leg when his horse skittered out from under him before he was completely off, then got kicked or bit by the horse when he thought he was safe on the ground. At least, all of those things happened to Andy the one and only day he tried to be a cowboy. By the time he got home, every inch of his body felt like he'd spent the day being flogged.

He was declared the clumsiest greenhorn the men had seen. Because Emmett Moss was his uncle, the men's ridicule was half-hidden behind their hands, but Andy got the message that he plainly wasn't cut out to be a cowboy. He slept till noon the next day, and when he finally limped out to the stable, Beau Cairn gave him a horse Uncle Emmett had decided was Andy's speed. Beau was an old man kept on because he'd once done good work, and Andy figured the same could be said of the horse. It was a nine-year-old dapple gray that Beau said already had its sand kicked out of it. Andy named the horse Kickapoo and spent the next few days riding up and down the river exploring his new home. His body adjusted to spending hours in the saddle, but he felt no inclination to work cows again. To his way of thinking, the romance of that occupation had been overrated.

He felt the same way about the land. The river was named Panal, which meant "honeycomb" in Spanish, but if Andy ever saw honey as muddy as this river he doubted that he'd eat any of it. Back home, the stand of trees around Uncle Emmett's house would have been called a *motte,* another Spanish word that meant "small grove on the prairie," which was a truer description of Uncle Emmett's ranch than *Bosque Grande. Bosque* was the Spanish word for "woods," which in east Texas meant a lot of trees, not a few. Away from the river, the range was rolling plains covered with mostly brown grasses. Of course, this was October, and Andy expected the land to green up come spring, but he couldn't see anything grand about it. He supposed the *grande* part was a figment of Uncle Emmett's ambition.

There were three towns along the Panal within a day's ride of Bosque Grande, though Andy hesitated to call them towns. Two hours south was River's End, a ramshackle collection of adobe saloons, houses that looked like hovels, and one store that sold everything from peppermint sticks to potbelly stoves. River's End was considered the most respectable town along the Panal. An hour farther south was Siete Rios. Andy hadn't gone there yet, but he'd heard it was a rough place with little to offer. A short ride north of Bosque Grande was Soledad. The village had once been a fort, and the old barracks were rented to Mexicans who farmed for Pedro Menard, who had bought the abandoned buildings and surrounding land from the government. The plaza had one saloon, owned by Foxy Strop. Because many of the men who spent daylight hours inside the saloon were drifters, Andy felt more comfortable in Foxy's place than anywhere else along the Panal.

He had been well liked back home. Out here, once people learned his name, there was no telling how they'd react. It hadn't taken him long, however, to understand that what they gave was aimed at his uncle and he was just the closest Moss to put it on. He hadn't yet found the right moment to ask Uncle Emmett the source of all that animosity, and the people who gave it didn't tarry long enough in Andy's vicinity for a conversation. He did know that to be known as a coward in this country was the worse fate to befall a man, so Andy went to town fairly often to prove he wasn't afraid to show his face. He also went out of pure and simple boredom on the days his sister didn't want him around. This had been one of those days. When Claire left the house to go for a walk, plainly expressing her desire to be alone, Andy saddled Kickapoo and headed toward Soledad.

The road north followed the eastern edge of the Panal, meandering along a cliff with the floodplain twenty feet below. In late autumn the river was a narrow sluggish stream between stretches of hardened sandbars that would have been easy to cross if a horse could get up and down the cliffs. Near Bosque Grande, a ford led to the western side of the river, where the road continued south. Andy had been told if he tried to cross at any point below the ford, he was apt to get mired in quicksand and disappear, horse and all.

The concept of quicksand intrigued him and he'd asked Uncle Emmett what it looked like. When he said it didn't look any different from the mud around it, Andy asked what it was that made it different. They'd been standing in the yard at the time, and Uncle Emmett squatted down and drew a map in the dust. A long, curving line represented the Panal. He used his thumb to mark the ford with a wide swatch, then used his finger again to draw a short line coming into the Panal just below the ford. That represented Gushing River, which was fed from a spring rather than rain or snow thaw in the mountains. The spring also flowed underground, Uncle Emmett explained, and quicksand was caused by water bubbling up from the bottom rather than sinking down into the soil. No one knew how deep the underground water was, but that it was deep enough to swallow a horse or cow had been proven more than once.

After studying the map for a minute, Andy had said, "I read a book before we came out here that said this whole country had once been an ocean. Ain't it strange to think the ocean could still be down there?"

Uncle Emmett stared at Andy with a suspicious frown.

His fantasy running with the idea, Andy said, "Maybe the ocean's full of monsters that eat horses and cows, so they deliberately make quicksand to trap 'em."

Uncle Emmett stood up. "This is the desert, boy, not no ocean. You'll never make sense of the world with such foolishness." He walked away fast, as if he was mad.

That conversation had made Andy wary of asking his uncle why folks didn't seem to like him once they'd learned his name was Moss; he was afraid Uncle Emmett would say he was dreaming up monsters again. Though Andy didn't invent the part about the ocean, his uncle hadn't gone to school past third grade and didn't give much credence to things learned from books. He was of the land and trusted only what he could see for himself, which didn't include words written by people he didn't know. Andy liked to read. Books were something else he'd left behind, never suspecting there wouldn't be any at Bosque Grande.

The trail veered away from the river to cross the prairie and meet the Texas Road, which came out of Soledad and disappeared in the flat expanse of the Llano Estacado. Andy always rode into town on the Texas Road. Just the name of it helped him sit up straighter in the saddle. A lone cottonwood grew at the junction, stately and proud. Today as he approached, he saw two horses grazing not far away. When he got closer, he could make out the shapes of the men in the tree's shadow. He didn't have to see their eyes to know they were watching him. A current of mutual awareness stretched taut across the glare of noon.

Andy looked at the horses again. One was a dark Appaloosa such as he had never seen, all charcoal gray except for white spots like polka dots on its rump. He'd heard of those horses and seen drawings in magazines, but the ones he'd seen were roan or bay, not anywhere near black. Andy knew he was looking at an expensive mount. The other horse was a brown mare. Not too many men rode mares because they were testy and unpredictable in season. This one was rangy and dull brown, the kind of horse cowboys called a cayuse for its lack of looks. Andy thought the two horses were an odd pair to be tethered together.

The men were sitting on rocks under the shade of the tree. Their hats were pushed back, their faces young, their clothes as unexceptional as the brown mare. They both wore gunbelts, but so did nearly every other man in the territory. Uncle Emmett never did and had forbidden Andy or his father to, saying being unarmed was their best protection.

Andy reined up just beyond the tree's shadow. "Morning," he said, raising his hand to tip his hat.

"Howdy-do," one of the men answered with a laugh. "Where you heading?" He looked to be about twenty, his hair a tawny blond, his eyes the color of sage honey held up to sunlight.

"Soledad," Andy answered.

"We was, too," the man said.

When he offered no explanation of what had stopped them, Andy said, "Couldn't help admiring that polka-dotted horse out yonder."

"Ain't no polka-dotted horse," the other man said with an edge of resentment. "It's an Appaloosa all the way from Montana."

Andy nodded. "You bring him down yourself?"

"What's it to you?" the man retorted. He looked to be close to his companion's age but taller and more muscled, definitely less friendly, his eyes the cold blue of slate.

"Nothing," Andy said. "Just noticed it, is all."

The first man laughed and said, "Man rides a flashy horse, it's apt to get noticed."

"Huh," the second man replied, glaring at Andy. "Where I come from, it pays a man to mind his own business."

"You come from Montana?" Andy asked.

"There he goes again!" the second man said to his companion, who was grinning. "He's slow on the uptake, wouldn't you say, Whit?"

"Ain't nothing wrong with being slow if you get there," he answered, winking at Andy.

Andy laughed, thinking the man named Whit was someone he could be friends with. "Don't s'pose you'd be int'rested in riding into town with me?"

"Could be," Whit said. "What're you gonna do there?"

"Have a beer at Foxy Strop's," Andy said, then added proudly, "he's my friend."

"That right?" Whit smiled. "I know Foxy. Tell him hello for me, will you?"

"What's the rest of your name?" Andy asked eagerly.

"Cantrell. This here's Jasper Stone."

Jasper nodded at Andy but didn't smile.

"I'm Andy Moss," he said.

"Sonofabitch!" Jasper said, jerking to his feet.

"The boy ain't wearing no gun," Whit said softly.

"Goddamn cowardly Mosses!" Jasper shouted. "Sonofabitch thievin' bastards!" He wheeled around and stomped across the prairie toward his horse.

Whit watched him a moment, then smiled at Andy. "Don't take it personal. He hates anyone carrying the name Moss."

"Why?" Andy asked.

Whit's honey-colored eyes scanned Andy's face as he said, "Ask your Uncle Emmett. Course, he'll put a slant on it that Jasper wouldn't, but if you look at it close you'll see the truth."

They both turned their heads toward the drumbeat of hooves and watched Jasper gallop away on his flashy Appaloosa, the speckled rump brilliant in the sunlight.

"That's a fine horse," Andy said.

"The one you're on ain't bad," Whit answered.

"My uncle gave it to me," Andy said.

Whit nodded. "Uncle Sam gave me that nag out yonder, so reckon we got something in common." He laughed, an easy, generous sharing of a joke instead of the ridicule Andy had learned to expect. "If I ride into Soledad with you," Whit asked, "will you buy me a beer?"

"I'd be pleased," Andy said.

Foxy Strop's Saloon was a long, narrow room so poorly lit Andy often wondered how the men at the tables could read their cards. As he and Whit stood just inside the door to let their eyes adjust from the bright sun outside, a dozen men shouted greetings to Whit.

"Howdy, boys," he answered, walking toward one end of the bar. He turned his back to the wall and leaned an elbow on the counter while he scanned his audience with a playful smile.

Foxy Strop was a short, fat man with a dark beard that glimmered with grease in the uneven light from the kerosene lantern. He glanced at Whit, then looked at Andy and said, "You're traveling in strange comp'ny."

Before Andy could answer, Whit asked, "Why do you say that?"

Andy looked at Whit, who was smiling though his eyes glinted hard in the lamplight.

Foxy's small, dark eyes were just as sharp. "Don't seem a friend of Jasper Stone would be drinking with no Moss."

Whit laughed. "I don't need anybody's enemies but my own. Ain't that the way you feel, Andy?"

Andy nodded, thinking he might use the same line with his uncle if the subject of enemies ever came up.

Foxy asked, "What kin I getcha?"

"Two beers," Andy said. He smiled at Whit as Foxy moved away to draw them.

"How do you like living at Bosque Grande?" Whit asked.

"I like it well enough," Andy said.

"Bet it's dif'rent from what you had at home."

He nodded, watching Foxy set the full mugs in front of them. Andy laid a dime on the bar, then leaned close to slurp the foam off the top of his mug.

Whit waited for the barkeep to leave them alone before he said, "You're from Paris, Texas, ain't that right?"

Andy looked up with surprise. "How'd you know that?"

"Everything concerning a Moss is gossip in these parts," Whit answered with a smile. His eyes scanned the room again, then he lifted his mug with his left hand, took a sip, and set it back down. "I know your mother died, so your father brought you here to live with your uncle, and that you got a pretty sister, and won't never make a cowboy."

Andy blushed.

"Don't worry about it," Whit said. "There's better ways to get by than pushing cows around."

"What do you do?" Andy asked.

Whit grinned. "A little of this, a lotta that." He winked and lifted his mug with his left hand again, took a sip, then set the mug back down.

"Are you left-handed?" Andy asked. Being as he was simple-minded, he thought the affliction of being left-handed would give him and Whit something in common.

Whit shook his head. "I keep my right free for more important things." He leaned back against the wall and asked, "What do you miss most about home?"

"My piano," Andy said. Quickly he lifted his mug and drank half his beer down, sorry he'd mentioned the piano.

"Celia's got one," Whit said. "You want to go over there and take turns on it after we finish our beers?"

"Do you play?" Andy asked, again surprised.

"I can tickle the bones to please my fancy," Whit said. "Bet you had lessons and all."

Andy nodded. "From my mother."

"That right?" Whit sipped his beer, then said, "My mother died, too."

"I'm sorry," Andy said. "Was it recently?"

"Seven years ago. Seven? Yeah, I'm twenty now." He laughed. "She said I'd never make it to twenty-one."

"Why'd she say that?" Andy asked, thinking Whit didn't look sickly.

"Oh well, she never knew nothing about boys," Whit said, his gaze roaming around the room again. "She was a good woman, though. Did her best by me, and you can't ask more'n that from a person."

His eyes had softened with a melancholy that tugged at Andy's heart. Impulsively he asked, "Would you like to come home for supper with me? You'll be the first guest I've brought."

Whit gave him a smile. "Why, then, I'd be honored."

The bat-wing doors creaked as someone came in, momentarily throwing slivers of light the length of the room to the bar. Andy watched Whit's eyes change again, this time glinting with the smooth sheen of a puddle hardening into mud.

"Howdy, Whit," a gruff voice said. "Ain't seen ya in the mountains for a spell."

"Ain't been there," Whit answered softly.

Andy turned around to see a huge man looming behind him. The man stood well over six feet and must have weighed two-fifty. His boots were tooled black leather with his pants stuck inside like men do in snake country, and he wore silver *conchas* in the band of his black, round-top Stetson. His hair was amber red and so long its kinky curls covered the breast pockets of his coat, which was also black with white stitching along the lapels. "Name's Rufus Bond," he said, sticking his hand out to shake with Andy.

Andy's hand was halfway up when Whit said, "Don't shake with him. You're apt to get lice."

Andy let his hand hover at half-mast, confused for a moment. But Rufus Bond jerked aside so he was facing Whit. "You got a nasty mouth, punk."

Whit laughed. "My ma was always telling me that. Guess I never did learn to heed her."

Rufus snickered with a sneer. "Why don'cha come up to Union and test your welcome?"

"You afraid to make your move down here on the Panal?" Whit asked with no apparent malice.

Andy noticed the room was quiet. Swallowing so hard he was sure everyone heard it, he asked, "Ain't we going to Celia's, Whit?"

Whit didn't take his eyes off Rufus Bond. "Yeah. The smell in here's changed on us, ain't it?"

Rufus took a step back but didn't reply to Whit's insult. They stared at each other another long moment, then Whit said, "Come on, Andy. Let's go tickle those bones."

Trying to match Whit's casual saunter, Andy followed him away from the bar. Except for their boots on the wooden floor, the room was silent. Suddenly a hand grabbed Andy's arm and jerked him down. He landed on his hands and knees, then looked over his shoulder to see Rufus Bond had drawn his gun. Three shots from the other direction erupted so close together they almost sounded like one. Andy watched the big man's head snap back three times before he crumpled, dropping his gun as he fell. Andy swiveled around on his butt to look at Whit standing just inside the door, a thin wisp of smoke curling out of the bore of his gun. Andy looked up at the man who had pulled him out of the way, intending to thank him, but the words died in his throat when he saw it was Jasper Stone.

"You coming, Andy?" Whit asked lightly, holstering his gun.

Andy pulled himself to his feet, looking at Rufus Bond's blood pooling beneath his flung-out red hair. It didn't seem there was much left of the back of his skull, but his forehead had a neat hole the size of a silver dollar. Andy turned away, feeling sick to his stomach.

Jasper Stone followed Andy toward the door as Whit said to the room at large, "I'll be at Celia's, if anyone asks."

He pushed through the bat-wings and Andy followed on their next swing, Jasper Stone on the one after that. They didn't speak as they walked east across the plaza, turned north up an alley, and followed it to a low adobe building with a blue door. Whit opened the door without knocking, which surprised Andy. Once they were inside, however, he saw from the many spittoons that it was a public parlor. The light was murky, but when he caught flashes of painted naked women it dawned on him what sort of establishment Celia's was.

The piano was pushed up against one wall, the other walls lined with horsehair settees. At the end of one was a vase of ostrich and peacock feathers taller than a man. Andy studied them, thinking surely no bird grew so big as to have six-foot feathers. They must be attached to sticks somehow. He didn't go look, though. He followed Whit to the piano and watched him sit down on the round stool. Its feet were glass balls gripped by iron talons.

"Afternoon," a feminine voice said from behind them.

Andy turned to face a young woman with an abundance of mahogany-colored hair. He'd never seen so much hair on a person. It was thick and wiry, falling like a hooded cape all the way to the backs of her knees. Beneath it, her body was covered with a white satin wrapper, luminous in the dim light, and it surprised Andy that the woman wasn't dressed though the day was half gone.

"Leave me alone, Celia," Whit said gently without looking at her. "All I want is to play the piano."

Celia glanced at Andy, her thin, pale face revealing no emotion. Then she looked at Jasper sitting on a settee, his long legs stretched out in front of him, his ankles crossed, his hands cupped open at his sides. He jerked his head for Celia to leave, and the woman spun on her toes and walked out.

Whit started playing a sad song, one Andy had never heard before though he knew the key was E minor. He moved away from the melancholy melody to take a closer look at the monstrous feathers. Sure enough, he could see where they'd been sewn onto sotol sticks. On the wall above them was a painting of a nude woman, blond and fat. A ribbon of pink satin seemed to float around her in such a way that one end hid the tops of her creamy legs. The background was all sky, as if she were a dream someone was having. Studying the huge mounds of her breasts, topped with what looked like candied cherries, Andy felt himself blush.

"Turkey in the Straw" suddenly exploded from Whit's fingers, a rollicking, kick-up-your-heels dance tune. Andy laughed, tapping his foot and grinning at Jasper. Whit was damn good on the piano, but Jasper acknowledged it only with a slow blink of agreement, as if Andy were dumb not to have known that. The door opened and Ephram Saunders strode in. He was a slight man, but no less imposing because of his stature. Beneath his hat, his jet-black hair was slicked straight back and his dark eyes were as sad as a prophet's. Having met him at Bosque Grande the week before, Andy knew Saunders was the U.S. marshal, with the entire territory as his jurisdiction.

Rather than stop playing, Whit went right into "The Yellow Rose of Texas." Andy glanced at Jasper, wondering if one of them should tell Whit the marshal was there. Jasper didn't move, so Andy didn't either. When Whit finished "Yellow Rose," he dribbled his fingers along the keys, creating an arpeggio of discordant chords, then suddenly he stopped and asked without turning around, "Whatcha doing here, Marshal?"

Andy wondered how Whit knew someone else had come in, then he guessed maybe Whit's nose had tipped him off. Even from across the room, Andy could smell the marshal's sweaty clothes. He remembered Whit saying Rufus Bond had changed the smell of the room, and Andy smiled to think the marshal had done the same. He wanted to make a joke about it but the intensity in Jasper's eyes stopped him. He was watching Saunders so warily Andy figured it wasn't the right time for a joke.

Whit thought otherwise. Turning around on the stool, he smiled and asked, "You come to see the elephant?"

Andy had once seen an elephant in a traveling circus. As many oddities as Celia's place held, he knew an elephant wouldn't fit under the roof, so it had to be a joke, though no one laughed.

"You know why I'm here," Saunders said, his voice as weary as his eyes. "Want to tell me what happened?"

"It was a game of two and I got there first," Whit said.

"He drew on you?"

"While my back was turned."

Saunders looked at Andy still standing by the peacock and ostrich feathers, beneath the pink lady floating in the sky. Andy thought the marshal must think he looked ridiculous in that setting, but Saunders merely asked, "Were you there?"

Andy nodded.

"Tell me what happened."

Andy looked at Whit.

"In your own words," the marshal barked.

Andy met his eyes. "Me and Whit had decided to leave. We'd almost made it to the door when Mr. Bond drew his gun. Whit fired in self-defense."

"Will you swear to that?"

"Yes, sir," Andy said.

Saunders looked at Whit a long moment, then asked, "If you had your back to him, how'd you know he drew his gun?"

"I heard it slithering like a snake outta the hole of his holster." Whit smiled. "It's a good sound to recognize."

Saunders nodded. "Did you know he'd been appointed a deputy sheriff?"

"I didn't see no badge. Did you, Jasper?"

Jasper shook his head.

"How about you, Andy?" Whit asked.

"I didn't see a badge," he said, realizing the import of what had happened.

"You best stay clear of Union," Saunders warned. "Red ain't gonna let it lie."

"Thanks for the advice," Whit said.

"Nobody wants to see you dead, Whit, but the way you're going, it's bound to happen."

Whit laughed. "I always heard the first law of nature is self-preservation. That's the one I followed today, and there ain't nobody in Soledad who'll fault me for it."

Saunders nodded again in that sad way he had. "There'll be an inquest tomorrow. I'd appreciate it if you'd show up."

"I'll see if I can fit it in."

"It'd behoove you to clear your name 'fore Red tracks you down."

"Ain't nothing wrong with my name."

Saunders muttered something that sounded like a curse, then spun around and stalked out.

Whit and Jasper met each other's eyes, and Andy had the feeling a lot was being said in their silence. Finally Jasper asked, "What'll you do now?"

"Andy's invited me home for supper," Whit drawled. "Reckon I'll go."

"Fuck!" Jasper said. Jerking to his feet, he followed Saunders out the door.

Whit stared after him, then gave Andy a smile. "Come play me a song," Whit said, standing up off the stool.

Andy slowly crossed the room and sat down, trying to decide what to play. He closed his eyes and began his mother's favorite, Chopin's Concerto no. 1 in E Minor. His right hand began the melody, rising up the keyboard to end in several trills before cascading back down, then climbed again accompanied by his left hand following like a shadow. The song flowed from his fingertips, all the correct stops and pauses perfect. When his right hand again ascended alone, he felt Whit kneel beside him, then Andy's left hand accompanied his right as they rose in partnership up the keyboard, dancing across trills to the highest keys and falling back down like rain to crescendo into a momentary silence. Again his right hand played alone, matriculating through more frantic trills until his left came in stern and steady as they climbed together. Andy kept his eyes closed, imagining the old music book open in front of him and his mother's perfume as if she were there and listening as intensely as Whit. Again Andy's right hand rose, lonely in its solitude. When his left joined in from the deepest keys, the harmony swelled into a magnificence that was lost in a poignant melancholy as his right hand finished alone. In the ensuing silence, Andy squeezed his eyes shut even tighter, feeling a sweetness vibrate between him and the man kneeling beside him.

Softly Whit said, "That's the most beautiful music I ever heard."

Andy turned on the stool and looked at him.

His lashes wet with tears, Whit laughed and said, "I'm hungry. Ain't you?"

4

In the shade along the river, Claire Moss was sitting on a hump of dirt beating the ground in front of her with a stick. The dust settled on her white frock like a film of age yellowing the hem of her skirt, but she couldn't see that it mattered. At eighteen, she was stuck on a ranch in the middle of a primitive territory populated with rube cowboys and old men. When she remembered the garden parties back home and the young gentlemen's faces as she smiled over her fan, she could cry. What fun was there here? She didn't have a blessed thing to do or anyone to do it with except her brother, and Andy was no company.

Gone half the time, too. She wished *she* had the freedom to go anywhere she pleased, but Uncle Emmett had forbidden her to leave the ranch without one of the hands riding along, and their company was worse than Andy's. They'd blush and stammer so badly it was a wonder they could get a word out, their eyes all the time avoiding her face as if it were an eyesore, though she could hardly fathom that.

The yard was surrounded by brown prairie, desolate land with nary a tree except around the house itself and along the river. She walked its banks nearly every day, the glare of the bright sun hidden beyond the broad brim of her bonnet so mostly she saw gnarled cottonwood trunks under the canopy of bare branches, the sandy riverbed, and the paltry flow of muddy water. The path meandered through wild wheat, the golden spears rustling with her passage. They were dry and prickly on her palms as she ran her hands lightly across the tops of the thistles, as dry as her hope for a husband in this empty land.

If her mother were still alive, Claire would have a companion in her solitude. But if her mother hadn't died, they wouldn't be here. Claire would be caught up in the whirl of her debutante season, her social calendar so full she wouldn't get enough sleep until the announcement of her engagement. Then she would bask in the envy of the unchosen, delight in the pleasures of amassing her trousseau, even travel to St. Louis on a shopping spree. When she came home, she would marry the richest and most handsome young gentleman in east Texas, and establish her place in society as his bride.

All that was lost to her now. If she caught a husband at all, it would likely be a man twice her age or an adventurer after her uncle's wealth. Her father had said they'd be rich in the territory, and she guessed they were, but she couldn't see what good it did. Money meant fine furniture and fancy frocks for parties, an elegant carriage to take her places worth going. None of that existed here. Uncle Emmett didn't even have a buggy. She was expected to ride a horse! His furniture looked as if it had been made by the cowboys, all rawhide and unvarnished wood. She got slivers if she touched it wrong! She'd brought trunks of fancy frocks but hadn't yet met a woman to admire them. The cowboys turned crimson at the mere sight of any skirt. She swore it wouldn't matter if she were wearing buckskin, for all they knew of fashion. Worst of all, she'd been burdened with the discomforting knowledge that the few educated men out here sought more than beauty and charm in her company.

She'd only met two who could put a sentence together in her presence. One was Robert Daggerty, who sold life insurance and wore so much pomade her perfume was overpowered. The second was Lash Cooper, who called himself a journalist. Uncle Emmett called him a drunk. Lash's compliments were flowery, there was no doubt of that, but rather than being poetic they reeked of self-interest in the same way Bob Daggerty's hair reeked of pomade. Meeting them had made Claire suspect that even if she found a man capable of winning her heart, she wouldn't know if he loved her or Uncle Emmett's ranch. Back home Claire had only her good breeding and beauty as assets, but they had been hers, given by God. She'd always told herself the lack of a dowry didn't matter because she had no intention of marrying a man who wanted her for the financial advantages she would bring. As

Uncle Emmett's niece, she doubted if being homely and mean-spirited would change her marriage prospects one whit.

Across the sluggish whisper of the river's current, Claire heard the staccato hoofbeats of a trotting horse. The other side of the floodplain stretched a hundred yards before reaching the cliff that separated it from the prairie, and the rider was still concealed beyond that cliff. She held herself immobile, the stick half-mast in the air as she watched for whoever was coming to emerge from the trees.

It was a girl. Younger than Claire but past the cusp of quickening. She was skinny, wearing a man's denim jacket and a brown skirt falling from her knee, crooked over the horn of her sidesaddle, to show the toe of a scuffed boot poking out from the stirrup. Her frock was homespun wool, and her brown hair was wound into a bun pinned at the nape of her neck, her face shadowed by the brim of a man's hat. Her yellow horse wore Uncle Emmett's brand: *EM* scarred into its left shoulder. When Claire irritably beat the stick on the ground in front of her, the noise caught the girl's attention.

She looked directly at Claire, revealing a pie-shaped face with an aquiline nose, thin lips turned down, and cheeks scattered with freckles as if she spent a lot of time outside. Her brown eyes were her best feature, large and oval and alert with intelligence, her thick tapered brows indicative of a strong will. The girl urged her horse into the current, the muddy water swirling against the animal's knees with languid resistance and splashing onto her skirt and the horse's belly. When they came out, she let the horse stop and shake itself as she looked at Claire, who expected the girl to fall off with the violent motion. But she kept her seat and kicked her horse to amble closer.

Claire stood up and watched the girl approach until she reined to a stop a few paces away, her yellow horse tossing its head and playing with its bit so the rowel spun with a wet noise. The girl said, "You must be Claire. I'm Lily Cassidy."

"How do you do," Claire said. Uncle Emmett had told her of Lily Cassidy, saying she had more savvy than most men and Claire would do well to befriend her. He had also mentioned Lily would be visiting soon, but that she'd been delayed because of problems at home. When Claire inquired as to what sort of problems, Uncle Emmett said her father had recently died and her mother was having a hard time getting on with life. Having recently lost her mother, Claire understood, probably better than Uncle Emmett, who had never married, had no children, and had left his parents and brother behind when he was eighteen. Claire thought that was evidence of a cold heart, though she liked her uncle well enough.

Lily's horse sidestepped impatiently but she reined it back with a firm hand. "You come down here to meet me?"

Claire shook her head. "I didn't know you were coming."

"Your uncle invited me to visit and help make you feel welcome. Didn't he tell you?"

"Yes," Claire said. "But we weren't sure of the day."

Lily nodded. "Where's your horse?"

"I walked," Claire said.

"Clear from Bosque Grande?"

Claire nodded.

"I ain't walked that far since I learned how. Can't you ride?"

"Of course I can," Claire answered testily. "I prefer strolling peacefully to fighting a horse the whole way."

"Do you now," Lily said softly. "Well, I ain't walking to Bosque Grande. You want to ride with me?"

"No, thank you. I'll soil my frock."

Lily's gaze dropped down Claire's form, taking in the gauzy white dress cinched tight with a scalloped red velvet belt, then rose to her wide straw bonnet held in place by a red ribbon tied in a big floppy bow beneath her chin. "You already got dust all over it. How come you're wearing white anyway?"

"This is one of my favorite frocks," Claire said, hurt.

"It's pretty," Lily said. "But it won't last in these thistles and thorns. Why don'cha come ride with me? I'll sit behind and let you have the saddle. How's that?"

Without waiting for an answer, Lily jumped down. Her horse bobbed its head and stepped back the full stretch of the reins. "Here now," Lily said, dragging it close again. She led it next to the mound of dirt Claire had been sitting on. "Be quick," Lily said. "My mare don't like standing still."

Having been raised to obedience, Claire responded to command. She lifted her skirts, stepped onto the mound, turned her back, and hoisted herself with both hands into the saddle, grabbing the mane when the horse moved. Lily stuck her own foot in the stirrup and propelled herself to sit astride behind the saddle. Her skirts were bunched up around her hips now, showing her black stocking above the man's scuffed boot hanging loose on Claire's side. As Lily gathered the reins, she said dryly, "You best use the stirrup."

Claire lifted her right knee over the horn of the sidesaddle and slid her left foot into the stirrup. Her skirt wasn't falling as it should, but she didn't dare let loose of the mane to straighten it.

"All set?" Lily asked.

Claire nodded, though the height of the horse frightened her.

Lily kicked it to ascend the steep trail up the embankment, leaning close against Claire as they climbed. Claire felt grateful to have the girl holding her. When they'd come out on top, however, Lily leaned back and let go, reining onto the trail toward the house.

On even ground, Claire let herself breathe again, then asked, "How's your mother? Uncle Emmett told me she was doing poorly."

"She's better," Lily said. "Thanks for asking."

"I'm sorry about your father," Claire said. "I lost my mother last year, so I know how you feel."

"Uncle Emmett told me," Lily said.

Claire felt a twinge of jealousy, hearing Lily refer to Emmett as an uncle. She'd felt privileged to be his only niece. Now it seemed she shared that honor with this rough girl who had no real claim to the appellation. Not one to beat around the bush, Claire asked, "Why do you call him uncle?"

"Him and my father were friends back in Texas, and Emmett's known me since I was born, so calling him uncle just naturally happened."

Claire nodded. "What part of Texas did your family come from?"

"Uvalde. You know where that is?"

Claire shook her head.

"It's southwest of San Antone, on the road 'tween there and El Paso. You ever been to El Paso?"

"No," Claire said.

In the ensuing silence, Lily studied Claire's face, guessing she'd be an exceptional beauty anywhere. On the frontier, she glowed like sunshine at dawn. Her hair, falling loose in curls down her back, was as golden as sunrise, her eyes as blue as the sky, her nose delicate, her lips full and flush, her complexion almost as white as her frock. Thinking Claire was bound to create a stir all up and down the Panal, Lily asked, "You met any of your neighbors yet?"

Claire shook her head. "I didn't know we had any."

Lily laughed. "They're well spread out, but they're there. Course we're two of the only three American girls in the county. There's Mrs. Homer up in Union, but she's married, so 'tween me and you and Elise Stone, we got our pick of the bachelors. Elise lives down by Siete Rios. Don't s'pose you've been there yet."

"I haven't been anywhere," Claire said.

"I'll take you down for a visit, if you like. Elise don't get out much on account of her brother, Jasper. He keeps her close at home. If he's there when we go, don't take nothing he says personal. He hates your uncle for unwarranted reason. Someday he'll see that."

"Why does he hate him?"

Lily sighed. "The Stone family built Emmett's house when they first come out here in sixty-seven. Jasper was only twelve then, but he killed a man, so his family abandoned their homestead and moved to Arizona. They didn't like it there, so decided to come back. In the meantime, though, Emmett had moved into the house and filed a claim on the land. The Stones couldn't do that 'fore they left 'cause the county hadn't been surveyed by the gov'ment and right of possession was all there was. So when they came back, they settled in Rocky Arroyo. All of 'em but Jasper have accepted it as fair. I reckon 'cause he was the cause of 'em leaving in the first place, he feels the loss as his own account. Ain't nothing to be done about the past, though. Sooner or later, Jasper's gonna understand that."

"Why did he kill that man?" Claire asked.

" 'Cause of a calf." Lily shook her head. "It couldn't have been worth more'n three dollars, but they quarreled over who owned it. When the man tried to rough Jasper up, he got hold of a gun and shot the bully. That was Jasper's first killing."

"You mean he's killed more than once?"

"Yeah. After the Stones were settled in Rocky Arroyo, he found his own spread higher up in the mountains. A man name of Miles decided he wanted the same land. Prob'ly he thought Jasper could be run off easy 'cause he was so young, but that was what you call a fatal miscalculation. One day Miles challenged Jasper to a duel. They stood back to back in the yard, counted off ten paces, then turned around and shot at each other. Miles missed, but Jasper didn't. He rarely does."

"How old was Jasper then?" Claire asked.

"Sixteen," Lily said. "He killed again a coupla years later, but that wasn't nothing more'n a saloon brawl. When men play that game, they gotta take the consequences. Now he's trying hard to be peaceable, and I admire him 'cause of it. He's got a temper, ain't no arguing that, but in all those cases he was in the right, though that don't necessarily count with the law. Jasper's twenty-three now, and considering that his family lost Bosque Grande 'cause of him, he goes out of his way to avoid fights. That's why he keeps his sister close at home, so nothing can happen that'll make him mad."

"Did he abandon his own spread after killing Miles for it?" Claire asked, thinking Lily was certainly giving Jasper the benefit of any doubt.

"He still owns it but he lives with his folks. They had nine children in the house when he struck out on his own. All but him and Elise died in the smallpox epidemic a few years back, so he stays with his folks and helps bring money in."

"That sounds admirable," Claire said.

"He ain't killed nobody for years now," Lily agreed. "But he spends too much time with Whit Cantrell, and I don't think Whit's gonna influence him in the right direction."

"Who's Whit Cantrell?"

"A local rowdy who come out of nowhere and has been raising havoc ever since. Makes his living off the monte tables more often'n not. He's killed three men just in the last two years."

"Why doesn't the sheriff arrest him?" Claire asked indignantly.

Lily laughed. "Ain't got the nerve, is the truth of it. Whit sashays real loose and only fools cross him. Rumor has it he's the best gun in the county, but I ain't seen him shoot, so I couldn't say. Folks like to talk about him, though. They say he killed a man in Santa Fe. If that's true, it brings his tally to four. When a man kills that many, there ain't nothing accidental about it, like with Jasper, who simply lost his temper and had luck with him at the time. Whit don't seem to have a temper. I've heard he smiles when he fights. That makes him a cold-blooded killer, but that he's got courage no one doubts. He tricks his foes with jokes and gets 'em mad, then shoots 'em while he's laughing. That kinda man's a lot more dangerous than one who has to get riled 'fore he fights."

"He sounds like a man of low character," Claire said.

"Yeah, I reckon," Lily answered, thinking Whit wasn't all bad. When her family had been stricken with pox, Whit was the only one who would come around to help her. Remembering Emmett's opinion, however, she said, "Jasper ain't got no business being Whit's friend, but you can't tell Jasper nothing. He's got a chip bigger'n a buffalo bull's."

Claire blushed, envisioning the image of Lily's metaphor. But though the girl's speech was crude and her dress rough, Claire appreciated being told the realities of her new home. Looking ahead at the trees shading the cluster of buildings comprising headquarters for the Bosque Grande ranch, she said, "I'm glad you came to visit, Lily. It's been lonely being the only woman here."

"How can you be lonely with all Uncle Emmett's cowboys around?" Lily asked, astounded at the notion.

"I don't like them," Claire said. "And if men kill each other as often as you imply, I can't see how their company can be safe."

"Ain't no reason for you to fear 'em, Claire. You got to let down your guard and enjoy who you are. None of 'em would dare cross any lines with the niece of Emmett Moss. That gives you more freedom than most girls have."

"Is that true?" Claire asked, intrigued with the notion.

"You bet." Lily laughed again, kicking her horse into a trot across the yard and right up to the portal. She slid off over the horse's rump, then helped Claire down before tying the reins to the hitching post. A pair of saddlebags held everything Lily had brought for her visit. She took them off her horse and followed Claire into the house.

Lily had been inside only a few times. The main door entered a hall that was long and gloomy because no light reached it except when the door was open. Through an arch to the left was the formal parlor, which had a small window looking onto the covered portal and another, even smaller, affording a view of the stable and corrals. Across the hall was the family parlor. It, too, had the same arrangement of windows, but the one to the side looked toward the river. The house had been built back when attacks by Apaches or Comanches were common, so all the windows were small and securely closed with wooden shutters.

Across the rear of the house was the long, commodious kitchen with a huge, walk-in pantry. Emmett had replaced the outside wall of the kitchen with a row of windows. Between the pantry and the formal parlor were four small bedrooms and his office. In front of the other side of the kitchen, working back toward the main door, was the dining room, a stairwell ascending to the roof, which was flat and surrounded by a parapet with gunports, then a small sitting room opening onto a small bedroom, and a larger bedroom the size of both the small sitting room and bedroom together.

Claire led Lily through the small sitting room and on into the tiny bedroom. "Uncle Emmett said you're to stay here," Claire said, drawing the drapes to open the wooden shutters and let light in.

Lily nodded, having been given this room the other times she stayed at Bosque Grande.

"I'm right next door," Claire said. "Come see."

Lily laid her saddlebags on the bed with her jacket and hat, then followed Claire through the sitting room and a connecting door to the large bedroom, noting the elegant furniture Claire had evidently brought with her.

"I always take a nap before supper," Claire said. "I rarely feel tired but an afternoon rest preserves a girl's beauty."

Lily stood just inside the closed door watching her undress. "I've never heard of such a thing," she said.

Claire smiled, crossing the room in her camisole and pantaloons. "Come join me. You'll feel better rested for the table conversation."

Lily laughed. "I don't need to be rested to talk."

Claire yawned, turning back the white eyelet comforter. "Sit with me, then, till I fall asleep."

"I'll dirty your bed with my dusty skirt," Lily said.

"Take it off, silly."

"My bloomers ain't no better, all crusted with horse sweat."

Claire slid under the covers. "Get a clean pair out of my chiffonier. My undies are in the top drawer."

Lily crossed the carpeted floor to the nearly black chiffonier with mother-of-pearl inlaid in a flower pattern on the doors. She slid open the top drawer and saw an abundance of lacy white undergarments. "I ain't never seen so many bloomers in my life," she said with a laugh.

"Uncle Emmett wrote that I wouldn't have much chance to shop after I got here so I'd best stock up at home." Claire sighed, remembering the fun of preparing for their journey. "I felt almost as if I were buying my trousseau."

"What's a trousseau?" Lily asked. She sat down on the floor and began pulling off her boots.

"Fancy new clothes a girl buys just before she gets married," Claire said.

Lily stood up and reached under her skirts to gently pull her sweat-encrusted bloomers away from the inside of her thighs. She walked across to the washstand, poured water in the basin and dunked her bloomers, then left them to soak as she walked back and studied the open drawer of silk and lace. Hesitantly, she lifted the top pair out and stepped into them. "They feel cool," she admitted.

"A lady always wears silk against her skin," Claire said. "Even the finest linen is too rough. Take off your frock so it doesn't get wrinkled."

Lily unbuttoned and stepped out of her dress, hanging it on the bedpost. "I ain't never seen clothes made of nothing but cotton and wool," she said as she sat down on the edge of the bed. "No, I saw black satin at my father's funeral, and Mrs. Homer has a frock of blue satin and another of copper-colored taffeta. They were all real pretty."

"How did you know what those materials were if you'd never seen them?" Claire asked.

"We sell ribbons of 'em in the store," Lily said.

"You have a store?"

"A small one at the mill," Lily answered. "Mostly we sell whiskey, though. I don't like doing it but can't make up my mind to lose the money it brings in."

"We had a store back home," Claire murmured drowsily. "It was doing real well before Mother died. Then Father started drinking and the bank foreclosed, so we lost the store and our house, too. Come lie down, Lily."

Lily stayed on top of the covers, wearing only her black stockings held with ribbons above her knees, her shimmy and camisole, and Claire's silk bloomers. Claire snuggled close, her hair smelling of a delicate, flowery perfume.

"This feels like home," she said. "I've always had girlfriends to cuddle. Haven't you?"

"No," Lily said. "I can't ever remember touching anybody who ain't kin." That wasn't entirely true. She certainly remembered kissing Jasper in the cave, but that was a secret she'd never confided to anyone, and Uncle Emmett often hugged her, though he was the same as kin so she didn't think it counted. She tried to imagine growing up in a city and having lots of girlfriends who shared her afternoon naps, but the notion struck her as odd. "Didn't you have no chores to do at home?"

Claire didn't answer; she was asleep.

The hospitality at Bosque Grande was renowned, attracting travelers from afar as well as local men looking for a free meal. Tonight, Lash Cooper, Bob Daggerty, and Woody Wheeler were sitting under the portal waiting to be called for supper. Cooper was an itinerant reporter who sold stories about local events to any newspaper that would pay him. As a drummer for the Territorial Life Insurance Company, Daggerty traveled all over the county and often stopped at Bosque Grande when he was on the Panal. Woody Wheeler was a perennial ne'er-do-well who wandered between the saloons at Siete Rios and Foxy's place in Soledad, begging meals and drinks wherever he happened to be. They were all eager for the brandy Emmett offered in his parlor before the evening meal, and conversation between them had died when Andy rode into the yard with Whit Cantrell. All three of the men stiffened, though they tried not to show it. Watching the two riders swing down by the corral and unsaddle their horses, Lash Cooper mused aloud, "Looks like Whit means to stay for supper."

Bob Daggerty snickered. "That'll give you something to write about."

"Maybe he'll kill someone 'fore he leaves to spice up your story," Woody Wheeler agreed with a chuckle.

Andy and Whit let their horses loose in the corral, then walked across the yard and stopped in the red light of sunset just beyond the shadowed portal. "This here's my friend, Whit Cantrell," Andy said proudly. "Whit, that's— "

"I know their names," he said with a smile. "Evening, boys."

"Evening," they all answered.

"Come on in, Whit," Andy said. "I want you to meet my sister."

Whit grinned at the men, then followed Andy into the house.

"Least he didn't bring Jasper Stone with him," Woody Wheeler muttered.

Lash Cooper said sadly, "Jasper wouldn't come here if his mother was dying in the parlor."

"I bet Emmett doesn't know," Bob Daggerty said, "that his nephew's made friends with Whit Cantrell."

"Why don't you go tell him," Wheeler taunted. "I saw him walking around to the back a few minutes ago."

"I saw him, too," Daggerty said, standing up. "I think he should be warned who Andy brought to his table tonight."

Cooper and Wheeler watched Daggerty walk out from under the portal and head toward the rear of the house.

"He's a real kiss-up," Woody said.

"Yes," Lash agreed.

A few minutes earlier, Emmett had paused in the backyard to study the pair of bloomers pinned to the clothesline. He knew they weren't Claire's because hers were all silk and frilly with lace. These were plain, unadorned cotton, reflecting the character of the woman who owned them. Chuckling, Emmett went into the kitchen and saw Lily at the table peeling potatoes. Cipriano was pulling a bird halfway out of the oven to baste. He looked over his shoulder and nodded at his boss.

"Smells mighty fine in here," Emmett said, giving his cook a smile of approval, then turning his attention to Lily. "Claire taking her afternoon nap?"

"Yes, sir," she said, deftly denuding a potato with a sharp, shiny knife.

"You'd rather peel taters, eh?"

"Ain't sleepy," she answered, tossing the potato into a pan of water in front of her and lifting another from the bushel off the floor.

Emmett looked at his rotund Mexican cook closing the oven. "How long before supper?" Emmett asked in Spanish.

"Una hora," Cipriano said. "No más. ¿'Sta bien?"

Emmett nodded, then moved a few steps closer to Lily. Gambling that she wasn't wearing the extra pair of bloomers she'd likely brought with her, he asked softly, "How's silk feel next to your skin?"

Her head bobbed up and her knife stopped as her face turned pink with embarrassment.

Emmett smiled that he'd won his bet. "Those bloomers cost a dollar fifty each, and she's got twenty pairs of 'em. How much money is that, Lily?"

"Thirty dollars," she murmured, concentrating on the potato.

"She says it's only a year's supply. What do you think of that?"

"I think she's lucky to have a generous provider," Lily answered, unwilling to be baited into criticizing her friend.

Emmett laughed. "The trick is to find her a husband just as generous."

"Plenty of men are generous," Lily said, dropping the potato into the pan and taking another from the bushel. "Most of 'em don't have that kinda money, is all."

"Can you think of one who does?"

"You in a hurry to marry her off?" Lily asked, puzzled.

"Just as soon do it 'fore she needs a new supply of undies," Emmett said, then chuckled again when Lily blushed. "Being as she's my niece, I don't get no pleasure outta whether she's wearing silk or cotton."

Lily stared at him, her astonishment at his topic of conversation overriding her embarrassment. Suddenly she felt off balance with a man she'd known all her life, and the sensation wasn't pleasant. She was saved from thinking of an answer by someone opening the door. They both turned to watch Bob Daggerty come in from outside.

Daggerty was always meticulously dressed, today in a shiny black suit, pale purple shirt, and black four-in-hand tie. His dark hair was slicked straight back to fall just above his collar in curls so drenched with pomade they seemed about to drip, and his equally dark eyes gleamed as if with a secret. Lily knew he sold something called life insurance. Since his policies only paid off after the buyer died, she'd always thought they seemed a sure loss of a gamble. After her father's death, however, she'd realized such a policy would have been a help to her mother.

"Smells divine in here," Daggerty said, looking back and forth between them. "How kind of you, Mr. Moss, to share your bounty."

"Don't take it personal," Emmett replied with a twinkle in his blue eyes. "My table's open to everyone."

"So it seems," Daggerty said. "I saw Whit Cantrell arrive a few moments ago. Apparently your nephew invited him."

Emmett frowned. "Like I said, I welcome all comers. You got a problem with that?"

"Indeed not. I merely thought perhaps you didn't know he was here and would appreciate being forewarned."

"I know my country and the men in it. Any of 'em who come in peace are welcome."

"An admirable sentiment," Daggerty murmured.

Emmett turned his back on the man and said to Lily, "Wanta go say hello?"

"Let me wash my hands," she said. Dropping the last potato into the pan, she stood up and carried the knife to the sink, washed it in a basin of soapy water, then laid the knife on the counter.

"*Gracias, señorita,*" Cipriano said as he glanced up from rolling biscuit dough.

"*De nada,*" she said, giving him a smile. When she looked back at Emmett, she saw an odd playfulness in his eyes as he offered her his arm. She took it and let him escort her out of the kitchen and along the dark hall toward the light in the parlor. Hearing Bob Daggerty follow behind them, she thought this visit was shaping up to be a strange one.

5

*L*eading his new friend into the parlor, Andy looked around, wondering how Whit saw it. The room was mammoth and masculine, with rawhide settees, tree trunk tables, and a huge rock fireplace with a blackened hearth. The ceiling was a herringbone pattern of latillas supported by massive vigas, the walls were plastered adobe adorned with only a few paintings of cattle and horses, and no curtains draped the deep window boxes closed with wooden shutters. Seeing no one else was there, Andy said, "She's probably resting. I'll go fetch her."

"All right," Whit said, dropping his sweaty dark hat on one of the settees.

Andy walked down the hall to his sister's room, feeling excited as he knocked. When Claire called for him to come in, he opened the door to see her in a pink wrapper at the dressing table, putting her hair up for supper. "Can you hurry?" he petitioned. "I want you to meet a friend of mine who's waiting in the parlor."

"What's his name?" she asked, sticking pins into the thick, blond braid perched on her head like a crown.

"Whit Cantrell," he said.

She froze, one pin halfway in, then whispered, "Where'd you meet him?"

"On the road to town. I asked him to supper. Won't you come say hello?"

She pushed the pin all the way in. "You had no right to invite him to our table, Andrew Moss. He's a gambler and a cold-blooded killer."

"Ain't true," Andy argued. "I saw what happened and it was self-defense. I told the marshal so."

She turned on her stool to face him. "What're you talking about?"

"Whit killing Rufus Bond. I was there and saw it."

"When?"

"Earlier today. In Foxy Strop's Saloon."

"Mother wouldn't like you going there."

"Aw, come on, Claire. Won't you make him feel welcome?"

"If you invited him, I suppose I must." She turned back to the mirror, surveying her hair. "It's a good thing Miss Perkins's School taught us how to hold our standards in bad company."

Softly Andy said, "You oughta meet him 'fore passing judgment."

She looked at her brother with surprise. "That's a wise thing to say, Andy."

"I ain't all stupid," he said, dropping his gaze to his boots, pigeon-toed on the purple roses woven into her carpet.

"Of course you're not," she answered gently. "Go on back to your guest. I'll join you in a moment."

She watched him walk out and quietly close the door, thinking it was a shame Andy had heard the talk about him being simpleminded. She guessed it could be true, though she hadn't considered him that before hearing it from someone else. She'd considered him deep because he thought about the world so much. Things other people took for granted were a puzzle to Andy, but whether that made him simple or deep she hadn't figured out yet.

Claire stood up and studied the frocks hanging in her wardrobe, wondering which would be appropriate for meeting a dangerous desperado. She selected the most modest of her evening dresses, a dark umber brown that closed high on the neck. After adorning the collar with a gold starburst brooch, she surveyed herself in the oval mirror standing in a corner. The dress was so dark, the brooch and her blond hair shone like sunshine. On impulse she pinned a silver crescent moon on her left hip, then smiled at herself in the mirror. Content with her appearance if not the world, Claire opened her bedroom door and walked down the hall to the parlor.

A young man stood up at her entrance. He was commonly dressed and dusty besides. His tawny brown hair was rather long and windblown, his square chin barely shadowed with a peach-fuzz beard, and his honey-colored eyes sparkled with fun above the warmth of his genial smile. Her impression was of a boy who had always been sheltered and hadn't yet learned how hurtful life could be, as if no one he loved had ever died and he'd been allowed to bask in the innocence of a childhood he'd outgrown but not left behind.

She looked around for the dangerous desperado, but saw only her brother pouring wine at the sideboard. He grinned and said, "Claire, this is my friend, Whit Cantrell. Whit, my sister, Miss Claire Moss."

She looked back at Whit, then burst out laughing. Covering her mouth with her hand, she struggled to stifle her amazed amusement but the best she could do was apologize between giggles. "I'm sorry," she strove to explain, "I hadn't expected you to look as you do."

"Yes," he said gently. "I understand."

"Mr. Cantrell," she said, advancing forward and extending her hand. "I truly am sorry. Welcome to Bosque Grande."

"Thanks," he said, shaking her hand with his own, which was nearly as smooth. "Pleased to meet cha. I heard you're pretty, but the gossip can't hold a candle to the truth."

"Sit down, both of you," Andy said proudly. "I've poured us all sherry."

Lily was still holding Emmett's arm when they entered the parlor. She could sense he was angry, but didn't know if it was aimed at Daggerty for carrying tales or at Whit for having the audacity to show up. She felt Emmett stiffen even more when they crossed the threshold and saw Claire sharing a settee with the outlaw. There was only enough room for his sweat-stained hat on the rawhide between them. Feeling a flash of surprise to see Claire smiling at Whit as if he'd just walked on water, Lily slid her hand free of Emmett's arm, half expecting him to throw Whit out.

Andy stepped forward from a shadowed corner. "Uncle Emmett, this is my friend, Whit Cantrell."

Whit stood up, smiling in his crooked way.

"We know each other well enough," Emmett drawled, his eyes on Whit. "Heard you got in a fracas up in Union."

"Wasn't nothing," Whit answered. "Evening, Lily."

"Evening," she said, crossing the room to pick up his hat and drop it farther along the settee so she could sit next to Claire. They glanced at each other, Lily with a frown of solemn warning, Claire with an impish grin.

Bob Daggerty came in from the hall, followed by Lash Cooper and Woody Wheeler. Emmett nodded at each of them, then crossed to the sideboard and poured himself a finger of brandy. "Help yourself," he said to the room at large, carrying his drink over to stand near Whit, who had moved away from Claire toward the shuttered window. Emmett watched the three men elbowing one another at the sideboard to get at the liquor, then he looked at Whit's nearly full glass and asked, "How do you like that sherry?"

"It's real sweet," Whit answered with a smile for Claire.

Emmett frowned, then looked at Andy, standing pigeon-toed

as he held his half-full glass. His mouth wore a stupid smile Emmett wished he could credit to the wine. "How'd you happen to meet this galoot?" he asked, striving to keep his voice pleasant.

Andy glanced at Whit, then looked at his uncle. "Met him on the Texas Road into Soledad. We hit it off."

"In what way?" Emmett asked.

"We both like to tickle the bones," Andy said with a grin.

"Only piano in Soledad is at Celia's place," Emmett said, looking at Whit. "The boy's a little young for that kinda entertainment, don'cha think?"

"Don't reckon I do," Whit said, "but we never left the parlor."

"You mean she lets you play her piano without paying her price?"

"Yeah, she does," Whit answered, his eyes dancing in fun.

Lily rose abruptly to her feet. "If you're gonna talk about that, Claire and I'll leave the room."

Emmett smiled. "Sorry I brought it up. Sit down, Lily. I don't want you to leave." He watched her smooth her skirts as she sat back down. The two girls were a contrast in textures, the one wearing silk adorned with gold and silver, her cheeks pale as marble, the other dull and plain but tanned by a healthy life outside and able to see reality through her feminine eyes. He moved back to replenish his drink, then said from there, "I heard Jim Daniels was visiting at the mill, Lily."

"He came calling on Mama," she agreed.

"That ain't the way I heard it." Emmett sipped his drink. "I heard he was courting you."

"Courting the mill for Henry Hart is more like it," Lily said, her eyes spitting fire that he'd mentioned her marriage prospects again.

Emmett chuckled. "Isn't Daniels a friend of yours, Whit?"

"Was once," Whit answered easily. "Ain't no more."

"Since when?" Emmett asked, watching him closely.

"Since he hired his gun to Hart."

"Seems a lot of men're doing that lately," Emmett said.

Whit smiled. "Don't it, though?"

Andy's father walked into the room, stopping just inside the doorway to look over the gathering. Andy said, "Dad, I want you to meet a friend of mine, Whit Cantrell. Whit, this is my father, Andrew Moss, Senior."

Whit was still holding his sherry in his left hand. He took a few steps across the room and offered his right to Drew, smiling as he said, "Pleased to meetcha, sir."

Drew shook with him but didn't smile. "Seems to me I've heard of you."

"Same here." Whit laughed. "The word around the county is Emmett sent home for reenforcements."

Drew frowned. "Nobody came from home except me and my children."

"I can see that," Whit said, looking at Emmett. "But that ain't the way the county's talking it up."

In a puzzled tone, Claire asked, "What are people saying?"

Whit looked at her and said, "I'll tell you the same thing I told your brother when he asked me to explain something similar: You best ask your Uncle Emmett." Then Whit smiled at the man as if they were friends.

Emmett studied the smile. "On which side are you likely to fall if it comes to that, Whit?"

"You aim to fight?" he answered.

"I don't aim to lay down for Henry Hart's pleasure. Do you?"

Whit shook his head. "I only lay down for my own."

"What're y'all talking about, Emmett?" Drew asked unhappily.

Emmett studied his brother, then said slowly, "Henry Hart's building a combine to take over the economy of the county. He operates mostly in the mountains, though. My range is down here on the Panal. I don't figure we'll cross paths for good *or* ill." He finished his drink. "Ain't that right, Whit?"

"Sounds right from your side of it, but Hart's got a habit of thinking all sides oughta be his."

"He can think what he wants. Getting it's something else."

"The problem with that approach," Whit said, "is it leaves nothing to do but react. I took pleasure bringing Browne Carson down, but it didn't change what he'd already done to Angus Bodie. Ain't there a motto about an ounce of prevention being worth a pound of cure?"

"Hart wouldn't dare threaten me," Emmett muttered.

"Long as your own skin's all you care about," Whit replied, "reckon that's true."

Unable to ignore Lily's stare, Emmett knew she was thinking of her father. "Supper's prob'ly ready," he said. "Let's find a more palatable topic over the table."

After supper Bob Daggerty, Lash Cooper, and Woody Wheeler sat under the portal smoking cigars. The family was in their private quarters, and the three men kept their thoughts to themselves as they watched Whit saddle his horse and lope out of the yard without a backward glance at them but with a wave for Andy, standing by the corral.

"Went smooth," Lash said, exhaling a fat smoke ring toward the stars.

"Whit must have been raised in a decent home," Daggerty said. "His table manners impressed me."

"Poor ain't necessarily crude," Woody Wheeler said with a belch.

Grimacing, Daggerty conceded, "Not in all cases."

"If I don't miss my bet," Lash mused, "Whit's lining up with Moss. Ain't that something?"

"Jasper Stone won't like it," Woody said, then chuckled. "Maybe him and Whit'll kill each other. That'd be a gain for the county all around."

Andy sauntered over to lean against a pillar of the portal. The men looked at him so pointedly, silently puffing on their cheroots, that he felt impelled to say something. Unable to think of anything else, he said, "I saw Whit shoot Rufus Bond in Foxy Strop's today."

"What?" Lash jerked his feet off the rail and leaned forward to hear better.

"Me and Whit was leaving," Andy said with a self-conscious smile. "Rufus Bond drew on him when his back was turned."

"Killed him?" Lash asked in a low voice.

Andy nodded. "Was self-defense. The marshal said so."

"Saunders was there and let Whit go?" Lash asked, astounded.

Andy laughed. "Whit said it was a game of two and he got there first. Anybody would have to agree with that."

The three men under the portal exchanged wary looks, then Woody Wheeler whispered, "Everybody does, when it's Whit Cantrell saying it."

Lash leaned back, puffing on his cigar. After a minute, he asked, "Did Whit say where he was going, Andy?"

"Siete Rios," he answered proudly. "To find Jasper Stone."

Lash stuck his cigar in his mouth and used both hands to heave himself out of the chair. "My nose is itching at a story, gentleman," he said, trundling from under the portal. "See you another day."

They watched him hurry across to the stable and disappear inside.

"Where's he going?" Andy asked.

Woody Wheeler snickered. "If you wanta stay friends with Whit," he said, standing up, "you best learn not to repeat what he tells you." He, too, walked from under the portal and toward the stable.

Andy watched him, then turned back to Daggerty. "I sure cleared the roost, didn't I?"

"Sit down, son," Bob said in a superior tone, "and let me give you some advice about your friend Whit."

"Don't guess I care to hear it," Andy said, turning away to enter the house.

Passing along the dim hall, he saw Uncle Emmett and Lily Cassidy alone in the family parlor. At his sister's room, he knocked on the door but received no answer. Thinking she was already asleep, Andy went to his own room and lay down in the dark. He smiled, remembering how the men had scurried off the porch. Whit had really said he was going back to Celia's, but if anyone asked, Andy should tell them he was riding down to Siete Rios. Andy wasn't sure why Whit wanted him to say that, but of one thing he felt certain: Making friends with Whit Cantrell was the most exciting thing he'd ever done.

*   *   *

Lily sat before the hearth watching Emmett puff on his pipe as he stood staring into the fire. She had been disappointed when Claire excused herself to bed so soon after supper, then pleased when Emmett invited her into the parlor. Neither Lily's mother nor brother were much for talking, and she enjoyed visiting with Emmett, who usually shared his thoughts freely with her. Tonight, however, he was silent except for the soft sucking sounds he made with his pipe. She told herself that if this was the usual evening entertainment at Bosque Grande, it wasn't much better than home. To break the silence, she said, "Too bad Whit didn't stick around."

"Why do you say that?" Emmett asked, not looking at her.

"He has a way of livening up a room," she said.

Emmett chuckled, laying his pipe on the mantel and turning to face her so his tall, spare frame was silhouetted against the flames. Towering over her where she sat in a chair with one foot tucked under her skirt, he said, "We've been friends a good long while, haven't we, Lily?"

"All my life," she answered, wondering where that topic would lead. Emmett had been in a strange mood all evening.

"When I invited Drew and his family to come live here," Emmett said, "I offered 'em a home for life. They're my kin and I don't begrudge giving 'em that, though I was careful not to include any promise of title to Bosque Grande. I *had* considered leaving the ranch to Drew's children, but a few weeks in their company convinced me it wouldn't work. Can you guess why?"

Lily could but considered it more politic to keep quiet, so merely shook her head.

Emmett chuckled as if reading her thoughts. "Andy's so simpleminded he'd be hard put to ramrod the chicken coop, let alone herds of cattle numbering eighty thousand head. Claire might catch a worthwhile husband, but her brother shows a flaw in their lineage that I attribute to her mother since no Moss has been simpleminded before. Can you guess what I'm building up to saying?"

"No, sir," Lily said.

Again Emmett chuckled. "I've decided to take a wife and start a family of my own. Being as I'm fifty years old, I don't figure I'll live long enough to see any of my sons grow up, so I gotta choose a woman I feel confident can raise 'em to fruitful manhood and mind the ranch till they take over."

Lily quickly sorted through the local women Emmett might consider. Other than Mexicans, the only widow was her mother, who had just turned thirty-four and still had some childbearing years left. Briefly Lily tried to imagine Emmett as her father, but her loyalty toward her real father rebelled at the notion. Then she told herself he would approve the match because Emmett's wealth would make a powerful difference in her mother's life, and her brother's, too. With resolution, she said, "Reckon every man wants a son to carry on his name."

"Ain't just my *name*," Emmett said. "I've done enough in the settlement of this territory to be included in the history books. I want more'n that."

"What do you want?" she asked curiously.

Emmett hunkered on his heels in front of her so their faces were at an even level. "I want to know the family I leave behind will keep Bosque Grande intact."

"It's the prettiest ranch in the county," she agreed.

He nodded. "I've got seven different kinds of fruit trees in my orchard that've never before thrived west of the Mississippi. Last fall I harvested millet with heads bigger'n any I've seen in the books, and last spring I planted alfalfa, a kind of wheat that'll put the native forage to shame once it gets established. What do you think of that?"

"I've always heard it's the best fodder for cattle," she said.

He nodded again. "But I've done even more, Lily. I've planted fifteen varieties of roses around the house, and three different kinds of willows along the river. Cattle and produce are all fine and well, but beauty's important, too. With flowers and such, beauty's a matter of appearance, but with people, it's something that comes from inside. Like you, Lily. You may not shine to the unwise, but to my eye, you're everything a woman should be. That's why I've always cherished you as my friend."

"Thank you," she answered, suddenly feeling frightened.

Taking one of her hands between both of his, he said, "Ain't no better foundation for marriage than a strong friendship."

"Reckon that's true," she murmured, silently willing him to stop.

Instead, he said, "Lily, I'm asking you to be my wife and the mother of my children."

She tried to pull her hand free. "You're joshing."

"I'm in earnest," he said, holding her hand tight.

She studied his weatherworn face, the brightness of his blue eyes, and the serious line of his mouth beneath his thick mustache. Grasping at straws to staunch her confusion, she asked, "What if I'm barren?"

He chuckled. "I know cattle well enough. People ain't much dif'rent, and I can tell a breeder."

Indignantly she asked, "How long you been sizing me up as a cow?"

He laughed more loudly. "I've been enjoying your company since you learned to talk, Lily. When you turned the cusp, even a hardened old bachelor like me couldn't miss seeing it."

She looked away. "You never mentioned none of this before."

"I know it's sudden but I didn't think you'd balk. I thought it would please you."

"It does," she said, still unable to look at him.

"What's the trouble, then?"

She felt as if she had a precipice at her back and one wrong step would be sure death. Meeting his eyes, she said, "You could have any woman in the territory, Uncle Emmett. Why me?"

" 'Cause you're smart," he answered without hesitation. "I've told you my life story while we've ridden the prairie, kicked around problems I'm having with men, even talked business and you've followed me every step of the way. You don't blush when I talk about castrating a bull or having a good mare in season, never need a pencil to tally profit by pound or acre, and I've never heard you waste breath on which bonnet or frock you'd wear for which occasion. On top of all that, you come from sound Texas stock, with nary a fool nor a coward in your lineage." He paused, then said, "You're the woman I want. Will you have me?"

She tried to look at him in the way she did Jasper Stone when she thought he wouldn't notice. Unlike Jasper, however, Emmett was old. Not a bad-looking man, but tough and crusty without the pale translucence to his cheeks that often tempted her to touch Jasper lightly with her fingertips. When she remembered him kissing her, she felt breathless. Thinking of Emmett giving her more than a fatherly peck made her stomach queasy. "What about love?" she whispered. "Ain't two people who get married s'posed to love each other?"

"I love you," he said. "Don't you love me?"

"You know I do," she said, feeling caught. "But I ain't got any kind of dowry."

"There's only one promise I'll ask above the marriage vows. If you agree to it, we'll call it your dowry."

"What is it?" she asked with trepidation.

"That you stay Mrs. Emmett Moss all your life and raise our children to keep Bosque Grande alive."

The severity of what he was asking slowly penetrated her mind. "But I'll be alone so long!" she cried, then hid her face in shame for having mentioned his death.

He took hold of her chin and forced her to meet his eyes. "I'll be leaving you with the prettiest ranch on the Panal and half a million dollars in banks in Santa Fe and St. Louis. Seems to me I'm offering a fair trade. You think I ain't?"

"It's more than I merit," she argued.

"I disagree. And I wouldn't ask if I didn't think you were capable. Do you accept?"

Lily thought of her mother struggling to keep the mill open with only hired men to run it. She thought of her brother, Theo, and how he'd never make a workingman's wage because of being crippled. And she thought of Theo's children, for surely he'd marry and have some, and how poor they'd all be eking an existence from what their father had been building before his life was cut short. Remembered, too, that Henry Hart had killed him yet not only still walked free but was now making a move on the mill, trying to intimidate her mother into selling at half value. Taking a deep breath, Lily said, "I'll want a promise from you, too, Uncle Emmett."

"That's fair. What is it?"

"I want vengeance for the murder of my father. Will you give me that as a wedding gift?"

Emmett stiffened as he considered her price. In the angry aftermath of Bob Cassidy's murder, he had considered killing Henry Hart, but prudence and time stopped him from redressing one death with another. All things considered, though, he admired Lily for throwing her trump card on the table when she was the pot. It proved she had the courage and grit to achieve what he asked, so he promised what she wanted in return. "I'll do it," he said. "Are we agreed, then?"

"Yes," she said.

He stood up and lifted her to her feet. "Give me a kiss to close the deal," he said.

She shut her eyes as he bent down and quickly brushed his lips against hers. His mustache tickled her nose and she giggled. He laughed, too. "I'll ride over tomorrow and speak to your mother. Can't see any reason why you shouldn't stay here till the wedding, can you?"

She felt a sudden loss, thinking of home. But she shook her head.

"Good," he said, breaking their embrace. "We best get some sleep. There's apt to be a stir when the news gets out."

She watched him leave the room, then sank into the chair and stared at the barely flickering fire. A tear fell across her cheek. Impatiently she brushed it away. Becoming Mrs. Emmett Moss was nothing to cry about. There wasn't a woman in the territory who wouldn't trade places with her in the blink of an eye. She had been given a great honor, a position of privilege and wealth. It was only when she thought of Jasper that she felt cheated. But he'd never shown any interest in her. And if Emmett's prediction came true, Jasper wouldn't live long anyway.

She wondered how long Emmett would live, guessed he had a chance at another twenty years. Which would make her thirty-five when she was widowed, a year older than her mother was now. Yet her mother often complained about losing the years she should have had with her husband. Lily wouldn't have the right to complain. Her only consolation was that her father's assassin would die before the blood of her maidenhood stained the marriage bed.

Feeling ancient, Lily left the parlor and walked through the dark hall to Claire's room. She knocked on the door, then went on in, thinking to wake her friend with the news, to share both the joy of betrothal and the melancholy of her lost love for Jasper, though now that must remain forever unnamed. But Claire wasn't in her room. Puzzled, Lily sat down to wait.

6

𝓣he breeze rustled in the leaves like children whispering secrets above Claire's head. She didn't hear Whit coming, neither his horse nor him moving through the dry grass. He appeared in front of her as silently as an apparition, his hat pushed back so she could see his face, his body taut with a predator's tension. Giving her a playful smile, he said, "I didn't think you'd come."

"I shouldn't have," she answered, stepping deeper into the darkness beneath the peach tree.

He followed her, slid his arms around her waist, and kissed her mouth. Affronted that he hadn't asked permission, she pulled free and slapped him. He laughed, turning around to study the pattern of shadows and moonlight filling the orchard.

She wanted him to kiss her again, but to ask as the boys back home would do, playing a game whose limits she defined. She had expected Whit to broach those limits, just not so quickly. Asserting control, she asked, "What was it you wanted me to tell my uncle?"

Whit faced her with a sly grin. "Nothing," he said. "I just wanted to see if you'd come."

"That's dishonest!" she accused. "You induced me here under false pretenses."

Softly he said, "You knew why I wanted you here."

"You told me you had a message for my uncle," she argued.

"He was right there. Don'cha think I could've told him anything I had to say?"

"I thought perhaps it was a delicate matter that required diplomacy."

He smiled. "It is."

"What is it?"

"You've got a pretty mouth," he said. "I'd kiss it again but for fear of getting slapped."

"You've changed the subject so we're talking about two different things."

"Are we?" He laughed softly. "Don't you think my kissing you is a message for your uncle?"

"Are you doing it because of him?"

"In spite of him," Whit said. "If you let me do it without slapping me again, you'd be doing that in spite of him, too."

"I would not. He has nothing to do with who kisses me."

"Can I kiss you again?"

"No! You've lied to me already and I've scarcely known you an entire evening. Why should I allow liberties to such a scoundrel?"

"Maybe 'cause you like 'em. The liberties, I mean."

"Maybe I don't," she said.

"You want me to leave?"

She bit her lip.

He laughed as he backed away from her.

"Don't go," she whispered.

He came close again, took her in his arms, and kissed her, delicately at first, then passionately, leaving her breathless when he let her loose. Tugging his hat low above his eyes, he said, "I'll be back another night."

She blinked and he was gone. There was nothing where he'd been but the pattern of moonlight and shadow moving with the breeze. Honing her ears, she listened for a long time but heard no trace of his leaving, neither his footsteps in the fallen leaves nor his horse in the distance. She raised her fingers to touch her lips, thinking he might have been an apparition after all except for how his kisses had changed her.

Back home when boys kissed her in the garden swing, she had often wanted them to do it again, but never before had she wanted so much from a man. She yearned to know all of Whit: his control when sharing a joke with a foe he was about to kill; his gentleness that pulled soft boys like Andy into friendship; his wisdom that induced powerful men like Emmett to ask his opinion; the worth of his character, which overrode his reputation so a girl like Lily could criticize him with admiration in her voice; his charm that made a woman like Celia allow him to play her piano without paying her price, whatever that meant. Each of those people knew a separate part of Whit Cantrell. Claire wanted all of him. Tingling with excitement, she walked back toward the house wondering how long she would have to wait for his next visit.

When she slipped through her bedroom door, she saw Lily sitting in the straight-backed chair waiting for her. Their eyes met across the dim room, lit only by moonlight falling through the open drapes. Seeing the tension on her friend's face, Claire suspected Lily was dwelling on the death of her father and worrying for her mother. Claire wanted to feel sympathetic, but she felt too happy for such somber thoughts.

Lily saw a glow on Claire's face that she envied, the carefree enjoyment of life possible only to a girl whose future was still unmapped. Curious, she asked, "Where've you been?"

"For a walk," Claire answered, crossing to the window and looking out at the orchard. She hugged herself with the thrill of remembering Whit.

"I wanted to talk to you," Lily said. "Hope you don't mind me waiting here."

Claire turned around to face her friend. "Why don't you sleep with me tonight? We can talk under the covers."

"I'd like that," Lily said, realizing with a sharper pang than usual what she'd missed by losing her sister to cholera shortly after their family arrived in the territory. Claire didn't have a sister either, but apparently her circle of girlfriends had been so close they'd served instead. In the whole county there was only one other American girl Lily's age, and Elise Stone was so shy Lily's boldness intimidated her. At one time Lily had hoped to become Elise's sister and break through the barrier erected by the difference in their characters, but that was a lost dream of childhood now.

Wearing one of Claire's frilly nightgowns, Lily slid under the covers and felt Claire's arms pull her close. For a moment, they simply held each other in the comfort of warmth, then Lily sighed and whispered, "Something happened to me tonight."

Claire giggled. "To you, too?"

Lily opened her eyes in the dark. "What happened to you?"

"Tell me yours first," Claire said.

Lily sat up and pushed her pillow against the headboard, then leaned on it as she twisted the length of her hair around her hand and watched the curtain lift and fall with the breeze. "After supper . . ." she began, then paused, suspecting once she named what had happened it would be irrevocably true. Maybe if she didn't tell anyone, Emmett wouldn't either, and they could pretend it hadn't happened.

"After supper what?" Claire prodded, watching Lily from where she lay under the covers, her blond hair flaxen in the moonlight, her face a chiseled cameo of perfection.

Lily took a deep breath and sighed. "Emmett asked me into the family parlor." She stopped again, meeting Claire's eyes. Impatient with herself, she spit it out: "He proposed marriage and I accepted."

Claire seemed to get more still somehow. Then she whispered, "But he's an old man, Lily."

"I know," she said, lifting her chin.

"Do you love him?" Claire asked.

"I've loved him all my life. He's been a second father to me and my brother. If not for Uncle Emmett, we might've gone back to Texas after my father was killed and lived off the charity of kin. Emmett helped us stay on. Now he's asked something of me and I didn't renege."

"Oh, Lily," Claire said, sitting up and hugging her. "Uncle Emmett will do well by you."

"I know," Lily said again, hiding her tears.

Claire kissed the top of her head. "Come lie down," she murmured, pulling her into the warmth beneath the covers. "The best part is you'll be living here with us. We'll be sisters, Lily. I've always wanted a sister."

"Me, too," Lily said, snuggling close to the velvet bow on Claire's breasts. "Tell me what happened to you tonight."

Claire sat up and smiled at the moonlit window as she pushed her blond curls away from her face. "In a way, it's like what happened to you, only you shine with virtue while I was naughty." She smiled at Lily. "Whit asked me to meet him in the orchard and I went."

"You didn't!" Lily said, sitting up abruptly.

"I even let him kiss me. Oh Lily, you can't imagine how his kisses made me feel."

Remembering Jasper's kisses, Lily could imagine it clearly. When she pushed them from her mind, she was left with anger that Claire would think her unworthy of receiving such joy.

Claire giggled again. "I told you I'd been naughty."

"More'n that," Lily said. "Whit Cantrell is dangerous. He'll get you in trouble if you don't watch your step."

Claire laughed. "If he'd kissed you like he did me, you'd be singing his praises, too."

"I don't guess he'll ever get the chance! I'm warning you, Claire. Any girl who allows him liberties gets her heart broke and then some. You won't be the first one in this county he's ruined."

"Maybe I'll be the last," Claire said. "Though I wouldn't call it ruined. Don't you think 'Claire Cantrell' has a ring to it?"

"Not a wedding ring! You'd be better off marrying Bob Daggerty and putting up with the smell of his pomade for the rest of your life 'stead of harnessing your wagon to Whit's horse."

Claire hooted with laughter. "I'd as soon marry an undertaker and live with the smell of embalming fluid as that pomade Bob Daggerty douses on himself!"

Lily laughed, too. "It's 'cause he never takes a bath. He thinks it covers his stink, but I'd snuggle up to ripe sweat over his pomade any day or night."

Claire smiled, opening her arms for her friend. "I'm glad you're going to be family, Lily," she said, pulling her close.

Lily had forgotten that she was betrothed to Uncle Emmett. She sighed, accepting her fate, then thought that if Claire did have a romance with Whit, he might bring Jasper around once in a while.

A pudgy man with wispy white hair and dark eyes as big as an owl's, Lash Cooper stopped just inside the bat-wing doors of the Seven Sevens Saloon in Siete Rios. His gray worsted frock coat still managed to create the effect of a man of means down on his luck, but everyone knew Lash Cooper wasn't that. Like a gambler riding his losses, he was broke more often than not. As he stood casting his gaze over the sports in the Seven Sevens, he was assessing which of them would be most likely to buy him a drink.

Spying Jasper Stone alone at the end of the bar, Lash wasted no time joining him. "Good evening, Jasper," he said. "Or perhaps I should say good morning, since it's well past midnight."

Jasper looked at him with hooded eyes. "What're you doing clear down here, Lash?"

He smiled. "Looking to have a drink among friends."

Jasper laughed. "Hey, Louie," he called to the barkeep. "Bring another glass for everybody's friend."

The men who heard him chuckled, all of them having been hit up for liquor by Lash at one time or another. Louie brought the glass, then returned to his conversation with Marty Turner as Jasper poured a fresh shot from his nearly full bottle of Magnolia Pike. When Lash chugged the drink down, Jasper laughed again and poured him another.

"I had the pleasure of dining with Whit tonight," Lash said softly. "You'll never guess where."

"I know where," Jasper said, turning his back to the bar and leaning on his elbows as he surveyed the room.

"Young Andy told me Whit killed Rufus Bond in Soledad yesterday. Is that true?"

"Why ask me?"

"Weren't you there?"

"What're you after, Lash? More'n whiskey, I'll warrant."

"I'm a journalist, Jasper, always in search of a story."

Jasper turned around and poured himself another drink. "You should've ridden north 'stead of south. Saunders is holding an inquest in Soledad and Whit promised to be there."

"Tomorrow?"

"Today," Jasper said, "if it's after midnight."

Lash emptied his glass and looked hopefully at the bottle. "Will Whit claim self-defense?"

"That's what it was," Jasper said. "He was walking out the door when it came down. He wheeled around and packed three bullets into the fucker's forehead, all the holes hitting so close together you could've covered 'em with one silver dollar."

Lash met Jasper's eyes in silent appreciation of Whit's skill.

"You mind?" Lash asked, reaching for the bottle.

Jasper shook his head.

"Red won't be happy," Lash said, filling his glass.

"Hart neither," Jasper agreed.

They each sipped their drinks, then Lash asked, "Will you be attending the inquest?"

"Whit's got Andy Moss to back him up. Don't guess he needs me in his corner."

Lash hesitated before asking softly, "Is Whit riding for Moss now?"

Jasper's blue eyes flashed cold. "Why didn't you ask him at supper, if you're so curious?"

"If he is," Lash persisted, "will you oppose him?"

Jasper fished into his vest pocket for a coin and slapped it on the bar. "Guess you'll have to wait and see." He downed his shot and walked out.

The barkeep hurried to collect the coin and bottle before Lash could touch either one, then returned to his conversation with Turner. Lash dawdled over his last drink, trying to make up his mind to ride all night to reach Soledad in time for the inquest. If Whit really showed, it would be worth reporting. Without him, it would be just another mundane procedure of an impotent court.

Jasper had said Whit promised to show. Against that, Andy had said Whit was riding to Siete Rios to meet Jasper. That obviously hadn't happened, and Lash kicked himself for believing Whit would tell Andy where he'd be when half a dozen men would pay a tidy sum to anticipate Whit's location. Lash now suspected Whit had deliberately used Andy to lead anyone interested on a wild goose chase, and it wasn't far-fetched to suspect Jasper of doing the same.

On the other hand, the Vegas *Optic* would pay seven-fifty for any story on Whit that carried a smidgeon of veracity, and Lash didn't have two dimes to rub together. He lifted his glass and licked the last drops off the bottom, then left for the six-hour ride to Soledad.

The next morning, Emmett took his brother with him and rode to the north range, where the cowboys were splitting a herd for shipment. Emmett and Drew sat on a knoll watching the work through a haze of dust raised by the cattle and horses on the prairie below.

"You know," Emmett said, "when I came out here in sixty-seven, I brought a herd of nine hundred head I'd gathered in Texas."

"I remember," Drew said, also remembering Emmett had asked him to go in on the deal and he'd refused because he thought it a foolish gamble.

"I trailed the herd up the Panal," Emmett said, "and turned 'em loose pretty close to where we are now, then rode up to Soledad, which was still a fort then, and sold the whole lot to the army to feed the Indians. Made twenty-eight thousand dollars on that drive."

"What'd you pay in Texas?" Drew asked.

" 'Bout seven thousand." Emmett smiled. "Garnered such a good profit, I made the drive again. By the time I got here, though, the army market was controlled by contracts. So I had to find me a new buyer. That first roundup, I drove a herd all the way to the San Carlos Agency in Arizona. Lost a lotta cows, which cut into my profit considerable. Was tough going those first years."

"I can imagine," Drew said.

"No, I don't think you can," Emmett answered, his eyes on the work below. "Long about seventy, I lost five hundred head of horses—pretty near my whole remuda—to the Mescaleros. I went to the army brass up at Fort Stanton and complained. They told me to file a claim against the gov'ment. Well, you know, I ain't ever been much for paperwork, and cows don't respect a man who's afoot. So I got my horses back."

"How'd you do that?" Drew asked.

"Hired a bunch of guns, rode into the Mescalero camp up in the Sacramentos, killed every buck we saw, then herded the horses back down here to the Panal."

Drew felt appalled, meeting his brother's bright blue eyes.

Emmett laughed. "I ain't been bothered by Apaches since, but the army don't like me much. Now Henry Hart's got the gov'ment contract. He came into the territory with the California Column and is tight with the soldiers, so an old rebel from Texas like me ain't ever gonna get the contract long as Hart's alive. But that don't bother me none. I trail my herds to Colorado and ship 'em on the railroad to Kansas City. They lose a bit of weight on the trail, even moving slow and giving 'em time to graze along the way. Once they're loaded on the trains, they're in transit thirty-nine hours. That takes considerable weight off 'em, and a'course I'm paid by what they weigh at the stockyards. Still in all, I'm making money."

"How much, if you don't mind my asking?" Drew said.

"I usually turn fifty, sixty thousand a year," Emmett drawled. "You know what it costs me to raise a cow?"

"No," Drew said, amazed at the amount of his brother's income.

"Running 'em on open range like I do, it don't cost me but eighty cents an animal per year." Emmett laughed again. "That's a right pretty profit, ain't it?"

Drew nodded.

"Thing of it is," Emmett said, "lately I've been wondering what I'm doing it for."

"The love of it, I imagine," Drew said.

"Yeah, there's that," Emmett agreed. He stood up in his stirrups. "*Listo,* Raul?"

Drew looked down at a Mexican cowboy yelling up at Emmett. Though Drew couldn't hear what the man was saying, Emmett yelled back, "Run 'em on by."

As Drew watched, the cowboys hurrahed a stream of cattle beneath where he and Emmett sat. Emmett kept his eyes pinned on the steers and cows passing beneath him. Half an hour later, the herd was separated into two groups. Raul spurred his horse onto the knoll beside Emmett.

"Two hundred yearlings at six bucks; sixty two-year-olds at nine; forty-five cows at eighteen; eighty-nine steers at twenty-five. That makes four thousand seven hundred seventy-five. Best add a dozen more steers, Raul, so they'll be sure'n bring an even five in KC."

"*Sí, señor,*" Raul said, reining his horse down the knoll into the herd again.

Drew stared at his brother in amazement. "You counted four different grades of cattle while they were running by?"

Emmett's eyes sparkled with fun. "After twenty years in the business, a man develops the knack."

Drew shook his head. "I doubt if many men do to that extent."

"Well, hell," Emmett said, slapping his brother on the back. "They don't call me Cattle King of the Panal for nothing."

"No, indeed," Drew said.

"Let's head home," Emmett said, turning his horse down the other side of the knoll. "What I wanted to tell you this morning, Drew, is that I've decided to get hitched."

"Married?" Drew asked in surprise.

"I been a bachelor long enough, don't you think?"

"No argument," Drew said, trying to emulate the easy way Emmett sat a saddle. He also tried to hide his disappointment that if Emmett took a wife, he'd likely have children, which meant Drew's children wouldn't inherit Bosque Grande.

As if reading his thoughts, Emmett said, "It's not so much a wife I'm wanting, but sons." He hesitated, then said, "I asked Lily to marry me. She said she would."

Drew bit his tongue, knowing Emmett could court any woman in the territory and most of Texas with guaranteed success. Why he'd choose such a homely girl was beyond his brother's ability to understand. But paramount in Drew's mind was the disappointment of his prospects for his own children.

"Don't tell nobody," Emmett said. "I ain't seen her yet today and she might've changed her mind."

"Do you really think that's possible?" Drew scoffed.

"There's always the chance," Emmett answered. "She can be stubborn about getting what she wants, and I ain't no spring chicken. There're plenty of roosters with cockier struts and bigger crows. If that's what she's aiming for, she won't be happy with me."

"What about Claire?" Drew asked miserably.

"Why, she's my niece! That'd be a sin, Andrew Moss."

"I didn't mean it like that," he protested. "You gonna find her a respectable husband?"

"Seems to me that's your job," Emmett said. "But I'll advise you to the best of my knowledge as to the pick of the field."

"And Andy?" Drew asked.

"Will always have a home at Bosque Grande," Emmett promised.

Drew nodded. "Reckon I'm beholden."

"Ain't no call for that," Emmett said. "They're my kin, same as you. But Andy ain't got the wherewithal to run a ranch. Surely you know that as well as I do."

"He's still a boy," Drew said in his defense.

"A dreamer is what he is. Maybe you oughta think of sending him to some school back East. Seems to me he's got the makings of a poet."

"I've never heard of any poet able to earn a living, but he might do well in the law once he gets his head out of the clouds and realizes money doesn't grow in his father's pockets."

"His uncle's neither," Emmett agreed. "But the lawyers I've known mix a great degree of arrogance with no small amount of cunning that leans toward crooked goals. I don't see Andy doing that. He's got a religious bent. The other day he asked me if we could go to services some Sunday, and he looked right perturbed when I told him we'd have to ride clear to Vegas or Santa Fe to find a church."

"Nothing wrong with a man being religious," Drew said.

"No, there ain't. But a lawyer cripples himself by following God's law over man's. Take this Edgar Homer up in Union. He used to be a preacher, and he's always spouting off about building a God-fearing community when he oughta be looking after his earthly survival. It's more threatened than his place in heaven. Regardless of what he says, though, he's after money same as the rest of us." Emmett chuckled. "His wife's the most fetching woman in the county. Have you met her?"

"No, I haven't had the pleasure," Drew said, watching his brother closely as their horses ambled along the trail. "In fact, I'm surprised, Emmett, to hear you mention a woman's charms. I didn't think you were interested in the feminine sex."

"I generally confine my int'rest to the professionals, is all," Emmett said, then laughed at his brother's amazement. "Did you think I'd been celibate all these years?"

"I guess I did," Drew admitted.

Emmett shook his head. "If a man don't get his rocks off least once a month, he's apt to go crazy and start killing folks right and left. I bet if you investigated most of these hellions with a gun, you'd discover they can't find satisfaction with a woman in bed."

"That's an interesting theory," Drew said.

"It's my own," Emmett answered proudly. "I suspect some of these killers would rather do it with men, but they can't admit that so take to killing outta pure frustration."

"Are you saying they *should* do it with men?" Drew muttered, offended at the thought.

Emmett laughed. "Nobody knows what happens behind the closed door of a bedroom, while a man killing folks right and left is hard to ignore."

"I agree with that," Drew said, "but the Bible specifically prohibits the crime against nature."

"Whose nature? By definition, God's unknowable, so it can't be His. And there's a helluva lotta murder in the Bible even though there's a commandment against it. Maybe there was a lotta sodomy, too."

"That's blasphemy, Emmett," Drew said, feeling ill.

"I don't care if it is," Emmett said. "I've seen bulls mount steers, so the so-called law against nature apparently wasn't meant for critters who can't read." They rode along in silence a while, then he asked, "What've you been doing with all your juice since Laura died?"

"I loved my wife," Drew answered indignantly.

"I know you did, but I'm talking about now. If you like, I'll take you into Soledad and introduce you to a whore named Celia. Whit Cantrell broke her in, and he's a mighty fine teacher judging by the results."

Drew was momentarily speechless. Then he caught a flaw in his brother's logic. "From what I've heard, Whit Cantrell is a prime example of a hellion with a gun, one of those men you say wreak violence because they can't find satisfaction with a woman."

"Whit's killings were justified," Emmett said. "I was thinking of fellows like Jasper Stone."

"I never met him," Drew muttered.

"Count yourself lucky. Whit's got an uncommon tolerance up to a point, but if Jasper don't like the least little thing about a man, he's apt to react with a twitch of his finger. He's one of those roosters with cockier struts I mentioned earlier. Lily's got her eyes full of him. I'd bet my ranch if she got him he couldn't get it up for her, but if I'm gonna make her happy, the first thing I have to do is knock Jasper Stone outta the game."

Drew stared at his brother, then finally managed to ask, "Do you mean you're going to kill him?"

"Hell, no! The reason I never carry a gun is so folks'll think I'm a peaceable man."

"You mean you're not?" Drew asked weakly.

"Do you think a man gets what I got by turning the other cheek?" Emmett shook his head. "One of the advantages of being rich, Drew, is having enough money to pay some fool to pull the trigger when you want it pulled. He bears the culpability before the law and you skate free. Henry Hart knows that. It's why I consider him a worthy opponent. But he considers me the same, so it ain't likely we'll lock horns." Seeing the incredulous look on his brother's face, Emmett reached across and slapped him on the back again. "This is the frontier, Drew. What d'you think 'wide open' means?" Without waiting for an answer, Emmett said, "Let's pick up the pace a bit. All this talking has set a fire in my loins for a trip to Soledad."

7

Three days later Whit Cantrell was ambling his broomtail along a ridge overlooking a herd of horses belonging to Emmett Moss. They were all branded with a bold *EM* on their right shoulder and would be known to be stolen if he took one. Whit was studying how he might alter the brand when he saw Emmett circling around from the far side of the herd.

Emmett saw him, too. Had probably seen him silhouetted against the sky considerably sooner than Whit had seen Emmett in the shadowed meadow below. Whit let his mare munch at a stand of fountain grass while he watched the old rancher spur his big horse to climb the trail up the ridge. The gelding was a black-stockinged bay that could give any horse in the county a run for the money, which was the exact quality Whit needed from his mount. The mare he was riding wouldn't win any prizes but she was better than she looked.

"Afternoon, Whit," Emmett drawled, reining up close so he was looking down on him.

"Emmett," Whit said with a smile.

"Heard they gave a party in your honor in Soledad the other day and you forgot to show up."

Whit laughed. "Hope I didn't ruin it for 'em."

"No, they went ahead anyway." Emmett waited for Whit to ask what the verdict had been. When he didn't, Emmett shifted his gaze to the fifty prime mounts in the meadow and tried to guess which one Whit had singled out. "It's a hard brand to alter, ain't it?" Emmett mused.

"I've noticed that," Whit said. "Now with cattle, once you butcher and skin 'em, all beef look the same. But a skinned horse wouldn't be no fun to ride."

Emmett studied Whit's honey-brown eyes dancing in fun, then said, "Self-defense. Foxy Strop testified on your behalf."

Whit smiled. "Was nice of you to let him tell the truth."

"What makes you think I had anything to do with it?"

"Foxy's your man, last I heard."

"He's not on my payroll," Emmett said.

"I know that. But most all the money changing hands in his saloon comes outta your pocket," Whit said, pausing to grin, "one way or another."

Emmett nodded. "Been up to Union lately?"

"No, I haven't," Whit answered. "I heard you and Lily Cassidy are getting hitched."

"That's true," Emmett said. "Who'd you hear it from?"

"It's the talk of the county. Guess I should offer congratulations."

"Only if you mean it."

"Lily's a flower with a stalk of steel."

"I'm surprised to hear you say that, Whit."

"Don't you think it's true?"

"Yes. But I always figured your taste in women ran more to appearances than substance."

"Well, now, I ain't looking for a wife, though, am I?"

"I've heard more'n one girl's been powerfully disappointed when she learned that too late."

Whit laughed. "You gonna invite me to the wedding?"

"Hadn't thought to have anyone but family," Emmett said, studying his herd of horses again.

"Why, Emmett, I would've expected you to have a big she-bang. After waiting fifty years to take a bride, seems to me you oughta celebrate."

"Maybe so," he said. "We ain't set a date yet."

"What's the holdup?"

Emmett nudged his horse a little to the left. "See that pinto out there by itself?"

"Yeah, I do," Whit said, letting his gaze follow Emmett's.

"Would you like to own it?"

"Looks like a good 'un, but I'll tell you what, Emmett, I wouldn't cotton to such a mount. All that white's liable to flash in the dark, making for a dangerous ride in the wrong circumstances."

Emmett met his eyes.

Whit gave him a teasing smile, then looked at the horses when he said, "If I was to pick a mount outta that herd, I'd choose that black mare grazing close to the stud. Ain't she pretty?"

Emmett didn't need to look to know which horse Whit meant. A three-year-old with long legs and strong haunches, she'd likely top out the fastest of the bunch. "Why is it you're so partial to mares?" he asked, unhappy because he'd intended to breed the black.

Still watching the mare, Whit said softly, "Reckon I got an affinity for the feminine mind. I can coax things outta females you wouldn't believe possible."

Emmett did believe it, suspecting Whit could seduce a princess if he put his mind to it. "She's yours," Emmett said.

Whit slowly shifted his eyes to meet Emmett's. "What for?"

"Just a present 'tween friends. No more'n that."

"We been friends a long time, Emmett, but you never gave me a present before."

"Consider it a gift from the largess of a generous bridegroom."

Whit laughed. "I'll accept it if you give me a bill of sale so no one can say I stole her."

"Why don't you come to the house for supper? I'll write one out 'fore you leave."

"I believe marriage is gonna improve you, Emmett," Whit said. "I'll just ride on down and catch her first. That all right?"

"I'll wait here," he said.

Whit spurred his horse down the slope of the ridge, not bothering with the trail. Emmett watched the scruffy nag nimbly descending the steep incline, thinking the mare was worth more than she appeared to be. She couldn't hold a candle to the black, though, and Emmett knew Whit had been wanting a better mount for some time. Living the life he did, it made sense to have a horse under him that could outrun most challengers. Knowing the black could do that, Emmett ruefully admitted he might be giving Whit the edge he needed to cut as wide a swath as he damn well pleased. That wasn't Emmett's intention, but he was keenly aware that the gift could ricochet out of control if he wasn't careful about playing his next card.

Whit loosed his lariat and swung the loop over his head twice before letting it sail to settle pretty as pie on the black's neck. Watching from the ridge, Emmett shook his head with scorn. Whit had the skills to be a top hand. That he rode the underbelly of the law wasn't a matter of circumstances but a clear-cut choice. His free and easy days were coming to a close, though, and Emmett saw no shame in using Whit before the outlaw put himself in an early grave.

Whit pulled his saddle off the broomtail and let it go, then saddled the black. She hadn't been ridden in a while and he had to fight her at first, but within minutes she stood quivering beneath him, waiting his command. Again Emmett shook his head that such talent should be wasted, but he wasn't truly sorry. Top hands weren't nearly as hard to come by as a man with the balls to kill Henry Hart. Emmett reined his horse downhill to join the outlaw on the prairie, then grinned at Whit's pleasure as they turned toward Bosque Grande.

"Tell me more about Whit Cantrell," Claire whispered to Lily. They were sitting on Claire's bed with her jewelry box open between them, bracelets and brooches and earrings and necklaces scattered on the white eyelet of her comforter.

"I don't know much more'n I already told you," Lily said, turning a sapphire to catch sun from the window. The blue gem reminded her of Jasper's eyes in the soft glow of lamplight.

"You must know something else," Claire urged.

"He's an orphan without any family," Lily said, putting the earring back and taking a bracelet off the bed. She ran her fingertip along the flowered vines engraved in the gold. "Jasper told me Whit's father was killed in the War of Rebellion fighting for the North, and his mother died when he was thirteen. Lash Cooper said that happened in Santa Fe, but I've heard other folks say Whit comes from Indiana. Whit told me he was born in Missouri. I've no reason to doubt him, but it don't seem likely his father fought for the North if they lived in the South." She shrugged, carefully placing the bracelet back in the box. "A lotta stuff about Whit is like that. Stories with pieces that don't add up."

"How did you first meet him?" Claire asked.

"Jasper brought him by the mill in the spring of seventy-six, before Whit killed those men in Union. I'd thought he was a drifter down on his luck, but when I heard he challenged Browne Carson on the street and beat him to the draw, I figured there was more to Whit than meets the eye. Browne Carson was a professional gunman, and what Whit did proved he wasn't no novice at it neither."

"Why did he kill him?" Claire asked.

"Browne Carson killed Angus Bodie, a friend of Whit's. There was more killing up in the mountains that Whit had a part in, but that was later. When I first met him, he helped me out when no one else would."

"How?" Claire asked.

Lily lifted a long necklace off the bed and ran the strand through her fingers, taking pleasure from the cool, smooth texture of the pearls. "We had a coupla bad years 'fore the killings happened. The summer of seventy-five, hordes of grasshoppers descended on the county. They covered our whole house—roof, doors, windows, everything. We couldn't see out, and couldn't go out but they didn't land all over us."

"How horrible," Claire whispered.

Lily nodded, rolling a pearl between her fingers. "They ate the county's entire harvest, as well as everything in our vegetable garden and everyone else's. When the grasshoppers landed on a fence, they ate the bark off the posts. Their noise was awful.

They're loathsome creatures. I get the shivers just remembering 'em."

"I've got them, too," Claire said.

"As soon as the grasshoppers were gone, everyone replanted their fields. Then we got cabbage lice." She shivered again. "They're tiny but there must've been millions of 'em, covering the leaves and sucking the juice out. Some people sprinkled ashes on their fields. We tried lime water, but nothing worked. They ate everything, so the county lost its harvest a second time. Doing all that work with nothing to show for it was discouraging, to say nothing of knowing we'd have to buy food all winter. Some folks needed to sell their harvest to have any money, but we had some put aside, so we were better off than most." Gently she laid the pearl necklace in the jewelry box, then picked up the silver pin shaped liked a crescent moon and pushed one of its points into her thumb. "After that we got fleas."

"Good heavens!" Claire exclaimed. "Did you have them yourself?"

"Everybody did. Wasn't no way to get rid of 'em. Inside the house, the tables and walls were covered with black specks that moved. You couldn't sleep for being bit, and you itched all day. Everybody was miserable. Mama swamped the house with lye soap as strong as her hands could bear every morning and night, but within an hour there'd be as many as before. All we could do was wait for the first freeze to kill 'em."

"My word," Claire said.

Lily laid the silver moon in the box and picked up a topaz pendant, an orange stone with black lightning shooting across its surface. "I don't know if there's a connection 'tween all them bugs or not, but the next summer we had an epidemic of smallpox." She sighed, flashing sun off the topaz. "The Mexicans said it was a curse from God for our wickedness, so they didn't do nothing to protect themselves. When a friend or relative died, they'd all go to the wake, then carry the disease home, spreading it around the county like wildfire. Hundreds of people died in the territory that summer, most of 'em children."

"How sad," Claire murmured.

Lily nodded. "Mama sent me to Junction to get a bit of scab from Old Man Clene. He got it from the doctor at Fort Stanton, who'd taken it off a child who recovered. He had to use a silver knife to cut it out 'cause silver's the only effective metal for doing it. I don't know why. That scab was so precious, I was given only a tiny piece of it in a cup of water, and I carried it home in my hands, walking 'cause I was afraid if I rode my horse I'd spill the cup."

"What did you do with it?" Claire asked with a grimace of repugnance.

"Used it to vaccinate everyone at the mill." Lily laid the topaz in the box, then picked up a ring with a ruby the color of fresh blood. "I scratched their upper arms till I drew a spot of blood that looked just like this, only smaller. You can't draw too much blood or the flow'll wash the vaccine out. I let a single drop of the scab water drip into the wound." Suddenly she laughed. "It was funny to watch the men flinch as I made such a small cut in their arm when there they stood wearing six-shooters none of 'em ever hesitate to use."

Claire smiled weakly.

"It was a real hot summer," Lily said, somber again. "Father had gone to Texas to bring back a herd of select heifers he wanted to breed to one of Uncle Emmett's imported bulls. 'Cause of no harvest the year before, the mill didn't have any work, and we closed the store to keep folks away, not knowing who carried the pox and who didn't. The men who worked for us stayed out on the range with the herd, so there wasn't nothing stirring at the mill. Not even a breath of wind, seemed like. I'd vaccinated everybody, but I was the only one it worked for, even though I'd done myself last when there wasn't hardly any of the scab water left. Maybe it was more potent 'cause it set longer. I don't know. But everybody else took sick."

"How terrible for you," Claire whispered.

"It was all of that," Lily agreed. "Black smallpox is the most vile disease I've ever seen. Mother was covered with pustules. Her breasts were a solid blister. Her hands and arms swelled up twice their normal size and she was black all over. She wanted me to open the sores on her hands but I'd heard you weren't s'posed to do that, so I refused. It was the first time in my life I hadn't done what she told me. She got her way by holding her hands over her head at night and letting the mice gnaw at the sores. We were overrun with mice. As if I didn't have enough problems, I had to bat mice off a chair every time I sat down."

"How did you bear it?" Claire asked, hugging herself in horror.

Lily snorted. "Didn't have no choice. I was the only one on my feet. Everyone else was sick in bed. My next to the youngest brother, Will, talked to angels. He said they were holding his hands and trying to lead him to heaven. I told him not to go, but he didn't pay any attention. John, my brother who was a year older'n me, was tormented by visions of his favorite horse being tortured. He kept saying Jack Crawford, our millhand, who was himself down with pox, had tied the hooves of John's horse together and was whipping him to run when he couldn't move 'cause of the ropes. John cried and wanted to help his horse so bad, I had to tie him to the bed. Theo was always slapping at centipedes he thought were running all over him, but I couldn't see any. Add, my baby brother, just cried and whimpered all the time but never said nothing. I felt like I'd died and gone to hell, and maybe I would've outta sheer exhaustion if Whit hadn't come along."

"Whit?" Claire whispered eagerly.

Lily nodded. "I'd only seen him a coupla times 'fore that and didn't know him well. When I heard his horse in the yard, I pulled myself to my feet, so tired I could hardly stand up, and I walked to the door and called out to him that we had the pox and he shouldn't come in. He swung right down without hesitating one bit. Said he had the pox as a child and was immune. I nearly cried at the great blessing of simply seeing someone who was healthy. Whit looked around the house, then told me to get some rest, that I appeared to need it." Lily half laughed. "I hadn't slept more'n fits and starts for days. When I woke up, Whit had soup simmering on the stove, and he was bathing Will and listening to him talk about the angels as if Whit believed Will was really seeing 'em. Will died that night. Add and John the next day. Mama was delirious and didn't know they were gone till after Whit buried 'em. I don't know what I would've done if he hadn't been there. I sure didn't have the strength to dig three graves."

"Oh, Lily," Claire breathed with compassion.

Lily shrugged. "Mama got better. Theo, too. Soon as Whit saw the worst had passed, he left for Soledad. I was sorry to see him go, and I didn't see him again till after he killed Browne Carson in Union. Whit was arrested for that. There were plenty of witnesses who said it was a fair fight, but they weren't allowed to testify at his trial. He was found guilty and sentenced to be hung but his friends got him outta jail. He came to the mill right after that, on foot 'cause he'd killed his horse running it so hard. The army was trailing him and he needed someplace to hide. My father didn't hold with harboring escaped crim'nals, but 'cause of what Whit had done for us the summer before, Father hid him above the gristwheel in the mill. When the soldiers came, it never occurred to them to doubt my father's word. Everyone knew he was an honorable man." She rolled the ruby earring around in her palm a moment, then let it fall into the jewelry box.

Softly Claire asked, "Is there still an order of execution against Whit?"

Lily nodded, then laughed. "Nobody's got the courage to serve it. He rides into Union whenever he pleases, and anywhere else, too. He lives on the run, though. Always moving, never staying the same place two nights in a row, telling stories about where he's going when he's got no intention to be there. It'd wear anybody else down, but I think Whit likes it." She met Claire's eyes with a solemn warning: "There's a lot to admire about Whit Cantrell, but he ain't husband material and never will be."

Claire thought a moment. "Isn't there a chance he could get a new trial and be exonerated?"

"There might've been once. But he's killed three men since Browne Carson. The latest was Rufus Bond, the sheriff's brother. The sheriff works for Henry Hart, and Hart controls the courts. Ain't no way Whit'll get a fair trial. If he lets himself be arrested, he prob'ly won't live long enough to see a courtroom anyway. They'll hang him on the old charge and not bother with the new ones. He's let it be known he won't be taken alive, and if he dies fighting arrest, he'll take some men with him. Everybody knows that and it makes 'em shy to act against him."

"But it's all so unjust, Lily," Claire protested with tears in her eyes.

Lily nodded. "Henry Hart paid William Wilson to kill my father, just like he paid Browne Carson to kill Angus Bodie. There won't be justice in this county till we get rid of Hart. Maybe when that happens, Whit'll get a new trial and clear his name, but like I said, I think he enjoys living on the wrong side of the law."

"I shall speak to Uncle Emmett on Whit's behalf," Claire said.

"Don't, Claire," Lily said urgently. "As things are now, Emmett likes Whit. That's why he can come and go on the Panal as easily as he does. But if Emmett suspects you have strong feelings for Whit, he'll withdraw his protection and Whit'll be thrown to the wolves. Bide your time. I expect a change to be coming. Maybe then you'll have a chance to win Whit's heart, but I'm still warning you that he ain't husband material, whether he's clear with the law or not."

"Why isn't he?" Claire asked.

Lily tried to think of a convincing answer. Finally she said, "Maybe 'cause he's been on his own from such a young age, he throws his fate to the wind and don't consider long-term consequences. A wife and children are about as long-term as it gets, and I don't see him ever choosing to settle down."

Claire gathered the pieces of jewelry still scattered on the bed and replaced them in the box, rearranging those pieces Lily had put in while she talked. When she was done, Claire snapped the box closed and met Lily's eyes. "With proper motivation, I believe Whit's capable of anything."

Lily smiled with bitter irony. "He's proved that several times over."

Lily and Claire were sitting with Andy under the portal when Emmett and Whit rode into the yard. Lily noticed right off that Whit was riding one of Emmett's horses. She hoped Whit's mount had gone lame and Emmett had happened along and loaned him another, not that the horse was a gift. She knew such a gift could only be a bribe, and she also knew the hook hidden under the feather of that lure. Lily didn't approve. If she hadn't cared what happened in the aftermath, she could have asked Whit or Jasper either one to do her bidding in regards to Henry Hart. But she did care, and that made her wonder how she'd expected Emmett to achieve her wish. It suddenly dawned on her that she'd assumed he was so powerful he could make it happen as if through magic. Kicking herself for being so childish, she frowned as Claire laughed when Whit gave her a smile.

Andy stood up. "Hey, Whit, good to see you."

"Howdy, Andy," Whit said, swinging down and tying his reins to the rail, then coming close to shake Andy's hand. He smiled at Lily. "I hear you're getting married. Am I gonna have to call you Mrs. Moss when it's done?"

"Don't be silly," she said, looking quickly at Emmett. But he had turned his horse toward the corral.

"Can you stay for supper?" Claire asked Whit.

"Your uncle already invited me," he answered. "What's that you're drinking?"

"Apple cider. Would you like a glass?"

"Yeah, thanks," he said, sitting in a chair on the other side of Andy. "Seen Foxy Strop lately?" Whit asked him.

"Haven't been to town since the inquest," Andy said. "He was there, along with everyone else in Soledad, and he testified that you shot Rufus Bond in self-defense." Andy took the glass Claire had filled and passed it to Whit, then said, "I would've testified but they wouldn't allow it on account of my age."

"I appreciate that, Andy," Whit said. He drank the cider down and passed the glass back.

"Where were you?" Andy asked, handing the empty glass to Claire.

"Would you like more?" she asked Whit, leaning forward to see past her brother.

"That'll do me," Whit said, then told Andy, "I was with Jasper." He leaned forward with his elbows on his knees to smile down the row at Lily. "Theo rode over to tell us about you getting hitched."

"Was he happy about it?" Lily asked softly.

Whit smiled. "Seemed to be, but Jasper was fit to be tied."

Lily stared at him.

"The way he carried on," Whit said, "you would've thought Emmett was fixing to elope with his sister."

"What'd he say?" Lily whispered.

"Nothing I can repeat in mixed company," Whit said.

"I haven't met Jasper," Claire interjected. "Why don't you bring him for supper sometime, Whit?"

He laughed. "I don't think he'd come, Claire, but I'll extend the invitation next time I see him."

"Why won't he come?" she asked, coyly pretending she didn't know.

"He thinks this house is haunted," Whit answered. He winked at Lily before turning his gaze back to Claire. "You ever hear anything odd in the middle of the night?"

"No," she said. "Haunted by whom?"

"Oh, the usual kinda spooks. You know, chain-rattling ghosts that howl in the dark."

"Goodness," Claire said with a laugh. "You'll make me afraid to be alone in my bed."

Whit gave her a smile.

"I don't believe in spooks," Andy said. "I don't think they're real. Do you, Whit?"

"Oh yeah," he said. "I've seen one."

"You have? What'd it look like?"

He smiled at Lily when he said, "It was a tall old man all covered with green, slimy moss."

She stood up. "I'll go see about supper," she said, hurrying away. But she didn't go to the kitchen. She went to her room and stood hugging herself in front of the window, wondering why Jasper had reacted to the news of her engagement with anger. Could it be she'd been wrong in thinking he had no interest in her? Had she traded the future she wanted for vengeance, and would Whit now die because of her? Lily sank onto her bed and held her head in her hands, wondering what she should do.

The three people on the portal watched her disappear inside the house, then Whit said, "She's taking on her duties right smart, ain't she?"

"I'll say," Andy said, glad she had left. "She's even gone so far as to tell me when I need a bath."

"If you need to be told," Claire said, "you should be grateful she bothers."

Andy felt hurt. To cover it, he smiled at Whit and said, "Too bad we don't have a piano."

"It surely is," Whit agreed.

"I hear you play well," Claire said.

"Only tunes I learned in bawdy houses, nothing like what Andy coaxes outta the bones."

"Bones?" Claire asked, puzzled.

"Keys," Andy said, as if she were stupid.

"Oh," she said. Then, smiling at Whit, "I suppose Andy does play rather well."

"Brought tears to my eyes," Whit said. "Didn't you, Andy?"

Andy nodded, proud to bursting.

"I imagine," Claire teased, "that's not an easy thing to do."

Whit chuckled. "Being in the presence of beauty always makes me cry. In fact, I can feel myself misting up right now."

"If so," Claire said softly, "I can't see it."

"You know a man never lets himself cry in front of a lady."

"Uncle Emmett's got a fiddle," Andy said, feeling left out. "You ever play one of them, Whit?"

"No, I never," he said, leaning back to look at Andy. "How about you?"

"Not yet, but Uncle Emmett said he'll teach me soon as he has an idle hour."

"Maybe after Lily's his wife," Whit said, "he'll spend less time on the range and more at home."

"Maybe," Andy said, not entirely happy at the prospect.

"Lily don't seem too tickled about getting married," Whit said, looking at Claire.

"What makes you think that?" she asked.

"Oh, I don't know. Maybe 'cause she's content to hide out here when, seems to me, any woman about to marry the Cattle

King of the Panal would strut her stuff so the poor folk could envy her good fortune."

"Lily's more modest than that," Claire said.

Whit smiled. "Funny, I never noticed it before."

They broke off talking as Emmett came out of the stable and walked across the yard toward the house. When he was close, he smiled and asked, "Ain't y'all hungry? By my clock, I figure it's suppertime."

Claire laughed. "Then it is, Uncle Emmett, since Bosque Grande runs by your clock."

He chuckled. "Where's Lily?"

"Seeing to supper," Claire said, "as befitting a wife."

"Best not let it get cold," he said, opening the door and holding it for the others.

Andy followed Claire inside. Hovering in a dark shadow of the hall to wait for Whit, Andy heard him say, "Never thought I'd see you hold a door open for me, Emmett."

"Just being a good host," Andy's uncle replied.

"A good host and a generous bridegroom all in one day," Whit said. "Makes me suspect I'm about to be hit up for a favor. I ain't opposed to that, but if I don't get a bill of sale for the mare first, she won't be a gift."

"We'll talk about it after supper," Emmett muttered.

"Talking won't change what I just said."

"I have your bill of sale in my pocket."

"Why don't you give it to me now, so it won't be an issue later?"

"I ain't signed it yet."

There was a momentary silence before Whit said, "I don't need you, Emmett. You're the one needs me. You think about that while we're breaking bread with your family."

"I will," Emmett said.

Whit came through the door and saw Andy had been listening. Whit gave him a wink and they walked down the hall toward the dining room together. Andy felt proud that Whit was his friend, but he could feel his uncle, following behind, wasn't pleased.

8

*C*laire could barely wait for supper to be over so she could have Whit to herself. Even then, it was an hour before Andy went to bed and left them alone on the portal. The November night was chilly, and Claire sat on the swing bundled in a thick shawl. Whit balanced on the rail, his left knee folded in front of him and his right leg straight to the floor, his jacket tucked behind his gun as if he anticipated needing the weapon without warning.

Though Whit sat in shadow, by the lamplight falling from the house behind them, Claire could see his gun. She had never held a weapon, and she wondered how it would feel to pull a trigger and send a bullet to take someone's life, to have enough faith in your convictions that you didn't doubt you were right. She had often thought she believed something to be absolutely true, then discovered it wasn't; but none of her actions caused irrevocable results. In the hours since her talk with Lily, Claire had formulated the questions she meant to ask when she next saw Whit. Now that they were alone, she began by murmuring, "May I ask you something?"

He turned his eyes away from the darkness of the yard and gave her a smile. "What is it you want to know?"

"Have you ever felt regret for killing a man?"

He shook his head. "The men I killed deserved it."

"Do you deserve the price you've paid for killing them?"

"What price is that?" he asked, his smile teasing now.

"Living the way you do, without a home or the possibility of a family."

He shrugged. "I ain't had those things since my mother died. Reckon I've forgotten what they're like."

Knowing she was risking rejection, Claire asked, "Is there anything that might make you want them again?"

"If I did happen across something like that," he answered, "I'd prob'ly walk away from it."

"Why?" she asked.

"Can't see any sense in wanting something that ain't possible."

"You could change," she said, "so those things were possible again."

He laughed softly. "A river can change course, too, but I've never seen it happen, have you?"

"I've heard of it happening," she said.

He nodded. "So've I."

"Come sit by me," she petitioned.

He hesitated, then joined her on the swing, leaving an empty space between them as he raised his left foot to the railing and pushed against it to make them move. Feeling her skirts lift in the breeze, she looked at his scuffed boot, cut by the strap of his spur, its rowel catching light, then again at the shadow of his gun on his hip. When she raised her eyes to his, he asked, "What sort of fellows did you know back in Texas?"

"They were nice boys," she answered softly.

"Not like me, huh?"

"I think you're nice."

He chuckled, sliding his arm around her shoulders to pull her close. She nestled her face against the rough suede of his jacket, inhaling his scent—faint sweat and the sweet smell of horses mingled with the oil off his gun—a perfume so powerful it made her feel dizzy. His fingers lifted her chin and she met his eyes as he leaned low to kiss her, then she closed her eyes and surrendered to wanting him. He broke the kiss only to start another, and this time he laid his hand on her waist. She moaned, then felt embarrassed to have made any noise. Again he broke the kiss, lowering his face to breathe heat on her bodice. She touched his arm to protest, but hung on instead as if he could save her from what he was doing.

Beneath the shawl, his fingers unbuttoned her frock, then slid between the laces of her camisole to caress her skin as he kissed her mouth, touching her tongue with his. Again he broke the kiss and met her eyes.

"Whit," she whispered, "I feel so afraid for you."

He pulled his hand out and sat up. "*For* me?" he asked.

"I don't want anything bad to happen to you," she said.

He studied her face as if he couldn't believe what he'd heard, then he moved back to the railing and watched her from there. She wanted to say she loved him but kept quiet for fear of driving him farther away. Neither of them said anything for a long time, merely watched each other across the distance he'd imposed between them. Finally she smiled and said, "I miss you already."

He nodded. "I'm leaving pretty quick."

"When will you be back?"

"I don't know. Your uncle wouldn't like me coming around too often."

"I would."

"Then I will."

"Maybe we can go for a walk in the orchard again."

He laughed softly. "You sure you want to do that, Claire?"

"I've never wanted anything more."

"Yeah, but like you said, I ain't got no future."

"You could have, if you wanted one."

"I wouldn't count on that if I were you." He turned around, his eyes scanning the yard.

She looked at the expanse of dust milky in the moonlight, the corral with the silhouettes of horses shifting in a lazy pattern of slowly bobbing heads with cocked ears, but she couldn't see that anything had changed to draw Whit's attention. Then she saw Uncle Emmett standing in the dark door of the stable, and she wondered how long he'd been there.

Without looking at her again, Whit said over his shoulder, "Go on in the house, Claire. Me and your uncle have business to discuss."

She rose with a rustle of her satin skirt, then boldly leaned down to kiss Whit's cheek. His eyes flashed up at her. She laughed and said, "I'm of age and can do as I please." Not waiting for his reply, she slipped through the door and closed it behind her. Then she hurried into the parlor and opened the shutters just enough to see Whit stand up and walk out to meet her uncle. Unable to hear their words as they came together in the empty expanse of the yard, she dropped to her knees and prayed with every breath that they would reach an agreement.

Emmett had seen Whit and Claire kissing on the swing. Though he wasn't pleased with what he'd seen, he figured he could use it to coerce Whit's hand. Smiling pleasantly, Emmett asked, "You leaving, Whit?"

"Wouldn't want to without that bill of sale you promised," Whit answered.

Emmett reached into the breast pocket of his jacket, pulled out a paper, and handed it over.

Whit held it up to the fading moonlight and read the written words, then slid the paper into his own pocket and met Emmett's eyes.

Emmett reached into another pocket for his pipe and a small leather bag. He filled the pipe, replaced the bag, tamped the tobacco with his finger, then struck a match on the sole of his boot and sucked the fire alive, all the time feeling Whit's attention as a quickening of the outlaw's blood. "Summer before last," Emmett drawled, emitting a fragrant cloud of smoke, "I was bothered by a whole lotta hornets. I kept killing 'em one by one 'fore I got tired of that game and went after the hive." He sucked with soft, puckering sounds. "Seems to me you've got the same problem."

"How's that?" Whit asked.

"Wasting time killing hornets. If you'd knock out the hive, I think you'd discover you could move on to doing something more important with your life."

"Which hive did you have in mind, Emmett?"

"The one that sent Rufus Bond to Soledad to bother you."

Whit smiled. "He didn't bother me none. Is that hive bothering you?"

Emmett nodded over his pipe.

"But it's clear up in the mountains and your range is down here on the Panal. Didn't you say just the other night you wouldn't cross each other's paths?"

"Things change," Emmett said. "Could profit you and me both if that hive took a fall."

"I never cared much for profit," Whit said.

"Yeah, well, right now you're young and fancy free. When you get a little older and maybe meet a girl you want to court," Emmett paused to smile, "something to offer might come in handy."

Whit hadn't broken his lock on Emmett's eyes, but he looked away now, toward the house huddled dark in the moonlight. When he looked back, Emmett saw a hunger in Whit's eyes that he'd never seen there before.

"Today up at the meadow," Emmett said between puffs on his pipe, "I wondered if you were looking over the horses or the land." He puffed in silence a moment, then said, "There's a creek running through that meadow. Would make a good homestead, don't you think?"

"Might," Whit said. "For a workingman."

Emmett laughed softly. "Well, if you're thinking about courting, you best make up your mind to become one."

Whit stared so hard that Emmett could almost see the wheels turning in the outlaw's mind.

"I can't allow my niece to be trifled with," Emmett said around his pipe, "so I'll just ask point-blank: Are your intentions honorable?"

Slowly Whit answered, "I hadn't thought that far ahead."

"Well, you think about it," Emmett said, knocking the bowl of his pipe against the palm of his hand and watching the embers scatter on the breeze. "I'd tell you to take as long as you need," he pocketed his pipe, "but I don't want any hornets spoiling my wedding." He gave the outlaw a smile. "Though I haven't spoken with Lily, I'm of a mind to set the date for Wednesday. You think you might be able to knock out that hive and be back by then?"

"Reckon I could," Whit said.

"If so, you'll be welcome at our celebration," Emmett said, extending his hand.

Whit shook with him and watched until the old man had disappeared inside the house, then he moved to where his new horse was standing tied to the corral. He tightened the cinch, untied the reins, and swung on. Ambling across the yard, he looked at the house again, feeling eyes follow him.

Whit couldn't believe Emmett would allow him to court Claire, but neither could he see why she'd be dangled as a temptation if discouragement was her uncle's aim. Whit also knew Henry Hart wasn't bothering Emmett, and he puzzled over why the rancher suddenly wanted that particular hive knocked out of the tree. The only reason he could come up with was Lily, and that Emmett wanted it done before the wedding supported Whit's suspicion that Lily had demanded vengeance for her father's murder.

Reaching the shadows at the edge of the yard, Whit whistled in appreciation of Lily's price. If Emmett was willing to buy his bride with murder, he might really pay for it with his niece.

Whit let his black mare lope through the trees and across the ford of the river, then turned south toward Rocky Arroyo, where he intended to run the proposition by Jasper.

Emmett walked through the dark hall and entered the sitting room in front of the bedroom he'd given Lily. For thirty-five years he'd slept on the ground when he was out on the range, on a pallet on the floor in a house or hotel, and he didn't figure habits that old could or should be broken, so he had no intention of bringing her to his room after the wedding. He'd given her the small bedroom because it also afforded her a private parlor to share with Claire.

Knocking on the bedroom door, he called softly, "Lily, I need to speak with you." Then he retreated to the cold hearth of the sitting room and set about refilling his pipe. He was taking his first puff when she opened her door. Wearing a peach silk wrapper Claire must have given her, she stopped on the threshold. For a moment Emmett wondered if Lily's prior lack of interest in clothes had been caused by not owning any worth admiring, then he decided he wouldn't mind if his wife learned to dress in style, so he smiled his approval, but she didn't smile back.

He thought she seemed frightened. He'd noticed it at supper, too, and could only surmise she was worried he might retract his proposal and cancel the wedding. To dissuade her of that, he got to the point. "I saw Claire granting liberties to Whit on the porch just now. They didn't see me, and I didn't say nothing to either one of 'em, but I want you to speak to her. Will you do it?"

"And say what?" Lily asked, her voice a tad tart for his liking.

He sucked on his pipe, trying to figure why she was riled. Calmly, he said, "Claire may have a few years on you, Lily, but you've got a much better head on your shoulders. She's lost her mother. As my wife, I expect you to fill that role. She'll listen to you. I've told her to."

"I've already advised her against Whit," Lily said. "Apparently she doesn't think your wish is her command."

Emmett sucked deeply on his pipe, never having encountered any serious resistance from Lily. He wondered if she'd taken Claire's contrariness to be as much a garment of femininity as her silk robe. Softly he said, "Advise her again."

"I'll do it," Lily said, "if you'll tell me why Whit's riding a horse wearing your brand."

Losing patience, Emmett asked, "Are you gonna demand tit for tat every time I make a request?"

"When we was just friends," she said, her breath ragged, "you took me into your confidence. You said my savvy was why you wanted to marry me. Now that I've agreed to be your wife, are you gonna stop sharing your thoughts?"

"I have no such intention. But what I shared before was offered freely. It wasn't pried outta me."

"I had no right to ask before. Now I do."

Emmett sucked on his pipe, but it had gone out and he got a bad taste in his mouth. He turned away and spit into the hearth, then took his time relighting the pipe, veiling his eyes as he considered what his capitulation would mean for their future. Emitting a cloud of smoke, he met her eyes and decided again that she was merely frightened. Suspecting it might be her anticipation of the wedding night that had put her on edge, he said gently, "I came across Whit looking over the breeding stock of my remuda."

If he'd stolen one of those horses, I would've had to go after him, so I gave him one to prevent that from happening." He sucked again, thinking he'd lied only about his motive.

But Lily knew him well. "So you gave him the horse for his protection," she said with a sting of sarcasm.

He thought back over what he'd said. "I guess you could see it that way."

"I want to see the truth, Emmett."

Clenching his pipe in his teeth, he asked in a low voice, "Are you calling me a liar?"

"Not yet. Did you use that horse to pay Whit to kill Henry Hart?"

Emmett stared at her for a long moment, then slowly took his pipe from his mouth and knocked the ash into the hearth, giving himself time to control his anger. Pocketing the pipe, he faced her again and said in a near whisper, "Let's get something straight, Lily. *If* I ever made a contract for murder, I'd be damn sure not to use that word. Since I'm doing your bidding on this account, it would behoove you to play the game in such a way that we got the best chance to come out on top."

"I don't want Whit to do it," she stated.

"Who'd you have in mind?" Emmett drawled.

"Guess I hadn't thought that far," she said.

"No, you left it for me to do, and that's what I've done. Whit's the best qualified, and being as there's already a death warrant against him, he won't lose nothing. 'Sides, I chose him 'cause he's fast. He'll be in and out 'fore anyone catches wind he's there. Don't all that make sense?"

She nodded with tears in her eyes. " 'Cept I feel like I've betrayed him."

"Nobody's twisting his arm, Lily. Whit likes this kinda game. He's been playing it awhile now without us having nothing to do with it. Ain't it better to use a man who's already got one foot in the grave than spoil the future of someone who's still got a chance to live a long life?"

"Are you saying he doesn't?"

"He's been running on borrowed time ever since he escaped jail. It's only his wiliness that's kept him around this long."

She closed her eyes, remembering how her father had hidden Whit from the soldiers. Now she was sacrificing him for her father's vengeance.

Watching tears fall across her cheeks, Emmett said gently, "You got a soft spot for boys like Whit and Jasper. That's the girl in you, liking roosters with a cocky strut. But roosters always end up on the chopping block. I've told you that before."

She nodded, then wiped her tears.

Emmett smiled with approval. "So will you speak to Claire?"

"Yes," she said.

"Good." Emmett smiled again, letting his gaze slide down and back up the silk wrapper. "I've set the wedding for Wednesday. That all right with you?"

"Reckon," Lily whispered.

"You need any help planning the party?"

"Claire's taken it outta my hands."

He chuckled. "Your mother'll be coming tomorrow. Reckon she'll be a help, too."

"How long will she be able to stay?" Lily asked, desperately wanting to see her.

"She'll be needing to get back to the mill pretty quick."

Lily nodded. Knowing he could hire men to run the mill if he had a mind to, she guessed he didn't want her mother living at Bosque Grande.

"See you in the morning," Emmett said, leaving her alone in the cloud of undulating smoke left by his pipe.

Lily returned to her room, shut the door, and walked across to the one window. It was long and narrow, closed with wooden shutters she swung open to allow moonlight in. Everything Emmett had said made sense. Whit did already have a death warrant against him, and if anyone could penetrate Henry Hart's bodyguards it was likely to be Whit. She doubted, however, he'd do it merely to own a new horse. None of his other killings had been done for money but for vengeance. Maybe this one would be, too; not only hers, but his own, since Hart was responsible for the death of Angus Bodie, a man Whit had held in high esteem. It was a deal between the men, and she was outside it. Maybe, even, her father had saved Whit from the soldiers just so Whit could some-day avenge him. If so, it would be justice on such a grand scale she had no right to interfere. At least Jasper wasn't involved.

It was an hour after dawn when Whit rode up Rocky Arroyo to the Stone homestead. Neither Jasper's horse nor Pa Stone's team were in the corral, and the buckboard was gone, so Whit guessed he'd missed everyone. He was sitting his new mare in the yard, fighting disappointment that he couldn't show her off, when Elise came out of the house onto the porch.

She was a slip of a girl, only thirteen, and seemed so delicate that Whit always tried to be quiet around her. Her dark brown braids fell sleek as silk all the way to the waist of her blue woolen dress. Whit remembered seeing it on her before, and also noticed she was filling out the front of it more than she had.

"Morning, Elise," he said with a smile, tipping his hat.

"Jasper's gone to town with my folks," she said.

"How come you didn't go with 'em?"

She met his eyes in silence, both of them knowing why. A small, towheaded boy came out of the house and hung onto Elise's skirt as he smiled at Whit. When Whit grinned and waved a hello, the boy shyly waved back.

Whit asked Elise, "How long ago did they leave?"

"Sunup."

His mare shifted beneath him.

"You've got a new horse," she said.

"Ain't she something?" He turned the black mare to parade up and down in front of the porch.

"Wearing Emmett Moss's brand," Elise murmured.

Whit laughed. "I got a bill of sale."

"She's real pretty, Whit," Elise said.

He stopped the horse and swung down. "You got anything left from breakfast you might spare?"

She nodded and went back inside the house. The boy stayed behind, watching Whit tie his mare to the hitching post.

"How you doing, Sammie?" Whit asked softly, extending his

hand because he knew the boy couldn't hear him. "You wanta come watch me wash up?"

Sammie held Whit's hand as they walked across the yard to the trough by the empty corral. After lifting Sammie onto the fence, Whit set his hat on the post, draped his jacket across the rail, dunked his face, and scrubbed the dust off. He dried his face with the sleeve of his shirt, then met Sammie's eyes. Whit laughed, turning his back so Sammie could slide off the fence onto his shoulders. He carried the boy across the yard and into the house, through the parlor to the kitchen.

A place had been set at the table. Eggs were cooking in fatback and coffee was simmering on a back burner, their aromas filling the room. Whit pulled out a chair and swung the boy onto the seat, then sat down beside him and watched Elise working at the stove. When she brought the coffeepot to fill his cup, Whit said, "Jasper's keeping you corralled too close."

Elise's blue eyes disappeared behind her lashes. "He's looking out for me, is all," she said, carrying the pot back to the stove.

"A girl deserves to go to town with her folks," Whit answered as he reached for the sugar bowl.

"I've been to River's End," she said. "This morning they were going to Siete Rios and Jasper thinks it's too rough."

"There's a rowdy bunch in Siete Rios, no argument," Whit said, spooning sugar into his coffee. "But ain't no man nowhere dumb enough to mess with Jasper's sister." He handed the bowl to Sammie, who licked a finger and dunked it in, then licked the white crystals off and smiled at Whit.

"Strangers don't know how Jasper feels," Elise said, watching the eggs as she moved them around with a metal spatula. "The other day, two men stopped here to water their horses. I was gathering eggs at the time, and when I came out of the chicken coop and was walking toward the house, one of the men said something to the other that Jasper didn't like." She looked over her shoulder at Whit, the spatula in her hand dripping grease. "Jasper almost beat him to death. I think he might've if the other man hadn't stopped it. He pulled Jasper off and Jasper knocked him down, too, then told both of them to get out and not come back. The second man said they surely wouldn't, helped the first onto his horse, and they left. I told Jasper I hadn't even heard what the man said, but he said that didn't matter." She concentrated on the sizzling skillet again.

Whit looked down at Sammie licking more sugar off his finger, then back at Elise. "It's lucky Jasper's such a good fighter, otherwise he'd get hurt taking on two men at once."

She slid the skillet off the fire, lifted the eggs and fatback onto a plate, then set it on the table along with a platter of cold biscuits. "When he gets riled, he's like a tornado touching down on the plains. I hope I cooked your eggs right." She started to leave.

"Won't you sit and talk while I eat?" he called after her.

She turned on the threshold, biting her lip as she met his eyes.

"I'm Jasper's friend," Whit coaxed. "He knows I wouldn't hurt you for the world, Elise."

"Reckon I can have another cup of coffee," she said, coming back to pour herself one at the stove. She set it on the table, then opened the drawer of the hutch and took out a tablet of paper and a thick-leaded pencil. Handing them to Sammie, she sat down and sipped at her coffee, hiding her eyes.

As he ate, Whit watched Sammie draw lines on the paper, fat circles that began to resemble a person. Jasper had found the boy one day wandering lost in their arroyo. The first noise they got out of him sounded like "Sammie," so that's what they called him, and they guessed his age at five or six, but no one really knew his name or how old he was, where he'd come from, or how his folks happened to lose track of such a little boy who was deaf.

Buttering a biscuit, Whit stole glances at Elise while he said, "There's a dance in River's End next Friday night. You think you might want to go?" He watched her as he laid the knife on his plate.

She kept her gaze on her hands in her lap. "Jasper wouldn't like it."

"I'm asking you," Whit said.

"I'd have to have his permission," she answered, still not looking up.

"I know that," Whit said. He sipped his coffee, then set the cup in the saucer again. "I ain't asking you to marry me, Elise.

You're a fine girl and I wouldn't be amiss to do that, but all I'm asking is for you to come to the dance. A girl has to get out and look over the field 'fore she can see the dif'rence in men and know which one's likely to make her happy. I'm only offering to show you the field. Will you come, if I square it with Jasper?"

"I'd dearly love to go," she whispered as if she were talking to her cup.

Whit nodded. "I figured as much. Since we've maybe got a date, think you could give me a smile?"

Slowly she raised her eyes and smiled at him. Whit chuckled, then started eating again as he studied Sammie's drawing. "Looks like a doll," Whit said.

"He draws it all the time," Elise said. "We think it must've been his favorite toy when he was with his folks."

Whit leaned closer to the boy and touched his shoulder to get his attention. "That's real pretty, Sam," Whit said softly, coating his words with a smile.

"Pretty," Sammie echoed.

Whit looked at Elise.

"He's learning to read lips," she said.

"Ain't that smart!" Whit laughed, and the boy did, too.

Slapping his tiny hand on the paper, he said, "Sammie!"

Whit studied the drawing of a floppy rag doll, fairly well done though it was missing an eye. "Looks like a girl to me. She's wearing a dress, ain't she?"

"Elise," the boy said.

She laughed.

Whit smiled at her. "Reckon that's an honor, wouldn't you say?"

She blushed and looked at her hands again.

Whit cleaned his plate and finished his coffee. "I'm riding to Union. When I get back, I'll talk to Jasper about us going to the dance."

"All right," she murmured.

He stood up. "Thanks for breakfast."

"You're welcome," she said, bravely meeting his eyes.

Whit held his hand down to Sammie. "So long, pardie."

"Pardie," Sammie whispered as they shook hands.

Whit laughed and walked out, calling back as he left the house, "Be sure'n tell Jasper I was by."

Putting on his jacket at the corral, Whit doubted that Jasper would allow Elise to go to the dance. But he figured it was time Jasper got used to the idea that his sister would soon be a woman wanting things he couldn't give her. On the off chance he actually let her go, Whit would have to convince Jasper to stay home, maybe by using the argument that it wasn't fair to Elise to make potential suitors face death to court her.

Swinging onto his mare, Whit decided to climb Rocky Arroyo into the mountains. The trail was rough and most folks preferred the road that followed Deep River. But considering the sheriff in Union always carried a death warrant for Whit in his pocket, Whit figured he had good reason to take the less traveled route.

9

Whit reached the outskirts of Union close to nine o'clock that night. Because the mountains rose so abruptly on the north side of the Río Pequeño, everyone lived south of the river. By following the old Indian trail that wound between the foothills and the crumbling edge of the riverbank, Whit was able to ride into the heart of town without being seen.

He tied his mare in a grove of black elder trees, loosened her cinch but left her saddled in case he needed to make a quick retreat. Taking his Winchester, he kept to the dark shadows along the river as he walked a hundred yards upstream to the back of Henry Hart's hotel. It was a long, low adobe building with a west wing. Hart's private quarters were in that wing, and a light shone from his bedroom window. Whit hunkered down in the tall weeds at the edge of the yard and waited for the man's last trip to the privy before turning in for the night.

Knowing Lily's father had been killed from ambush, Whit figured turnabout was fair play. That made him wonder, though, if he wasn't earning the same fate for himself. He considered it a fair-to-middling way to die. The element of surprise eliminated fear, and if the shooter was half good, death came fast. It beat being hung, which entailed a period of waiting and then having an audience at the end. He supposed dying of simple old age would be best, but he'd never known anyone who lived long enough to enjoy that pleasure. If death could ever be considered a pleasure. He guessed in some cases it was. His mother's succumbing to consumption had been a relief, as much to her as him. Sick people generally suffered a long decline before giving up the ghost, while death delivered from a gun tended to be quick. Whit expected that to be his fate, and he figured Henry Hart must expect the same.

Whit felt strange, though, sitting cross-legged in the dark cradling his Winchester in his lap. Killing Rufus Bond had brought his tally to five, but all those fights had been finished before Whit had time to contemplate his choices. Even killing Browne Carson wasn't something he'd planned but a fight that erupted after he chanced upon the man on the street. In each of those cases, seeing his opponent dead when the smoke cleared was hard evidence that Whit had made the right move. He'd dismissed the killings and would have forgotten them if everybody else wasn't constantly reminding him. This waiting for his prey, however, was an entirely different proposition.

He told himself that Henry Hart had done the same, then remembered it hadn't been Hart who pulled the trigger. It had been Browne Carson who shot Angus Bodie, William Wilson who shot Bob Cassidy. Carson had bragged about it to Jim Daniels and Daniels had told Whit. Neither of them commented on it; they'd simply met each other's eyes, acknowledging the game had changed if a man would shoot another from hiding. Daniels had once been part of the Siete Rios bunch, but now he'd gone over to Hart, who was gouging the county by controlling the price of everything from whiskey to thread. Nobody liked him, though Whit supposed he paid well. Daniels had implied as much the last time he and Whit talked. It was to the credit of their friendship that that conversation happened at all. Daniels had come to deliver a warning. Now that he was a deputy, he'd said, the next time they met he'd be obligated to serve the death warrant on Whit. They agreed to avoid each other's proximity in the hope that moment never came.

After tonight, Whit knew there'd be a mad scramble for the reins of power. It was anybody's guess who'd catch 'em first. Maybe the county would run free so everybody could breathe easy for a spell. Maybe it would run amuck and smash up a lot of lives before the reins were caught. Emmett Moss wouldn't catch 'em; his aversion to politics was well known. The next most powerful man in the county was Sheriff Red Bond, who hadn't liked Whit even before Whit killed Rufus, the sheriff's brother. Whit had been cleared at the inquest, but he'd already earned a death warrant for the killing of Browne Carson, which the sheriff could use to justify shooting Whit on sight. Killing Henry Hart would increase the sheriff's rancor. Even though he'd likely benefit by Hart's death, he'd also worry that he might be next.

Looking at it honestly, though, Whit couldn't see that his life was apt to be much different if he killed Henry Hart. Since the sheriff had vowed to get him anyway, Whit stayed alive only as long as he escaped Red's clutches. In a fair fight, he could take Red as easily as he had Rufus, and sometimes Whit felt tempted to force the confrontation just so he'd be done with it. But he couldn't help wondering if farther on down the road he wouldn't have to kill whoever replaced Red. Hart had been responsible for issuing the death warrant in the first place, and Whit couldn't see why the new sheriff wouldn't do Hart's bidding just like Red did. So for the moment Whit's strategy rested on avoiding the law rather than forcing a fight.

Knowing Red didn't have the nerve to attack him point-blank, Whit also knew an ambush would succeed only out of pure luck because he didn't have a home or a routine like most men did. On the other hand, he was known to frequent Celia's bordello, which put her at risk, and if he collected what Emmett promised, Claire would be in jeopardy, too. That was Whit's strongest doubt about this deal: Why would Emmett put his niece in danger, unless the Cattle King of the Panal was powerful enough to thwart even the sheriff and the courts?

Whit knew indictments for murder sometimes moldered in courthouse basements unserved and forgotten. He'd never heard of that happening with a death warrant already signed by the governor, but the world was constantly changing. A new governor might be induced to annul the warrant. So as long as he stayed alive, he had a chance to outlast what currently passed as the law. It meant living on a constant alert of defense, whereas killing Hart and then facing Red would clear the field of opponents so Whit could relax for a while, maybe even long enough to contemplate marrying Claire. That was an intriguing notion. It wouldn't be possible unless Union County found itself a new sheriff who danced to Emmett's tune, but that wasn't beyond the pale of possibility. Still, Whit kept coming back to the suspicion that Emmett wouldn't allow his niece to marry a man with a death warrant against him no matter how the political climate might change.

The dark yard in front of Whit was suddenly slashed by a furrow of light as Henry Hart came out the back door. He left it open and followed the path to the privy. Whit raised his rifle. It was already cocked. He sighted down the barrel and positioned his finger a scant increment above the trigger, watching Hart disappear inside the wooden latrine.

Whit waited, barely breathing. He thought of Claire and how soft the inside of her thighs must be, then wondered if he'd ever touch them without remembering this moment of watching the door of a privy, and he thought of Lily's blood staining the sheets on her marriage bed because of the blood he was about to spill. Emmett would gain a wife; Whit another warrant for murder. Even if he escaped and no one knew what he'd done, Emmett would know; even if he married Claire, he'd be free only as long as Emmett allowed it. Maybe his life wouldn't be different if he killed Henry Hart, but as things stood now, Whit didn't dance to anyone's tune but his own. He still had a chance to change the melody. It might be a slim chance, but it was wide open compared with living under another man's thumb for the rest of his life.

Henry Hart opened the door of the privy and closed it behind himself, then walked halfway across the yard and stopped to admire the stars. He even turned his back to his open bedroom door so he was silhouetted against the light. Not knowing there was a rifle aimed at him, a finger on a trigger that could send him to hell, Hart smiled at the heavens. Sympathizing with the man's appreciation of beauty, Whit lowered his rifle and uncocked it.

The sound was the same as a rifle cocking, and Whit dropped fast as Hart pulled his pistol and fired into the dark. Whit snickered in the dust as he slithered through the brush. Beyond the six-gun's range, he stood up and ran, barely able to contain his laughter. He didn't think Henry Hart would ever visit the privy in comfort again, and that tickled Whit. He laughed about it all the way back to Rocky Arroyo.

The sky was rosy with dawn when he ambled onto the Stone homestead and found Jasper feeding the horses in the stable. He watched Whit ride in, then went back to forking hay into the mangers. Whit unsaddled his pretty black mare, tethered her in a stall, and went to the bin for a scoop of oats. Jasper leaned on his pitchfork and watched, not saying anything. Whit smiled when his mare nickered at the oats he dumped in her trough, then he returned the scoop and sat down on a wooden box before he asked, "Did Elise tell you I came by?"

Jasper nodded.

"She tell you I asked her to the dance on Friday night?"

"You should've asked me, not her," Jasper said.

Whit smiled. "She's the one I want to dance with."

"You never mentioned wanting it before."

"Well, she's growing up quick, ain't she, Jasper?"

He scowled.

"Pretty, too," Whit said. "Somebody's gonna take her dancing sometime. Why not me?"

"It ain't you I'm bothered about," Jasper retorted. "It's all the other galoots eyeing her."

"Pretty girls usually like being admired," Whit said. "Why deny her that?"

"If you had a sister," Jasper replied, "you'd understand my point of view."

"I doubt it," Whit said. "You and I don't see women the same."

"You see your own pleasure, is all."

Whit chuckled. "They're pleasurable creatures. Can't see why I shouldn't enjoy 'em when they're in front of me."

" 'Cause when they're not, they never cross your mind."

"That ain't true," Whit said softly. "I've been thinking about Claire Moss a good bit lately."

Jasper snorted with disdain, then stuck the pitchfork into the mound of hay at the end of the aisle. "I see your horse is wearing Emmett's brand. You fixing to marry into the family?"

"Funny you should mention that," Whit said. "Emmett offered me Claire's hand in exchange for knocking a hornet's nest outta the tree."

Jasper frowned.

"This particular nest was in Union," Whit said.

Jasper's frown deepened. "What do you mean *was?*"

"Oh, it's still there. I had it in the sight of my rifle, then decided to let it be. Not on account of not wanting Claire, and not on account of deciding the fall wouldn't be justice."

"What was it on account of, then?"

Whit tried to put it together, but the best he could come up with was, "It seemed like a short chute to nowhere."

Jasper thought a minute, then asked with sarcasm, "Ain't that what your life is anyway?"

Whit shook his head. "Some of it's sashaying around a dance floor with a pretty girl in my arms. Come to think of it, Jasper, I ain't ever seen you do that. Maybe if you tried it once or twice, you'd understand why Elise thinks it might be fun."

"I got nothing against dancing," Jasper said. "It's what follows that I don't like."

"You seemed to like it well enough the last time we were with Celia."

"She's a whore."

"There ain't all that much dif'rence between what whores and good girls want. No more'n between what a man wants from a whore and what he wants from his wife. It's mostly a matter of how many men she does it with."

"I don't want Elise doing it with anybody."

With a smile of forgiveness, Whit asked, "Don't you think that's her decision?"

"She's only thirteen, Whit!"

"I know that. But since it's gonna take you a while to get used to the idea, I thought I'd start it simmering in your mind so when it comes to a boil you think of her 'stead of yourself."

Jasper glared at him in silence.

"It's like with Lily," Whit said lightly. "A man can't be both a brother and a husband to the same woman."

"I ain't Lily's brother," Jasper muttered.

"That's true, and Emmett's about to be her husband. I was invited to the celebration." He paused, then said, "On one condition."

"What condition?"

"I knock that hornet's nest outta the tree."

Jasper thought a minute. "Why didn't she ask me 'stead of Emmett? I would've done it without demanding nothing in return."

"Don't reckon she wanted it on your hands, Jasper. 'Sides, I can't recollect you giving her much encouragement to ask anything of you."

"Hell," he grumbled.

"Yeah, pretty much," Whit agreed. "You want to come to the wedding with me?"

"You gonna tell her you didn't do it?"

"Emmett's the one who asked me. Reckon I'll tell him."

"What if he don't tell her? You gonna let her marry him thinking it was done?"

"It's no nevermind to me who she marries. Does it matter to you?"

Jasper turned around to pick up the pitchfork and drive it into the hay several times with a vengeance. Leaving the handle quivering from his thrust, he said without looking at Whit, "Caring for a woman don't mean I oughta marry her."

"I feel the same," Whit said softly.

"No, you don't," Jasper said, wheeling around to meet his eyes. "You don't have any idea what I'm talking about. You fuck women without a second thought. It ain't the same for me."

"I know," Whit said.

"What do you know?" Jasper asked.

"That we oughta go to Lily's wedding and say what we feel when we get there." When Jasper just stared at him, Whit smiled and said, "Maybe we can visit Celia 'fore we come home and share a roll in the hay."

Jasper's eyes were hot with pain. "You do know, don't you?"

Whit felt tempted to ask what he was supposed to know, but he decided Jasper had been pushed enough for one day. With another smile, Whit said, "Let's go up to the house and get some breakfast. I'm starved."

On Wednesday morning, Elise watched Jasper ride away with Whit, wishing she could go to the wedding, too. She hadn't been out of Rocky Arroyo in over a fortnight, and that was merely to accompany her mother on a visit to the Beckworth spread just a few miles upriver. Clarissa, Old Man Beckworth's daughter, now Mrs. Ben Reed, was expecting her first child, and Elise's mother was the only midwife on the lower Panal. Returning from that visit, she'd predicted a difficult birth for Mrs. Reed. So no one was surprised that Wednesday afternoon when Ben rode a lathered horse into Rocky Arroyo and shouted that Ma Stone was needed at the Beckworth spread. Pa drove her in the buckboard, leaving Elise home alone with little Sammie.

The shadows lengthened across the yard as Elise worked in the kitchen to make supper. When she had it on the table, she left the house to look for Sammie, knowing she couldn't simply call him as she'd do with anyone else. She'd seen him go into the barn an hour before, so she walked across the yard drying her hands on her apron. The barn door was open and she stepped inside, letting her eyes adjust to the lesser light as she tried to spot the boy's head of nearly flaxen hair. The barn seemed empty, yet she felt his presence. Knowing that she had to put herself in his line of vision to catch his attention, she walked down the aisle, peering into each stall she passed as doves murmured from the rafters: *who-cooks-for-you? who-cooks-for-you?*

"Sammie?" she called, though she knew it was useless.

Beyond the grain bins, the door to the tack room stood open. It was darker inside so she hesitated after stepping across the threshold, her eyes searching all the nooks and crannies where a small boy could hide. Then she saw him crouched behind a jumble of broken harness waiting to be mended, his mouth open in silent terror.

"Sammie, what on earth?" she whispered, hurrying to hold him and soothe the fear that drove him to hide.

He shook his head with urgent warning and looked at something behind her. As she whirled around, a burlap bag was dropped over her head and a man's hard arms trapped her in his grip. She struggled to breathe inside the dusty bag, her face pressed close to his chest as she kicked with her feet. She heard him chuckle, then grunt as her foot struck his shin. Pulling her foot back to do it again, she kicked at thin air while he held her with both hands. What felt like a rope was pulled tight just below her breasts, pinning her arms at her sides, then her feet were knocked out from under her and she fell to the floor. She lay still, breathing dust from the burlap as she tried to think what to do.

"Our ace is a jackass now," the man said.

"Ain't so bad," another man said.

His voice was familiar. Frantic with fear, she couldn't name who owned it. Then she remembered: Buck Robbins. Trying to decide if she should let on that she knew who he was, she heard Sammie run, then the rustle of clothes as they caught him. A hand smacked against flesh, and she heard a soft thud. There was a moment of silence in which she tried to pinpoint where Sammie was, then she smelled blood and the other man said, "It's done."

Struggling to her feet, she shouted, "My brother'll kill you for this!"

As rough hands pushed her back down, Buck growled, "Mentioning your brother ain't likely to help you right now."

"Why not?" she cried where she lay on the floor. "Whatever he's done, are you so cowardly that you take your grudge out on children?"

"You ain't no child," Buck answered. "I can see that plain."

A fresh fear struck her heart. "He'll kill you," she whispered.

Buck snickered.

"Let's go," the other man said.

"Not yet," Buck answered.

"Ain't no call for that," the other man said, disgust thick in his voice.

"It'll cinch it sure," Buck said.

"What it'll cinch is your death," the other man said.

"Best way to keep a woman quiet," Buck said, his voice coming closer, "is to fill her with shame."

She tried to get up but was pushed back down. Rolling away, she hit the impediment of a foot. She rolled the other way and hit another foot, telling her the man stood astride her. Then she heard Buck's laughter as he bent close and flipped up her skirts. When he yanked her drawers off, she screamed, though she knew it would do no good.

Andy had been told to stay out of the way until three o'clock, then come in for his bath and change into his suit for the wedding. He'd just as soon skip the whole thing if given his druthers. No one else seemed especially happy about the wedding, either, and he couldn't figure why it was happening.

When his father first told him Uncle Emmett intended to marry Lily Cassidy, Andy thought he was joking. The girl was young enough to be Uncle Emmett's granddaughter, and none too pretty besides. The little time Andy had spent in her company convinced him she could be formidable despite being tiny, so he guessed Uncle Emmett was marrying her for her gumption. She surely had a lot of that. Within two days of meeting Andy she was bossing him like a mother, and he'd seen her upbraid a cowboy for leaving the garden gate open, tongue-lashing him up one side and down the other until the poor man was crimson with shame. On top of that, the cowboy was Shiloh Pook, Uncle Emmett's top hand.

Andy didn't think Lily had the right to tear into a man like that, especially one who didn't work for her. But when he told his father how he felt, adding that maybe Lily's visit would be detrimental to the smooth running of the ranch, Andy's father said Lily did have the right since she would soon be Uncle Emmett's wife.

Andy forgot the upbraiding of Shiloh Pook in contemplation of this news.

When he recovered from his stunned surprise, he asked, "What's he marrying *her* for?"

"I suspect," his father answered with a smile, "it's partly because she has the courage to chastise a six-foot-tall cowboy wearing a gun."

Andy didn't consider that courageous but uppity. Shiloh Pook could snap Lily's spine across his knee with one hand. His restraint was the only reason she could treat a grown man as if he were an irresponsible child, so to Andy's way of thinking, any honor in the situation was owned by the man who tolerated the girl's audacity. Andy keenly anticipated the day he became a man and could shrug off women telling him what to do.

Today, however, he gladly followed their orders and escaped the hectic bustle inside the house. Mrs. Cassidy was actually washing the parlor windows, as if Andy hadn't gotten them clean enough yesterday. Theo, only a year younger than Andy, was arranging bouquets of roses in the kitchen. Andy almost envied him the task. The roses were beautiful, red and pink and yellow and white, fragrant and lush, the last crop before the first freeze, which Uncle Emmett said would come any night now.

Claire said it was a good omen that the freeze had waited long enough for Lily to have roses at her wedding. That seemed right to Andy, though Lily had wistfully told Claire she'd always wanted lilies of the valley at her wedding, which she'd imagined would happen in springtime. Claire had momentarily looked sad, then brightened and said the roses were appropriate since Lily was marrying a cattle king. Andy had piped up that lilies of the valley were poison anyway, so not fit for a wedding, to his way of thinking, and Lily had burst into tears. That's when Claire told him to make himself scarce.

"Fine by me," he said, walking down the hall, intending to go out through the kitchen.

Theo was there, arranging the bouquets in pitchers, mixing the colors in some and keeping them all one color in others. The kitchen smelled like a bordello, reminding Andy of the piano at Celia's. He'd been about to invite Lily's brother to ride into town when Theo, not seeing him, turned away from the table and limped over to the counter for more water, dragging his right leg across the floor. Andy felt a surge of pity, then ducked back the way he'd come and left the house through the front.

He saddled Kickapoo and rode alone into Soledad, intending to have a beer with Foxy Strop, who was always quick with a disparaging remark about women. Andy figured after that he might go to Celia's and ask if he could play her piano. He'd never been there without Whit, though, and Andy wasn't at all sure he could garner the courage to walk through that blue door by himself.

The prospect of seeing Whit again was Andy's only hope for brightening the day, but the guests weren't due to arrive until four. Wondering how Whit was filling the hours in between, Andy thought for the first time that maybe he was old enough to strike out on his own. Whit had done it when he was a year younger than Andy. Whit's situation was different in that he didn't have a choice in the matter, but Andy thought Whit had done well for himself. He also suspected Whit was sweet on Claire. The last time Whit visited, Andy had left them alone on the portal not because he was sleepy but because he was trying to be a good friend. Just before closing the door, he'd looked back and Whit had winked at him, so Andy figured he'd done the right thing. If any wedding had to happen, he wished it was Claire marrying Whit. He would be a joy to have around all the time, exactly the opposite of what Andy expected from the new Mrs. Moss.

Reining his horse north on the Texas Road, he ambled past the tree where he first met Jasper and Whit. Andy hadn't seen Jasper since then, but he remembered how Jasper had pulled him out of the way when Rufus Bond drew down on Whit. That still puzzled Andy. If Jasper hated all Mosses as much as he claimed, why had he bothered to get Andy out of the line of fire? Probably he'd done it to save Whit the grief of having hurt a boy he'd befriended. Whit wouldn't have taken that lightly. He had deep feelings he camouflaged behind his constant jokes and smiles. Andy suspected Jasper had powerful feelings, too, only he camouflaged his behind a gruff mask of anger. Maybe everybody had such feelings they'd learned to hide one way or another. Andy had always thought he alone had to do that.

As he followed the road's meandering curve through the out-lying huts of the poor folk, he felt he was finally growing up. The children playing in the dusty road watched him ride by, and he wondered if he looked like a man to them or just an older boy. Women worked sweeping dust out through their open doors or washing clothes in kettles over fires in the yards, and a few old men sat idly under the portals. They all watched him ride by but no one called a greeting. He guessed they knew who he was and it was their dislike of Uncle Emmett that made them slow to be friendly.

He rode past the row of adobe barracks and entered the broad expanse of the plaza. Foxy Strop's Saloon was kitty-corner across what had been the old fort's parade ground. Despite the early hour, some men were gathered under the huge cottonwood tow-ering over the saloon. They were brawling, three of them gang-ing up on one. Andy saw the victim's face as he tried to lunge free. It was Foxy they were joshing. At least the three men were laughing, though Foxy seemed to be sincerely trying to escape. On the other side of the plaza, a hundred yards away, a small fire flickered in the middle of the north road.

Andy couldn't figure why anyone would build a fire there. He stopped his horse and looked away from the brawl to the shad-owed portals ringing the plaza. The few men standing beneath the portals were so engrossed in watching the fight that they hadn't noticed Andy. He nudged his horse closer, then stopped again, watching the three men hog-tie Foxy as if he were a steer, his hands and feet bound close together in front of him. Andy didn't know the men. Three horses were tied to the dilapidated fence around the old orchard, twenty or thirty feet past the fire in the road. Andy looked back in time to see one of the men yank Foxy's trousers down, pulling his drawers, too, to bunch around his ankles. Foxy was bellowing like a stuck pig, thrashing on the ground but unable to get up.

Andy considered intervening, but because of Uncle Emmett's rule against wearing guns, he was unarmed. He hadn't yet had a shooting lesson, so he wasn't even carrying a rifle on his saddle like everyone else did, including Uncle Emmett. Andy was also a skinny, green kid while the three men were burly and all wearing guns. One of them walked toward the fire. To Andy's horror, the man lifted a branding iron out of the coals and carried it back toward Foxy. Foxy howled, watching that red-hot iron come closer. Andy swallowed hard.

The other two men flopped Foxy facedown and held him while the man pressed the iron into his buttocks. Foxy screamed, his body flailing beneath the impact, then shuddering like creamed whey dropped in a bowl. When the man lifted the iron, a huge red *EM* was emblazoned on Foxy's butt, the first leg of the *M* seared into his crack. He slumped limp, moaning with his face in the dirt. The men stood up laughing. Then they left Foxy there, abandoning the iron and the fire as they swung onto their horses and trotted down the road out of sight.

Andy looked again at the people under the portals. They were lined with men now and a few women, too. He saw Celia standing with another woman in the mouth of the alley leading to the bordello. They were wearing only wrappers. A breeze lifted Celia's robe and Andy saw the pale outline of her leg inside the dark cloth. Not looking at him or even at Foxy, she was staring toward the southwest corner of the plaza. Andy followed her gaze and saw Whit and Jasper sitting their horses watching him. Andy tried to smile, but his stomach felt queasy and he didn't guess his smile amounted to much.

When Whit nudged his horse forward, Jasper followed along. Andy looked back at Foxy. Some men were helping him now. They had cut the ropes off and were carrying him to a water trough. They dumped him in and he howled like a Comanche as Whit reined his horse to a stop alongside Andy.

Meeting Whit's eyes, Andy blurted out, "Why didn't you help him?"

Whit slowly smiled before he asked softly, "Why didn't you?"

"I don't have a gun," Andy said. "You could've stopped 'em!"

"Not without killing 'em," Whit said.

Andy looked back at Foxy being lifted out of the trough. His face was twisted in pain, his round belly quivering above his shriveled little cock, dangling from a mat of fur, his pants still bunched around his ankles. Andy looked at Jasper watching Foxy being carried inside the saloon, the men holding him facedown and the red letters blazing on his butt. Jasper's chiseled lips were set in a straight line of indifference. As he shifted his gaze to Andy, Jasper's dark blue eyes were cold.

"They burned him," Andy whispered.

"Branded him," Jasper said, "with the mark of his owner."

Andy looked down at the scarred *EM* on the shoulder of Whit's black mare.

Whit laughed and said, "I got a bill of sale."

Andy blinked back tears. "How can you joke?"

Whit grinned. "That ain't no joke. You want to see it?"

Andy shook his head in confusion, then looked at the fire flickering red and gold in the sun. "They branded him 'cause he's friends with Uncle Emmett?"

"It ain't the friendship they hold against him," Whit said. "Foxy's a spy, carrying news he picks outta private conversations. Nobody likes a spy, least of all your Uncle Emmett, though he uses 'em often enough."

Andy studied Whit's face as if he could read understanding on its features. Whit suffered the scrutiny with ease, then asked, "How come you ain't home helping get ready for the festivities?"

Jasper cleared phlegm from his throat and spit in the dirt.

"The women kicked me out," Andy said.

Whit chuckled. "We was heading over to Celia's to get a bath. Care to join us?"

Andy nodded, then reined his horse to fall in step beside Whit's. Jasper followed them, his eyes so sharp Andy felt as if they were branding the back of his skull. Celia and her friend watched them come. When they were close, Whit reached down and lifted Celia into the saddle in front of him. "I need me a bath, Celia," Whit said, nuzzling her neck. "Will you scrub my back?"

Her giggle made Andy blush. He reined his horse beside Jasper's. Watching Whit with Celia, Jasper looked like he was about to spit again. The other woman followed behind as they all ambled down the alley toward the bordello.

10

*L*ily stood in her mother's wedding gown surveying herself in the oval mirror in Claire's room. The gown's white satin had mellowed with age to a pale butter color that did nothing to enhance Lily's complexion. The sleeves were the huge leg-of-lamb style of the antebellum South, ballooning from the shoulders to the elbows, then tight to the wrists. The bodice was covered with lace to display a discreet view of the bride's décolletage, and the waist was cinched above a voluminous bell skirt draped over hoops.

Lily thought her body appeared to be nothing more than a hanger for the sumptuous dress, and that the overabundance of lustrous satin shamed the thin, dull crown of her braid on the top of her head. Even the silk spray of lilies of the valley that Claire had cleverly fashioned and pinned to Lily's temple emphasized the homeliness of the face beneath the flowers.

Having heard it said that all brides were beautiful, Lily guessed she was about to break the mold. If she went through with the wedding, that is. Emmett had yet to deliver her price. He said news of her satisfaction would arrive with the wedding guests. Which meant if he failed her, she would have to cancel the wedding the moment before she walked down the aisle. She wasn't sure she could muster the courage to do that, and she suspected he didn't believe she could either. So she didn't know if she was marrying a man of integrity who kept his promises or a man willing to trick her into becoming his wife. Once it was done, there was no recourse. She'd heard of women who divorced their husbands, but that was a disgrace she would never inflict on her family.

With none of the joy she'd anticipated feeling on her wedding day, Lily walked to the window and peered out through a crack in the drapes. Beyond the flowerless lilac bushes inside the picket fence, she could see a wide strip of hard-packed dirt and the still-green weeping willows dragging their leaves in the dust along the river. She caught a flash of pink among the trees, then saw Claire emerge from their shadows and gaily pirouette with her arms held high, the silk of her pink gown floating like clouds before falling to kiss the ground around her feet. Though her skirt was full, its generosity was subtle compared with the antebellum exaggeration of the wedding gown. Lily felt like a toothpick inside the huge skirt. She was on the verge of changing into her best blue frock when she saw Whit Cantrell follow Claire out from under the willows.

Lily gasped with apprehension that his arrival brought the news Emmett had promised. Without stopping to think, she slid the window open its full height and stepped through it, dragging her hooped petticoat and satin skirt behind her. She ran nimbly in the satin slippers, holding her skirts out of the dust and watching her path lest she stumble or tear the gown on the shrubbery. At the picket gate, she had to lift her hoops flat against her body to squeeze through the narrow passage, revealing her lace pantaloons. Blushing at her own immodesty, she kept her eyes on the ground as she ran to where Claire and Whit were standing, so it wasn't until she'd stopped in front of them that she saw Jasper. His dark blue eyes were full of sorrow.

"Why, Lily!" Claire admonished in fun. "It's bad luck to let a man see you in your wedding dress before your husband does."

Lily shook the notion off as if it were a chill and met Whit's eyes.

"You look beautiful, Lily," he said as if he meant it.

She dismissed that possibility. "Have you been to Union?"

Whit glanced at Jasper, then looked back at her. "Yeah, I was up there day before yesterday."

"Did you do it?" she whispered.

His smile teased her. "Do what?"

"What are you talking about?" Claire asked, the fun in her voice dying as she spoke.

"A special present Lily wanted," Whit said. "Ain't that right, Lily?"

"I didn't ask it of you," she said.

"He did, though."

"Who?" Claire asked with pique.

"Did you do it?" Lily nearly wailed.

"I didn't want to let you down, Lily," Whit said.

"You should've asked us in the first place," Jasper interjected angrily. "We wouldn't've demanded this in return."

Lily sank into the dust and hid her face in the satin skirt of her gown.

"What on earth?" Claire whispered, leaning low to tug at Lily's arm. "Get up, Lily. You'll ruin your dress! Why are you crying? Poor sweetheart, let's go inside. Help me get her inside!" she begged of the men.

"Don't reckon Emmett would like me touching his bride," Jasper said. "Though he didn't mind buying her with blood."

Lily looked up through her tears. "Tell me it wasn't yours," she implored.

"I would've answered Lily Cassidy," Jasper said. "But Mrs. Moss ain't got the right to ask me nothing."

Lily pressed her fist to her mouth as she watched Jasper turn around and disappear beneath the trees.

"Sorry," Whit said softly. Then he, too, turned his back and followed Jasper.

Lily moaned, leaning low into her satin skirt, now stained with tears.

Beside her, Claire whispered, "What on earth happened?"

Lily raised her head and stared into the emptiness beneath the trees. "It's done," she said with resolution. "Now there's nothing left but the funeral."

"Funeral?" Claire echoed. "You mean your wedding?"

Lily nodded. "Only trouble is, I'm afraid I'm gonna take a long time dying."

"Let's go inside," Claire entreated, tugging at her arm again.

Lily let Claire help her to her feet and lead her across the bright expanse of yard. Ignoring the bustling people in the kitchen, she leaned on Claire as they crossed the room and walked down the hall. Claire locked the bedroom door as Lily studied her dust-streaked reflection in the mirror. "It's done now," she said again. "I can't renege."

"What's done?" Claire asked.

A knock sounded on the door, then Theo called, "Lily, are you ready?"

"Not quite," Claire called back.

Unable to staunch her tears, Lily wet a towel at the basin and wiped her eyes, then squeezed them shut and said, "Slap me, Claire."

"What?" Claire whispered.

"I gotta stop crying. Slap me so I can."

Claire whimpered in confusion.

"Do it hard," Lily said. "Please, I need you to."

Claire took a deep breath and slapped Lily's left cheek with the palm of her hand.

"Do the other," Lily said, managing a smile, "so I'll be a pink-cheeked bride."

Claire slapped the right cheek, making it glow, too.

Lily opened her eyes and studied herself in the mirror. Thinking she looked like the most pitiful bride in God's creation, she said, "I'm ready now."

Claire opened the door and whisked Lily's brother inside. Dressed in a new black suit, his damp hair slicked behind his ears, Theo fingered the red rose in his lapel as he said, "You look real pretty, Lily."

She shrugged. "Is everything set?"

"Let me wipe off your dress," Claire hurried to say. Taking the damp towel from where Lily had dropped it, Claire whisked it down the satin skirt.

"How'd you get your dress dirty?" Theo asked.

"It came out of the trunk this way," Lily said.

"I thought you washed it."

"What do you know about dresses, Theo Cassidy?" Lily scoffed.

"Not much," he admitted. "Why're you mad?"

"I ain't," she said.

Claire dropped the cloth in the basin of water, rinsed off her fingers and was drying them when Theo said, "You don't have to do it, you know." Slowly Claire turned to look at Lily. She seemed so distressed, Claire couldn't keep herself from agreeing with Theo. "He's right," she said. "You still have time to call it off."

"I gave my word," Lily said. "I won't go back on it."

"Pshaw," Claire tried to say gaily, "plenty of girls break their engagements. It isn't the same as breaking a vow."

"In this case, it is," Lily said. "Are you ready, Theo?"

"If you are," he answered, stepping close.

Lily took hold of his arm. "Don't let me faint," she whispered.

"You've never fainted in your life," he teased.

"I've never gotten married either," she said.

Claire lifted the two bouquets of roses off her vanity, a pink one to match her dress, a white one for Lily.

Lily looked at all the white flowers, then at the red bud in Theo's lapel. "Trade with me," she said. Before he could argue, she exchanged the center white rose in her bouquet for his red bud, still closed tight. It stood alone within a circle of emptiness, which was how she felt.

The satin of her gown rustled like a thousand rattlesnakes as she and Theo followed Claire down the hall. When she stopped, poised in the arch to the formal parlor, a hush fell over the people crowding the room. Then Emmett's violin began to play the wedding march, and Theo escorted Lily down the aisle. Accompanying his limping gait, she looked at no one.

When she stood before Judge Houghton, Emmett finished the song and lay his violin aside, then took his place. She felt his eyes but couldn't meet them. The judge announced the purpose for the gathering, paused a moment, then asked if anyone knew of a reason why this marriage should not take place. Lily willed with all her heart for Jasper to step forward and object, but the moment passed in silence. The judge began the exchange of vows, and Lily made hers without a tremble in her voice, though her knees felt weak. When she was pronounced a wife, Emmett had to lift her face to receive his kiss. She didn't return it. Holding his arm as they walked back down the aisle, her eyes searched the faces watching her, but neither Jasper nor Whit were there.

The celebration passed her by. Never had she received so many kisses, seen so many smiling faces whose joy she couldn't share. Plates of food were given her, which she accepted then set aside. Numerous cups of punch were offered, but she sipped only a little. The men, including her husband, spent the afternoon and evening in the family parlor, smoking cigars and drinking whiskey, while the women and children, what few were there, stayed sequestered in the mammoth formal parlor, festooned with so many roses the air was sultry.

Cipriano kept delivering more food from the kitchen, and Lily's mother stayed busy serving the guests and clearing both rooms of the constant accumulation of dirty dishes. Lily sat on a rawhide settee positioned with its back to the cold hearth. Since the day was unseasonably warm, a fire hadn't been lit and the front door stood open to welcome any late arrivals. Smoke from the men's cigars drifted out of the family parlor and curled in wafting blue clouds as it floated through the hall and out the door.

Theo and Andy stood between the two rooms, Theo leaning with his back to the wall, Andy moving restlessly to and fro. Lily was glad to see the boys were at least making an effort to become friends, though she saw few smiles grace their faces. Theo would occasionally look in at her, his expression one of puzzled concern. Andy never so much as glanced in her direction. When he wasn't looking at Theo, he was watching the men or staring out the front door.

Since the expanse of Lily's skirts made it impossible for anyone to sit beside her, Claire had perched on an ottoman nearby. After family, Bob Daggerty was the first to present himself to the bride. When he leaned low to kiss Lily's hand, she almost swooned from the scent of his pomade.

"What a great day!" he exclaimed, standing straight again and smiling at Claire, who quickly looked away. Bestowing his attention on Lily again, he said, "The ceremony was as beautiful as the bride." Seeing her wince, he asked Claire, "Don't you agree, Miss Moss?"

She merely smiled and nodded.

"You yourself look especially ravishing," Daggerty said. "That nubile pink suits you perfectly."

Claire turned her head toward the door as if she hadn't heard him. Looking back at Lily, Daggerty said, "The sunshine outside is as brilliant as I'm certain your happiness will be, Mrs. Moss." Then he beat a quick retreat to join the men across the hall.

Claire collapsed against Lily's knees to camouflage her laughter.

"What's *nubile* mean?" Lily whispered. "It sounds indecent."

"Marriageable," Claire answered between giggles. "I guess he wants to wed my dress."

Lily smiled, thinking Bob Daggerty had more chance of that than marrying Claire. Looking up, she saw Augustina Menard, the wife of Soledad's *patrón,* beaming down at her.

"Dear little Lily," Mrs. Menard simpered, "how blessed you are to make such a match. Years ago, I'd hoped one of my daughters might catch the Cattle King of the Panal, but I finally decided he was among those peculiar men destined to die in an unmarried state."

Unable to think of a reply, Lily looked at Claire, who was biting her lip as she fussed with the roses in her bouquet.

"Isn't it amazing," Mrs. Menard continued, "that Emmett didn't go to Santa Fe or Texas and take his pick from the beautiful debutantes of high society? Despite his advanced age, most girls would have jumped at the chance to be his wife."

Collecting her wits, Lily answered, "Reckon he's too old to want a girl who'd jump at nothing."

"Yes, perhaps," Mrs. Menard murmured. Spying the platter of hot *buñuelos* drenched in honey Cipriano was carrying into the room, Mrs. Menard said, "Best wishes, dear, for your happiness." Then she hurried to the *buñuelos* and took three on her plate before Cipriano had let go of the platter.

Mrs. Menard's youngest daughters, Bianca and Petra, smiled shyly as they curtsied in front of Lily. Both girls were barely in their teens, dark like their mother, and dressed to the teeth. Bianca complimented Lily's gown, Petra the spray of flowers in her hair, then they moved away to sit near their mother, though they didn't eat. Lily suspected their corsets were too tight to allow it, and from the way they watched the men across the hall, that they'd come merely in the hope of catching husbands for themselves.

Lily shifted her gaze to Abigail Broussard, approaching with a sad smile. Celia, her youngest daughter, had been considered the prettiest girl in the county and might have caught Emmett's eye if she hadn't been ruined before she was old enough to be courted, though she'd been Lily's age when Whit seduced her. After Celia's grandmother died and left her an inheritance, she opened a bordello in Soledad. Though she could have chosen a more lucrative town for her business, rumor had it her love for Whit kept her in his vicinity.

"Congratulations, Lily," Mrs. Broussard said, then asked rhetorically, "Who could have guessed Emmett Moss would choose you?"

Pitying the widow for living within a day's ride of her daughter's shame, Lily answered mildly, "It surprised me, too."

"Indeed," Mrs. Broussard replied. "I'm certain your mother's bursting with pride. My mother was one of the wealthiest widows in New Orleans, you know. My match displeased her, though my husband was a good man, may he rest in peace. But I came from one of the best families and once had my own ambitions for Emmett's eventual marriage."

"I know," Lily said gently.

"Well, it's certainly a stroke of luck for you," Mrs. Broussard said, blinking back tears. "I wish you all the happiness in the world."

"Thanks," Lily said. When Mrs. Broussard had joined Pedro's wife at the platter of *buñuelos,* Lily leaned close and whispered to Claire, "She really wishes I'd die of worms."

Claire giggled and whispered back, "I can't imagine why she'd think Uncle Emmett would have chosen such an old woman, but she's jealous of you. It's plain as a cock's crow at dawn."

Lily considered telling Claire that Mrs. Broussard's jealousy was for her daughter's sake, a girl who had been ruined by the crow of the very cock Claire admired. But feeling certain Whit wouldn't compromise Claire as he had Celia, Lily had decided to let them find what pleasure they could in their romance. She certainly no longer had any intention of doing Emmett's bidding on that account.

Lash Cooper walked through the front door. As he greeted Theo and Andy, Lash looked longingly at the men drinking in the family parlor, though he had enough manners to pay his respects to the bride first. He crossed the room and leaned low to give Lily a congratulatory peck on her cheek. "I regret missing the ceremony in which you became Mrs. Moss," he apologized. "I was detained in Soledad because Foxy Strop met with an unfortunate mishap and I wanted to write the story for publication. I tarried only long enough to mail my missive to the *Optic* in hopes I might quickly receive remuneration enabling me to buy you a gift, dear Lily."

"Please don't, Lash," she murmured. "I doubt I'll be in need of much of anything from here on out."

"Which speaks to the munificence of your husband. I can't imagine a more worthy woman to be his bride. Your father would be proud of you, Lily."

She looked down at the single red rose in the center of her bouquet, suspecting her father would be ashamed if he knew what she'd done in the name of his vengeance. Pushing that from her mind, she asked, "What happened to Foxy Strop?"

"He was badly burned," Lash answered, "but he'll recover. You should be joyous today, so please don't trouble yourself about it."

"I've never met him," Lily said. Knowing Lash was craving a drink, she added, "Emmett'll be glad to see you."

Lash smiled. "Ah, Lily, you have such a good heart. Please accept my sincere wishes for your sublime happiness."

She watched him scurry into the family parlor to lap up the whiskey provided in abundance, then she smiled sadly at Claire and said, "Lash is a good friend of mine, but I'm afraid he thinks his best friend is liquor these days."

Claire nodded, then whispered, "Uncle Emmett calls him a drunk."

"He wasn't always," Lily said.

Manny Tucker, Emmett's ramrod, made a polite appearance. He was a squat, dark man with a barrel body and a forbidding demeanor. Standing stiffly before Lily, he extended gruff congratulations along with the crew's welcome to the new mistress of Bosque Grande. With him was Shiloh Pook, which surprised Lily. Not long ago she had upbraided him for leaving the garden gate open, exposing the vegetables to scavengers. As he stood holding his hat in his hands, she let her gaze slide up his tall, well-muscled frame to meet his blue eyes beneath a curly flop of sandy-brown hair she thought was in need of a trim.

"Just wanted to say, ma'am," he offered in a gravelly voice, "that this house has been lacking a woman's touch and I think you'll be good for Bosque Grande."

"Thank you," she said with surprise. He was already turning to go, so she called, "Mr. Pook?"

"Yes, ma'am?" he asked, facing her again.

"Reckon I lost my temper 'bout the garden the other day."

A hint of a smile played on his lips. "That ain't a hard thing to do," he said. "And you were right. I should've closed the gate."

"What was it, if you don't mind my asking, that you went into the garden to get?"

He looked around warily, and his eyes were definitely laughing when they met hers again. "Promise you won't tell Cipriano?"

"I swear it," she said, raising her right hand as proof.

"I snitched some strawberries," he said. "Cipriano likes to preserve 'em for jam, but I got a powerful love of strawberries hot off the vine."

She laughed, the first bit of joy she'd felt all day. "If any more come up missing," she said, "I promise I won't tell who took 'em."

"Thank you, ma'am," he said, then walked out with Manny Tucker to return to the bunkhouse, where the cowboys had a more raucous party in progress.

That snippet of Shiloh Pook's humor was the high point of Lily's day. For hours, she sat in the parlor receiving the perfunctory attention of a string of men she'd never met before. Associates of her husband's, they showered her with gifts she didn't open, compliments she believed false, and best wishes for her future she credited to the giver's hope of gain.

Except for Lily's mother and brother, only Emmett's friends, his family and employees attended the celebration. Because of the enmity for Emmett along the Panal, no one came from Siete Rios or River's End. None of her former neighbors and few of her father's past associates from Union made the journey; those who did were Emmett's guests, not hers. More an enemy than a friend, Sheriff Red Bond came without a gift, his congratulations oily with insinuations that her marriage improved her station far beyond anything her father could have provided. Emmett's lawyer, Edgar Homer, bowed low to kiss Lily's hand, then bid her to remember his fondness for her father if the day should come when she again found herself without masculine guidance through the perils of the world. Disliking his allusion to the age difference between herself and Emmett, Lily turned without a reply to the lawyer's wife.

Suzanne Homer was resplendent in a taffeta frock of such a brilliant yellow it made Lily's gown look faded. Keenly aware of her own sallow complexion, Lily felt jealous of the blush that yellow provided to Mrs. Homer's cheeks, and how it brought out golden highlights in her auburn hair. Claire had momentarily left the room, and Suzanne sat on the vacant ottoman as if to accentuate the comparison between herself and Emmett's bride.

"Though I suspected it the day of your visit," Suzanne said with a mischievous smile, "who else could have guessed that Emmett would choose you when he decided to marry?"

"Nobody, I reckon," Lily said, remembering how uncomfortable she'd felt during that visit.

"Indeed," Suzanne answered with a delicate snort of amusement. "I suppose he's hoping you'll give him children?"

Lily shook her head. "He didn't mention daughters."

Suzanne laughed with forthright pleasure. "You may be a match for him yet." She leaned closer, engulfing Lily in a tempest of heavy perfume. "Don't be frightened by what happens tonight, my dear," Suzanne whispered. "Being inexperienced as you are, it will no doubt take a while to learn to curb the beast that exists in every man."

Lily stared at the lawyer's wife. Thinking her speech wouldn't calm anyone's fears, she suspected the woman's remark had the opposite intention. "It hadn't crossed my mind to be scared," Lily answered defiantly.

Suzanne's smile implied she found that statement so frivolous it scarcely merited recognition. "Emmett is a man's man," she said, settling back with a slither of her taffeta skirts. "I doubt you'll find his sensitivity overwhelming."

"Your kindness is, Mrs. Homer," Lily retorted. "And your perfume's about to make me puke."

Suzanne stood up. "I'll leave you then to catch your breath. Lord knows you'll need it."

Lily watched her walk out and cross the hall to where the men were gathered. After a moment, a burst of laughter erupted from the room, making Lily's ears burn with the suspicion that Mrs. Homer was sharing her opinion of the bride's innocence as a joke. On the pretense of visiting the privy, Lily escaped to hide in her room. When Claire came to find her, Lily feigned sleep, so Claire quietly left her alone. And then, as if the day had been an exhausting chore of physical labor, Lily did fall asleep, only to be awakened by her husband opening her door at midnight.

11

*E*mmett had deliberately avoided Lily all evening. Shortly before midnight, he glanced out the window and saw Whit talking with Andy in a patch of moonlight by the corral. Emmett excused himself and was out the door before he saw Jasper Stone in the shadows behind Whit. Walking toward them, Emmett felt Jasper's hatred rankle across the decreasing distance.

Shouts of drunken enjoyment erupted from the cowboys' party in the bunkhouse, but the big house was demurely quiet as Emmett stopped in front of the three young men. He looked at his nephew and said, "Your sister needs you in the house."

Andy started away, then turned and called back to Whit, "You gonna be around awhile?"

"Prob'ly not," Whit answered. "But I'll most likely sleep at Celia's tonight if you want to see me."

Andy blushed, glanced at his uncle, then walked toward the house without saying more.

Emmett loaded his pipe and carefully tamped the tobacco, struck a match on the fence post, and sucked smoke into his mouth as he looked at the two men watching him, one with an amused smile that could mean anything, the other with anger in his eyes. Taking the pipe from his mouth, Emmett asked in a friendly tone, "How come you boys ain't inside enjoying the party?"

"We was fixing to leave," Whit answered. "Just kind of waiting around to see if you'd mosey out to say hello."

Emmett felt irritated by Whit's bedeviling smile, wishing he'd just come right out and say whether he'd been successful or not. Jasper's presence could mean Whit hadn't done it and wanted a backup when he delivered the news, or it could mean Jasper simply hadn't been able to stay away from Lily's wedding. Unable to resist doing some bedeviling of his own, Emmett asked him, "Ain't you gonna congratulate me on taking a bride?"

Jasper's eyes were as cold as iced-over slate. In his years on the frontier, Emmett had known all kinds of killers. Some were powder kegs waiting for a fuse, some had a misbegotten grudge against the world and would square off with any part of it, and some had legitimate grievances they exaggerated to justify their wrath. A few had all of those things compressed inside a mind as lethal as a steel trap. In Emmett's estimation, Jasper Stone fell in that category.

Though he had a smidgeon of a legitimate grievance for the loss of his family's homestead, the fact remained that they had abandoned it to the precarious protection of a caretaker who held only a quit-claim deed to the improvements, not the land it-self. Emmett had bought that deed for pennies compared with what it was worth, then filed a claim on the land as soon as the government legitimized titles. In Arizona, Jasper had heard of the government's survey, but he'd arrived mere days too late to claim the land.

Whether it was a day or a decade was irrelevant to the law, and Emmett's claim was proved in court, another procedure that cost him pennies since he kept a lawyer on permanent retainer. Jasper's attorney had taken a great deal more from the Stones. Public opinion supported them and resented Emmett, who ran his immense herds on open range. Though it was technically pub-lic domain and he used hired guns to enforce his exclusive right to that range, he justified the guns as being necessary to defend his investment. Everything Emmett did was within the letter of the law, but Jasper was a sore loser.

It was Whit who answered Emmett's question. "Reckon we're just hoping," he said, "for Lily's happiness."

"So'm I," Emmett said, exhaling smoke. "Did you make that trip to Union?"

"Yeah, I did," Whit said. "But it was a waste of time."

"How's that?" Emmett asked pleasantly, clenching his teeth on the stem of his pipe.

"It was the damnedest thing," Whit said, as if baffled himself. "I rode all the way up there and primed the tumble to fall the way I wanted, then decided not to do it."

"What made you decide that?" Emmett asked, emitting a cloud of smoke to hide his displeasure.

"I'm my own man," Whit said with an easy smile.

Emmett took his pipe from his mouth and hit the bowl against the palm of his hand to knock the ashes out, then pocketed the pipe before he met Whit's eyes again. "A man can't get by in this world without friends."

"I got friends," Whit said.

Emmett looked at Jasper, who didn't seem nearly as amused as Whit by what was coming down. Looking back at Whit, Em-mett said, "Your friends won't be much help when you're caught riding a stolen horse."

Whit grinned. "I got a bill of sale."

"You mean the one taken from my office last week?"

Whit laughed. "You know how easy it'd be for me to kill you right now?"

Again Emmett glanced at Jasper, then he looked back at Whit and said, "You'll hang if you do. You know that for a fact, and I don't think you're so stupid as to shoot a man everyone knows is always unarmed. I'll give you the mare on the condition that I never see you again."

"You already gave her to me," Whit said. "So you ain't giving me anything tonight, Emmett."

"Yes, I am. I'm giving you fair warning that after I walk away from this talk, you're my enemy and I'll do everything in my power to bring you down."

Emmett waited a minute to allow Whit to change the way things stood. When he made no move in that direction, Emmett turned and started away, but a hand reached out and took hold of his arm. He looked over his shoulder into Jasper's slate-blue eyes, as cold as death.

"If I ever hear of you hurting her," Jasper said quietly, "I'll kill you."

Emmett met Jasper's eyes a long moment, then looked down at his hand until he let loose and took a step back. "That's two threats against my life I've heard from you boys," Emmett said. "Ain't a person in this county would take exception to my shooting either one of you on sight."

Whit smiled. "You'll need a gun to do that, Emmett."

"Not in my own hand," he said, then turned and stalked toward the house.

He didn't glance back as he crossed the yard, but just inside the door he turned around to watch Whit and Jasper ride out. Emmett shut the door, then looked into the formal parlor and saw the women had gone to bed. With a sigh, he returned to the dregs of his party. Only the confirmed drunks were left, bunched around the liquor table. Given their inebriated state, Emmett didn't have to try hard to disguise his mood. With a few ribald jokes and thinly veiled insults, he cleared the room.

Not waiting to see his guests safely on their way, he walked down the dark hall and through his office to his bedroom. He went inside and closed the door, then remembered this was his wedding night and he had to consummate his marriage. With the attitude of completing one last chore before he could sleep, Emmett reentered the hall and walked through its gloom to Lily's room, pushing through her door without knocking.

She awoke to the sound of his entrance. Sitting up, she lit the lamp on the bedside table, then watched him take off his jacket and hang it on a hook on the wall. He sat down on the dressing stool in front of her vanity and tugged off his boots. When he stood up again, he unbuttoned his vest as he said, "I don't believe, Lily, I got much chance of getting you outta that dress without help."

As he hung up his vest, she said softly, "I can't do it on my own either."

"Com'ere," he said, facing her.

She stood up and crossed the room to turn her back to him, feeling his fingers unfasten the long line of hooks and eyes running from the nape of her neck to well past her waist. When he'd finished, she walked to the closet, opened the door, and stood in its shadow as she stepped out of the dress. She hung it up, thinking only that she never wanted to see it again. Untying her petticoats and hoopskirt, she let them fall to the floor. Then she looked over her shoulder at Emmett.

He smiled, half done with unbuttoning his shirt.

She reached for her nightgown, draped it over the top of the door, then pulled her shimmy off and dropped it on the closet floor. After quickly unlacing her camisole, she tossed it onto her shimmy, ducked under the hem of her nightgown, and pulled it down fast. Standing on one leg at a time to peel off her stockings, she dropped them, too, on the floor, then closed the closet and faced her husband.

He was already in bed, the blanket as high as his hips, his chest covered only with a thick mat of silver hair.

Lily forced herself to cross the room and blow out the lamp on the bedside table. The moon barely lit the room through the cracked heavy drapes, but her eyes adjusted as she slid under the covers beside him.

He moved closer, reaching to pull up her nightgown, then chuckled. "You still got your bloomers on," he said, taking hold of the waistband and tugging them down.

She lifted her hips to help him.

" 'Attagirl," he said, leaning to kiss her. His mouth tasted sour with whiskey and smoke. When she squirmed in repugnance, he lifted his head. "I don't like kissing much either," he said, then slid his hand between her legs and nudged them apart.

She buried her face in his shoulder so she couldn't see.

"You know, for a girl," Emmett said in a tone of imparting information, "the first time always hurts."

"I know," she whispered.

Emmett caressed her most intimate place, then slid his finger inside. She couldn't keep from jerking away. "Here now," he said, as she'd heard him say many times to a disobedient horse. Rising to his knees, he waddled to the end of the bed, took hold of her hips and positioned her in front of him, then spread her legs wide. She told herself he was her husband and had a right, but she didn't like it.

Touching her again, he said, "Reckon you ain't gonna get wet. I've never had a virgin before. Maybe that's just the way it is." He leaned low above her, his breath stale.

She turned her face aside, feeling his thighs press against hers. Then she felt it, hard and dull as a table knife cleaving her in half. When he thrust deeper, she recoiled away, but he pulled her back and did it again. "It'll be easier next time," he said, his breath like kerosene.

She remembered Jasper gently unwrapping the blanket from around her in the cave, how sweet he had tasted when he kissed her mouth, and how he'd kissed her breast, too, making her tremble with wanting him. She tried to pretend he was on top of her, but Jasper's touch had been tender. When Emmett tore her open, she bit his shoulder to keep from screaming, then felt blood as he kept pummeling into her. Though she whimpered for mercy, he seemed to have forgotten who she was. After a long time, he lifted himself above her and their skin came apart with an ugly sucking sound, then he held himself on stiff arms as he panted while his sweat dripped cold on her breasts. His face was contorted as if he had a stomachache, and his open mouth emitted odorous grunts with each stroke. Finally he shuddered and exhaled as if he were dying, then dropped his weight on top of her and lay still while his member slowly slid out with a flood of seed.

After a while, he jerked as he inhaled a snore, and she realized he was asleep. Carefully she maneuvered herself out from under him and onto the floor. Sitting with her knees drawn up to allow the soothing cool air between her legs, she stifled a sob. Then she stood up and walked across to the washbasin, poured water, and dunked a cloth to dab gently at her bruises. She stuck the cloth as far inside as she could, then stopped, realizing she was trying to wash his seed from her womb and she had no right to do that.

Dropping the cloth in the basin of water pink in the moonlight, she walked across to the window and stared out at the willows along the river. Silently she whispered Jasper's name, knowing this night would have been wonderful if she'd been his bride. *He never asked me!* she cried in silence. *Emmett asked, and I accepted. It's done.*

Struggling to find some shred to sustain her, she remembered that not only her blood had been shed in the usual sacrifice of marriage. Henry Hart was also dead. Her vengeance had been achieved. But she felt no joy. Instead of being Jasper's bride, she was his executioner. Sinking onto the floor in front of the window, Lily curled herself into a knot of regret.

It was nearly dawn when Whit and Jasper trotted their tired horses into the yard of the Stone homestead. To their surprise, lights shone from every window in the house. Jasper spurred to a gallop and swung off before his horse had completely stopped. He ran up the steps in front of the porch and disappeared in the blaze of light as Whit slowly ambled forward.

The smell of death emanated from the house. Knowing the loss of any of the four people inside would break Jasper's heart, Whit felt wary of sorrow. He could handle anger with one hand and glide the currents of humor like a bat in a breeze, but mourning was an emotion he'd sealed off after his mother's death.

He caught Jasper's Appaloosa and tied it with his black to the rail, then quietly walked up the steps and through the open door of the house. Inside, Ma Stone stood with a wooden spoon at half-mast in her hand, as if she meant to beat the air into batter. She was a plump woman, small and round with lustrous dark hair always worn in a braid on the top of her head, her complexion as creamy as warm milk. Her eyes were dark moons swimming in a red sky as she looked at Whit, her mouth a compressed line of control.

Pa Stone sat in the rocker in front of the fire, a formerly vital man now suddenly old. His long, thin body was collapsed in on itself as if his shoulders wanted to meet his hips. In the flickering light of the dying fire, his face was frozen in grief. Whit looked back at Ma Stone, then down the hall leading to the bedrooms. Jasper came out of Elise's room and met Whit's eyes through the long, narrow passage. Whit had seen Jasper angry to the point of rage before, but never had he seen such a fury of wrathful vengeance as he witnessed now. It was cold beyond passion, dead to any sense of caution, a silent cunning toward murder with no regard of consequence. Jasper emerged from the hall and headed for the door.

Whit lightly caught hold of Jasper's arm and stopped him, asking softly, "Where you going, Jasper?"

"Union," he answered.

"What for?"

"To kill Buck Robbins."

"Why?"

Jasper's mouth opened but uttered no sound.

Still holding onto Jasper, Whit looked at Ma Stone.

"Was Buck Robbins done it," she said. "Elise recognized his voice."

"Done what?" Whit asked, forcing someone to name it.

"There was another one," Ma Stone said, "but Elise didn't know him. They killed Sammie." Her voice broke and she sobbed when she cried, "They cut his throat, poor little boy, then Buck Robbins had his way with Elise."

Whit's grip tightened on Jasper's arm, communicating allegiance. "When?" Whit asked.

"Yesterday," Ma whimpered through her tears. "Mr. Reed rode over to fetch me 'cause his wife's time had come. Pa drove me there, so Elise and Sammie were alone."

Thinking hard, Whit said, "Don't make sense. Why would Buck Robbins kill Sammie?"

"Maybe 'cause he was his," Ma said, "and starting to talk."

Whit met Jasper's eyes and spoke softly, measuring his words to penetrate Jasper's rage. "Go feed and water the horses, Jasper. We gotta let 'em rest 'fore we ride clear to Union. Let's think this through and move smart when we go."

Jasper took in air as if he'd been holding his breath, then let it out in a great sigh of grief. Only when he nodded did Whit let go of his arm. As soon as he was out the door, Whit turned back to Ma. "Can I talk to Elise?"

"I don't think she'll want to see you, Whit," Ma answered.

"Is she awake?"

Ma nodded, spilling tears.

Whit walked down the hall and pushed through Elise's door. She lay flat on her back in the middle of her low child's bed, the quilt pulled up to just under her chin, her cheek bruised and her eyes red from crying. Seeing Whit, she rolled onto her side and pulled the covers over her head. He wanted to hold her, to comfort and soothe her, but didn't guess she was eager to feel a man's touch just then. Even so, he couldn't talk to a faceless bundle hidden under the blankets. He sat down and coaxed gently, "Look at me, Elise."

She shook her head beneath the covers.

"You can't live the rest of your life buried under blankets," he said.

She sniffled, then finally turned and pulled the quilt down just enough to show her eyes.

He gave her a smile, though he felt heartsick. Gently he said, "Your ma told us you heard Buck Robbins's voice. Is that right?"

She nodded, squeezing her eyes shut tight.

"Who else?"

"I don't know," she whispered.

"Tell me everything you remember 'em saying."

She shook her head and met his eyes. "I don't want to remember, Whit."

"You got to," he said. "Facing it down is the only way to put it behind you."

"I can't ever," she whimpered, tears running from her eyes. "Jasper wouldn't even touch me."

"Only 'cause he was afraid of hurting you more, Elise. 'Sides, it's hard to touch someone hidden under the covers without feeling you're invading where they don't want you to be." Seeing some of the terror melt from her eyes, he lifted his hand and tugged the blanket off her face, then kissed his fingertip and laid it lightly on her lips.

She turned her head and kissed his palm.

"Yeah, Elise," he whispered, cupping her face with both his hands as he leaned close and kissed her cheeks, her teary eyes, her forehead, and the tip of her nose. "There's still plenty of love in the world," he said. "Don't let a coupla men's ugliness make you think we're all worthy of fear."

Her arms came out and held him tight.

He lifted her up against him, rocking her gently.

"Oh, Whit," she moaned, "I feel like Jasper's mad at me for letting it happen."

Whit stroked her hair, a tangled dark mass he'd never seen unbraided before. "He's mad, but not at you, Elise. He'll get over acting like he is once we've dealt justice."

She pulled away and met his eyes. "Don't let him get killed 'cause of me!"

"I won't," he promised. "Now tell me everything you remember."

She shivered as she lay back down and tucked the covers under her chin again. "Just before it happened, the other man argued against hurting me, but Buck said it would cinch it sure. What'd that mean, Whit?"

"I don't know yet," he said, his mind racing with possibilities.

"Whit?" Elise moaned. "Why'd they kill Sammie? Why would anyone kill a little deaf boy who couldn't even talk?"

"To keep him that way, maybe," Whit said.

Elise lifted a corner of the quilt and wiped her eyes. "Right after they'd caught me and put the bag on my head, I heard the other man say, 'Our ace is a jackass now.' Does that make sense to you, Whit?"

"Not much," he said, "but I've heard it before."

"From who?"

"Ernie Kessel."

"He didn't hurt me, Whit, but I think he's the one killed Sammie. I heard him say it was done, then when Buck started with me and Ernie argued against it, that's when Buck said it would cinch it sure."

"He was right about that," Whit said, having decided what that meant. "Can you remember anything else?"

She shook her head, biting her lip to keep from crying.

Whit stood up. "Try'n get some sleep. We won't be leaving for a few hours yet." He turned away and left her alone.

Ma was waiting in the hall. She met Whit's eyes as they passed each other in the door, but neither of them spoke. Pa still sat in front of the hearth. Whit walked across and laid a hand on the old man's shoulder.

"All my life," Pa said, staring into the barely flickering fire, "I've split my guts to turn the other cheek. I don't have any fight left, Whit, but if I did I'd ride with you."

"The women need you here," Whit answered. "Me and Jasper'll take care of it."

Pa nodded. "We've left the children home alone many times and nothing like this ever happened before. I wish now we'd taken 'em with us."

"Regret ain't no use," Whit said.

"No," the old man said, "but it's hard to let loose of knowing I could've prevented what happened. Ben Reed come riding in on a lathered horse shouting his wife was in labor. You know Ma's been looking after her, and been saying all along Clarissa'd have a hard time, being as small as she is and this being their first. She didn't, though. She popped it out easy as pie. A boy. We weren't gone more'n three or four hours. Looking back on it, the very moment we were sharing congratulations with Ben and the

Beckworths, this tragedy was happening here. Hard to figure, ain't it, Whit?"

"Yeah, it is," he agreed.

"We love you as if you were our own," the old man said. "You know that, don't you, Whit?"

"It's made me proud," he said.

"We've buried seven children in the cemetery out yonder."

"I know," Whit said.

"All of 'em were babies, the oldest younger'n Elise is now."

"I know."

"Jasper's our only son who lived to manhood." He looked up and met Whit's eyes. "Don't let him be taken, too, Whit."

"It's a mean game they're playing, Pa Stone. I can't make no promises about the outcome, but I'll do my best to bring him home alive."

"Your best is up to it," Pa said, patting Whit's hand, then letting his own fall in his lap to lie helplessly still.

Whit walked out and crossed the yard to the stable. He found Jasper in the tack room, hunkered over the blood on the floor. Whit leapt up to sit on a barrel and lean with his elbows on his knees as he studied the stain of Sammie's death. Meeting Jasper's eyes, Whit said, "Elise heard the second man say his ace was a jackass. What's that mean to you, Jasper?"

"That Ernie Kessel's about to die," he said.

12

$\mathcal{L}$ ily woke up when Emmett lifted her off the floor. As he carried her across the room, she saw over his shoulder that it was dawn outside the window.

"Didn't mean to kick you outta your bed," he said, laying her in it and tucking the covers close around her body. "I won't be sleeping here again. Reckon I had too much to drink or it wouldn't have happened last night."

With sudden fear that her sacrifice had been for nothing, she asked, "Didn't I please you?"

He smiled, his crow's-feet crinkling around his eyes in the way she remembered loving when she'd thought of him as her uncle. "You did fine," he said. "It's never as pleasurable for women as it is for men, but the first time's always hard for a girl. I didn't expect you to like it, Lily."

"Then why won't you be coming back to my bed?" she asked, struggling to understand.

He sat down on the edge of it and gave her another playful smile. "I didn't say I wouldn't be back but that I wouldn't be sleeping here. I've been a bachelor too long and gotten used to sleeping on the floor. Why, I've got a crick in my spine this morning from lying on feathers all night. As for the other, we'll do it till you're with child. After that, I won't bother you again."

She studied his weatherworn, pox-scarred face with its bristly salt-and-pepper mustache and pale blue eyes, which she had known all her life as a font of kindness. "Ain't there s'posed to be more?" she asked.

"More what?" he answered.

She shook her head in confusion. " 'Tween married folks, ain't there s'posed to be a love of," she hesitated, searching for the right word, then finished weakly, "cuddling?"

"We'll have plenty of that," he said. "But like I mentioned already, I'm set in my ways and accustomed to sleeping alone. Right now, you prob'ly still have girlish notions about marriage, but as time goes by, I think you'll prefer it this way, too."

"I hope you're right, Uncle Emmett," she whispered.

He chuckled. "You best stop calling me 'uncle.' Makes our marriage sound like a sin."

"It's one of the things *I'm* accustomed to," she answered, "but I won't do it again. I'm gonna try hard to be a good wife to you, Emmett."

"You already are," he said. "You're right, though, to think the accommodating comes mostly from the wife. You're part of me now, Lily, an extension of my will in the same way a good horse does its rider's bidding. That's the union spoken of in the vows. As for the other," he paused to smile, "what you call cuddling, a good woman sees it as a duty to her husband and an act necessary to the fulfillment of her destiny as a mother. So don't be dwelling on your disappointment. If you *had* liked it, *I* would've been disappointed and doubted my choice of a bride." He stood up. "I'm riding out to the north range today. See you tonight."

She nodded and watched him go, then looked at the dawn beyond her window as she tried to accept what he had said. She knew the part about the union was right. After all, he hadn't become a Cassidy; she'd become a Moss. Everyone knew a husband and wife were one person, and that person was the man. But Lily remembered her mother's fondness for cuddling, how when her father hinted at it during the day, her mother's eyes had shone with anticipation. And when he returned from a journey, the next morning her mother's face seemed as smooth as a river stone, as if what they'd shared under the covers had washed away all the rough edges she'd accumulated in his absence.

Lily decided her parents' marriage had been uncommonly blessed and such comfort wasn't to be hers. Since Emmett had chosen her precisely because she was strong enough to stand alone, she must form herself in the mirror of his expectations. Most of all, she must never again allow herself to remember how she'd felt with Jasper in the cave in the mountains.

"We gotta think this through," Whit said.

Jasper stood up and walked over to stare out the door of the tack room into the stable, filling with the first light of morning. "I can't figure it, Whit," he mumbled.

"You're letting yourself be blinded by hurt," Whit said.

His voice husky, Jasper asked, "How do you figure it?"

"Sammie's father wanted him dead 'fore he learned how to talk. Who do Buck and Ernie work for?"

"Henry Hart," Jasper said, turning around.

Whit nodded. "Elise got in their way, but Sammie's the one

they were after. When Ernie argued against hurting Elise, Buck said it would cinch it sure. What do you reckon he was talking about?"

Jasper shook his head.

"Getting us to ride into an ambush," Whit said, "by tearing hellbent into Hart's stomping ground so the sheriff can shoot us down, me on the old death warrant and you for being with me. That way, Hart wouldn't have to worry about us getting retribution. We ain't gonna do what they want, though. We're gonna make 'em come to us."

Jasper frowned. "How?"

"By letting on that Sammie's still alive. More'n that. We'll spread the news that the shock of being attacked brought his voice back and what he's saying ain't pretty to hear."

Jasper considered the plan, then said, "Might work."

"It'll work good enough to get 'em to come make sure."

"Ain't gonna be easy," Jasper muttered, "just sitting here waiting for 'em to show again."

"It's the easier side of an ambush," Whit said. " 'Sides, I think it'd mean a lot to Elise if you stayed close by awhile."

Jasper jerked back around and kicked hard at the wall. After a moment, he said with tears in his voice, "I wanted so bad to protect her."

"What happened wasn't no fault of yours," Whit said. "We best get Sammie buried and the grave hid right quick, or our story won't wash."

Jasper wiped his eyes with his sleeve before turning around again. "I'll go along with that part of it. But I can't wait too many days, Whit. Folks won't believe it of me anyway."

"I don't think it'll take 'em long to show up."

"You gonna be the one to spread the news?"

Whit nodded. "I'll ride up the Panal far as Soledad, telling everyone along the way. Then I'll hightail it back here and we'll be ready for 'em."

"You'll only tell about Sammie, right? You ain't gonna say nothing about Elise?"

"I'll just say they hurt her, and you're sticking close till she gets better. Someone'll tell Buck and Ernie the story I'm spreading. They won't be eager to face Hart without the job being done, so they'll wait for me to get back, thinking you and me'll ride to Union together. That's when they'll come here, after they think we've left."

Jasper nodded. "I'll wait till you get back, but if they don't show pretty quick, I'm going after 'em."

"I'll be with you," Whit said.

Standing at the bar in Foxy Strop's Saloon, Lash Cooper could scarcely believe what Andy Moss was telling him. It was early Friday morning and they were alone except for Woody Wheeler, who had been hired to tend bar while Foxy recovered from being branded. Lash sipped the beer Andy had bought him, then asked Woody, "You hear about this?"

Woody nodded. "Whit was here yesterday."

Lash looked back at Andy and prodded him for details. "Have you heard Sammie talk?"

"No, sir," Andy said. "But Whit has. And he says the boy's tale is none too pretty."

"Wouldn't repeat it, though, huh?"

"Whit said it's up to the Stones to decide who to tell."

"When'd you see Whit?"

"Yesterday about noon. Elise is still in bad shape and Jasper's staying at her side till he knows she won't die. Otherwise he would've already gone after the scoundrels."

"He knows who they are?"

Andy nodded. "Elise recognized their voices."

"Whit didn't mention their names, I don't reckon."

"No, sir. But he said Sammie named his father and told how he was mistreated till he ran away and Jasper found him."

"But Whit wouldn't say who he named?"

"No, sir."

"Did he mention whether or not Elise had been defiled?"

"No, he didn't. Can a girl die from that?"

"Sometimes, depending on how it was done." Lash sipped his beer again. "Where'd you see Whit?"

"At Bosque Grande, like I said. He was riding up here to see a man about some business that couldn't wait, otherwise he'd have stayed with Jasper."

"Reckon he would," Lash said.

"Claire and Lily were all for riding over to Rocky Arroyo and offering to help, but Whit said it'd be best to let things settle down first. He said Jasper's taking it hard and not fit for company."

"Jasper dotes on his sister. Everyone in the county knows that."

"Whit said he won't hardly leave her side."

"Ain't that something," Lash said.

"It's pitiful." Andy sighed. "I haven't met any of Jasper's folks, and he's not easy to warm up to, but I wouldn't want to hear about that kind of trouble falling on anybody."

"No," Lash agreed. He drained his beer and smiled at the boy. "Would you be so kind as to buy me a shot of whiskey?"

"Sure," Andy said, digging into his pocket for two bits. He laid the coin on the bar. "I gotta be getting home, though."

"Give my regards to the new Mrs. Moss," Lash said.

"I'll do that," Andy said, walking out.

He didn't go home but to Celia's, hoping to find Whit. Even though his black mare wasn't at the hitching rail, Andy had figured out that Whit didn't like to announce his presence wherever he was. Andy tied Kickapoo to the rail and went in anyway. The parlor was empty.

He sat down in front of the piano and folded it open. The white keys sparkled in front of him like a pathway to pleasure, something he sorely needed just then. He caressed them into a soothing melody to ease the hurt he felt for the Stones. He didn't even know them, yet he felt as if he did. Whit was hurt, too. Andy had seen it in his eyes, and maybe that was enough of a connection. Or maybe all people were connected whether they knew one another or not. Maybe pain was like a pebble thrown into a pond, the force of its fall rippling to touch every drop of water before the pebble hit bottom. The same didn't seem to be true of joy. If Andy heard of someone suffering even a thousand miles away he felt bad enough to cry, but if he heard of someone equally far away being happy it didn't make him laugh. When he finished the song, he let his hands fall in his lap without having found the peace he'd sought.

"That was beautiful," Celia said behind him.

He turned on the stool to face her. She was a pretty woman, her abundant mahogany-colored hair tied with a ribbon behind her neck. She wore a white wrapper left open to reveal a frilly black garment such as Andy had never seen before. Her breasts nearly escaped from the top of it, and its lacy skirt barely covered the beginnings of her thighs.

"Have you seen Whit?" she asked.

"Not since yesterday noon," he said.

"I've seen him since then. Ain't it awful what happened at the Stones'?"

"Yeah," Andy said.

"If a man feels an urge," she bit off, "he oughta come here. Ain't no excuse to force himself on an innocent girl."

"No, there ain't," Andy agreed, thinking Whit had told Celia what he wouldn't tell Claire and Lily, though somehow they'd known without his having to say it.

"It's gonna be the end of Whit," Celia said.

Andy blinked with surprise. "What makes you say that?"

" 'Cause he'll help Jasper take vengeance and the law won't let 'em get away with it."

"Maybe you're wrong," Andy said. "Any man who'd hurt children deserves vengeance being delivered."

She nodded. "That just means Whit has finally found a cause he can justify throwing his life away for."

Andy studied her, puzzled. "You make it sound like he's looking to die."

"He acts like it most of the time." She walked to the sideboard and opened a bottle of whiskey. "Want a drink?"

"No thanks," Andy said, watching her pour herself one. "I oughta get home."

Celia downed the shot, then faced him with a smile. "Did you come just to play my piano?"

"I was hoping to catch Whit," he said.

"Ain't we all," she said with a bitter laugh. "If you play me another song, I'll give you a free ride."

Andy felt himself blush. "Aren't you Whit's girl?"

She shrugged. "He shares me with Jasper. I'm sure he likes you as well."

Andy was tongue-tied, trying to imagine Celia in bed with both Whit and Jasper.

She laughed again. "You've never had a woman, have you, Andy?"

"No, ma'am. I haven't felt the inclination yet."

She nodded. "Well, when you do, let me know. In the meantime, you can play my piano whenever you want."

"Thank you," Andy said. "I gotta get home."

"Tell your Uncle Emmett I said hello. Tell him just 'cause he's got a wife now don't mean he has to stop visiting me."

Andy stared at her.

Again she laughed. "You leaving or not?"

He nodded and walked out to his horse, swung on, and ambled along the road south. Not wanting to go home, he decided that when he reached the ford he'd cross the river and keep heading south toward Rocky Arroyo in the hope of finding Whit with Jasper.

Lily and Claire were riding toward Rocky Arroyo, too. Though their avowed purpose was to offer comfort and sympathy to the women, Lily knew Claire was hoping to find Whit. When Lily had argued against making the trip, however, Claire insisted she would cross the prairie alone, so Lily agreed to go because she felt responsible for the pampered girl.

Lily had grown up on the frontier with men who were rough but often no less kind because of it. Most of them anyway; she'd met plenty who weren't kind. The fact that some of those men could hurt innocent children didn't surprise Lily, though she suspected what had happened to Elise carried no more weight in Claire's mind than an excuse to see Whit. Surely if it did, she wouldn't go gallivanting across the country alone and unarmed, as if the mishaps that could befall a girl had no more impact than those found in the romantic novels she was constantly reading.

Lily thought Claire and Whit had a lot in common, which was odd given the difference in their upbringings. Claire had been raised in a genteel home by doting parents; Whit had been orphaned at an early age and learned to fend for himself. Yet somehow those disparate childhoods had created two people who never considered consequences. They followed their whims and laughed at danger as if it didn't truly exist. Duty and prudence never entered their minds.

Lily had been raised with a strong sense of both. Prudence protected a person from undesirable consequences, and duty gave order to life, which otherwise would be a chaotic rampage of self-indulgence. The worst men she'd known were motivated by exactly that, and nothing good ever came of them. She still hoped for something good for Whit, and she suspected marrying Claire could provide the station he needed to make a success of his life. Lily also believed that if Whit joined the family, Emmett would use his power to keep the law at bay, not only for Whit but also his friend Jasper. So for the first time in her life, she denied her duty, acting against what she knew to be her husband's wish in regard to Claire and Whit.

The autumn was proving to be a warm one, the bright sun denying the approach of Christmas, only a month away. Crossing the Panal, the two women came out on the other side with the bellies of their horses dripping water on the sand. Lily urged her palomino up the embankment to gain the road on the crest, then reined around and watched Claire holding her horse back so it worked twice as hard to climb the hill. Lily thought the scene a perfect illustration of Claire's ineptitude for frontier life. That she had fallen in love with a man who was a product of that frontier and adept at surviving its challenges was an irony that would have been funny if the stakes weren't so high.

Lily turned away from the sight of Claire's delicate progress and looked south toward their destination. Even if their visit was short, they wouldn't be home in time for supper, and Lily wondered what Emmett would say about their absence. She turned her horse and looked north toward the range where he was working. Far in the distance, a buggy was coming toward her. It moved fast, two men on the seat, the driver holding a whip he used often. He was burly, his shoulders wide and his bulk occupying more than his share of the seat. The other man held a rifle between his knees as if he anticipated the sudden need of defense. He was slight, his face shadowed by a dark hat, the rifle a line of silver dissecting his silhouette in half.

Lily felt a prick of recognition she didn't want to admit. She heard Claire's horse gain the crest and come to a stop, but Lily didn't take her eyes off the men approaching at a fast clip. They were still fifty yards away when that prick exploded her apprehension as if it were a boil that had festered too long.

Henry Hart tipped his hat as the buggy sped by, Sheriff Bond whipping the horses so they wouldn't break their stride. Lily stared through the dust they raised on the road until the black canopy of the buggy disappeared in the distance. As the initial numbness of shock gave way, she felt rage and humiliation ricochet with doom into every cell of her body.

"Lily, what on earth?" Claire whispered with baffled concern.

Lily kept staring at the dust drifting to fall on the now empty road. Struggling to remember what had been said the afternoon of her wedding, she saw again Whit's trickster smile as he confessed he didn't *want* to let her down, then heard Jasper say she should have asked it of them in the first place. When she'd pleaded to be told he hadn't helped Whit, Jasper had answered only that Mrs. Moss didn't have the right to question him. Reading their aversion as guilt, she hadn't even asked Emmett if it had been done. He had lied to her! Taken her under the pretense of having delivered her price when he hadn't.

"Lily?" Claire whispered.

Lily looked at the stricken concern on Claire's face, realizing her own must be as pale as if she'd seen a ghost. But the man was alive.

"What's wrong?" Claire asked. "Who were those men?"

Lily forced her tongue to work. "Henry Hart and Red Bond."

"Who are they?"

"Bond's the sheriff. Henry Hart's the man who killed my father."

"Oh," Claire said. "Yes, I understand. It must be awful to see him ride by and tip his hat as if he were a gentleman."

Lily reined her horse onto the trail toward home. Except it wasn't home anymore. She lived at Bosque Grande. And she wasn't going up the Deep River Road but south to Rocky Arroyo, a place she had once hoped would be her home. She would see Jasper, knowing he knew she'd been bought with a promise that wasn't delivered. Damn Whit for twisting his words so you had to look underneath what he was saying! Damn Jasper for walking away from her when she was crying in the dirt on her wedding day! Either one of them could have saved her from the betrayal now curdling in her heart. Damn them both!

Claire watched the rigid set of Lily's face testifying to her ability to control emotions so fierce they could set the prairie on fire. Unable to imagine the torture of facing a person who had wronged her so terribly, Claire thought she herself would have spit in the man's face. Maybe even used the rifle Lily carried, pulled the gun and shot the man dead rather than let him add insult to injury by tipping his hat as he sped by. At the very least, Claire would have cried. Lily rode on showing no more emotion than a searing pain in her eyes. Claire admired her fortitude, but mostly she felt sorry that Lily's path had chanced to cross that man's so soon after her wedding day.

13

*A*ndy moved along at an easy lope. The prairie was flat, stretching to a distant ridge of mountains smoky blue on the western horizon. Bunches of red fountain grass bowed in the wind among tufts of yellowed buffalo and grama grass, gray-green creosote, and a few scrawny mesquite trees, their bare branches black. Andy wondered if the wind ever stopped on the prairie. He hadn't known it to, and he'd been here two months now. At first the wind had made him cranky, the way it kept buffeting night and day, but now he supposed he'd miss it if it stopped. As lonely as his life had become since moving to the Panal, he found the wind a companion on his solitary rides.

At the junction, he took the road leading south. The westerly road followed Deep River into the mountains, passing Cassidy's Mill. Andy would like to go there someday. He'd never seen a gristmill, and he thought if he and Theo spent more time together they might be friends. Though their liabilities were different, it seemed a cripple and a simpleton should find some common ground. Andy missed having a friend he could chum around with, someone who didn't think being simpleminded meant he had nothing to offer.

Whit didn't seem to find any fault with Andy. And though Jasper held a grudge against anyone named Moss, he treated Andy the same way he treated nearly everyone else. No one received much kindness from Jasper but he didn't generally make trouble except to stomp off in anger every time the name Moss came into a conversation. Despite that, he'd pulled Andy out of the line of fire the day Whit killed Rufus Bond, so Andy figured he could ride onto the Stone homestead without getting shot even if he was a Moss.

He kept thinking about Sammie, the little boy who'd been so badly treated by his father that he ran away. Andy couldn't figure why God would give a child such a heavy burden, then let something so awful happen after he'd found a good home with the Stones. He'd asked Lily what the boy looked like, and she'd said he was towheaded with blue eyes. Andy suspected he and Sammie could get along. The boy's prior silence would have created a feeling of isolation that Andy could understand. So besides hoping to find Whit with Jasper, Andy was looking forward to meeting Sammie.

As he traveled farther south along the river, the cottonwoods thinned out and pretty soon he saw two riders in the distance ahead. They were small, one on a plain bay and the other on a flashy palomino. After a moment he recognized that they were women because of their oddly shaped silhouettes, caused by their knees crooked over the horns of their sidesaddles. The chance of another woman riding a palomino along the Panal was slim, so Andy knew they must be Lily and Claire. He spurred his horse to catch up.

When he was still a good stretch away, Lily turned her horse to see who was coming. Claire did, too. Andy kept Kickapoo at a gallop until he was almost on top of them, then reined up so sharply that Lily's palomino reared and spun around before she settled it down again. Glaring at Andy, she said harshly, "That ain't no way to come up to folks on the road."

"Sorry," he said, thinking he'd intended to show off how well he was learning to ride, but it had been Lily who displayed the superior skill. Though Claire's horse was so old and docile it barely blinked at the commotion, she was hanging on with both hands. Still, she seemed to understand his intent because she smiled and said, "You're doing fine on that horse, Andy."

He grinned. "Where are you going?"

"To visit the Stones," Claire said.

Andy's smile slid into a frown. "Whit told you not to."

"Whit doesn't understand how women need each other in times of trouble," Claire said. "I'm sure Mrs. Stone and Elise will be glad for our company."

Andy looked at Lily.

She shrugged and said, "I tried to talk her out of it but she said she'd come alone."

Andy thought Lily was in an especially bad mood, making him wonder if marriage agreed with her. Looking back at his sister, he suspected she was really going to see Whit. But since his own reason was the same, Andy decided to play along with the sympathy line. "I figure I could talk to little Sammie and maybe cheer him up."

"He can't hear nothing," Lily said, as if Andy were stupid not to remember that.

"He can see, though, and I can make faces." He made one at her. Claire giggled, but Lily just looked away. "In times of trouble," Andy said, "folks need to laugh."

"Well, don't make him split his stitches where Mrs. Stone sewed him up," Lily said, reining her horse around and ambling on.

Andy followed behind, not wanting to hinder their conversation, something he suspected he did since they always got quiet when he came around. But nothing was said as they eked out the miles in deference to Claire's fear of going faster than a walk. He wondered if the slow pace was what had spoiled Lily's mood, or if she really was unhappy being Mrs. Moss. This was only the third day of her marriage but Andy couldn't see that much had changed. Uncle Emmett was still gone most of the time, and Lily had neither moved into his bedroom nor he into hers. Andy's room was kitty-corner to his uncle's, and last night he'd heard Emmett snoring as usual. Maybe they didn't sleep together because of his snoring. Some nights it kept Andy awake.

Finally Lily turned off the road onto a trail that led into an arroyo full of white rocks. A few miles up the canyon, the trail stopped in the yard of a homestead. The house and barn were built of logs, not the adobe Andy had seen everywhere else along the Panal. He wondered if Jasper had brought the logs down from the mountains himself, maybe with Whit's help. Though when Andy thought about it, he couldn't remember Whit ever mentioning any kind of work. Neither Jasper's Appaloosa nor Whit's black were in the corral, but Andy hoped they were out of sight inside the barn.

Lily rode straight up to the porch steps and called hello with a quiver in her voice that Andy hadn't noticed being there before. He guessed she was feeling trembly about what happened to Elise, it being a tragedy only girls could suffer and therefore fully understand. After a minute, a small, dark-haired woman wearing a white apron over a brown dress opened the door and stepped onto the porch. Her gaze flew from Lily to Claire to Andy, then settled on Lily.

"Afternoon, Mrs. Stone," she said softly. "This here's Claire Moss and that's her brother, Andy. We heard of your trouble and rode over to offer our sympathy and any help you might need."

For a long moment Mrs. Stone didn't speak. Then she said in a husky voice, "Thank you kindly, Lily. I appreciate your coming all this way, but there's nothing to be done now except wait out the hurt."

"Maybe we could help you pass that time a mite more pleasantly," Lily said.

Jasper came through the door and stood behind his mother, laying his hands on her shoulders as he looked at each of the visitors. He, too, settled on Lily when he said, "Thanks for coming, but we ain't receiving comp'ny."

Claire said, "Andy thinks he can cheer Sammie up. Won't you let him try?"

Mrs. Stone paled and turned around, pressing her face into Jasper's shirt, her shoulders shaking as she cried. Jasper held her close and murmured words too soft for the others to hear. Seeing how gentle he was with his mother, Andy felt his heart go out to Jasper. After a moment, Mrs. Stone nodded and hurried into the house, closing the door.

Jasper met Andy's eyes and said, "Sammie's asleep. Maybe you can come back another day."

No one said anything for a long moment. Then Lily asked in a voice raw with hurt, "Will you let us water our horses 'fore we go?"

"Help yourself," Jasper said, nodding toward the corral behind them.

They turned their horses and ambled across the yard to the trough outside the fence. Jasper came over and leaned his back against it, his eyes scanning the distance all around.

From atop her horse, drinking at the trough, Lily asked, "How's Elise?"

Andy watched Jasper flinch. When he looked at Lily, his blue eyes were as sharp as knives of tempered steel but his voice was dull when he said, "As well as can be expected."

"Was she hurt bad?" Lily asked.

"She'll be all right," Jasper mumbled, studying the distance again.

The horses lifted their heads, dripping water from their

mouths that fell noisily into the trough. After a minute, Claire asked, "Have you seen Whit?"

Jasper's eyes flashed with scorn. "Why don't you pull your skirts out of the mud, Miss Moss, 'fore he trips over 'em?"

"I don't consider him mud," she answered haughtily.

"Your uncle does."

"Oh, hush, Jasper," Lily said, sounding like a mother scolding her child. "Ain't no need for you to come 'tween Claire and Whit if they want to be together."

"Is that your husband's opinion," he asked coldly, "or your own?"

"My own," she said.

"Bet he don't agree with you."

"He don't rule the world," she said.

Jasper's smile was vicious. "You just figure that out? Or did you decide to believe it the day after your wedding?"

Lily whimpered as if he'd struck her. "Why didn't you tell me Whit didn't do it?" she cried. "I came begging for one word from you to stop me. You didn't give me that word, Jasper, even though it would've been the truth!"

He shrugged. "If you ain't happy with your price, I ain't the one you oughta complain to," he paused, then drawled with sarcasm, "Mrs. Moss."

"Is that all I am anymore?" she asked angrily.

"It's all you are to me," he said.

She yanked her horse around and kicked it into a gallop out of the yard. Hearing Claire leave, too, Andy watched Jasper stare after them. When he finally looked at Andy, there was so much sorrow in Jasper's eyes that Andy gave him a smile of sympathy.

"Go on," Jasper said, jerking his head toward the women. "They shouldn't be crossing the country alone."

Feeling proud that Jasper considered him a man capable of protecting women, Andy nodded and turned his horse out of the yard. He galloped to catch up, then reined back beside Claire, both of them watching Lily disappear ahead. Andy looked at his sister and asked, "What was that all about?"

Claire sighed sadly. "Nothing you'd understand."

"How can I learn anything," he asked, "if nobody'll answer my questions 'cause they think I'm too stupid to understand?"

She glanced at him with surprise, then returned her gaze to study his face as if she'd never seen it before. Finally she said, "Promise you won't tell anyone?"

"I promise," he said.

She sighed again. "Lily's in love with Jasper. I think he cares for her, too. That's why he's so mad about her marrying Uncle Emmett."

"Why did she?" Andy asked, astounded.

Claire looked at him with an expression of exaggerated patience. "Some girls don't have the luxury of marrying for love. They have to think of the best interest of their family."

"You mean she married Uncle Emmett for his money?"

"Her brother's half crippled and her mother a widow. It fell on Lily to provide for them. What would you have done in her place?"

"I don't know," Andy said, suddenly feeling compassion for the homely girl who bossed him around. "But I still don't understand why she couldn't marry Jasper. He's got a ranch. It's not as big as Uncle Emmett's, but Jasper's got enough to take a wife if he'd a mind to."

"That's just it," Claire said sadly. "He didn't ask her."

"Why not, if he cares for her?"

Claire shrugged. "Only he can answer that."

Andy nodded. "But what did she mean about begging Jasper for the truth?"

"I don't know," Claire said. "I was there at the time, but I didn't understand it then and I don't now. Guess it's just something between the two of them. You must never ask her or him either, Andy. It's one of those private things that're best left alone."

"I won't ask 'em," Andy promised. He wondered how many other private things existed that he'd never seen before, and if the fact that he hadn't seen them meant he really was stupid.

Lily was waiting for them at the junction, her face pinched and her eyes red as if she'd cried the whole way.

"I'm gonna visit my mother," she said as soon as they reined to a stop. "Andy, you take Claire home. Will you do that? Not leave her alone out here?"

"Sure," he said, only stifling his resentment that she doubted he would because of what he'd just learned.

"Don't you want us to ride with you, Lily?" Claire asked.

She shook her head, tears falling across her cheeks, then yanked her palomino to half rear as it spun around.

As they sat watching her gallop away, Andy said, "She's sure good on a horse."

"Yes, she is," Claire agreed, turning her staid, old mount onto the road and ambling at a snail's pace north toward the ford.

Andy followed along, assuaging his impatience at the gait with the thought of what Jasper had said about not leaving the women alone. He worried slightly about Lily. But knowing she had a rifle, he figured she had better protection than any he could offer. Suddenly Andy's eye caught movement in the cottonwoods along the river. He picked a rider out of the shadows, then recognized Whit. Andy waved and yelled as he spurred his horse to meet his friend and grab a few minutes alone before Claire caught up.

Whit laughed a greeting. "Hey, Andy! What're you doing way out here?"

"Taking my sister home," he said, jerking his head at her slowly coming along the trail. "She and Lily rode over to offer the Stones comfort, but it doesn't seem they want any."

Whit nodded, watching Claire amble closer. "Where's Lily?"

"She decided to visit her mother."

Whit nodded again. "Tell you what, Andy. I'll take Claire home. Why don't you ride back and wait for me at Jasper's?"

"I don't think he'll want to see me, Whit. He pretty near threw us out just now."

"Tell him I sent you, and that I'll be there directly." Whit looked away from Claire and met Andy's eyes. "It's important that Jasper ain't left alone too long. So I'm counting on you to stay with him till I get back."

"All right," Andy said, pleased to be needed. He reined around and grinned at his sister. "Whit's gonna take you home. Reckon you'd rather go with him anyway."

A smile spread across her face as she looked at Whit. "I'd be pleased," she said.

He chuckled, a soft sound deep in his throat.

"Where are you going, Andy?" Claire asked.

"Back to Rocky Arroyo." Before she could ask why, he galloped away, leaving Whit to explain.

Claire watched her brother disappear in the dust cloud kicked up by his horse, then she looked back at Whit.

He gave her a smile and said, "You look mighty pretty sitting that horse."

"Thank you," she answered, returning his smile.

As Whit reined his horse into a walk alongside hers, she said, "We rode over to be with Mrs. Stone and Elise, but Jasper chased us off."

"There's a reason for that, Claire. When this is over, I'll tell you what it is."

She nodded. "Jasper was real sharp with Lily. They remind me of that poem 'Evangeline.' Have you ever read it?"

"No, I haven't."

"It's about lovers who are always missing each other because they're traveling different directions."

"Sounds like it fits," he said.

Boldly she asked, "Do you think it's also true of us?"

He smiled. "We're traveling the same road now."

"Yes, we are," she said, happy with his answer.

"There's a cove in the river down below that's real pretty. Want to see it?"

"Very much," she said.

He turned off the road and meandered through the brush toward the river. She followed him until he spurred his horse to descend the embankment at a run, kicking stones that beat him down. Claire hesitated, then held her horse back to take the descent carefully. When she joined him on the floodplain, he grinned and said, "It takes my breath away just looking at you."

She laughed, pleased beyond measure.

"The cove's right down here," he said, reining his horse south. "Keep close or you'll get bogged in quicksand."

She felt a thrill of danger, following his lead through a world that looked benign but lurked with bogs. After a few minutes, the floodplain widened into a natural cove against the bank. Lush grass covered the ground, still green in the lee of the cliff. Whit swung off and turned to lift her down. He held her waist a moment longer than necessary, smiling into her eyes, then turned away and tethered the horses to the roots of a cottonwood protruding out of the bank. Untying his bedroll from behind his saddle, he carried it to the deep grass in a dark shadow, unrolled the blanket and spread it flat, then gestured for her to sit down. She did, carefully arranging her skirts to fall in graceful folds around her, then taking off her bonnet and laying it aside. When she looked up, he was still standing a scant distance away, watching her. "Aren't you going to join me?" she asked.

"I don't know as I should." He laughed. "I think I'll just stand here and admire you for a while."

"As pleasant as that prospect is," she answered, "I'd rather have you closer."

"Would you?" he teased.

"Yes," she said.

He dropped down to sit cross-legged in front of her and lift a strand of her hair to drape behind her shoulder as his gaze lingered on her breasts beneath the dark bodice of her dress. Then he raised his eyes to meet hers.

"It's been too long since I've seen you, Whit," she murmured.

"I saw you yesterday morning," he said.

"Yes, when you brought the news of what happened to Jasper's family. That was a somber visit."

"I saw you the day before at Lily's wedding," he said.

"But you didn't stay for the ceremony or the party afterward. Why not?"

"It wasn't you I was avoiding, but your uncle."

"Why?" she asked.

"Let's just say me and Emmett don't see the world the same."

"Is it so important that you do?"

"Oh, yeah. Everything Emmett believes is important, even when he's wrong."

"Such as?"

"Oh, it mostly concerns politics and business. Stuff that had its start 'fore you came here. Don't reckon you'd understand even if I tried to explain, but I'd rather talk about something else."

"Me, too," she said. "Tell me again how pretty you think I am."

He leaned back on his elbows. "You must've had a lotta men tell you that, Claire."

"A few," she said. "But none of them meant more to me than you do."

He smiled. "Jasper thinks I'm loco to think about you."

"He told me," she said.

"Today?"

She nodded.

"Well, you know, he's funny about women. I can't hardly figure him out myself."

"It's obvious he cares for Lily. Why didn't he ask her to marry him?"

"He loves his sister too much."

"You mean in the wrong way?"

"No, there ain't nothing wrong about it. It just fills his mind. He tries to enjoy himself in town, with harlots and all, but to Jasper, if a girl lays with a man, even her husband, she's less in his eyes."

Claire frowned, trying to understand.

"You mad 'cause I mentioned harlots?"

"No," she said. "But it doesn't make sense that he holds that against married women, too."

Whit nodded. "It seems Jasper thinks he and his sister were conceived through immaculate conception, like what happened to the Virgin Mary. I don't know. Ma Stone's such a good woman, maybe he's right."

Claire laughed. "That would mean Jasper is Jesus Christ. Do you think he is?"

Whit shook his head, an amused smile playing on his mouth.

"You don't feel the way Jasper does about women, do you?"

"No," Whit said. "It's a natural inclination and it don't seem nature would give it only to men. Women who say they don't like it just haven't met the right man, to my way of thinking. The right man can make a woman feel things she couldn't imagine on her own."

"I have a vivid imagination," Claire said.

Whit smiled. "Have you ever thought about doing it?"

"Yes, I have."

"What did you think?"

"Well, back home, I mostly thought it was gruesome. I mean, when I first learned what it entails, I felt ill. I don't suppose that's something a man can understand, but for a woman, it's an infringement on her sovereignty. Do you know what I mean?"

"I think so," he said.

"Even when I met a man I liked, back home, I thought it would be something I'd do to please him, and to have children, of course, which is every woman's destiny, unless she's barren or not chosen." Claire paused to lick her lips, which were suddenly dry. "Since meeting you," she whispered, "I've thought about it differently."

"Yeah? How've you thought about it?"

"As something I'd like very much to do."

He smiled. "That's a good sign, Claire, that you'll be a treasure to the man who has the luck to win you for his bride."

"Who do you think he might be?" she asked, reaching to the edge of the blanket and snapping off a stalk of wild wheat. The thistle felt like velvet against her cheek. "Before we came out here, I had a dozen young gentlemen trying to win my hand."

"I bet you did," Whit said softly.

"But here, there aren't hardly any men except old ones like my uncle and rough drovers who'd probably prod a girl the way they do a cow."

"There's me," he said.

She ran the tip of the thistle around her lips as she met his eyes, the golden brown of honey. "I like you a lot, Whit."

"I like you, too, Claire," he said, not moving to kiss her as she expected.

She bounced the thistle impatiently against her knee.

He chuckled, that soft laughter from deep in his throat she loved to hear. Then he asked gently, "Will you take your dress off for me?"

She raised her head imperiously. "Will you be good if I do?"

"I usually am."

She laughed. "I bet that's a lie, Whit Cantrell. I bet you're usually bad with girls."

"I've never had one tell me so."

"What do they say?"

He shook his head. "I ain't the kinda man who carries tales."

She smiled, tossing the thistle into the grass. Then she stood up and unbuttoned her frock, pulled it over her head, and dropped it on the blanket. He leaned close to untie her petticoats. When they fell, she stepped out of them and kicked them aside. He rose to his knees and tugged her to kneel in front of him as he unlaced her camisole, opened it, and kissed her breasts, bare in the dappled sunlight falling through the trees. She closed her eyes and inhaled deeply of this new pleasure, smelling the wild wheat all around them, hearing the ripple of the river and doves murmuring from the far shore. He raised his mouth to hers, kissing her deeply as he lay her beneath him, then he left her alone.

She opened her eyes to see him on his knees unbuckling his gunbelt. He laid it nearby, took off his jacket and vest and tossed them aside, pulled out his shirttails and took off his shirt, then sat down to pull off his boots, the spurs jingling like silver. When he stood up, he took his handkerchief from a pocket of his trousers and dropped it on the blanket beside her. Puzzled, she stared at the handkerchief so long that when she looked back at him, he was naked except for his socks. She had seen baby boys, but never a man filled with desire, and suddenly she felt frightened.

He dropped to his knees and said, "You can touch it."

She hesitated.

"It doesn't bite," he coaxed.

Carefully she lifted a hand and ran her fingertip from the nest of dark, curly hair to the firm, smooth crown. It rose against her palm and she jerked her hand away in alarm.

He laughed, lowering himself beside her and kissing her as he tugged her bloomers off over her feet. When he nudged her legs apart and touched her there, she whimpered with an instinctive renewal of her fear.

"I won't hurt you," he murmured, his lips moving against her mouth.

As if his kisses were sunlight, he dappled them across her breasts and down her belly until his tongue played in her navel. She giggled, and he moved lower as he parted her thighs, then touched the place between them with his tongue. Feeling the heat in her loins like quicksand pulling her into pleasure, she held tightly to his shoulders until she realized her nails were digging into his flesh. She forced herself to relax, concentrating on laying her palms lightly against the taut curves of his muscles while he tasted the inside of her. She marveled at his desire to do that, then opened her legs wider to give him more room. Yet he tarried there only a moment before he slid up to kiss her mouth again. She tasted herself on his tongue as he shifted his legs between hers and penetrated the crevice he'd left wet. When her hips bucked in revolt, he murmured close to her ear, "I lied, Claire. It always hurts the first time."

"I don't want it to!" she cried.

Raising his face above hers, he asked, "You want me to stop?"

She shook her head.

Yet when he thrust inside, she couldn't prevent a whimper from escaping her throat. He drove fast and hard as her impulse to kick him off was swamped with the need to suck him deeper despite her pain. The pain waned as her desire rose toward a consuming crescendo suddenly cut short when he quickly withdrew. Startled, she opened her eyes to watch him catch his seed in the handkerchief.

"Why did you *do* that?" she accused.

He finished cleaning himself and let the handkerchief drift away on the breeze before he met her eyes. "So you won't get pregnant."

"I *want* your baby, Whit." She held her arms to entice him back. "I want lots and lots of your babies."

He filled her arms, caressing her again as he kissed her cheeks, her eyes, her nose, and her ears. "Whit," she whispered with each kiss. "Whit, Whit," as if his name were a ladder to salvation. Finally she giggled and asked, "Is that your only name?"

He raised himself above her and shook his head. "I have three of 'em: Whittaker Claiborne Cantrell."

She smiled. "I have three, too: Claire Rebecca Moss. But I wish my name was Claire Cantrell. Would you like that?"

"Oh, yeah," he said, kissing her on the mouth this time. Then he sat up and let his gaze scan the world as if he were looking for anything that might have changed.

It had all changed for her. "I love you," she murmured, "Whittaker Claiborne Cantrell."

He met her eyes and nodded. "We're something, ain't we? The two of us?"

"What are we?" she whispered.

"Something new," he said.

14

Rosemary Cassidy seemed to have aged ten years since her husband's death. Formerly a plump woman with lustrous black hair, she was now thin and her hair was streaked with gray. She wore it twisted in a severe bun that revealed her face, plainly creased with sorrow. Giving her daughter a bittersweet smile, Rosemary said, "I bet there ain't a girl in the world who shortly after her wedding didn't run home to her mama looking like you do right now."

"Did you?" Lily asked, trying hard not to cry.

Rosemary nodded as she carried the coffeepot from the stove to fill their cups on the kitchen table. "It took me longer'n it did you, but one day I decided I didn't want to be married to your father anymore, so I went home."

"What had he done?" Lily asked, watching her mother return the pot to the stove.

Rosemary came back and sat down across from her daughter, then gave her another melancholy smile. "He had a friend I didn't cotton to. Man name of Evan March." She shrugged. "Evan was loud and backwoods country and I could barely tol'rate listening to him talk. That partic'lar week, he was at our house ev'ry night, sharing our supper and sitting with us on the po'ch. Finally I told your father I didn't like Evan and didn't want him coming around so much. Your father listened but didn't give me an answer one way or t'other. When Evan showed up again the very next night, I put my foot down. Your father refused to tell him he couldn't stay for supper, so after I'd laid it on the table, I went out the back door and walked home. Seven miles through freezing cold, and I was crying the whole way." She laughed softly at the memory.

"What happened?" Lily asked, warming her hands around her cup as if feeling the same cold.

"Oh, I was sitting in the kitchen talking to my mama, same as you are now, and she told me she'd done pretty near the same thing shortly after her own wedding. The way she 'plained it, girls always go into marriage with stars in their eyes. We're bound to be disappointed when we wake up and discover what we've done to ourselves, the gist of it being we signed a lifelong contract of indentured servitude to a man who seemed a prince 'fore we married him but after the ceremony we saw as just another man not much dif'rent from the ones we didn't marry." Rosemary smiled. "The truth my mama helped me understand is that if a person ain't happy with the contract, changing the principals won't make much dif'rence."

"But you loved Daddy," Lily argued.

"Yes, I did. But that don't mean I couldn't've loved another. It's sharing the love of life that counts."

Lily frowned. "So you went back to him?"

Rosemary nodded. " 'Long about ten o'clock, your daddy came knocking on my parents' door. I heard him ask my father if I was ready to come home yet." She laughed at herself. "I flew outta that kitchen into his arms, and I never left him again."

"Did Evan March still come around?"

Rosemary nodded. "After I set myself the task of understanding why your father valued his company, I was able to see that for all his rough ways Evan was a man of honor and integrity. Few such men exist in this world." When her daughter remained silent, Rosemary said softly, "Emmett Moss is one. He and your daddy were close as brothers when we lived in Texas. And Emmett has stood by us as if we were kin."

"We are now," Lily mumbled, staring into the dark coffee in her cup.

"Your daddy would be pleased with your match, Lily."

"Do you think so?" she asked, looking up again. "Don't you think he'd rather I have someone my own age?"

"I'm sure we all would," Rosemary said, "but life don't always give us what we want."

"I'll be a widow 'fore I'm old as you," Lily said.

"The territory will be more settled by then," Rosemary answered. "I'm sure you'll have ample opportunity to remarry if that's what you choose."

Lily shook her head. "Emmett made me promise I'd stay his widow all my life."

Rosemary stared. "He had no right to ask any such thing."

"I didn't give it without asking for something worth as much in return."

"What did you ask?" Rosemary whispered.

Lily sat up straight and met her mother's eyes when she said, "Vengeance against Henry Hart."

Abruptly Rosemary stood up and backed a few steps away, her face pale.

"Emmett promised it," Lily accused, "then didn't deliver."

"Good for him," Rosemary pronounced. "Nothing's gained by vengeance. You'll only bring more hurt on everyone concerned."

Lily stared at the condemnation on her mother's face. "I thought you'd take my part."

"In murder? Did you really think that?"

"I traded my life for it, Mama!"

"Then you've doomed yourself to misery."

Lily held her forehead in her hand, feeling freshly betrayed.

"It's not too late," Rosemary said, sitting down again and reaching across the table to clutch Lily's other hand. "Emmett hasn't done it yet. Withdraw your request, ask for anything else, but don't begin your married life with murder in your bed."

Feeling a clammy swamp of despair, Lily muttered, "Can't see how it could be any worse'n what's there now."

Rosemary gripped her daughter's hand more tightly. "Listen to me, Lily! I loved your father as my husband and knew him as a man. He wouldn't want you to avenge him."

Lily raised her head. "Maybe that's why you can't understand what I'm saying! You loved Daddy. I used to love Emmett when he was my uncle. As my husband, I hate him."

Rosemary let go of her daughter's hand and leaned heavily against the back of the chair. "How could you, after loving him so long?"

"I cringe whenever he touches me, but the nights are the worst. Him grunting and sweating on top of me turns my stomach."

Rosemary smiled weakly. "You must be patient, Lily. Emmett was too well set in his ways to take a bride so late in life."

"I feel like one of his cows, hog-tied and helpless while he sticks his iron into my flesh. The first night I thought I'd been murdered. I told myself it was justice 'cause I'd avenged Daddy. Then I discovered I can die every night and each time feels like the first. Now I've found out Henry Hart's still alive! I'm the one who's dead."

Rosemary slumped in her chair. "You can have the marriage annulled, Lily. Or get a divorce. We can bear the shame. You don't have to stay with Emmett."

"It's too late," she said. "The only man I'll ever love hates me 'cause I'm a Moss. Even I did leave Emmett, Jasper could never forget who had me first."

"Jasper Stone? You'd trade him for Emmett Moss?"

"In the blink of an eye."

"Oh, Lily," Rosemary moaned. "I always thought you had good sense, but what I'm hearing now don't make any sense. As

Jasper's wife, you'd be a widow just as quick, prob'ly with children and no money to feed 'em. Emmett's rich. No matter what else, you and your children will never go hungry."

"Don't love count?"

"Learn to love Emmett. Jasper Stone's a killer! Do you really think he'd be gentle with you in bed?"

"I know he would. I've been there with him." Seeing the horror on her mother's face, Lily quickly said, "We didn't do more'n kiss. I was a virgin on my wedding night. But when I'm lying under Emmett, I can't stop remembering how tender Jasper was."

"That's why girls ain't s'posed to be experienced," Rosemary said, "so they won't have nothing to compare their husbands to. Emmett's a good man. If he don't tickle your fancy in the same way Jasper did while compromising your virtue, the fault's yours, Lily. As for the other, I pray to God that Emmett refuses to honor your request."

Lily stood up. "Reckon I'm ready to go home now."

"It's nearly dark!" Rosemary protested. "You can't be riding clear to Bosque Grande tonight."

Lily looked at her mother with scorn. "I ain't got nothing left for anyone to take." She took her hat off the table, settled it on her head, and pulled the chin strap tight. "Who knows, maybe Henry Hart'll rape me on the way home so Emmett has a good reason to kill him."

"Oh baby," Rosemary moaned, rising, too, and opening her arms to hold her daughter close. "You're only fifteen. You've still got your whole life ahead of you."

"I'll live it as Mrs. Emmett Moss," Lily muttered into the lost comfort of her mother's embrace, "the wife of a liar and a cheat."

"You don't have to," Rosemary said, holding Lily's shoulders to look into her face. "You can come home if that's what you want. You'll always be welcome here."

Lily shook her head. "My home is Bosque Grande. It's all I got in my bargain, and I ain't ever giving up my claim."

*   *   *

Andy rode into the Stone homestead alone. He didn't call a hello as he sat his horse in the middle of the yard, afraid he wouldn't be welcome. Finally Jasper came out on the porch and studied him for a long moment before descending the steps and walking close to stand by Andy's knee. Then Jasper just looked up in silence, waiting for an explanation.

"We met Whit on the road," Andy said. "He took Claire home and asked me to come stay with you till he gets back."

"You mean he took Claire and Lily home," Jasper said.

Andy shook his head. "Lily went to visit her mother."

Jasper snorted. "Don't you have no qualms about leaving Whit alone with your sister?"

"Would you?" Andy asked.

"No, but the two cases ain't the same." Jasper looked down the trail as if he could see Whit and Claire in the distance. When he looked back at Andy, some of the hard glint was gone from his eyes. "Go ahead and put your horse up," he said, "then come on into the house."

Andy turned toward the corral. He had swung down and was loosening his cinch when Jasper joined him.

"On second thought," Jasper said, walking past on his way to the barn, "maybe we'll ride over to Cassidy's Mill and see if we can catch Lily 'fore she leaves."

Andy's hands stopped in the middle of untying his cinch as he watched Jasper disappear inside the barn. Guessing whatever he and Lily had been arguing about needed to be settled before Jasper could let it rest, Andy retied his cinch and swung back on his horse, then looked at the house while he waited. Although he had been thinking earlier that he'd like to see Cassidy's Mill, he wasn't keen on riding along. He'd rather stay and meet Sammie. It would also be dark in an hour or two, and he'd never ridden at night. But Whit had said it was important that Jasper wasn't left alone, so when he rode his Appaloosa out of the yard, Andy followed him.

They didn't take the trail but cut north across country, skirting the foothills of the Sacramentos. The prairie was a rolling terrain alternately cut by arroyos and humped ridges stretching east toward the river. Jasper knew his way, zigzagging to catch the best places to cross the arroyos, sometimes spurring his horse to jump them, other times scuttling down the banks with the Appaloosa half sliding on its haunches, then climbing up the other side, the Appaloosa almost on its knees. The rough ride challenged Andy's skill, but Jasper didn't seem to be in the mood for conversation anyway. After a while, Andy let himself fall back as if he were giving Jasper privacy when in truth he was having a hard time keeping up.

Kickapoo grunted with exertion as they climbed an especially steep hill. Jasper had stopped on the crest. When Andy reined up beside him, Jasper didn't take his eyes off the scene below. Andy followed his gaze into the shadowed canyon, its floor cluttered with huge rocks of black lava. Four men were squatting around a meager fire. Andy looked back at Jasper and saw a muscle in his jaw quiver with tension.

"Who are they?" Andy whispered, though the men were too far away to hear.

Without taking his eyes off them, Jasper said, "Buck Robbins and Ernie Kessel, for starters." He reached behind himself and pulled his Winchester from its scabbard.

"Are they dangerous?" Andy asked, wishing he had a gun, too.

"They won't be in a minute," Jasper said.

He cocked the rifle and raised it to his shoulder, then squinted down the barrel and pulled the trigger.

Andy held his horse tight as he watched one of the men fall. The others lurched to their feet as Jasper cocked his rifle and fired again. The deafening boom was so close to Andy's ears that he forgot himself and slacked his reins enough that his horse turned away from the noise. By the time Andy yanked Kickapoo around, they were fifty yards away from Jasper, who had already cocked his rifle again. Andy looked at the canyon and saw a second man down just as Jasper fired and a third was flung backward. The last man dived for the sagebrush. Jasper emptied his rifle into the swaying bushes as the man crawled away. Then everything was quiet, a cloud of gunsmoke wafting between Andy and the men lying motionless below.

Jasper began reloading his rifle from the bullets on his belt. Kickapoo sidestepped and tossed his head, nickering nervously, but Jasper's Appaloosa stood stock-still. Nudging Kickapoo back along the crest, Andy felt a twinge of admiration that Jasper had been able to train his horse to stand under gunfire. But when he looked at the three men sprawled below, Andy felt sick. "Are they dead?" he whispered.

"You bet," Jasper said, his voice as heavy as an anvil.

"What'd you kill 'em for?"

"I had my reasons. Think the last one got away?"

"I don't see how he could've."

Still watching the men below, Jasper asked, "Will you do me a favor?"

"Reckon," Andy said, wary of denying him.

"Ride down and untie their horses so they can go home," Jasper said.

Andy stared at him, not moving.

Finally Jasper looked at him. "Go on. I'll keep you covered in case that last scoundrel's still alive. Then you go home and keep your mouth shut about what happened here. Understand?"

Andy looked around at the prairie, empty for miles, unless the last man was still alive. Then he looked back at Jasper and nodded. Still, Andy felt more needed saying, so he asked, "Ain't you gonna see Lily?"

Jasper shook his head. "Don't reckon I got nothing to tell her now."

Wanting to ask if he was in love with Lily, Andy kept quiet, figuring this wasn't the time.

"Go on," Jasper said, giving him a friendly smile.

Andy smiled back, thinking the warmth of Jasper's regard was worth having, especially after witnessing the power of his wrath. Feeling pretty good riding down the hill knowing Jasper was up there looking out for him, Andy guessed he was experiencing a moment of what it felt like to be Whit. It felt cocky, free, and bold. But when he saw the coffeepot, testifying to the men's innocent intentions, Andy felt like a frightened child. He fought back tears as he looked at the men.

One lay facedown; the other two were on their backs. Blood pooled into the sand around them, and their eyes were blind to him riding by to where they'd tethered their horses, never guessing they wouldn't ride them again. Andy tugged the reins free and waved his hat to spook the animals into a run. He didn't make any more noise than he had to, figuring the dead deserved that much respect.

When he looked up, Jasper was sitting his Appaloosa silhouetted against the red sky of sunset. He raised his rifle in a salute, then turned back down the other side of the ridge and disappeared.

Andy dug in his spurs, wanting to escape the smell of blood and the dead eyes, which seemed to watch him with malevolence. He galloped Kickapoo all the way to the trail, slowed to a lope as he approached the river, then splashed across at a butt-breaking trot. Under the first dark after twilight, he rode into Bosque Grande and reined his lathered horse to a heaving stop in the strip of light falling through the open door to cut across the yard. Sensing more than seeing Claire and Whit on the swing of the shadowed portal, Andy quickly asked, "Is Uncle Emmett home?"

Whit stood up and walked out to meet him. "No, he ain't. What put such a burr under your tail, Andy?"

"Nothing," he said, swinging down. "Will you help me put my horse up?"

"Glad to," Whit said. Giving Claire a smile, he called, "We'll be right back."

Andy led his horse toward the stable with Whit close beside him. Neither of them spoke until they were inside and Andy lit the lantern just beyond the door.

"I went to Jasper's like you said," he began. "First he told me to come on in, then before I got my cinch untied, he said we'd ride to Cassidy's Mill to catch Lily if we could."

"He left the homestead unguarded?" Whit asked incredulously.

"Mr. Stone was there, I reckon. But that ain't important, Whit. It's what happened when we were riding to Lily's."

Whit waited, watching him closely.

"We come over a hill," Andy said, "and saw four men sitting around a fire at the bottom of it. They were making coffee, is all." He hesitated.

"Did Jasper say who they were?"

"Said two of 'em were Buck Robbins and Ernie Kessel. Didn't mention the other names if he knew 'em."

"Sonofabitch," Whit whispered. "What'd he do?"

Andy's voice broke when he said, "Jasper killed 'em, Whit!"

Whit stared a moment, then asked, "All of 'em?"

Andy nodded. "Least three. The fourth crawled into the bushes and we couldn't tell if Jasper hit him or not. He emptied his rifle into where the man was and it ain't likely he escaped, but I wasn't about to go poking into those bushes to find out. Jasper told me to let their horses loose, then come home and keep my mouth shut. I figured you'd want to know, though."

Whit was silent so long, Andy felt compelled to say, "He picked 'em off like tin ducks at the fair, Whit."

Whit nodded. "Jasper's the best shot in the county, no doubt about it."

"Why'd he kill 'em?"

Whit studied Andy a moment, then said, "They're the ones hurt Sammie and Elise."

"Oh," Andy said. "That makes me feel a little better."

Whit was watching him warily now.

"Nobody saw it happen," Andy said. "And I ain't never gonna tell."

Whit smiled. "I knew you were one of us the first time we met, Andy. Go get yourself a bath and soak a good, long while. I've generally found it helps to face the world clean after something like this."

"What're you gonna do?"

"Find Jasper. Did he go home or on to Lily's?"

"Home. Said he didn't have nothing to say to her after what happened."

"No, I reckon not." Whit shook his head. "This changes the game, that's for damn sure."

"What game?"

"Someday I'll let you in on it, Andy. Right now, the less you know, the better off you are." He touched Andy's shoulder. "Thanks, kid. See you around."

Andy watched Whit walk out, then a minute later heard his horse gallop away. Unsaddling Kickapoo, he remembered Whit had told him to take a bath. It sounded like a good idea, but Andy guessed this would be the first bath he ever asked for. As he led Kickapoo into a stall, the door behind him opened, and he looked over his shoulder to see Claire coming into the stable.

Andy wanted to hide but she'd already seen him. As he watched her approach, he questioned why he felt ashamed. He'd done nothing wrong. Then he realized his promise of silence was beginning to make him feel as guilty as if he'd helped Jasper kill those men.

Claire stopped at the end of the stall and said with a teasing smile, "Whit told me to give you a bath, but you don't look especially dirty to me."

"I have a headache," Andy lied. "He said a long, hot soak's the best remedy."

She smiled. "Isn't he sweet?"

"Reckon," Andy mumbled.

"I'll go up to the house and start the water boiling," she said.

Andy watched her leave, amazed that she hadn't noticed he was different. He guessed if he could fool her, he could fool anybody. So maybe Whit was right: After a bath and some supper, maybe what had happened would fade like a bad dream.

It didn't. The bath changed nothing except that his body was clean. Cipriano served fish for supper, a huge bass with eyes as dead and vacuous as those of the men in the canyon. Only family were at the table, and Uncle Emmett was angry because Lily still wasn't home, so their usual playful banter was missing. They ate in a silence broken by the scraping of silverware on the plates, a sound that kept Andy on edge. No one seemed to notice he didn't have much of an appetite.

After supper everyone dispersed to their bedrooms. Andy lay staring at the darkness above him, tormented with visions he couldn't shut out: Jasper methodically cocking and firing his rifle;

the men's blood coagulating on the sand around them; the expressions of surprised agony frozen on their faces; the pain in Whit's eyes as he learned what Jasper had done. Even though he said Jasper was justified, Whit had still been worried that the game was irrevocably changed. Andy didn't even know what the game was, but he knew he was different.

Late in the night he heard a horse trot across the yard. Guessing it was Lily, he got up and snuck quietly through the kitchen, out the back door, and around the house toward the stable. Though he had no intention of breaking his promise of silence, he thought maybe he could ease some of his misery by talking to Lily. If she knew that Jasper had wanted to see her, that he'd felt badly about their quarrel and wanted to resolve it but something had prevented him from riding to Cassidy's Mill, Lily would feel better. Andy thought he could say all that without breaking his promise, and maybe by giving Lily this small gift of reassurance, he could feel that something good had come from the day.

Silently he crossed the yard toward the light falling through the open door of the stable. Just as he reached it, however, he heard Claire speaking in such an urgent whisper that he stopped to listen.

"We tarried along the river coming home," she said, "and one thing led to another."

"What do you mean?" Lily asked sharply.

Claire giggled. "It was wonderful. I've never felt so many good things all at once. He's beautiful, Lily, isn't he?"

"He's a villain if he did what I think you're saying."

"He did." Claire giggled again. "But he's not a villain. Be happy for me, Lily. I'm finally a woman."

"A fool is what you are! No decent man will marry you unless Emmett gives you a dowry; then you'll be bought and sold like cattle!"

"Maybe Whit will marry me," Claire said, her voice hurt.

"Whit Cantrell ain't got the means to care for a wife. He doesn't even have a home. He lives in a cave! Is that where you're gonna spend your happy-ever-after?"

"Why can't he live here?" Claire asked.

"There's a death warrant against him, and someday we'll have a sheriff with the courage to serve it. What will you do then, even if you are Mrs. Cantrell?"

Claire sniffed and said, "I thought you were my friend."

"I am. That's why I'm trying to make you understand that Whit ain't got nothing to offer."

"I love him," she said.

"So do half the girls in the county. Even Elise Stone's been in love with Whit since she got her first petticoat, but what he did to you is the same as what was done to her."

"It's not!" Claire insisted.

"The only dif'rence is you were willing and Elise wasn't. That puts you in the company of harlots like Celia Broussard. She was a good girl 'fore she fell in love with Whit. Now she's a whore running a brothel in Soledad. She's still in love with him, but you know what he does? He shares her with Jasper. All three of 'em in bed at the same time. Is that the kinda future you want?"

"I don't believe you," Claire said. "Besides, how would you know that unless you were there, too?"

Andy heard a slap, then his sister cry out.

"I know a lot," Lily said, her voice cold, " 'cause I keep my eyes and ears open. I don't often repeat what I know, but I know it just the same. The world ain't a romantic novel, Claire. Anyone with sense knows Whit Cantrell ain't gonna live long. A woman needs a husband who'll be around to provide for her children."

"Is that why you married an old man?" Claire asked with tears in her voice.

"His money'll do the job."

"I'm not for sale," Claire said.

"No, you give it away," Lily retorted. She stormed out of the stable, not seeing Andy standing in the shadow behind the door.

Watching her stalk toward the house and disappear inside, Andy sank down to sit in the dirt. He remembered Jasper asking with scorn, "Don't you have no qualms about leaving Whit alone with your sister?" "Would you?" Andy had answered, and Jasper had said, "No, but the two cases ain't the same." Why weren't they? Celia had said Whit liked Andy as much as Jasper, but Whit wouldn't ruin Jasper's sister. Was it because Jasper would kill any man who did that, or because Whit's liking a man wasn't the same as respecting him? Whit had claimed he'd known Andy was one of them from the start. Evidently that was a lie. Whit wouldn't ruin the sister of a man who was truly his friend.

Andy stood up and walked in to look down at Claire crying on the floor. When she raised her eyes to his, he said, "I heard what you and Lily were talking about. It's my fault for leaving you alone with Whit."

"There's no fault to it, Andy," she said, wiping her tears with the hem of her skirt. "Lily's just jealous because I was deflowered by a man I love. There's no greater blessing for a girl in this world, so don't go blaming yourself when no wrong's been done."

"Why were you crying, then?"

"I was crying for Lily," she answered. "And because the hurtful things she said proved she isn't my friend."

"Doesn't what Whit did prove he's not my friend either?"

"Of course not, Andy. Whit's real fond of you. He's told me so."

Andy wanted to believe her, but remembering the three dead men in the canyon, he couldn't see how any good could come from this day.

15

Whit rode hard for Rocky Arroyo. He loped into the yard and was walking his black mare in a circle to cool her down when Jasper came out on the porch carrying a rifle. They stared at each other a long moment before Jasper closed the door and descended the steps as Whit swung off his mare. When they were close, Whit said softly, "I saw Andy."

Jasper nodded. "Come put your horse up."

Whit led her across the yard and through the corral gate

Jasper held open, then waited until he'd gone inside the barn and lit a lantern. When Whit led his mare in, Jasper was forking hay into a manger. Whit unsaddled and tethered his mare in the stall, then came out and sat down on the covered barrel full of sweet-smelling sorghum. Neither he nor Jasper looked toward the tack room, but both were keenly aware of the dark beyond its door. Jasper stood kicking the toe of his boot against the bottom slat of an empty stall, the thump and accompanying jingle of spur like a drumbeat presaging action.

Finally Whit said, "I trust Andy to keep quiet. Do you?"

"I don't trust any Moss," Jasper answered, yanking himself around and flopping back to lean against the fence, his arms along the top slat on both sides of his body.

"Andy's dif'rent," Whit said. "So's Claire."

Jasper snorted in disbelief. "Did you fuck her on the way home?"

Whit nodded. "It might've been about the same time you was pulling the trigger. Ain't that something?"

"I don't know what."

"Me, neither," Whit said. "Strikes me peculiar, is all."

"After Andy left," Jasper said, "I rode back to Black Canyon and looked for the fourth man. I didn't find him."

Whit made a clucking sound of regret. "Do you know who he was?"

Jasper nodded. "Their horses were grazing alongside Agua Negra Creek. All four of 'em."

"Andy said you saw Robbins and Kessel. Who were the other two?"

"Jack Elkins and Jim Daniels. Daniels is the one who got away."

"Four of a kind, all hearts," Whit said, managing a smile at his pun. "Elise only heard two."

"I figure the others were keeping watch."

"Maybe."

"What the hell, Whit? You saying I took more'n I deserved?"

"I ain't saying nothing, Jasper, 'cept I'm behind you in whatever comes next."

Jasper nodded. "Appreciate it."

"Daniels'll drag his butt to Union and swear out a warrant."

"Maybe he didn't recognize me."

"You pinned Robbins and Kessel. Sight works both ways."

Jasper shrugged.

"A posse'll be here by sunset."

"They won't take me alive."

"Your family'll be caught in the crossfire."

"I'll go to my spread further up the mountain."

"And fight till they kill you?"

"It beats hanging."

"You could surrender in town, where the sheriff'll have to protect you till the trial. If Elise testifies, they'll call it justifiable homicide in defense of your family."

"I won't put her through that."

"Don't you think it's her choice?"

"No."

"Seems to me she'd rather endure a few hours of embarrassment than a lifetime without a brother."

"You'll take care of 'em, won't you, Whit?"

He shook his head. "I'll be with you."

"On the gallows?" Jasper scoffed.

"If you're convicted, I'll break you out and we'll high-tail it to Mexico."

"I ain't running," Jasper said.

"Don't it beat dying?"

"No."

"Okay," Whit said. "If we're going for broke, let's bet against the dealer."

"What do you mean?"

"Shoot the hive outta the tree. When what passes for law falls with it, things might resettle in a more livable arrangement."

Jasper shifted his gaze to the door of the tack room.

"This is how I've got it figured," Whit said. "Either those boys intended to ambush us on our way to Union, or they were waiting in Black Canyon to come back here and finish the job. Either way, they was just hornets, Jasper. It's the hive who sent 'em."

Jasper's eyes were dark.

"The posse'll come down Deep River," Whit said. "We'll go up Rocky Arroyo and make our move while the sheriff's chasing us down here. Hart's best men'll ride with the posse. He'll be as open as he's apt to get."

Jasper nodded. "I'll go tell my family what to expect."

"Let 'em sleep," Whit said. "My mare needs rest, too. We'll wait a few hours 'fore we leave."

Jasper blew out the lantern, then moved through the dark to the haystack. The rustle of hay told Whit where he was. After a minute, Jasper asked, "Do you really think Hart was Sammie's father?"

"I can't figure any other reason for what happened," Whit said.

"Maybe it was 'cause of us," Jasper said.

"What do you mean?"

"On account of you setting yourself against Hart and everybody knowing how I feel about you. Maybe all this was just a way to knock *us* outta the tree."

"What do you think everybody knows?"

Jasper was quiet a long time. Finally he said, "My feelings ain't natural."

"Who says?"

Jasper snorted. "The Bible, for one."

"I never read it," Whit answered. "What does it say?"

"A lotta shit."

Whit smiled, though he knew Jasper couldn't see him in the dark. "Why pay any attention to it, then?"

"I wouldn't if I thought . . ." He stopped.

"Thought what?" Whit asked.

"Hell, Whit. Don't you know what I'm getting at?"

"Reckon I do. Want to know what I think?"

"Yeah," Jasper said, his voice barely above a whisper.

"I think you oughta go up to the house and say your good-byes. If you don't, I'm apt to join you in that haystack and tarry so long we'll both be caught with our pants down when the posse comes."

Jasper laughed. "That'd be a fate worse'n hanging." He stood up and moved toward the door.

"Tell your folks adios for me, too," Whit called. "We may not be back for a while."

Sheriff Red Bond had barely settled at his desk with his morning cup of coffee when Jim Daniels limped in off the street. Daniels was filthy, his trousers snagged with thorns and his dusty face streaked with sweat. He glared at the sheriff, then sat down on the bench beneath the window and tugged at one of his boots.

"What the hell you doing?" Red barked. "This ain't no bath-house."

Daniels winced as the boot came off, revealing his sock, soaked with blood. "I walked all the way from Black Canyon, Sheriff, so cut me some slack."

Red frowned. "Somebody steal your horse? Is that why you're here?"

Daniels shook his head and pulled off his other boot, dropping it on the floor and staring at his bloody socks. "My horse was run off with those belonging to Ernie Kessel, Buck Robbins, and Jack Elkins. They're all dead."

"Dead? How?"

Daniels's eyes were hot with anger. "Shot from ambush. Picked off with no warning from a ridge overlooking our camp."

"In Black Canyon?" Red asked, stalling to let the news settle in his mind.

"I said so, didn't I? Hart sent us to Siete Rios to do a job. We hadn't finished and were waiting for a good time to go back and get it done when we were attacked for no reason. The shooter used a rifle. Ours were on our horses and he was outside a six-gun's range, so he picked us off like ducks on a lake."

"Did you recognize him?"

Daniels nodded. "Jasper Stone done the shooting. Whit Cantrell was with him."

"You saw 'em plain?"

"I saw Stone. They were on a ridge, like I said, and Cantrell was just far enough along it that I couldn't make him out for sure, but everybody knows they're thick as thieves."

"What everybody knows and what you saw are two dif'rent things, Jimmy."

"After it was all over, the second man came down into our camp to let our horses loose. I was a good stretch away by then, running for my life, but I know Whit well and this fellow had the same build. Who would you think it was?"

Red didn't answer, savoring the advantages of believing it was Whit.

"Fucker ran our horses toward the Panal," Daniels continued, "then rode off in the same direction. I didn't dare try to catch 'em, figuring Whit meant to do it and sell 'em for profit. Not only the horses but the outfits and rifles, too. Seventy-three Winchester repeaters worth fifty bucks each, Red. Horses worth at least a hundred a piece. That's a tidy profit for a few minutes' work."

"Will you swear in court it was Stone and Cantrell?"

"I'll swear it on a Bible now."

"I ain't got a Bible. But I'll take your affidavit of the facts."

"I just told you the facts."

Red pulled out a sheet of paper and dunked the nib of his pen in ink. "Tell me again. I gotta have something to show the judge 'fore he'll issue a warrant. Then I'll raise a posse and we'll hit Rocky Arroyo when the Stones are sitting down to supper."

About nine o'clock that night, Whit and Jasper rode into Union on the old Indian trail north of the river and tethered their horses behind Henry Hart's hotel. Crouching in the shadows beneath the trees, they studied the grounds around the low adobe building, the back rooms dark but possibly occupied. The wing of Hart's private quarters showed only one lamp lit in the parlor.

"How many men you figure to be inside?" Whit whispered.

"Six or seven, give or take a dozen," Jasper answered.

Whit chuckled. "So it's none or an army. I'm ready."

"Let's go, then," Jasper said. He stood up and casually sauntered across the moonlit yard.

Whit watched for any reaction. Seeing none, he followed his friend. Jasper used his knife to jimmy the lock on the door, gaining them entry to the hotel's empty kitchen, scrubbed clean for the night. They stood a moment listening to the silence, then quietly walked to the interior door. Jasper peered through its small, round window. He beckoned for Whit to follow. They crossed the dining room with its chairs upside down on the tables, then stopped in front of the door leading to Hart's private parlor.

Jasper drew his gun and slowly turned the knob. Whit glanced behind, through the eerie camouflage of chair legs like a spindly forest to the moonlit street beyond the windows.

In Hart's parlor, Joe Graham slept in a chair with his chin on his chest. Whit and Jasper crossed the carpet and entered the hall to the bedrooms. When a floorboard creaked under their weight, they stopped and listened, then continued to the last door in the northwest corner. They stood on each side of the door and listened again, then Whit turned the knob.

In the second it took them to slip inside, they saw Henry Hart asleep in a tangle of white sheets on a massive four-poster bed. Whit quickly eased the door closed, but not before noting the location of the bedside lamp. When Hart rolled over, they waited until they heard a muffled snore before they approached the bed from opposite sides. Covering Hart's mouth with one hand, Jasper pressed the barrel of his pistol against Hart's temple as Whit struck a match and lit the lamp. Hart lurched awake, his eyes bulging with fear.

"Get up," Jasper said, taking his hand off Hart's mouth. "If you make a sound, I'll kill you."

Whit drew his own gun and stepped away to give the man room. His flaxen hair silver in the lamplight, his eyes calculating for any chance he could grab, Hart kept glancing back and forth between them as he slid out of the bed on Whit's side wearing a white nightshirt, his skinny legs and bare feet pale.

"Get dressed," Jasper said.

"If you try to wear any weapons, though," Whit added, "we'll take you naked."

"Where're we going?" Hart asked, clumsily stepping into his trousers.

"Gonna take a ride," Whit said. "Such a pretty night. Shame to waste it sleeping."

"There's a posse looking for the both of you," Hart said.

Whit smiled. "Bet they ain't looking in the mountains."

"What do you want?" Hart asked, stuffing his nightshirt into his trousers.

"Right now," Whit said, "we want to get outta here with all three of us alive. You reckon we can?"

Hart buttoned his fly and reached for his jacket. Whit beat him to it, hefted it for the telltale weight of a gun, then handed it over with a smile.

"I've got a guard in the parlor," Hart said. "How'd you get in?"

"Graham's asleep," Jasper said.

Hart frowned as he sat on the bed and picked up a boot.

"I've heard," Whit said, "that you got a cellar under this room. That true?"

Hart shook his head, working his foot into the boot.

"It ain't gonna help if you lie to us," Whit said. "I know the man who built this wing, and he told me there's a cellar under this room with a tunnel leading out. How do we get there?"

"I don't know what you're talking about," Hart said.

"That's two lies," Jasper said. "You're gonna lose some teeth with the third."

Hart looked at him. "If you're gonna kill me, I'd just as soon you do it here."

"What reason would we have to kill you?" Whit asked.

"None," Hart said. "But that's never stopped either one of you before."

Whit chuckled. "A man's always got a reason for murder. It may not be a good one, but after the fact, the reason don't matter a whole lot to whoever's dead. Sometimes a man can die just 'cause he won't tell the fellow with a gun where the door is."

Hart looked back and forth between their guns. Meeting Whit's eyes, he said, "The trapdoor's under that round table in the corner."

Whit moved to the corner and holstered his gun, then set the table aside carefully so the silver candlestick on top wouldn't fall over. He flipped the small rug out of the way to reveal a three-foot square cut in the floor, the door hinged and an iron ring set in a groove for a handle. Lifting the door, he stared at a flight of wooden steps leading into the pitch-black cavern of the cellar. He lit the candle with a match from the box beside it and took the candlestick with him as he descended the stairs.

The cellar was cold, the air acrid with a stench of filth. The rock walls seeped humidity from the river, dampening the dirt floor of a room twenty feet long and fifteen wide. One end was a jail with a wall of iron bars, its door standing open. Whit walked closer and held the candle high as he peered into the cell. A pitiful pallet and unemptied slop bucket were its only furnishings. On the pallet lay a rag doll missing an eye. Hearing footsteps on the stairs, Whit set the candlestick in the dirt and drew his gun, then watched Hart emerge into the flickering light. "What's this?" Whit asked. "Accommodations for special guests?"

Hart's smile was snide. "I keep guests there sometimes."

"No one you care much about, from the looks of it."

"No, comfort's not my aim for the men I put there."

Jasper descended the steps and took a quick look around. Nudging his gun into Hart's back, he asked, "How do we get out?"

Hart walked to a barrel wedged into a corner. He rolled the barrel aside, revealing a tunnel at the bottom of the wall.

"You go first," Whit said to Jasper.

He holstered his pistol and crawled into the tunnel.

"How long 'fore he's out?" Whit asked.

Hart shrugged. "A minute."

"We'll give him two."

"From what I understand," Hart said with an ingratiating smile across the length of the dungeon, "Jasper did the shooting at Black Canyon. I may be able to convince the sheriff to drop the warrant against you as an accessory, but not against Jasper as the principal. You're hurting your own chances by helping him with whatever you think you're doing tonight."

"You already got a death warrant against me," Whit said. "I ain't losing nothing by helping my friend."

"That warrant's ancient history. It'll never be served."

"Funny it's still on the books, then. Let's go."

Hart fell to his knees, then disappeared into the tunnel.

Whit holstered his gun and picked up the one-eyed doll. Looking at the battered face, he remembered Sammie's drawing and how the boy's eyes had laughed when Whit said it was pretty. "Pretty," Sammie had echoed, the first word Whit ever heard him say. With a moan of pain, he stuffed the doll into his coat pocket, then walked out of the cell and crawled into the tunnel after Hart.

As soon as he was inside the passage, Whit smelled fresh air. Though it was permeated with dust, he breathed deeply away from the stench of the slop bucket. The tunnel opened into a root cellar lit by moonlight shining through the cracks in its wooden door. Jasper held his gun on Hart as Whit stood up, drew his gun, and pulled the wooden latch out of the lock on the door, then pushed against it. The hinges creaked as it swung open. He waited a moment, listening for any reaction outside. Hearing none, he climbed the steps in a crouch, then poked his head up and scanned the view. They were behind Hart's stable, within sight of the black elder trees sheltering their horses. "Let's go," Whit whispered, preceding them out.

Hart came first, his expensive suit covered with dust from the tunnel. Whit was dusty, too, but he hadn't noticed it until seeing Hart, who was usually so dapper. Whit smiled, thinking the man was apt to get a lot more dirty before dawn. When Jasper came out, he used his gun to nudge Hart toward the black elders.

Whit took a short rope out of his saddle pocket and tied Hart's hands behind his back. Jasper tied his handkerchief around Hart's mouth, then tightened the noose of his lariat around Hart's neck. Jasper and Whit mounted their horses and forded the river, Jasper trailing Hart behind him like a steer led to slaughter.

At the east edge of town, Whit crossed the road alone, watching all around for anyone who could get in their way. The road was empty, the whole town asleep. He beckoned Jasper to follow, and they spurred their horses into the shelter of the forest. Hart ran to keep up as they climbed the low ridge of mountains between Union and the Deep River Valley. When he fell, they stopped only long enough for him to gain his feet, then they rode on with Hart gasping to breathe through the gag in his mouth. On the crest, they waited, giving him time to catch his breath.

Descending into the valley, they rode east to Cassidy Canyon.

Within its shadows, they again waited for Hart to recover, then climbed south up the canyon and followed the trail that meandered through the Sacramentos to the mouth of the cave. When they swung down, Hart collapsed, his chest heaving and his clothes soaked with sweat.

Leaving him there, Jasper and Whit led the horses inside the cave, unsaddled and fed them, then went back out just as the sun began to spill warmth into the clearing. Jasper walked into the forest to relieve himself. Hart lay still, his hands tied behind his back, the noose around his neck and the gag in his mouth as he watched Whit stretch, limbering his muscles after hours in the saddle.

"How you feeling, Henry?" Whit asked with a smile.

Hart mumbled an inarticulate curse through the gag.

"What's that?" Whit teased. "I couldn't make out what you said."

Hart struggled to stand up, not seeing Jasper return behind him. Just when Hart gained his feet, Jasper tripped him so he fell on his back in the dust. Jasper reached down and yanked the gag off. Hart kicked at him, but Jasper was already out of range.

"Why are you doing this?" Hart bellowed.

Whit pulled the doll from his pocket, straightened the skirt, and winced at the sorrow of the one-eyed face. He looked up at Jasper, who was staring at the doll. "I found it in the cellar," Whit said.

Jasper spun on Hart and kicked him hard in the gut. He curled himself into a ball, moaning in pain. When Jasper picked him up and threw him toward the forest, Hart was as limp as the rag doll. Jasper sat him up against a tree and used the tail of the noose to tie his chest to the trunk, then backed out of range of his feet.

Hart breathed hard, glaring alternately at each of them.

Whit set the doll in front of Hart, nestling it in the dirt just beyond his feet so its one eye faced him. "What's this doll's name, Henry? Can you tell us that?"

"I've never seen it before."

Coming at him from the side, Jasper kicked him in the mouth. Hart cried out, spitting blood, then looked at him incredulously.

"That was your third lie," Jasper said.

"Sammie!" Hart shouted.

"That's the doll's name?" Whit asked.

Hart nodded, then spit out a tooth.

"But it's a girl doll," Whit said.

"Samantha was the boy's mother."

Whit shook his head. "I pride myself on knowing every woman in the county, and I never heard of one by that name."

"She moved on before you came here."

"Leaving her boy with you?"

"That's what she did."

"How about it, Jasper? You ever hear of him having a woman named Samantha?"

"Long time ago," he muttered.

"Okay," Whit said. "What was the boy's name?"

"He didn't have one."

Whit winced, then asked Jasper, "What do you think his name was?"

Jasper drew his knife from the sheath on his belt and hunkered on his heels behind the doll. "I bet his name was Henry Hart, Junior."

Watching sunlight glint off Jasper's blade, Hart shouted, "He was an idiot! What was I s'posed to do with him?"

"He was deaf," Jasper said. "He wasn't stupid." He played the sunlight on his blade, then asked, "What do you think, Whit? If I cut off Henry's ears, would he be deaf or just dead?"

"If no one stopped the bleeding," Whit answered, "he'd prob'ly be both."

Hart's eyes darted back and forth between them.

"Maybe," Jasper drawled, "I oughta cut his throat like they did Sammie's. Then he'd for sure bleed to death."

"Help me!" Hart pleaded, his eyes pinned on Whit. "Don't let him kill me!"

Whit shrugged. "Jasper ain't following my orders."

"That's right," Jasper said. "I'm not like the men you sent to Rocky Arroyo. What do you think, Whit? Maybe I oughta use my knife to do to Henry what his men did to my sister."

"I didn't tell 'em to do that!" Hart shouted.

"You paid 'em," Jasper said.

"Only to kill the boy. That's all I wanted."

Jasper and Whit met each other's eyes. Looking back at Hart, Whit said, "You admitting that's all we wanted." Then he sighed and took a step away. "It's time to finish it, Jasper."

He nodded. "Ain't you got a bag of beans in the cave?"

"Yeah," Whit said.

"Dump 'em out and bring me the bag."

Whit walked inside and emptied the fifty pounds of black beans into the dirt. They fell with a crisp rustle into a hill of wasted nourishment. He remembered buying the beans and how proud he'd felt that he had enough food to see him through winter if it should happen that his luck at the poker tables failed. The really cold weather hadn't started yet, but he didn't expect to be eating any of those beans or playing poker, either one. What was about to happen would be irrevocable.

No more so than Jasper killing those men in Black Canyon, but Whit hadn't been there. He could stop what was about to happen here. Convince Jasper to high-tail it to Mexico by tempting him with the promise of sharing his bed. Whit knew he could get some señoritas on the side so he wouldn't feel deprived. Maybe he could keep up the pretense long enough that he and Jasper might someday be able to come back. But then what? Say Adios, Jasper, it's been fun?

Whit told himself that even though his tryst with Claire could see him through a lot of lonely nights, abandoning Jasper would haunt him forever. On the other hand, though neither he nor Jasper had any future in the county, living a lie in Mexico was throwing what future they had to the dogs. Eventually Jasper would remember it wasn't Whit's inclination. Whit would probably say it himself, sick to death of the pretense. So the fine friendship they shared would end in a squalid squabble over where they put their cocks. They'd kill each other, one way or another. This was better than that. Kill Hart, who surely deserved it. Face death from the posse that would surely track them down. Die like men, fighting alongside each other. Jasper was the best friend Whit had ever had. Since Jasper had given him that, Whit carried the bag out of the cave and handed it over with a smile of acquiescence.

Jasper stood up and cut the rope holding Hart to the tree. He cut Hart's hands loose, then backed away, sheathed his knife, pulled his gun, and laid it in the dust. "I'll give you more of a chance than your men gave Sammie," Jasper said. "You see where my gun is?"

Hart nodded, rubbing his wrists, burned red from the rope.

"If you get to that gun and shoot either one of us," Jasper said, "we'll let you go."

Hart looked at the gun in the dirt, then at Whit. "Do you agree to that?"

Whit nodded.

Hart looked at the bag and rope now in Jasper's hands. Jasper smiled. "Hold still," he said. Dropping the bag over Hart's head, he tied the rope with a bow around his neck. "Okay," Jasper said. "The game's on."

He came close to Whit and held out a hand for his gun. As Whit gave it to him, they shared a smile, then they both watched Hart fall to his knees and crawl toward Jasper's gun in the dirt. Jasper took a step closer and kicked the weapon a few feet away. Hart raised his head, trying to hear where the gun stopped. He crawled toward it. Jasper let him get a grip, then kicked the gun out of Hart's hand. Hart howled with pain, so didn't hear where the gun landed.

"It's five feet behind you," Jasper said.

Hart lurched around and crawled toward it. Groping on the ground, he found the gun and picked it up. Whit and Jasper moved. Hart's head swiveled back and forth as he cocked the hammer, trying to pinpoint where they were.

"How's it feel?" Jasper asked, ducking and taking a step to the left.

Hart fired a bullet into thin air. He whimpered, cocking the gun.

"If you were my sister," Jasper said, ducking and moving again, "you'd be screaming right now." He ducked and moved a second before Hart fired. "How's it feel, Hart," Jasper taunted, "to be raped in the dark?"

Hart bellowed and fired again, hitting nothing.

"I'm over here," Jasper said, standing still.

Hart swiveled the gun in both hands and cocked the hammer.

"Right here," Jasper said.

Hart fired, but missed.

Jasper laughed. "He ain't much good, is he?" he asked, meeting Whit's eyes as Hart cocked the gun.

Whit smiled and said, "No, he ain't."

Hart swiveled the gun and fired at Whit's voice. Whit ducked, hearing the bullet whistle past. Jasper slowly walked toward Hart, who kept turning his head, trying to see through the bag. Jasper leaned close and said, "Right here."

Hart raised the gun and fired point-blank at Jasper's chest, but the gun was empty. Jasper yanked the bow of the rope so it fell loose around Hart's neck. Hart dropped the gun and pulled off the bag. He stared into the barrel of Whit's gun in Jasper's hand. Jasper smiled, then pulled the trigger. The bullet took out one of Hart's eyes and a good portion of his brain.

Jasper tossed Whit his gun, then bent down and picked up his own. As they both reloaded from their belts, Whit asked, "You feel better?"

Jasper looked at Hart and said sadly, "Somehow it ain't never enough."

Suspecting the man Jasper wanted to kill was the one who loved Whit in what was considered the wrong way, Whit said, "I know of a cave on the other side of the Panal where we could hide out for a while."

"The one in the Crevice?" Jasper asked.

"Yeah," Whit said.

"It's part of Bosque Grande," Jasper said. "Might as well go home to do it."

"Might as well," Whit said.

16

*L*ily was sitting in her room wearing a yellow quilted wrapper over her nightgown as she waited for her husband. Emmett had been furious about her night ride home from the mill, adamant that he didn't want her crossing the country alone. Her statement that she'd always done it had carried no weight. She hadn't been married then, and apparently the daughter of Robert Cassidy had been protected by his reputation in a way the wife of Emmett Moss wasn't. When Lily argued that no man would risk Emmett's wrath, his last words on the subject were, "You'll do as I say."

She hadn't mentioned encountering Henry Hart on the road, unable to see what difference it made since she'd decided to stay with Emmett anyway. Eventually someone would mention Hart in conversation, and her lack of surprise would tell Emmett she'd known all along. In the meantime, she was curious to see if he displayed any contrition for having breached their contract. So far she hadn't detected so much as a smidgeon.

It puzzled her because she'd always considered him an honorable man. But when she remembered their trip to Union to witness the hanging of William Wilson, she also remembered the many men who had approached Emmett on the street and petitioned his help. He evaded them by promising to talk about it later at Bosque Grande, a promise he told Lily he never meant to keep. She should have seen that as the warning it was. Instead she'd sloughed it off by feeling proud that he found her worthy of his confidence. Now, on the other end of the stick, she understood a false promise to be a lie.

After supper, Emmett usually sequestered himself in his office to keep his accounts. She didn't know what they entailed, but apparently the paperwork was enough to occupy him several hours each night. When the weekly mail arrived from River's End, she glanced through the many envelopes from faraway places. Assuming the letters came from brokers and lawyers connected to the cattle business, she felt curious as she laid them on Emmett's desk. If eventually she was to manage the ranch on her own, she should be learning the business, but she didn't know how to broach the subject since it meant alluding to his death. So she held her tongue on that topic, too.

Lily felt lonely. When no visitors came to avail themselves of Emmett's hospitality, she decided people were granting the newlyweds a period of privacy. She supposed Claire would forgive her in time, and Andy would come out of his shell and start riding to Soledad again, bringing back news of what was happening along the Panal. People would visit, carrying gossip and spicing the supper table with their jokes and stories. As it was, the family ate in near silence. Accompanying his brother on horseback all day exhausted Drew to the point that he was unconversational at supper and went to bed right after leaving the table. So Lily spent her evenings alone, with only Emmett's nightly visits to punctuate her solitude.

About nine o'clock on this particular night, he opened her door and closed it softly behind himself, then walked across the darkness of her room to look out the window as he stood beside her. She glanced up at him, steeling herself for what lay ahead by trying to find some semblance of affection in his face. Failing, she looked out the window again.

"I'll be leaving 'fore dawn tomorrow," he said. "Reckon I'll be gone a few days."

Lily suppressed a smile, trying to hide her pleasure at the prospect of his absence. "Where're you going?"

"There's a posse in Soledad," he said, still not looking at her. "Since I know the country around here better'n most, Sheriff Bond asked me to ride along."

Suddenly suspecting this was the reason no one, including Whit, had visited Bosque Grande all week, she asked with dread, "Who're they chasing?"

Emmett walked across the room, lit the bedside lamp, took off his shirt, and faced her bare chested before he said, "Whit Cantrell and Jasper Stone."

Noting a smug victory in his voice, she asked, "What've they done?"

"Murder. Jasper shot three men without bothering to give 'em fair warning. Whit was there and watched him do it."

Emmett was definitely gloating. Struggling to control her anger, she said calmly, "They must've had good reason."

"Ain't no good reason for cold-blooded murder, but what we've been able to learn comes from a statement the sheriff got from Jasper's family. Whit's in it up to his neck. He's the one rode up and down the Panal carrying the story about Sammie being attacked, but the boy was already dead when Whit told that tale. Jedediah Stone said they were hoping to lure the killers back to try again by letting on that Sammie was still alive. The Stones say it was Buck Robbins and Ernie Kessel that killed the boy, and they were two of 'em that Jasper gunned down from ambush, but whether they were guilty or whether Jasper killed the boy himself is still unknown."

"Jasper loved that boy!"

"Uh-huh. Well, the family buried him in an unmarked grave so they was trying to hide something. Then Jasper and Whit found four of Hart's men in Black Canyon. Jasper killed three but the fourth got away. He's the one swore out the deposition. Coming down Deep River Valley, the posse saw buzzards near the top of Cassidy Canyon. When they rode up there, they found Henry Hart's corpse, shot in the head. The tracks of two horses were found near the body, and no one doubts it was Jasper and Whit who killed him."

"Especially you," she said.

"Ain't got nothing to do with us, Lily. Whit killed Hart for his own reason. Don't seem Jasper needs a reason to kill nobody. He's a rabid dog that's gotta be stopped."

"He's not!" she cried.

"I know you're partial to him, and I'm sorry for it. But if you look at him head-on, you'll see he's the worst kinda killer there is. His family come out here in the first place 'cause Jasper killed a man in Texas when he was still a sprout. Then they left here 'cause he did it again. Since they've been back, he's killed more and nearly stomped two men to death 'cause they said something disrespectful about his sister. Now he rides with Whit, who's already got a death warrant against him."

Impatiently she swiped at the tears on her cheeks. "If they did kill Hart, it was at your request."

Emmett shook his head with a sly smile. "The deal I made wasn't consummated."

She hated him for using that word. "Are you telling me you didn't have nothing to do with Hart's death?"

"That's exactly what I'm saying. After I spoke with Whit, he came back without doing it. That broke our contract. Refusing to return the horse I'd given him as a down payment made him a thief. When I told him so, he laughed." Emmett shook his head. "His taking the whole thing as a joke severed any responsibility I have in the matter."

"What about your responsibility to me? You knew before our wedding night that you hadn't paid my price. That makes what you did rape."

He smiled. "Now, Lily, a man can't rape his wife. It's a legal impossibility." He sat down on her bed to take off his boots, dropping first one, then the other, before he stood up and looked at her again. "I didn't have nothing to do with the murder of Henry Hart, but since he's dead, I figure your price has been paid. Maybe you should consider it a gift from Whit and Jasper. It'll likely be the last thing they give anybody."

Knowing the answer, she whispered, "You're gonna kill 'em, aren't you?"

He shook his head. "The sheriff's gonna do it."

"I'll testify at their trial that you paid Whit to kill Hart."

"I wouldn't allow that, Lily, but I don't reckon they'll be taken alive. Even if they are, your testimony wouldn't be pertinent 'cause the warrant's for the three men killed in Black Canyon. That's the crime they'll be hung for."

She stood up. "Please don't let this happen, Emmett."

"It's outta my hands but I wouldn't intervene if I could. Now come to bed and let's say no more about it."

"I can't," she whispered.

"You can and you will. Don't make me beat you to take my rights."

She looked at the door, calculating her chance to get past him.

Emmett took off his belt and doubled it up in his hand. "If you don't get in bed right now, I'll give you a whipping as an ounce of prevention."

She considered climbing out the window behind her, but didn't know where she would go in the dark, barefoot and wearing her nightgown. Numbly, she forced herself to move toward him.

" 'Attagirl," he said. Still holding his belt, he untied her wrapper, then dropped them both on the floor. "Get in bed," he said, unbuttoning his trousers.

She climbed under the covers, wishing she could disappear beneath them as she rolled away and hid her face in the pillow. He blew out the lamp, and a moment later she felt his weight beside her. Taking hold of her shoulders, he turned her to lie flat on her back, then pulled up her nightgown.

"Soon as you're pregnant," he said, hefting himself on top of her, "we can quit doing this."

In the kitchen before dawn, Emmett found Andy sitting at the table working his way through a plate of fatback and eggs. "I'll have some of that, Cipriano," Emmett said in Spanish, sitting down across from his nephew. "What're you doing up so early, Andy?"

Andy took a drink of coffee before he said, "I want to ride with you and the posse."

"Who told you 'bout that?"

"Manny Tucker."

Emmett frowned, thinking his ramrod should have known to keep quiet. "What'd he say?"

"That you were leaving 'fore dawn, and that he didn't think Whit and Jasper would be taken alive."

"So why do you want to go?"

"I'm a Moss," Andy said, watching Emmett's eyes warm with

affection as he'd hoped they would. He concentrated on cleaning his plate, not wanting to push his luck under his uncle's scrutiny. In truth, as confused as he felt about Whit and Jasper, Andy figured they needed at least one friend in the posse.

"All right," Emmett said. "I'll give you a rifle 'fore we leave."

Andy looked up from his plate. "Thought you didn't want me carrying a gun."

"We're going hunting, boy. Can't hunt without weapons."

"I guess not," Andy said, but he had no intention of shooting anyone.

When he followed his uncle out of the house, five men were waiting in the meager warmth of the stable, their horses ready to go, Andy's among them. "Put a scabbard on the boy's saddle," Emmett said. While Manny Tucker did it, Emmett walked into the tack room and came out with two Winchester rifles. He handed one to Andy and said gruffly, "It's fully loaded. You know how to use it?"

"Yes, sir," he said. "I've been practicing."

After sliding the rifle into the scabbard, Andy rode out beside his uncle, feeling uncomfortable at point but not knowing how to avoid it. By his own declaration, he was a Moss. That meant he was expected to stay at Emmett's side and act in accord with what Emmett wanted. The first part Andy could do. As for the second, he'd have to wait and see what happened.

They rode east across the prairie, dawn still a rosy glow beyond the distant ridge of mountains. When they cut across the Texas Road, the posse was waiting on the other side. Without a word, Emmett's men fell in with the others while Sheriff Bond nudged his horse alongside Andy. Bond was a burly, redheaded man wearing a silver star on the lapel of his coat. It was his brother whom Whit had killed in Soledad, and Andy didn't reckon the sheriff had any notion of mercy. Glancing around the other grim faces, he recognized Woody Wheeler but no one else he'd ever seen in the company of Whit or Jasper. Andy guessed that left him alone in taking their part, unless Shiloh Pook spoke up. He seemed the only one among the men who didn't want to be there.

Although the posse was after Jasper for killing those men in

Black Canyon, and Whit for aiding and abetting Jasper, Andy knew Whit hadn't done it. But if he told anyone, he'd not only break his promise of silence, he'd have to say Whit was with Claire. On top of that, Andy would be accused of being Jasper's accomplice. Though he hadn't believed it at the time, he could see now that merely running off the horses, and especially not telling anyone, made him guilty. On the other hand, if Andy failed to say he'd been the one who was there, no one was likely to believe it hadn't been Whit.

None of the posse talked much. The sky kept getting lighter as if it were any other day, but the intense purpose among the men proved otherwise. There was an edge flashing between them like the blade of a knife catching sun, glinting off their eyes with what Andy saw as a mean disregard of compassion. He remembered his uncle saying you couldn't hunt without weapons, and a dread grew in Andy's mind as he realized that what he felt around him was the intention to kill.

Andy wanted to be with Whit and Jasper more than the posse. Yet he also felt angry with Whit because of Claire. That she'd wanted and enjoyed it lessened Whit's wrong, but it wasn't the injury to her that Andy needed redressed. He needed to know Whit respected him as much as Jasper, whose sister Whit would never compromise. Knowing he was due an explanation from the man who claimed to be his friend, Andy wished he and Whit could have worked all this out. Now he was riding with Whit's enemies while feeling angry about something no one else on the posse even knew had happened.

The sun was pushing noon when the posse reined up on a plateau that looked no different from the prairie they'd been crossing since dawn. Everyone dismounted, and Sheriff Bond whispered when he told one of the men to stay with the horses. Uncle Emmett jerked his head for Andy to follow him. He started to, but Emmett stopped with an expression of strained patience.

"Best bring your gun," Emmett said with ill-disguised disgust.

Quiet snickers fluttered among the men, making Andy blush as he turned back for his rifle. He followed his uncle into what looked like open prairie. After walking a hundred yards, Emmett dropped to the ground and slithered through the dry grass, dragging himself with his elbows. Andy did the same. They crawled a few yards more, then suddenly came abreast of a cliff overlooking a narrow canyon.

On the bottom of the far side was a cave emitting a curl of smoke from a campfire inside. Two horses were hobbled a few yards away: a flashy Appaloosa and a black mare wearing Uncle Emmett's brand. The posse lay in a line along the edge of the cliff, their rifles pointing at the half-moon of darkness below. Andy wondered if it was the cave Lily had said Whit called home.

Emmett whispered, "Shoot to kill the first man out. The other'll surrender right quick after that."

As the order passed down the line, a few chuckles ran with the words. Andy felt ill. Lying between his uncle and the sheriff, he had his rifle in position but his wasn't cocked. In the noise of everyone else's gun, no one would notice his was silent.

The sun was warm on their backs, filling the canyon below with a merciless glare. The Appaloosa and black munched at the sparse grass growing on the sandy floor, mincing tiny steps in their hobbles, flicking at flies with their long black tails. The dark mouth of the cave remained empty except for the wisp of smoke escaping into the sky. A honeybee whined by Andy's ear. He slapped at it, hitting his face with a smack, and the Appaloosa raised its head and looked straight at him. The black did, too, then both horses turned and nickered toward the cave as the posse heard Whit's laughter, echoing easy and pleased against the walls of the canyon.

Andy gritted his teeth to keep from yelling a warning. His hands were so sweaty he couldn't keep a grip on his rifle. To his uncle, he whispered, "How'd you know they were here?"

"Was a calculated guess," Emmett answered. "Last winter, me'n Whit sat out a blizzard in that cave. Being as we're just across the county line, I figured he'd think they were safe."

"You mean we're outside the sheriff's jurisdiction?" Andy asked.

"Don't worry about it, kid," Bond whispered from the other side. "Neither of 'em's gonna be alive to complain."

"That ain't right," Andy said to his uncle. "We gotta give 'em a chance to surrender."

His eyes on the cave, Emmett said, "You heard my order. Whichever one's left will have that chance."

"Not if it's Cantrell," the sheriff said.

"I'm hoping it is," Emmett answered. "We already got a death warrant against Whit. Jasper might walk if it comes to a trial."

"That's why we oughta kill him here," Bond said.

"We'll kill no man who surrenders," Emmett said, his eyes hard on the sheriff.

The two men stared at each other as Andy flattened himself between them.

Though wrapped in his blanket, Whit felt cold inside the cave. The slap outside had told him they were no longer alone. He'd laughed to cover the noise, knowing there was no way out alive, but he figured that had been true since they made up their minds to kill Henry Hart.

"What's funny?" Jasper asked, hunkered over the meager fire he'd built from the scant supply of driftwood inside the cave.

"Us," Whit answered.

Jasper didn't look up from warming his hands over the flames.

Whit could see the horses grazing in the sunlight, and he envied them not only their warmth but the food they were finding. He and Jasper had been in such a hurry to get out of the county, they hadn't bothered to bring any food. Now Whit wondered why they'd bothered to run. At least in the Sacramentos they'd had fifty pounds of black beans and plenty of firewood. Here they had only the protection of being outside Union County.

Whit rolled onto his side and propped his head in his hand. "We should've gone to Mexico."

Jasper's dark blue eyes flashed beneath the fans of his lashes, as delicate as a girl's. "I don't like Mexicans much," he muttered, returning his gaze to the fire. "I sure as hell don't want to live in their country."

"Who do you like, Jasper?" Whit teased lightly.

Again Jasper's eyes ducked up from under his long, silky lashes.

Keeping his tone playful, Whit asked, "You want to fuck?"

Jasper stared at him.

"This might be our last chance," Whit said.

Jasper didn't answer, meeting his eyes.

"We can do it either way," Whit said. "I'm game."

"I'm not," Jasper scoffed. "I don't know what you're talking about."

"Forget it, then," Whit said, lying back down and watching the smoke curl along the ceiling. When he closed his eyes, he heard Jasper move, then sensed him coming close.

"Reckon I'll water the horses," Jasper said.

Whit looked up at his friend standing above where he lay wrapped in his blanket.

Jasper hunkered on his heels, the canteen suspended between his knees. "I've thought about it, but I always pushed it from my mind, not guessing it was anything you'd want."

"I'd do it for you."

"Maybe I wouldn't want you doing it just for me."

Whit smiled. "Then you'd have to let me do it back."

"Have you ever?"

Whit shook his head. "But I figure it ain't much dif'rent from what we did with Celia, only she wouldn't be between us."

Jasper looked down. "You knew I wanted it even then."

Whit lifted his hand from under the blanket and touched Jasper's knee. Jasper flinched but didn't move away, so Whit lightly ran his fingertips along the inside of Jasper's thigh, stopping halfway up. Jasper watched Whit's hand, then met his eyes. Whit smiled.

Abruptly Jasper stood up. "I'll think about it," he said. "Right now I'm gonna water the horses."

"Don't," Whit said. "There's a posse out there."

Jasper looked over his shoulder at the horses in the sun. "You sure?"

"Pretty sure."

"How long they been there?"

"Half an hour, maybe."

Jasper sighed. "You're right. We should've gone to Mexico."

Whit laughed.

Jasper sat down cross-legged in the dust, dropping the canteen aside. "They got us pinned, don't they, Whit?"

"Looks like it." He tossed his blanket off, then swiveled around to put his feet up on the wall of the cave, crossing his ankles as he rested his head in Jasper's lap.

Jasper touched Whit's cheek, then smoothed a strand of his hair behind one ear.

Whit smiled up at him. "Helluva pinch, ain't it?"

Jasper nodded. "Must be a way out."

"Let me know if you come up with one."

"You'll be the first person I tell." As Jasper looked over his shoulder again, studying the situation, he laid his palm flat on Whit's chest. "I could run out one way and draw their fire while you went the other direction."

"They'd shoot us both down," Whit said.

"Damn, Whit. I got you into this."

"Man makes his own decisions."

"Maybe I can get my horse inside. If we both ride out shooting, we might make it."

"Beats starving to death," Whit said.

They held each other's eyes a long moment, then Whit sat up. Still they watched each other, mere inches apart. Finally Jasper smiled and gained his feet. "Don't go anywhere," he said.

"Hadn't thought to," Whit answered.

Jasper walked across to his saddle and hunkered down, studying the view through the mouth of the cave. Whit figured he meant to get his rope to lasso the Appaloosa, and that it wouldn't work. The posse would see what was happening and either shoot the rope or the horse. Jasper probably figured it that way, too. He loved his horse, so he hesitated. Whit waited, knowing his mare was green-broke and there was no way he could coax her into the cave without a fight, also knowing she couldn't carry the two of them as well as Jasper's stud.

Suddenly Jasper slid his rifle out of its scabbard. Cocking the weapon in motion, he strode through the mouth of the cave. Too late Whit sprang to his feet and pulled his gun, hearing what sounded like a score of rifles shatter the quiet.

Jasper kept going straight into the guns. Whit saw him fall, then continue to jerk as bullets peppered his body with lead.

Whit sank to his knees, watching the blood of Jasper's sacrifice flow from a dozen wounds into the sand of the canyon. As silence slowly settled like dust, Whit stood up. He took a step back, then realized he had no where to go.

17

*I*f he ain't already dead," Sheriff Bond grunted, "he soon will be."

Andy lifted his head from where he'd ducked it close to the stock of his rifle when the shooting erupted. Jasper lay sprawled on his back in front of the cave, his blood flooding the sand. The Appaloosa and black were quivering in fright a hundred yards up the canyon. Emmett had been the first to fire. All the posse followed suit, except Andy, who hid his face in shame.

Emmett shouted, "Whit? It's Emmett Moss. You've no chance to escape. Surrender and you won't be harmed."

"Till I'm hung, you mean?" Whit yelled back.

"We ain't after you for that but the murders in Black Canyon."

After a minute, Whit yelled, "I wasn't there."

"If you can prove that," Emmett shouted, "you got nothing to fear."

"The hell he don't," Sheriff Bond muttered. "If he surrenders, I'm serving that death warrant against him."

"You can do your duty in Union," Emmett retorted. "Down here on the Panal, you'll do as I say."

"You mean you expect me to haul him all the way back to Union if and when he surrenders?"

"I do," Emmett said.

"Waste of time," Bond mumbled.

"It's the law," Emmett growled. "Now that Hart's dead, you're gonna have to start enforcing it by the book 'stead of his whim."

"Reckon that depends on who replaces him," Bond drawled.

"Till someone does, I'm filling the gap," Emmett said. "If you wanta keep your badge, I suggest you start acting like a lawman."

Bond looked away, then shrugged. "Okay, I'll go along with what you want. I'd rather hang Cantrell than shoot him anyway."

"Why don't you tell him that?" Emmett suggested. "Not in those exact words, but if you offer your protection back to Union, he might believe it."

Bond hesitated, then shouted at the cave, "This is the sheriff, Cantrell. If you surrender, I guarantee your safe passage to Union."

Only silence answered him.

"Whit!" Emmett yelled. "This is your last chance. If you don't come out in five minutes, we'll shoot you down when you do. Make whatever decision you can live with."

"I got five minutes?" Whit called back.

"Yes!" Emmett shouted.

"I ain't got no watch."

"I'll let you know when the time's up."

Whit laughed. "That's right nice of you, Emmett."

Andy bowed his head and prayed for Whit's surrender. After what seemed like an hour, Emmett shouted, "What's it gonna be, Whit?"

Andy lifted his head and opened his eyes. All along the line of men on the cliff, rifles cocked. Then it was so quiet Andy could hear his pulse pounding in his ears. Finally Whit shouted, "I'm coming out."

"Leave your guns behind," Bond ordered.

Whit walked into the now shadowed canyon, his empty hands at his sides as he squinted up at the men on the cliff.

"Put your hands above your head," Bond told him.

Whit raised his right hand.

Though he might have been aiming his gaze at the voice, Andy could have sworn Whit was looking right at him.

"The other hand, too!" Bond shouted.

Whit smiled as he dropped his right and raised his left.

"Quit clowning around!" Bond yelled.

As if he were climbing a ladder, Whit held one hand up at a time. He kept dropping it as he raised the other, wearing a shy smile as if he wasn't sure his audience would get the joke.

Emmett chuckled. "Guess only shackles'll stop him."

"They're on their way," Bond grunted, pushing himself to his feet.

Andy stayed with Emmett on the cliff while the posse followed Bond down a switchback trail to the floor of the canyon. Cautiously they approached Whit, some with their rifles in position, others with their six-guns drawn. Whit ignored them, smiling up at the cliff and playing the game with his hands until the sheriff yanked his arms behind his back and locked his wrists in manacles.

"Ain't you gonna come down?" Whit shouted at the top of the cliff, his voice ricocheting off the canyon walls. "I always heard I had the right to face my accuser."

"Your accuser's Jim Daniels," the sheriff snarled, the canyon amplifying his words though he spoke softly. "He's still in Union resting up after walking all the way there from Black Canyon."

Whit didn't shift his gaze. Softly to his uncle, Andy said, "I wanta go down."

"All right," Emmett said.

They stood up and descended the trail to the floor of the canyon, then crossed the sand to where Whit stood surrounded by the posse. He smiled at Andy, but Andy couldn't raise a smile back.

"So what's this about?" Whit asked.

The sheriff answered him. "You're under arrest for the murder of Buck Robbins, Ernie Kessel, and Jack Elkins in Black Canyon. Jim Daniels was with 'em and has sworn out a deposition saying he saw you and Stone shoot 'em down."

"I wasn't there," Whit said.

"Can you prove that?" Emmett asked.

Whit glanced at Andy, then looked at Bond. "If I do, it'll prove your witness wrong, and that'll make your killing Jasper murder. Which of your men are you gonna hang, Sheriff?"

"A posse's exempt from prosecution while acting in the line of duty," Bond said.

"Even when they make a mistake?" Whit asked.

"Wasn't no mistake," Bond said.

"If you can prove you weren't with Jasper," Emmett told Whit, "now's the time to say so."

Whit gave him a sly smile. "Thing of it is, if I say where I was, it'll soil the reputation of a lady." He looked at Andy. "You think I should do that, Andy?"

"Leave the boy outta this," Emmett barked. "He's here as a Moss, not your friend."

Whit let his gaze slide down to Andy's boots, pigeon-toed in the sand, then back up to meet Andy's eyes. "Is that true?"

Andy couldn't figure what Whit wanted him to say.

Emmett answered for him. "He's my brother's son. That makes him a Moss."

"And a Moss always keeps his word, don't he?" Whit teased.

Andy decided Whit was saying he should keep quiet. Stacked against Whit's freedom was Claire's virtue, and his freedom was doubtful anyway since the sheriff already had a death warrant against him.

"If you know something, boy," the sheriff said, "you best speak up."

Confused by the playfulness in Whit's eyes, Andy said, "I don't know nothing!" Then he felt a piece of himself die when Whit's eyes turned deadly earnest.

"Course not," Emmett told the sheriff. "You got an eyewitness and don't need more'n that." He shifted his gaze to Whit. "I ain't surprised, though, that the likes of him would try to drag a simpleminded boy into complicity."

Andy cringed in shame for having sided with the men who thought him stupid rather than with the one who'd named him an equal. Turning away, he saw Woody Wheeler raise his rifle and take aim at Whit.

"No!" Andy cried, lunging for Wheeler.

The gun fired when they fell. As the bullet ricocheted off the canyon wall, everyone ducked. Andy sat up from where he'd tumbled in the sand, staring in outrage at Wheeler.

"He deserves to die!" Woody shouted. "He's ruined half the girls in this county, my sister among 'em."

"We ain't after vengeance for sisters," Bond shouted. "And he's gonna stay alive till we get him to Union."

No one else said anything as Andy looked at his uncle, then the sheriff, then everyone else watching, all of them astonished at what he'd done. Finally Andy looked at Whit.

He smiled. "Thanks, Andy."

"Before we're through," Wheeler said, jerking himself to his feet, "you'll be wishing he hadn't stopped me."

"Enough of that!" Bond barked. "Someone fetch those horses yonder, and y'all go up and bring ours down. We'll ride out from here." He glared at Wheeler. "You, too, Woody. Get moving."

Wheeler picked up his rifle, threw an evil look at Andy, and followed the other men back up the trail.

Andy stood up and brushed the sand from his clothes. In a way Wheeler was right: They were after vengeance for sisters, at least he and Woody were. Yet Andy didn't want to be with Woody on anything. He wanted to be with Whit. Knowing there was one sure way to prove that, he was about to speak when Emmett came over and laid his arm on Andy's shoulders, guiding him away.

"You done good, Andy," Emmett said, speaking softly. "All we gotta do now is deliver Whit to jail and let justice take its course. You believe in justice, don't you, boy?"

"Yes, sir," Andy answered.

"Then let the law do its work. It ain't a Moss concern no more."

"There's something you don't know," Andy said.

Emmett stopped and faced him out of earshot of the others. "Tell me now."

Andy wanted to make things right, but what came out of his mouth was the thing most wrong. "Whit had his way with Claire."

Emmett scowled, his eyes piercing fiercely into Andy's. Finally he asked, "Is that what came between you and him?"

"Yes, sir," Andy said.

Emmett nodded. "You're right to feel angry on your sister's behalf. But it ain't got no bearing on what's happening here. That's a family matter and we'll deal with it when we get home. Don't you think that's best?"

"But Whit was with her when Jasper killed those men."

Emmett's frown deepened. "You know that for a fact?"

"Yes, sir. I was the one with Jasper. But I didn't do nothing. I was just there."

Emmett eyes were like ice. "Don't say nothing more. Whit's already got a death warrant against him. Implicating yourself won't do nothing but land you in jail. Is that what you want?"

"No, sir, but I feel I should tell the truth."

"Whit's a cardsharp experienced at twisting people into doing what he wants. Don't let yourself fall into his game."

"Is that what's happening?" Andy asked.

"You bet," Emmett grunted. "Stick with kin. We'll never betray you like he has."

"I like him, though," Andy argued weakly. "He's my friend."

"You think a friend would ruin your sister? Or let you take his place at a killer's side, compromising you and her both to give himself an alibi?" Emmett shook his head. "Whit Cantrell ain't your friend. You're a Moss. Don't ever forget it."

"No, sir," Andy said miserably.

Emmett clapped him on the back. "All right," he said. "Let's join the others now, and you keep your place among men, hear me?"

"Yes, sir," Andy said. But when he was back among the men, only Whit Cantrell gave him a smile. The others seemed embarrassed to have Andy among them. Looking away from their averted faces, he saw Jasper tied prone over the back of his beautiful Appaloosa. Andy wanted to cry but knew he couldn't let himself.

*　*　*

As the posse rode through the sunset toward Soledad, Andy let himself drift far behind the others. He followed at such a distance he guessed they forgot he was there, but he could hear their voices drift back on the wind. One man said Cantrell wouldn't likely make it to Union but would be lynched along the way. Another bet Whit would die trying to escape before he'd face being hung. Woody Wheeler said however Whit Cantrell died would be too good for him. Andy remembered all the times he'd seen Woody with Whit, and how Woody hadn't let on that he hated Whit until Whit was defenseless. There was something so puny about that it made Andy wonder if he was any better, claiming Whit as his friend, then denying it when the chips were down.

At the edge of the village, Andy reined to a stop and let the posse disappear around the first cluster of buildings. He sat a long time in the quiet of the prairie, wishing he hadn't told his uncle about Whit and Claire. Emmett was right in saying it had nothing to do with what was going on; at least it hadn't until it'd been told. Now Andy knew that any mercy his uncle might have delivered had been canceled by what he had said. He couldn't understand why Whit hadn't demanded he tell everyone the truth back at the canyon. He should have confessed from the start that he'd been the man with Jasper that day. No one would believe him now. They'd think he was lying to help Whit. So it was done, and whatever happened here on out was beyond his control.

He heard a horse coming toward him, then saw Uncle Emmett emerge from the shadows. Emmett reined up close and studied Andy a moment before saying with a semblance of gentleness, "You best go on home, boy."

"Why?" Andy cried in alarm. "Isn't Whit all right?"

"He's in jail, under guard. I told Bond not to let Woody Wheeler stand watch, so Whit'll make it through the night. I'm riding up to Vegas to bring the marshal back if I can. He'll guarantee Whit's safe passage to Union. I want you to go home. Don't say nothing to the women about what you told me. I'll deal with it when I get back."

Andy nodded numbly.

"I know this is hard, boy," Emmett said. "I should've guided you better and warned you against thinking Whit was your friend.

Since I didn't, reckon it's just as well all this happened 'fore you got in too deep." He turned his horse and looked back toward town. "The truth of it is, I once liked Whit myself. I owe him enough that I'll do what I can to ensure he's not lynched." He looked at Andy. "You go on home and stay with the women till I get there."

"Yes, sir," Andy said.

Emmett turned his horse north and kicked it into a lope across country. Andy wondered why his uncle didn't take the road, then guessed Emmett knew a shortcut. Feeling heavy with melancholy, Andy nudged his horse on into Soledad, avoiding the plaza and following back alleys to Celia's house. He tied Kickapoo to the empty rail and walked into the empty parlor. The piano beckoned with a memory of sweet comfort. Sitting down, he opened the keys, then began Chopin's Concerto no. 1 in E Minor.

He remembered Whit kneeling at his side when he'd played this song, and how there had been tears in Whit's eyes when the concerto was done. In that moment Andy felt he'd found a true friend. None of what happened since had changed that. He tried to pinpoint what exactly had changed, other than the obvious. He felt so lonely he guessed maybe that was it: Both he and Whit were alone. He wondered if Whit could hear Celia's piano from inside the jail. Comforted by that thought, he felt again as if Whit were beside him, but this time, when the last note echoed into silence, he heard Celia say, "We're closed tonight."

Andy turned on the stool and saw her standing in the door that led deeper into the house. Her eyes were red from crying and her face the most forlorn he'd ever seen. It wasn't hard for him to imagine Claire's face looking the same when she heard the news.

Celia said, "Didn't I tell you this would happen?"

"You told me," he said. "But Whit isn't dead yet."

"He will be. The sheriff took Jasper's body home to his folks and won't be back till tomorrow. Whit'll be lynched 'fore dawn, mark my words."

Andy stared at her, remembering his uncle had left town, too, riding cross country to fetch the marshal from Vegas. The country was cut by arroyos, and Emmett's horse was already tired.

There was no way he could get there and back by dawn. Making up his mind, Andy asked, "Do you have a pistol, Celia?"

"What do you think you're gonna do, kid? Break Whit outta jail?"

"If I can get him a gun, maybe he'll do it himself."

"You'll just postpone the play," she said sadly, "and get yourself in the same trouble he's in."

"Nobody'll lynch the nephew of Emmett Moss. And I rode with the posse, so I got a chance of getting close to the jail. If I end up inside it, least Whit won't be alone."

Celia studied him, then finally said, "Come with me."

Andy followed her down the dark hall to the last room. A lamp was already lit inside. He stopped on the threshold and saw a sumptuous featherbed with a mirror on the ceiling above it. The covers were rumpled, the air heady with a heavy perfume. He watched her open a trunk and lift out a gunbelt with a six-gun in the holster. The belt was loaded with cartridges, all the loops full. Celia carried it over and placed it in Andy's hands.

"If you live through this," she said, "come back and I'll give you a free ride."

Andy glanced at the bed, feeling himself blush.

She laughed bitterly. "Get outta here 'fore someone sees you and figures out where you got that gun."

Andy buckled the belt around his waist as he walked down the hall. The gun felt heavy on his hip. Seeing the parlor was still empty, he slipped out and quickly mounted his horse, then trotted into the shadows. A raucous racket came through the open door of Foxy Strop's Saloon, the posse inside loud with drunken bravado. Their horses milled within the common corral. Hay had been forked onto the ground and some of the horses were still eating. Andy saw Whit's black mare among them. He edged closer and stood in his stirrups to look all around. Seeing no one, he swung down and tied Kickapoo to the fence, then went into the barn, hefted the first outfit he saw, and carried it into the corral.

He worked fast to saddle Whit's horse, then led it out to his and walked them both through a back alley to the dark shadow under a cottonwood near the river. The banks were steep, the water a starlit flow through its channel. He left the horses there and sauntered back to the plaza, trying to act casual wearing a gun on his hip.

Soledad's jail was left over from the fort, an adobe hut at the east end of a row of quarters. It had one small window high in the back, grated with rusted iron bars. Andy skirted the hut and peered around a corner to see the guard in front. It was George Salinas, one of Uncle Emmett's men. Silently Andy returned to the back of the hut and stood beneath the window, trying to figure a plan. If he called out to Whit, the guard would hear him. Andy crouched down and searched the dirt for a pebble to throw, but his fingers found only dust.

From inside the jail he heard a sound that puzzled him. Slowly he stood up and listened more intently. Whit was crying. Probably with his face pressed against his drawn-up knees, the way the quiet mewling was muffled, as if against cloth. Andy decided Whit was crying for Jasper. Probably his family, too, who didn't yet know Jasper was dead.

Suddenly Whit began whistling the melody of Chopin's concerto. It amazed Andy that Whit remembered it so accurately. Listening to the song, Andy felt haunted by a memory of his mother. That made him think of Claire, who took joy from the light in Whit's eyes. It was pitiful to think women could find joy only in men while most men had such a small capacity to give it. Even Uncle Emmett, who loved music and was so successful among men, couldn't do for Lily what Whit did for Claire: make her eyes shine like the stars. Whit had done that for Jasper, too, though Andy doubted that Jasper had ever been able to admit it. Still, he'd followed Whit, who was younger and without any family or property. Whit was a miracle, a penniless orphan who loved life more than anyone Andy had ever met.

He walked away from the jail to circle around the row of barracks. Ambling back as if he were simply on his way to fetch his horse from the corral, he saw George Salinas watching him come. As if he intended to pass without speaking, Andy looked away.

"Hey, kid," George called. "I thought you went home."

"I'm going now," Andy said, stopping in front of him.

George looked at the light spilling from the doorway of the saloon along with the boisterous noise of the men inside. "It's colder'n hell out here," he said. "Why don't you stand guard a few minutes while I go over and get a drink to warm me up?"

"Guess I could do that," Andy said, sensing George hadn't noticed he was now wearing a gun. They were so common on men, it was taken for granted.

"I won't be long," George said, handing Andy his rifle. "If anything happens, fire a coupla shots in the air and we'll all come running."

"How many bullets are in it?" Andy asked, accepting the rifle.

"Hey, you're learning, kid," George said with a grin. "It carries a full load, so you'll have enough to handle whatever happens. But like I said, we'll all be here 'fore the echo of your first shot dies in the wind."

Andy nodded, cradling the rifle in his arms. "Don't be long," he said.

"Nah. Just a coupla drinks to warm my innards," George said, then walked away.

Waiting until George was inside the saloon, Andy pressed his face against the wooden door and whispered, "Whit?"

"Yeah," Whit said, close on the other side.

"I got a gun for you," Andy said, "and your horse tied with mine by the river, but I don't know how to get you out."

"I appreciate your wanting to do it," Whit said.

"It won't count for much if I can't figure out how."

"Does to me," Whit said. "What kinda lock they got on the door?"

"Padlock and chain."

"I figured as much," Whit said, "by the sound of it after they shut me in. It's dark in here, Andy. I ain't got no light."

"Cold, too, I reckon," Andy said.

"Yeah, and I'm so hungry I can hardly think. You gotta shoot the padlock, Andy."

"They'll be here in a minute if I do."

"I'll be out in less than that. If you give me the rifle, I can scatter 'em while I make a run for it."

"If you kill any of 'em, they'll hang you sure."

Whit laughed. "You think they won't anyway?"

"I'll tell 'em the truth. I'm sorry I didn't before."

After a minute, Whit said, "Wouldn't've done any good. They know we're friends."

"Even so," Andy said miserably, "I should've tried."

"This is better," Whit said. "You ever pick a lock?"

"Never."

"You got a knife?"

"No, I don't."

"What've you got?"

"A six-gun and rifle."

"How big a chain is it?"

Andy looked at it. "Not too big."

"Put the rifle in and twist it around, see if you can break it."

Andy did, leaning his weight against the rifle, but the chain held. "Didn't work, Whit."

"How about the hinges? Can you get 'em out?"

Andy looked at them. "If I had a screwdriver, I could."

"Damn!" Whit said. "There's gotta be a way."

Andy scanned the wooden door set in the adobe wall, then saw something gleam on top of the lintel. Standing on tiptoe, he gasped when his fingers touched the cold metal of a key. "Goddamn," he said for the first time in his life.

"What?" Whit whispered.

"They left the key on the lintel!"

Whit laughed. "Reckon they wanted someone to get in, don'cha think?"

"They weren't thinking it'd be me," Andy said. He turned the lock, dragged the chain free, and opened the door.

Whit pulled him close in a hug, laughing softly. Breaking the embrace, Whit said, "Give me your gunbelt."

Andy leaned the rifle against the wall, unbuckled the belt, and handed it over.

"Lock the door again," Whit said, "and wait for the guard to come back. When he does, high-tail it for home. Maybe I'll see you there."

Andy was already closing the door, the chain in his hand. He looked over his shoulder at Whit buckling the gunbelt. "You're coming to Bosque Grande?"

"I wanta say good-bye to Claire."

Andy snapped the padlock shut and picked up the rifle. "Whit, it was on her account that I didn't tell the truth."

Whit nodded.

"I felt it meant you didn't respect me the same way you did Jasper. You wouldn't have done that to his sister. Why'd you do it to mine?"

"I ain't got time to explain, Andy, but I didn't mean no disrespect to you or Claire. Did she say I hurt her?"

Andy shook his head. "She said it was a blessing to be deflowered by a man she loves."

Whit smiled. "I love her, too, Andy. Think she might come with me?"

"I think she'd like to."

Whit chuckled. "Where're the horses?"

"Straight down the alley, under the biggest cottonwood alongside the river."

"I owe you my life," Whit said, then he was gone, ducking behind the corner of the jail.

Andy listened to his footsteps running away, the soft jingle of his spurs making a glad sound until they were lost in the quiet of the night. It was broken by rude laughter from the saloon. Andy looked down the plaza at the light falling through the doorway, thinking George Salinas must be pretty well warm by now. When he saw George come out, Andy steeled himself to lie, something he'd never been very good at.

"All quiet?" George asked, coming close and reaching for his rifle.

"As a graveyard," Andy said, handing it over.

George laughed. "Thanks, kid. You go on home now, but I'd appreciate it if you don't tell your uncle you stood my watch for a while. If neither of us tells, nobody'll know."

"What about the men in Foxy's?" Andy asked.

"Aw, they're so drunk, come morning they won't remember seeing themselves there."

"You think they'll wait there till morning?"

George's eyes narrowed as he considered the implication of

Andy's question. Finally he said, "Half of 'em are already passed out on the floor. I don't expect 'em to be moving anytime soon. After that, it ain't my problem. Your uncle told me to stand first watch, then high-tail it back to Bosque Grande."

Andy looked at the door of the jail. "I hope he makes it to Union."

"He's gonna be hung either way," George said. "What dif'rence does it make which tree he swings from?"

"Not much, I guess," Andy mumbled.

"Go on home, kid," George said kindly. "You did a man's work today. You can be proud of that."

Andy nodded, suppressing a smile. "See you at Bosque Grande."

"You bet," George said. "Thanks again, kid. That whiskey'll keep me warm the rest of my watch."

Andy walked toward the corral. Only when he figured his silhouette was lost in the shadows did he veer toward the river. Whit's horse was gone. As Andy swung onto his own, he remembered he still had the key to the jail. He'd slid it into the pocket of his jeans after opening the lock, then forgotten to put it back. Digging it out, he threw it into the river, thinking the loss of the key would delay the lynch party at least a few minutes as they pondered the same problem he and Whit had. Andy smiled with satisfaction as he turned Kickapoo south toward Bosque Grande.

18

*L*ily was awake when Emmett returned home. Though she hadn't expected him so soon, she knew from her dread that the horseman crossing the yard must be her husband. When she heard his footsteps approach through the hall, she reached for a match and lit the bedside lamp just as he opened her door and met her eyes. He looked so weary, she felt a surge of hope.

Emmett quietly closed the door, lifted a chair and set it close to her bed, then sat down. Holding her gaze with his own, he stated flatly, "Jasper's dead."

Tears welled into her eyes.

"He was killed trying to escape," Emmett said softly. "The posse knew he'd make that choice, and they were ready. In the long run, it's best. A bullet's kinder'n a noose."

She nodded, the tears spilling across her cheeks.

"Go ahead and say it," he told her. "Name how you felt about him, so we can put it behind us."

"I loved him," she said.

"Say his name."

"Jasper," she whispered. "Jasper Stone."

Emmett stood up. "Jasper Stone is dead and will soon be buried. Someday I will be, too. When I am, I hope you can remember my virtues as generously, and forgive my flaws as willingly, as you do his."

Watching him return the chair, then start for the door, she asked, "What happened to Whit?"

Emmett turned back, his hand on the knob. "He's in jail in Soledad. Tomorrow he'll be taken to Union to be hung."

After watching the door close behind him, she extinguished the lamp, then walked across the cold floor in her bare feet to open the shutters and look out on the moonless night. She remembered the translucent quality to Jasper's cheeks, and how often she'd felt tempted to touch him though she rarely had. Remembered the dark blue of his eyes, the melancholy of his smiles, the anger in his voice the last time they'd spoken. With a certainty beyond logic, she knew that if she hadn't married Emmett, Jasper would be alive.

If he hadn't come to her wedding, he would have been home to protect Elise and Sammie. If they hadn't been hurt, he wouldn't have killed those men in Black Canyon. If he'd killed them at Rocky Arroyo, no one would doubt he'd done it in defense of his family. If in fact he and Whit had killed Henry Hart, they'd done it for her. She could see no other reason why they would suddenly act against him. It all came back to her. Her fault, her grievous error in demanding vengeance. Now she was left with the bitter knowledge that she had traded not only Jasper's life but Whit's, too, for a victory as empty as an unfilled grave, as empty as her life stretching for decades of regret from this moment of grief.

Emmett crossed the hall and entered his brother's room without knocking. Drew was asleep, so Emmett sat on the edge of his bed and shook him awake.

"Emmett," Drew mumbled. "Let me light the lamp."

"Don't. What you're about to hear is better said in the dark."

"What is it?" Drew whispered.

"It's about Claire. Whit Cantrell had his way with her." Emmett waited to let that sink into her father's mind, then said, "Now don't go getting riled, Drew. It's done and can't be changed. By morning, Whit's gonna be dead. The posse killed Jasper Stone trying to escape. If that don't happen with Whit, they'll lynch him. He killed the sheriff's brother, so believe me on that. What we gotta consider is that Claire's gonna be heartbroke when she gets the news. We gotta step softly in consideration of her feelings, knowing there's nothing to be done about the wandering of a young girl's heart except eliminate temptation from the field. I've done that. Are you listening, Drew?"

"Cantrell had his way with her?" Drew echoed mournfully.

"Did you hear the rest of what I said?"

"I want to be there when they lynch him."

"I understand how you feel, but we can't let on we knew it was gonna happen 'fore it does. So keep your mouth shut at breakfast, and she'll never suspect we had anything to do with it."

"Do we?"

"Only in the sense that I could've brought him here to prevent it from happening. I didn't figure you'd want me to do that."

"No!"

"In most cases I don't approve of lynching, but when it's to our advantage, the best thing is to look the other way. We'll have our vengeance without anyone being able to lay it at our feet."

There was a moment of heavy silence before Drew asked, "So you don't want me to say anything to Claire?"

"Let's wait and see if she comes up pregnant. If she does, we'll find her a husband. If not, we can sweep the whole thing under the rug."

"I'm her father. I should do something."

"Would beating her for it help how you feel?"

Drew sighed. "No, I don't think it would."

"Then let it be." Emmett stood up. "You with me on this, Drew?"

"Yes," he said.

Emmett walked out and went next door to Andy's room. Finding it empty, he muttered a curse. He'd never felt so much sorrow in his house. Lily was crying for a man unworthy of her tears, as Claire would be soon. Drew was heartbroken with disappointment, and unless Emmett missed his bet, Andy was playing a hand in a game that could only bring more grief. Emmett left the house and crossed the yard to the stable.

Taking his Winchester out of the scabbard on his saddle, he carried it and a blanket across the yard to where the buckboard was parked. He climbed into the bed of the wagon, wrapped himself in the blanket, and leaned into a corner. From there he could watch the yard, the stable door, and Claire's bedroom window. He admitted his suspicions might be wrong, both about what Andy was doing and what Whit would do if he were let loose, but whatever happened at Bosque Grande that night, Emmett would see it coming.

Andy rode at a leisurely lope toward home. He felt good about letting Whit out, figuring he'd made amends for not speaking up when Whit was arrested. He still felt bothered about Claire, though, and wished he'd had a chance to talk it through with Whit. But even Andy recognized that the middle of a jailbreak was no time for a long conversation.

Feeling Kickapoo tire beneath him, he felt nudged with a doubt he couldn't quite name. As he let his horse slow to a walk, he wondered why his uncle hadn't changed mounts before starting for Vegas. Then it hit him: Uncle Emmett wouldn't ride a tired horse all that way. Not on such an urgent errand. He'd lied about where he was going. Had he done that because of Claire, leaving the field wide open for Whit to be lynched?

Andy wondered how long it would take the posse to discover Whit was gone. Maybe they already knew. Maybe they were riding hard behind Andy right now. He urged Kickapoo into a trot again, then realized the posse would have no reason to think Whit would go to Bosque Grande. Nobody but Andy knew about Whit and Claire—except Uncle Emmett. Maybe he'd gone home, knowing Andy would let Whit out and Whit would visit Claire. Was Emmett so smart he could predict what Andy would do before he knew it himself? If so, Whit was riding into a trap.

Andy kicked in his heels, wishing he had spurs like the cowboys wore to goad their horses into action. He'd thought spurs were cruel, but they were nothing compared to the rest of life. Whit had been safe in jail until Andy was tricked into letting him out. That must be what happened. It had all been too easy. George Salinas hadn't noticed Andy was wearing a gun, yet no Moss ever did. Maybe George only pretended not to notice. It seemed a stretch to think he wouldn't when they'd talked about the load the Winchester carried. Hadn't it been awfully convenient that George left Andy alone to guard the jail? Maybe the key had been left on the lintel not so a lynch mob could get in without breaking the lock, but so Andy could.

Uncle Emmett had said Whit was experienced at twisting people into doing what he wanted, but Andy had always heard it took one to know one. Emmett was probably waiting at Bosque Grande for Whit to show up, knowing he'd be clear with the law for killing a man who'd escaped jail. Andy couldn't figure why Emmett had gone to all this trouble rather than kill Whit at the canyon, but his inability to figure that out didn't mean it wasn't true.

Andy galloped into the yard and reined up in the middle of it, his horse dripping sweat as he looked around. The house was dark. No sign of anyone awake. Maybe he'd been wrong. He walked Kickapoo in a circle to cool him down; once, twice, three times around the yard. Nothing seemed amiss. When Andy leaned from the saddle to open the stable door, it moaned in the quiet. Inside he dismounted and lit the lantern, then walked down the aisle until he saw Uncle Emmett's big bay in a stall. So Emmett *had* come home. Andy looked worriedly out the open door. All was still and silent. He unsaddled Kickapoo and rubbed him down before letting him drink, then tethered him in a stall and gave him a scoop of oats. Kickapoo munched contentedly, enjoying his hard-earned rest while Andy sat on a wooden box and held his head in his hands.

Whit had lied to Andy before about where he was going. If he'd done it then, protecting himself from ambush, he'd do it tonight of all nights. He wouldn't come here fresh from breaking out of jail. But the fact remained that Uncle Emmett was here, so he'd lied to Andy, too. Nobody trusted him. Then he remembered that Jasper had trusted him not to tell anyone about Black Canyon. Doing that had made Andy guilty of aiding and abetting Jasper in those murders. Now he'd helped Whit escape jail. If anyone found out, Andy would be arrested. If they would've hung Whit for helping Jasper, they'd hang Andy for helping him and Whit both. Hearing the soft tread of a footstep, Andy looked up at Uncle Emmett carrying a rifle into the barn. Their eyes met across the length of the lamplit aisle.

Whit was standing under the willows along the river when Andy galloped into the yard. As Andy walked his horse in a circle, Whit watched the shadows for any change. Nothing moved except Andy. Finally he rode into the stable, leaving the door open. Whit waited for him to come out again and go into the house. If he was met with lamplight, Whit would know he'd lost his chance to see Claire. Instead Andy lit a lantern in the stable and stayed there.

Whit could see that Claire's window was open a crack at the bottom. The white gossamer of her curtains lifted and fell with the breeze like a hand beckoning him inside. He was about to move when he saw a man stand up in the buckboard parked in a corner of the yard. Holding his breath as he watched Emmett vault over the side of the wagon and walk toward the stable carrying a rifle, Whit told himself to make tracks. Then he heard the soft rhythm of voices floating out the barn door. He wondered what Andy was telling his uncle. Whatever it was, Emmett wanted to hear it: He closed the stable door, dousing the yard with darkness.

Whit bolted for Claire's window. Quietly he raised the sash and stepped inside, then waited for his eyes to adjust to the lesser light. Telling himself he'd stay only a minute, kiss her once and be on his way, he crossed the room to her bed and covered her mouth with his hand as he sat down. "Claire, it's Whit," he whispered to her frightened eyes. When he took his hand away, she smiled and sat up to hug him close.

She smelled like heaven. He kissed her hair, her neck, her cheek, her mouth. She opened it hungrily and welcomed his tongue. He pulled back, searching her eyes for what she knew.

"Come lie here beside me," she said, lifting the covers.

"I'm too dirty," he said. "I just come to say adios."

"Where are you going?"

"Mexico, I reckon."

"Why?"

Realizing she hadn't been told anything, he said, "Jasper's dead."

"Oh, Whit!" she moaned. "How did it happen?"

He shook his head, pushing the vision of Jasper's death from his mind. "I'm starved, Claire. Can you get me something from the kitchen without waking anybody up?"

She rose and lifted her wrapper off the foot of her bed. He caught a glimpse of her nightgown, a flash of white lace and ribbons. "What would you like?" she asked, tying the sash tight.

"Whatever you can get your hands on without making any noise. Be quick, though. Emmett's in the stable and could come in anytime."

"I'll be right back," she said, and was gone.

Whit returned to look out the window. Light through the cracked stable door fell in slivers across the yard, telling him Andy and Emmett were still talking inside. About what? Whit walked back to the bed and leaned his face close to the pillows, inhaling Claire's scent. He sighed, then sat down and looked at her room. A rich girl with a lot of stuff, she'd never be happy with him, not in Mexico or anywhere else.

She slipped through the door, bringing him a loaf of bread and a pie. The pie had been cut into pieces, half of it gone. He lifted a slice and took a bite of mincemeat, reminding him it was almost Christmas. Feeling Claire's eyes, he didn't look up till he'd finished the pie, then he tore a hunk of crust off the bread and met her gaze while he chewed.

She smiled. "You must have been hungry."

"Ain't eaten for days." He lifted the pitcher of water off her nightstand and drank without using the glass, then wiped his mouth with the back of his hand. "I gotta go, Claire. Thanks for the food. Was good to see you one last time."

She set the empty pie plate and bread on the floor, snuggling close as she whispered, "Stay a minute longer, Whit."

He unwound her arms, stood up, and walked to the window, looking out to see that the light still shone from the stable. What was Andy saying to Emmett? Emmett saying back? Was Andy keeping Emmett there to give Whit time? How much did he have? He looked at Claire.

She'd taken off her wrapper. Her nightgown was luminous, her blond hair falling in a tumble of glory across her breasts to her waist. Whit went back and kissed her again. She tugged him to join her in bed. "I can't, Claire."

"Please," she coaxed.

His spurs caught on her covers as he lay down beside her. Knowing he shouldn't, he sat up again to tug off his boots. She stood on her knees to pull her nightgown over her head, then waited naked as he took off his gunbelt and laid it beside her pillow. Lowering himself on top of her, he felt her heat meld to his body. She was the one who unbuttoned his trousers, took him out, and guided him inside her. He moaned with his need as she whispered his name close to his ear. He shushed her with his mouth, then heard the bedsprings sing their unmistakable song. Quickly he finished, covering her mouth with his hand when she cried out under his sudden depth of penetration. She trembled beneath him as they held each other's eyes. Hers were full of love. He couldn't say what she saw in his, but he felt sorrow, knowing he had to leave her. With regret he broke their connection, stood up to button his trousers, then sat down again to pull on his boots.

"Please don't go," she pleaded.

He heard footsteps in the hall. Taking his gunbelt from beside her pillow, he whispered, "Meet me at our place on the river tomorrow. Don't let anyone follow you." Then he stepped through her window. The light was gone. He eased around the corner of the house. The yard was empty. Sauntering across its vast expanse, he moved slowly to keep his spurs quiet. Under the shadow of the trees, he swung onto his mare and walked her until they were far enough away that Emmett couldn't hear her galloping hooves.

Emmett opened the door to Claire's bedroom, seeing her window with the curtains hanging outside like a flag of someone's hurried departure. He crossed the room and looked out at the empty yard. Turning back around, he held his anger smashed in his throat as he said, "Light a lamp, Claire."

When she did, he saw the empty pie plate and torn loaf of bread on the floor by her bed, her nightgown and wrapper beside them. He looked at his niece with her blankets pulled up to her chin, then stepped closer and yanked the covers off, revealing her nakedness. With a growl of anger, he thrust his hand between her legs. She whimpered in fear, then cried out when he slapped her.

"I'll kill him," Emmett said. "You can count on that."

She shook her head, her eyes pleading. "No, Uncle Emmett. I love him."

He picked up her wrapper, tore the sash free, and used it to tie her hands to the brass headboard. Throwing the covers on the floor, he said, "Maybe after you've spent a night in his scum, you'll feel dif'rent."

He walked out, leaving the lamp burning and the window open to the cold wind. In the hall, he took the key off the lintel and locked the door, then pocketed the key and turned around to look at Andy cowering against the wall.

"This is what's come of your mercy," Emmett said. "If you think the strap I laid on your butt in the stable wasn't enough, I'll give your sister the same. Is that what you want?"

Andy shook his head, licking blood off the corner of his mouth where the gag had cut him as he screamed.

"Then go to your room," Emmett said. "And don't poke your nose out till I say so. Do you understand me, boy?"

Andy nodded, slinking down the dark hall to his door. Inside, he turned the lock and lit a lamp, then lowered his trousers and looked over his shoulder into the mirror at the bloody welts on his butt. Their pain was nothing compared with his shame for having told Emmett the truth, not only about the jailbreak but about Whit and Claire in the first place.

Andy's only consolation was that Whit was free. Emmett had expected him to be lynched by dawn. Had wanted it to happen that way. So the key left at the jail hadn't been for Andy after all, but for the lynch mob. Emmett never had any intention of riding to Vegas. He'd come home, expecting Andy to be here. Andy was so stupid, he'd thought Emmett knew about the jailbreak before being told. But Emmett had only suspected, and only that because Andy wasn't home. Andy could have lied. He could have said almost anything other than the truth and ended up better off than he had. His whipping had been deserved, not because he was wrong, but because he was stupid.

19

At five o'clock the next morning, Emmett was sitting at the kitchen table finishing his breakfast when Lily came in. Instead of her usual, upswept style with curls on her forehead, her thin brown hair was pulled away from her face and tied in a tight bun at the nape of her neck. Though the severity did nothing to diminish her homeliness, Emmett approved of what he saw. Her eyes were clear and her expression calm, denoting a resignation to the loss of childish notions.

Cipriano was working at the stove, cooking breakfast for the hands who ate in the bunkhouse. He had worked for Emmett for twenty years, and one of the cook's prime assets, in Emmett's view, was his ignorance of English. Seeing Lily in the door, Cipriano said, *"Buenos días, señora. Siéntese, por favor. ¿Quiere café?"*

"Sí, gracias," she murmured, sitting down across from Emmett and meeting his eyes with no discernible emotion.

He gave her a smile. "Morning, Lily. You look like you passed the night profitably."

She didn't reply, but she smiled at Cipriano as he set a cup of coffee in front of her.

The coffee's fragrance mingled with that from the huge skillet of frying fatback and the aroma of biscuits wafting from the oven to create a cozy warmth in the kitchen. Emmett sincerely wished he could enjoy this comfortable respite with his wife without the burden of more bad news. But as he watched her pour cream into her cup from the small pewter pitcher, he had to say, "Whit escaped jail last night and came here to visit Claire in her bedroom."

Again Lily met his eyes without speaking, though he thought he caught the curl of a smirk on her lips. As if to hide it, she looked down to pick up a spoon and stir her coffee.

"I didn't see him," Emmett said, measuring his words to stem the anger Lily's smirk had aroused. "He was quicker'n a coyote in a henhouse, but the evidence was plain he'd eaten his fill. I tied her to her bed."

This time Lily's brown eyes flashed with scorn above a definite lilt of disdain on her mouth.

"I've locked her in her room," Emmett said, "and I want you to make sure she stays there."

Lily sipped her coffee, meeting his eyes. Setting her cup

down, she smiled as if at the misstep of a fool, but Emmett didn't know if it was aimed at him or Claire.

Cipriano pulled three pans of a dozen biscuits each from the oven. Their fragrance filled the kitchen as he poured scrambled eggs into a skillet, which hissed when the eggs hit the grease.

Emmett asked, "Will you do it?"

"A wife," Lily answered, "is an extension of her husband's will in the same way a good horse does its rider's bidding rather than its own."

He recognized the advice he'd given her on the first morning of their marriage, but he felt certain he hadn't uttered it with her tone of sarcasm. Returning tit for tat, he said heartily, "I'm glad you've come around to understanding that, Lily."

She lifted her cup and sipped her coffee, veiling her eyes with her lashes.

The outside door opened and Beau Cairn came in to fetch breakfast for the hands. An old cowboy Emmett kept around out of pity, Cairn's legs were bowed from decades of sitting a horse, his face as weathered as the land. Surprised to see Lily at the table, he took off his hat and mumbled, "Morning, Miz Moss."

"Good morning, Beau," she said, giving him a smile that made Emmett feel jealous.

Cairn nodded at Emmett. He nodded in return, then watched the old man heft the skillet of fatback in one hand, a cauldron of beans in the other, and carry them out the door, left open. Cipriano followed with the platter of biscuits and a huge bowl of scrambled eggs.

Emmett lifted his cup but discovered it was empty. Lily rose and brought the pot to pour them both more coffee.

"Thanks," Emmett grunted.

She returned the pot to the stove, then resumed her seat and busied herself with the cream and her spoon.

"Andy's gonna be as melancholy as Claire over the next few days," Emmett said, blowing on his coffee to cool it. "Keep him occupied so he don't dwell on the mistake he made befriending Whit." He sipped his coffee, burning his tongue. "If I'd known Whit had weaseled himself so deep into my family, I would've stopped it. Now all I can do is ride the repercussions. But I've got a ranch to run. Even though it's winter and the work's slacked off, there's still plenty to do. Can I trust you to keep a tight rein on Andy and Claire?"

"You want me to keep him locked in his room, too?" she asked.

Emmett shook his head. "I've told him not to come out till I say so. You can do that for me. You might look at his bottom, too, if he'll let you. I whipped him hard last night."

"For making friends with Whit?" Lily asked incredulously. "Pretty near everybody in the county's done that at one time or another, including you."

Emmett felt pleased he'd finally raised some emotion from her. "He's the one let Whit outta jail," he said smugly. "I tell you that in confidence, Lily. It surely ain't nothing we want folks believing of Andy."

"I can't hardly believe it myself," she said.

"He told me he'd done it. Do you think he'd lie about something like that?"

She shook her head.

"He also told me Whit had his way with Claire 'fore last night. Did you know that happened?"

She hid her eyes.

"Answer me, Lily!"

"I hadn't realized it'd gone so far," she murmured.

"If Claire turns up pregnant, I'll have to find her a husband. You got any ideas?"

"No," she said. "Unless—"

"Unless what?"

She met his eyes. "Claire's in love with Whit. Why can't she marry him?"

Emmett snorted in disbelief. "Whit Cantrell's been sentenced to execution."

"You could convince the governor to give him a pardon. Everyone knows he didn't get a fair trial in the first place."

"You flatter me, Lily. But even if I did have such power, I wouldn't use it to help him." Emmett finished his coffee and stood up. "Will you do what I ask in regard to Claire and Andy?"

She nodded.

"Good," Emmett said. Fishing the key to Claire's room out of his vest pocket, he laid it on the table and said, "See you tonight." Lily stared at the key while she listened to him walk out. She lifted her cup, then set it back down without drinking any. Even with milk, the coffee turned her stomach, something it had never done before though she'd always drunk it black. She knew what that meant, but the prospect didn't make her feel glad. After she felt certain Emmett wouldn't come back, she stood up and dropped the key into her own pocket, then left their cups on the table and walked down the hall to knock on Andy's door.

When she received no answer, she called softly, "Andy, it's Lily. Can I come in?" Still hearing no answer, she opened the door. The room was empty. "Lord have mercy," she whispered, "doesn't that boy have any sense?"

She crossed the hall to Claire's room, unlocked and opened the door. Claire was asleep, naked on the bed, her knees drawn up close to her breasts for warmth, her hands tied to the headboard with a sash. Quickly Lily stepped into the room and closed the door, then walked across to where the wind was blowing the curtains in through the open window. She closed the window and drapes. Turning in the subdued light, she saw the empty pie plate and half-eaten loaf of bread on the floor next to Claire's nightgown and wrapper.

Not wanting to wake Claire by untying the sash, Lily covered her with the blankets, then sank into the window seat and watched her sleep. She thought Whit must have been starving to come here fresh from breaking out of jail. But he could have been fed in a dozen homes along the Panal, so the hunger he came here to satisfy wasn't physical. Jasper's death must have devastated Whit. Perhaps even more than her because she'd rarely seen Jasper while Whit had been his constant companion. He must feel as he had when his mother died, except that maybe this second loss hurt even more, making him believe he would always lose those he cherished. So he'd come to see Claire, knowing their love was doomed but savoring its preciousness while it was his.

Caught in a dream, Claire whimpered and tugged at the sash

binding her wrists. The golden girl with abundant prospects had fallen in love with an outlaw who had no future, while Lily, a homely girl with a sharp tongue, had supposedly married well. Claire had let herself be ruined and now likely wouldn't marry at all, yet she had love, and Lily did not.

She stood up and carried the empty pie plate and dry loaf of bread to the kitchen. Cipriano was washing dishes. He eyed the plate and bread, but said nothing. She set them on the table and asked him to make a tray of breakfast for Señorita Moss, who was ill in bed. Cipriano looked sympathetic and said he would make oatmeal sweetened with honey.

" *'Sta bien,*" Lily said. "*Gracias.*"

She returned down the hall to knock on Drew's door. He opened it, quickly slipped out, and closed it again, but not before Lily saw Andy asleep in his bed. She smiled at Drew with pity. He had come here after the death of his wife thinking that living on a ranch would be good for his children. So far they'd both met with disaster. "How's Andy?" she asked gently. "Emmett told me what happened."

"He had no right to do it," Drew rasped. "I'm their father. I should be the one to dispense discipline when needed. Emmett's too hard. Andy's bottom is cut to ribbons." His voice broke and he looked away, embarrassed.

"I'm sorry," Lily murmured.

Drew met her eyes. "I tried to see Claire but her door's locked. When I knocked and asked her to let me in, she said Emmett took the key. I asked if she was all right and she said she was, but it sounded like she'd been crying. Did he whip her too, Lily?"

She shook her head. "Did Andy tell you why Emmett whipped him?"

"He tried, but I couldn't make sense of it. Something about being friends with Whit Cantrell. Goddamn son of a bitch!" He stopped. "I'm sorry to swear in front of you, Lily, but this is all his fault. My children were good kids back in Texas."

"Whit ain't bad, Drew. He's just had a lotta bad luck."

"I wish he would've kept it away from my children! Now Claire's ruined and Andy was crying last night about how much he loved him. An outlaw! Sentenced to execution! Emmett told me he wouldn't make it to the gallows, though, that he'd be lynched this morning in Soledad. Don't guess you've heard if that happened?"

Feeling herself pale, Lily whispered, "Emmett told you Whit would be lynched?"

Drew ran his hand through his unruly shock of gray hair, uncombed from bed. "I wasn't supposed to say anything. Not about that or Claire being ruined. You won't tell Emmett I told you, will you, Lily? I'm beholden to him for taking us in. Don't know what I would've done if he hadn't. I hit the bottle pretty hard after Laura died. She was my wife and their mother."

Lily nodded. "I won't tell him, Drew."

"I lost everything I had back in Texas, Lily. Let it slip through my fingers 'cause they were wrapped around a bottle all the time. When I wrote Emmett and asked if we could come here, I thought it was the best thing to do. Now I'm not so sure. I quit drinking before we came 'cause I knew Emmett wouldn't approve. If I could do it for him, don't you think I should've been able to do it for my children?"

"Isn't that what you did?" Lily asked.

His eyes blurred with gratitude, then he frowned again. "Maybe. But look at them now."

"This will pass, Drew. They're young, and they'll bounce back."

"Claire's older than you are. But you're wise beyond your years. I guess that's why Emmett chose you for his bride."

She sighed.

"You're not happy, are you? I'm sorry, I have no right to say any such thing, but I can't help having noticed you've changed since becoming his wife."

"Don't all girls change after marriage?" she asked bitterly.

He nodded. "I suppose. Have you seen Claire? Is she all right?"

"She's asleep," Lily said. "You stay with Andy. I'll look after Claire."

"God bless you," Drew said. "She's missed her mother. We all have. But this is the time in Claire's life when a girl especially needs a mother's guidance. If Laura were still alive, none of this would have happened." He smiled weakly. "We'd still be in Texas. Claire was to make her debut this season."

"We're a long way from that," Lily said. "But life on the Panal's life just the same. We gotta remember what we have, 'stead of dwelling on what we've lost."

Drew's face brightened. "Laura's always telling me that." He looked toward the kitchen. "Is she making breakfast?"

Lily stared at him, then whispered, "Laura's dead, Drew."

"Yes, of course," he said, looking down at his robe and pajamas. "I'll get dressed. That always sets things right again."

Lily watched him go back inside his room and close the door. With a deep sigh, she crossed the hall and walked into Claire's room. She was awake, watching Lily come in. Quickly she closed the door, crossed to the bed and untied Claire's hands. As Lily pulled the sash loose, Claire whimpered, "Uncle Emmett struck me!"

"You're lucky he didn't do worse," Lily said.

"He did!" Claire cried. "He touched me down there!"

Though she shuddered with an intimate knowledge of Emmett's rough touch, Lily asked sternly, "What'd you expect him to do?"

"Stay out of my bedroom! He had no right to come in, or to strike me either. He's not my father."

"Put your nightgown on, Claire," Lily answered. "Cipriano's bringing you breakfast. I told him you're sick in bed."

"I'm not staying in bed," Claire said, standing up. "You may be stuck in this house, but I'm not."

"Emmett gave me orders to keep you here."

"That's your problem. When I tell my father what Emmett did, we'll move into town."

"He already knows."

A knock sounded. Claire leapt back in bed and pulled the covers up to her chin as Lily opened the door to Cipriano. *"Gracias,"* she said, taking the tray from his hands. He kept his gaze on the floor to avoid seeing Claire in bed.

"¿No quiere nada más, señora?" he asked.

"No, gracias," Lily said. She closed the door, then faced Claire. "The first thing I want you to do is eat this breakfast."

"I'm not hungry," Claire pouted.

"Put your nightgown on," Lily said, "so you can sit up in bed while you eat."

Claire peevishly did it, then glared at Lily settling the tray on her lap.

"Eat," Lily said. She walked to the window and lifted one drape to peer through the sheer curtain at the yard.

"I hate oatmeal," Claire said.

Lily dropped the drape and faced her. "Maybe you'd like some mincemeat pie and a crust of bread."

Claire stared at her, then lifted the spoon and began to eat.

"Do you have any idea where Whit is?" Lily asked.

Claire shook her head, spooning oatmeal into her mouth with a grimace of distaste.

"If you do," Lily said, "I might be able to take him a message." Holding the empty spoon over the bowl, Claire watched her.

"Do you know what happened yesterday?" Lily asked.

Claire laid the spoon down and sighed. "Whit told me Jasper was killed, but not how it happened. I'm sorry, Lily. I know you loved him."

Lily pushed Claire's sympathy away to concentrate on the task at hand. "He was killed by a posse. Whit was arrested and put in jail."

"What on earth for?" Claire whispered.

Lily smiled sadly. "You don't know anything about him."

"Why don't you tell me?" Claire demanded, sliding the breakfast tray off her lap.

"I've already done that. Apparently you weren't listening."

In a softer tone, Claire said, "I'm listening now, Lily."

"Okay," she said. "Whit helped Jasper kill the men who raped Elise and murdered Sammie."

"My God," Claire moaned. Then, puzzled, "I thought Sammie was only hurt."

Lily shrugged. "Andy let Whit outta jail."

"Andy did?" Claire laughed. "Good for him."

"Emmett whipped him for it."

Claire bit her lip.

"Whit'll be hung if he's caught," Lily said.

"Hung?" Claire whispered.

"Lynched, most likely. If you know where he is, you best tell me."

"What will you do?"

"Tell him Emmett knows he was here. That if he comes back, he'll be caught. His best chance is to high-tail it to Mexico. If he makes it, you might be able to visit him there. But if he doesn't go now, you'll lose that chance."

"How far is Mexico?" Claire asked.

"A day's ride." Lily waited a minute, then asked, "Did he say he'd come back, or ask you to meet him somewhere?"

"Meet him," Claire said.

"Where?"

"How do I know you won't betray him?"

Lily stood up. "If you can't see I'm trying to help, Claire, you'll deserve what you get, but Whit won't. He'd be in Mexico already if he hadn't stopped to see you. Now he's waiting another day for you to show up, but if you step foot off this ranch, I'd bet my last dollar Emmett'll have you followed, so all you'll take Whit is his death. Is that what you want?"

Claire stared at her a long moment, then whispered, "There's a cove in the river south of the ford."

"I know the place," Lily said. "If you love Whit, stay here."

"I do and I will, Lily. Give him my love, won't you? Tell him godspeed, and that I'll come to Mexico as soon as he writes and tells me where he is." She bit her lip. "Does Whit know how to write, Lily?"

"I don't know," she answered. "But I'll tell him what you said."

Lily waited until Cipriano had left the kitchen, then gathered a small shank of smoked ham and some biscuits left from breakfast. She wrapped the food in a linen towel she hid inside her jacket as she crossed the yard to the stable. Inside she saddled her palomino, then took a box of forty-four bullets from the tack room, hoping they were the right caliber, and slid them with the food into her saddlebags. She led the horse out to the mounting block, feeling eyes watch as she settled herself in the sidesaddle. At the line of willows between the yard and the river, she saw Shiloh Pook standing guard with a rifle.

She stopped and smiled down at him, remembering they'd bantered the day of her wedding about stealing strawberries from the garden. Pook was tall and muscular, an imposing man except for his unruly hair. Its sandy brown burst from beneath the brim of his hat in such a riot of curls that Lily felt tempted to attack them with scissors.

"Why aren't you out on the range, Mr. Pook?" she asked innocently.

"Your husband wants me to keep a watch on the house," he answered. "Whit Cantrell escaped jail last night, and Emmett's worried he might show up here."

"I don't think that's likely, do you?"

Pook's sky-blue eyes didn't betray his thoughts. "Cantrell's unpredictable," he said. "You think it's a good idea to be riding alone?"

She laughed as if the question were silly. "I've known Whit for years. He wouldn't hurt me if we did happen to cross paths, but I s'pect he's in Mexico by now, don't you?"

"I hope so, Miz Moss," Pook said. "Did you know Jasper Stone was killed yesterday?"

"I heard," Lily said, veiling her eyes.

"Jasper and Whit were like brothers, so it's possible he might try'n take vengeance 'fore leaving the county. Since your husband headed the posse that killed Jasper, it ain't too long of a stretch to think Whit might feel ill-will toward anyone connected to Emmett."

Lily's horse sidestepped away but she reined it back. "I thought the sheriff led the posse."

"He was more like along for the ride. I was with 'em, and I don't think Whit had any doubt Emmett was the leader of that particular pack."

She looked into the trees as her horse bobbed its head, playing with its bit. When she looked back, Pook was watching her closely. The kindness in his eyes encouraged her to ask, "Was Jasper's death quick?"

"More'n likely," Pook drawled. "He didn't make it far past the mouth of the cave where him and Whit were holed up. It was a while 'fore Whit surrendered and the posse got to go down. Jasper was peppered with bullets, so I don't see how he could've lived long. And he sure wasn't moving after he fell."

She held her reins tight, fighting for control. "I don't understand, Mr. Pook. Jasper made a run for it while Whit stayed in the cave?"

"Neither one of 'em did no running. Near as I can figure, Jasper was coming out for their horses when the posse opened fire."

"Without warning?" she whispered.

"Those were their orders," Pook said. "I didn't fire myself. Wasn't fair, to my way of thinking."

Through clenched teeth she asked, "Was it my husband who gave that order?"

Pook looked down to tug the brim of his hat lower above his eyes before meeting hers again. "I like my job, Miz Moss. 'Fore yesterday, there wasn't no part of it I didn't like."

She nodded. "I understand, Mr. Pook."

He smiled. "Enjoy your ride, Miz Moss, but keep a sharp eye. With men riding every which way scouring the country for Whit, anything's liable to happen."

"I will. Thank you," she said.

He stepped back under the trees as she reined her horse onto the trail to the river.

The sky was overcast, a chill on the wind. In another two weeks it would be Christmas, but she felt none of the joyful anticipation that usually preceded that holiday. Wondering if its thrill was another thing lost with childhood, Lily forded the river and climbed the west bank, then turned south. It felt good to be moving. To be still would allow her sorrow to pull her into a depth as deadly as the quicksand pits lurking along the water's edge. To survive, Lily had to keep moving. Helping Whit was doing that. When it was done, she'd have to find something else.

She reined up above the cove, unable to see anyone there. Urging her horse to take the decline, she ambled onto the dry grass under the cliff, sat a moment looking around, then saw the darker silhouette of a black horse beneath the shadow of a cottonwood leaning at a precarious angle off the edge of the bank. After tying her reins so her horse could graze, she jumped down and stood waiting until Whit appeared from where he'd been hiding. She met his eyes across a distance of fifty feet, hearing the ripple of the river and a crow cry in the trees above.

Whit came close and took her in his arms. "Jasper's dead," he whispered.

She nodded, her face against the soft suede of Whit's jacket.

He lifted her chin and met her eyes, then kissed the tears from her cheeks before he backed away and said gently, "Sit down, Lily. Why'd you come?"

"I brought some food," she said, settling cross-legged on the grass. "And a box of bullets."

He sat down beside her. "Did Claire send you?"

"What're you doing, Whit, playing with a rich girl? Emmett's fit to be tied."

Whit chuckled. "That'd make it worthwhile right there."

"Is that why you're doing it?"

He shook his head. "What I feel for her ain't got nothing to do with him."

"Emmett's keeping her locked in her room. I told her if you made it to Mexico, she'd be able to visit you. That's the only reason she told me where you'd be. Emmett's got Shiloh Pook guarding the yard. He told me the country's crawling with men looking for you."

Whit smiled. "How's Shiloh doing?"

She stared at him. "If you don't vamoose, they'll kill you like they did Jasper!"

Whit looked away to watch the river running south as he said softly, "The first time me and Jasper crossed paths was way up in the Sacramentos. Some kinda spark was struck, and we decided to share the trail a ways. Guess that's what we did." His eyes were sad when he gave her a crooked smile. "The next day, we was waylaid by Apaches." He chuckled at the memory. "We was watering our horses at a crick, and the first indication of any Apaches in the vicinity was an arrow hitting the dirt at my feet. I grabbed my rifle and looked up at two bucks on the hill above us. Only one of 'em was shooting, so I took aim at him, but I missed. Since the other buck kept out of it, Jasper did, too." Whit shook his head. "Me and that buck were having a time trying to hit each other. I took a shot and missed, then he fired an arrow and missed, so I took another and he did, too, both of us missing again. Jasper commenced to criticizing my style. First he said I was aiming too high. When I missed again, he said I'd shot too low. The next time, he said I was pulling right, and the next, left. Finally I lost patience and shouted, 'Who's fighting this Indian?' 'A damn poor shooter, from what I can see,' Jasper said." Whit laughed, a soft easy sound full of love and forgiveness. "I finally hit the buck and he and his friend disappeared over the rise of the hill, but I'll tell you what, Jasper taught me how to shoot that day."

Lily stared at him. "You're the best shot in the county, Whit."

"Only 'cause Jasper's gone," he said.

She sighed. "Are you gonna join him, or go to Mexico and stay alive?"

"You really think Claire'll come see me down there?"

"If you let her know where you are."

He looked at the river again, then turned back to give Lily a playful smile. "If me and Claire got married, you and me'd be kin. Wouldn't that be something?"

"Yeah, it would, Whit. But it ain't gonna happen if you don't make tracks fast."

He stood up. "I'm on my way."

"Let me give you what I brought," she said, standing up, too, and walking over to where her horse grazed beneath the cliff.

He accepted the food and bullets, then laid them down to take hold of her waist and lift her into the sidesaddle. "Texas Lily," he said, smiling up at her. "Do you think you'll ever go home?"

"I am home," she answered.

He nodded. "I meant back to where you came from, but reckon you're right. I hope we see each other again."

"Me, too," she whispered, though he was already sprinting away, her gifts in his hand.

She watched him untie his horse, swing on, and spur the black up the steep incline of the riverbank, then she turned onto the trail leading to Bosque Grande.

20

*L*ily entered the house through the back door, intending to explain the missing shank of ham to Cipriano. She had decided to tell him she'd given it to a needy traveler without mentioning the wayfarer's name. Cipriano, however, wasn't alone in the kitchen. Emmett was there, and from his disgruntled expression, Lily guessed the missing ham had been discovered.

"Where were you?" he asked without prelude.

"I always take a morning ride, Emmett," she answered, striving to keep her voice light.

"Cipriano tells me the shank of ham he planned on putting in the bean pot's gone."

Lily gave the cook an apologetic smile. *"Perdoneme, Cipriano. Le doy a un pobre."*

" *'Sta bien, señora,"* he murmured.

"Dejenos," Emmett said curtly.

Cipriano hurried out the door, obeying Emmett's command to leave them alone.

"Was the poor person you gave it to Whit?" he asked.

"Yes!" she said, then cried out when he slapped her.

"You defied me!"

"I didn't! Claire's still in her room."

Emmett nodded, his eyes fierce. "Following the letter and ignoring the spirit of the law ain't good enough, Lily. You knew my wants."

"Are yours the only ones that matter?"

"Damn straight! This is my ranch and what I say goes!"

"I'm your wife. That makes it my ranch, too."

His mouth opened in silent amazement.

Lily laughed. "If you thought I was just another one of your cows to breed, Emmett Moss, you've got another think coming."

"A wife obeys her husband!" he thundered.

"I won't," she retorted. "You got what you wanted: Jasper dead and Whit run outta the country. I know it was you who gave the order to kill Jasper. You did it 'cause of me, didn't you?"

"I did it 'cause he was a mad dog outta control. Where'd you see Whit?"

"I won't tell you."

"I can follow your tracks to where you met him, and his from there. When I find him, I'll kill him."

"Why?"

"Should've done it at the Crevice. Some misbegotten notion of mercy stopped me."

"Mercy's never misbegotten. It was your better judgment stopped you."

Emmett shook his head. "It was a mistake." He strode toward the door, then turned around. "I don't want you leaving the yard. Do you understand me?"

She shrugged. "Don't reckon I should be riding anyway since I'm pregnant."

He stared at her, then said in a low voice, "You chose this moment to tell me you're pregnant?"

She nodded. "I'm hoping the beginning of a new life will sway you to spare one."

"It only goads me to make sure my child don't share the world with Whit Cantrell." He stalked out, slamming the door.

Lily sighed, then turned to see Claire edging around the corner. "It's rude to eavesdrop on a quarrel 'tween married folk," Lily accused.

Claire smiled weakly. "You're so brave, Lily. I could never stand up to Uncle Emmett like that."

"I wouldn't've had to if you owned any sense. Get back in your room 'fore he sees you're out."

"Will you come with me?" Claire asked. "Tell me about Whit?"

"He's on his way to Mexico. You oughta get on your knees and pray he makes it."

Claire nodded. "I will," she whispered.

Lily listened to her run to her room and close the door, then she moved to stand on the threshold and look through the long, dim hall dissecting the heart of the house. Jasper and his father had built it, laying the adobe with their own hands. They'd made it large to accommodate several generations, and they'd made it strong to withstand marauding Apaches and all the evils white men could do. Counting the rooms in her mind, Lily realized there were thirteen, and she wondered why they had chosen an unlucky number. She vowed it wouldn't be unlucky for her. Despite the lack of love in her marriage, she intended to thrive in this house. After all, Whit had called her Texas Lily, and Emmett had said a Texan was a man who had the courage to stand his ground at any cost. Lily wasn't a man, but she meant to stand her ground.

On Christmas Eve, Beau Cairn brought into the parlor a piñon pine he'd cut in the mountains. Lily and Claire decorated the tree with red velvet bows, strings of popcorn, and tiny white candles on the tips of the boughs. Claire had made an angel for the top, fashioning a tiny body out of a stuffed stocking and covering it with a white silk gown sewn from an old shimmy. She embroidered the angel's face with a scarlet mouth, rose-spotted cheeks, round sapphire eyes, and golden arched brows. A gold ring that had once belonged to her mother was pinned to the angel's head as a halo above the hair of yellow yarn.

Andy stood on a chair and placed the angel at the top of the tree. When he climbed down, they all stood back to admire their work. "It'll look magical," Andy said, "when the candles are lit."

"If you had your piano," Claire said, "you could play us some carols."

"I wish I'd brought it," he said.

Lily looked at Emmett's violin above the mantel, remembering Andy had once tried to learn how to play it. But he hadn't touched the violin since Jasper's death. She sighed. "Call your father, Andy. I'll tell Cipriano we're ready for the cocoa."

She walked toward the kitchen feeling lonely. Her mother and Theo had been expected for Christmas, but a blizzard kept them home. The yard of Bosque Grande was buried under a foot of snow, and more had fallen on the mountains, making travel by wagon impossible. The kitchen was fragrant with chocolate simmering on the stove and *biscoquitos* still warm from the oven. Cipriano was frosting a coconut cake. *"¿Está listo?"* Lily asked.

"Sí, señora," he answered, his face pink from the heat of the stove.

"When you bring them to the parlor," she said in Spanish, "stay with us a moment. We have a gift for you."

He looked at her with surprise. *"Gracias, señora."*

Lily smiled and went to her room for the gifts she had wrapped in red satin and tied with white ribbon. She had no gift for her husband, who this first Christmas of their marriage was riding with a posse. In the parlor, she arranged the presents under the tree, then began lighting the candles. In a few minutes, Claire returned with her gifts, Andy with his, then came Drew, looking embarrassed at the sizes of the boxes he placed under the tree. Just as Lily finished with the candles, Cipriano came in with a tray bearing the coconut cake, cinnamon cookies, and a pewter pitcher of cocoa. Andy blew out the lamp and they all *ooh*ed at the beauty of the tree.

"Let's sing a carol," Drew said, unaware he was echoing their earlier comments. "It's a pity, Andy, that we didn't bring your piano, or that Emmett isn't here to play his violin, but we can sing without accompaniment."

"What'll we sing?" Andy asked.

" 'O Come All Ye Faithful'?" Drew suggested. "Maybe it'll bring Emmett home."

So they sang the carol, the three young people wishing for Emmett to return defeated, his brother alone hoping for success.

They sang "Silent Night" and "Hark the Herald Angels Sing." Then Andy lit the lamp and Lily began the presentation of gifts with Cipriano's. He unwrapped the package to discover a white chef's hat. Puzzled, he examined it.

Claire laughed and stood on tiptoe to place it on his head. "It's what the cooks in fancy restaurants wear," she explained. "I made it myself." She frowned. "It's a tad lopsided, but they always look that way."

After Lily translated Claire's words into Spanish, Cipriano beamed, thanked the family profusely, then left them alone. The gifts were passed around. Lily gave two pinning combs carved from mesquite to Claire, a braided rawhide lariat to Andy, and a writing quill to Drew. Claire gave her favorite gold bracelet to Lily, a harmonica to Andy, and a ream of the best stationery she could find in River's End to her father. Watching Drew strive to show pleasure at the poor quality of the paper, Lily remembered that on their shopping trip to River's End she and Claire had visited the Stones.

Elise had been ill, her parents aged beyond their years, their house cold, as if Jasper alone could warm them. Lily and Claire had walked with Mr. Stone to the family cemetery and saw Jasper's grave next to Sammie's, both marked with bare wooden crosses.

"We've ordered monuments," Mr. Stone said, "but they ain't finished yet. The tombstone carver's been busy lately."

Lily nodded, having heard that five men had died in the mountains since Henry Hart's death. The county was in a convulsion for control, and it seemed those in contention for power knew no other way to subdue their enemies than kill them. While the sheriff accompanied Emmett in pursuit of Whit, the lawless elements rode without rein. The most recent to die had been Edgar Homer. Appointed by the governor to replace Hart as territorial representative, the lawyer had been assassinated by a shot through the window as he was eating supper at home.

"Sheriff Bond's back now," Mr. Stone said. "They tracked Whit to the Mexican border but the sheriff couldn't cross it, a'-course, so he brought most of the posse back and the others went on. I hope you don't mind my saying so, Miz Moss, but it's a pity the way they're hounding that boy. Reckon they're thinking Whit's gotta die to justify them killing Jasper. He was wild, but he didn't deserve what he got."

In the parlor on Christmas Eve, Lily shook her head, trying to clear her mind of politics and the grief of Jasper's family.

Andy gave red velvet boxes of chocolate truffles to Claire and Lily, and an envelope of expensive pipe tobacco to his father. Drew gave new clothes to everyone, frocks he'd ordered made in Vegas for the women, and a store-bought suit for Andy. They all gushed with praise of their presents as they ate the cake and cookies and drank their cocoa, the continual onslaught of compliments a desperate attempt at gaiety in honor of the holiday.

After that, they extinguished the lamp and sat in only the light from the tree and the fire in the hearth, enjoying the warmth of family snug at home on a snowy night. When the candles on the tree were burned to nubs, and the cake and cookies were half gone, the remaining cocoa cold, they heard the muffled hooves of horses crossing the yard. Drew rose eagerly and looked out the window, then announced that Emmett had returned. No one answered him. They waited in silence, hoping to hear that Whit had escaped.

They heard the front door open, then Emmett stomping snow from his boots. He left his hat and coat in the hall and entered the parlor in a rumpled jacket and vest, his trousers limp from having been lived in for weeks, his face chapped and red from the cold. Meeting Drew's eyes first, Emmett gave his brother a nod that Lily understood to mean his trip had been successful. She suppressed a moan of grief as she rose to greet her husband.

"Merry Christmas," she murmured, standing on tiptoe to kiss his cheek, determined not to let the past spoil the future of their child.

Emmett chuckled with pleasure and slid his arm around her waist to keep her at his side. "I hadn't realized it was. Y'all are a sight for sore eyes, though. My, don't that tree look pretty. And presents, too. I've brought nothing, but I'll make up for it in the days to come. Merry Christmas, everyone."

They all murmured responses, waiting to hear his news.

"Is that cocoa?" he asked. "Warm it on the fire, will you, Lily, while I thaw my bones?"

She moved away from him to nestle the pewter pot in the coals of the fire. Staying near the hearth so she could hear the simmer as soon as it started, she sat on a three-legged stool and smoothed the skirts of her best dress, a dark blue frock already tight at the waist.

Emmett sat down in her chair as the others resumed their seats and waited expectantly.

He smiled at each of them in turn. "A man couldn't ask for a prettier family scene to come home to." He looked at Lily. "Reckon the weather kept your mother and Theo at the mill."

She nodded, disguising her anger that he would delay the news they were all breathless to hear.

"Pass me those cookies," he said. "And I'll have a piece of cake, too. Ain't eaten since early this morning."

Lily stood up and handed him the platter of cookies, then returned to the table to cut a slice of cake. In the silence she heard the cocoa simmer, so she took the pot from the fire and filled him a cup. He'd finished all of the cookies when she gave him the cake and cocoa. She carried the empty platter back to the table and stood beside it, watching him as they waited.

"Good cake," he said around his first bite. "Did Cipriano bake it?"

"Yes," Lily said.

He slurped the hot cocoa into his mouth, set the cup down, and continued eating the cake. Finally he scraped the last smidgeon of frosting off the plate and set it aside. "Is there more cocoa, Lily?" he asked, his teasing eyes telling her he knew how desperately they were waiting to hear his news.

She carried the pot over and refilled his cup.

"Put that pot back and come sit on my knee," he said.

She obeyed him, keeping her spine rigid. Not satisfied with that, he pulled her close to lean against his chest so she could hear his heartbeat and the working of his throat as he swallowed the cocoa, even the rumble of his stomach digesting the cookies and cake. With one hand on her hip, he used his other hand to swirl the cocoa in his cup as he said, "Seventy-nine's gonna be a good year for this family. All our troubles are over. There's nothing but blue skies ahead."

Claire was pale, biting her lip. Andy stared at the carpet between his pigeon-toed boots. Drew waited with a smug smile.

"Reckon y'all are ready for sleep," Emmett said. "I am, too, so I'm gonna say what you're waiting to hear. If anyone's got any hard feelings to share or shed, get it done tonight. Tomorrow's Christmas and a day of joy."

"Just say it, Emmett," Lily whispered.

He held her close as he leaned forward and set his empty cup on the floor. Then he settled back and looked at each of them except Lily as he said, "We tracked Whit to the Mexican border. The sheriff refused to cross it, so me'n Shiloh Pook went on alone." He paused. "We caught Whit, and we hung him."

Claire gasped, then hid her face in her lap as she cried.

"I consider it justice done," Emmett said. "Any of you got something to say?"

"I agree it was justice," Drew said.

"For what?" Andy asked, his voice breaking.

"Now, Andy," Emmett said sternly. "I know you thought Whit was your friend. You tried to save him, thinking that, and it would've been an honorable thing to do if he'd truly been your friend. But I don't believe he was, and I didn't believe the lie you told trying to protect him. It'll be best for the family if you don't repeat it."

"What lie?" Lily asked, trying to sit up straight.

Emmett held her down. "Andy told me he was the second man at Black Canyon that day. Look at him crying. Anyone with eyes can see he couldn't have no part in such a brutal act of murder."

"I didn't do it!" Andy shouted. "I was just there!"

"No, you weren't," Emmett said. "Whit put you up to saying that. As confused as you are, maybe you do believe it now. But get it outta your mind, boy. The truth is Whit helped gun down those men, and that's what we hung him for."

"You hung him for loving me!" Claire accused through her tears.

Emmett shook his head. "Whit was an alley cat incapable of love. I'm sorry, Claire, but you and Andy gotta face the truth. Whit took advantage of you both, and yes, maybe my vengeance had something to do with that. It turns my stomach to know he weaseled his way into your hearts. I acted to make sure he won't do it again, to you or any other young'uns so innocent they can't see the truth." He stood up, setting Lily on her feet but holding her close with his hand on her waist. "Whit Cantrell is dead. That's the fact we're all gonna live with. Tomorrow's Christmas. Tonight I'm gonna sleep with my bride." He met his brother's eyes. "They're your children, Drew. Comfort them as best you can." He smiled at Lily. "I got my own on the way." Lifting her in his arms, he carried her out of the parlor.

Drew watched his son and daughter cry over the death of a man whom he considered unworthy of their grief. He cleared his throat and said kindly, "I know this is hard, children, but what Emmett did was right. When you've lived a few more years, you'll come to understand that. Claire, we have to hope you aren't in the same condition Lily is. If you are, we'll find you a husband. It'd be best if you aren't. That's what I'm praying for. Andy, be a man and admit your mistake. A friend wouldn't ask you to lie for him, or accept your doing it even if you offered. Like Emmett said, tomorrow's Christmas. Let's all put on a happy face to show your uncle we're grateful he chose to share his home when we'd lost ours. Go on to bed now. Tomorrow all this will be in the past." He stood up and walked from the room.

Andy listened to his father leave, then looked at Claire crying into her lap. He wanted to comfort her, but since what had happened was his fault, he couldn't find the words. After a while, she stood up and left him alone without a backward glance. He felt so sad. If he had a piano, he could let his sorrow flow through his fingertips, but he'd left his piano behind, believing music wasn't manly. He remembered Whit crying at the beauty of Chopin. Remembered him crying in jail, then whistling Chopin's melody as a cure for loneliness. Andy couldn't understand why their friendship had led to this immense weight of guilt he must bear alone.

If Andy hadn't been so eager to share his new friend with his family, Claire might never have met Whit. If Andy hadn't left her alone with Whit that day, she wouldn't have been ruined. Whit would have ridden to Rocky Arroyo and kept Jasper there, so Jasper wouldn't have been in Black Canyon when those men stopped to make coffee. If Andy had admitted at the Crevice that he'd been the one with Jasper that day, Whit wouldn't have been arrested, Andy wouldn't have let Whit out of jail, and Whit wouldn't have visited Claire in her bedroom that night. If Andy hadn't felt so confused, he wouldn't have told Emmett about Whit and Claire in the first place. If he hadn't been so stupid as to think Emmett already knew, Andy wouldn't have confessed to letting Whit out of jail, enraging Emmett to the point that he wouldn't stop until Whit was dead.

Andy remembered Whit's hug of gratitude in the jailhouse door, and Jasper's smile at Black Canyon, finally ceding Andy recognition. Remembered Jasper's rifle salute from on top of the hill, and Whit saying he'd known Andy was one of them from the start, something Jasper had proved by pulling Andy out of the way when Whit shot Rufus Bond in Foxy's saloon. He remembered watching in anguish as Jasper was killed by the posse, and he thought of Whit being hung alone with only his enemies watching.

Andy looked up at the vigas crossing the ceiling. Jasper had cut those logs and laid them in place to support the roof. Lily, who loved Jasper, had given Andy a rope for Christmas. The last candle flickered out on the tree, so the room was lit only by a red glow from the coals in the hearth. Jasper had built that hearth to warm his family. He had died because he defended them. Whit had died alone, swinging in the cold with no one to catch him.

Andy chose the same chair he'd used to place the angel on the tree. He took the cake knife, climbed onto the chair, and methodically pierced through the latillas to the plaster until he'd dug a passage big enough to thread a rope over the top of the viga. When he returned the knife to the plate, he noticed that no one had covered the cake. It would be stale by morning, but he didn't guess anyone would feel like eating it anyway.

He uncoiled the rawhide lariat Lily had given him. Standing on the chair, he guided one end of the rope through the passage in the plaster, tied the rope to the viga, then fashioned a loop in the short end dangling free. He didn't know how to make a noose to break his neck when he fell, and he wondered if Whit had been hung with that mercy, or if he'd strangled with only a loop to slowly cut off his air. Andy slipped his loop around his neck, tightened the knot in back, then looked at the angel Claire had made. Their mother's ring was the halo above the angel's head. "Help me, Mama," Andy whispered, kicking the chair out from under his feet.

Kicking nothing, strangling as he twisted, the parlor flashing by first one way, then the other. He had to force his hands away from the viga to let himself hang without mercy. Pinning them between his thighs, he lurched hard and kicked the tree over so it fell to the floor. Good thing the candles are out, he thought, or I might burn to death. Then he smiled, feeling a rush of pleasure from where his hands pressed high between his thighs. Oh, he thought. Is this what sex feels like? This shot of pleasure up my loins? He laughed with the last of his breath. Yeah, Whit, he thought. Now I know. And I didn't even need Celia to teach me. Then he fell limp, his hands falling free, the blood vessels in his eyes exploding to blind him as he died.

21

$\mathcal{T}$he summer of 1879 was the driest anyone in Union County could remember. So little rain had fallen, the prairie grasses were as withered as if it were winter. Cattle grew gaunt, trekking half a day toward the mountains in search of forage, then the other half back toward the river for water. The Panal was diminished to a lazy curl through the center of its sandy bed, the rush of melting snow after the spring thaw a memory as if of a dream. Deep River was bone dry.

Drought had descended from day after day of bright sun. In

April, the mercury hit eighty and stayed there. By July, eighty felt cool. The thermometer at Bosque Grande read ninety-one the morning Lily and Claire drove out of the yard to visit Cassidy's Mill. Lily held the reins of a single bay mare hitched to a runabout with six jugs of water in the boot. Both women wore gauzy white dresses with the sleeves pushed up above their elbows, stockings rolled down below their knees, and the flimsiest of petticoats and shimmies. They carried smelling salts in their reticules against swooning, and wooden fans to cool their faces beneath the broad brims of their straw bonnets.

If Emmett had been home, he would have forbidden the trip since both women were seven months pregnant, but Emmett was in Vegas attending a meeting of the Southwest Cattlemen's Association. Though Lily thought the notion foolish that two big-bellied women could fall prey to the scalawags infesting the county, she conceded that accidents could happen and neither she nor Claire were agile enough to do much of anything but sit. So in deference to her husband's wishes that she not travel unprotected, she allowed Shiloh Pook to accompany them on the drive. He rode a dun horse beside the buggy, staying out of the dust stirred up by the wheels, and he wore a six-gun on his hip, carried a rifle in his saddle scabbard, and kept a vigilant gaze on the country they passed through.

It was midafternoon when they arrived at Cassidy's Mill. The cottonwoods along the dry riverbed drooped in a windless silence broken only by the buzzing of flies. In the corral, two scrawny horses endured the heat with their heads close to the ground. The broad canyon leading into the mountains, where Lily remembered her father's cattle grazing on lush grass, was now brown and empty. Shiloh swung down and was tying his horse to the hitching rail when Rosemary Cassidy edged out of the house carrying a rifle. She looked him over with a stern frown, then smiled as she saw the women in the buggy.

"Why, Lily! Bless your heart. And Claire! You both look 'bout ready to pop or faint, I don't know which. Come on in and get outta this heat. Not that it's much cooler in the house, but some."

Lily allowed Shiloh to hand her down from the buggy as her

mother leaned the rifle against the wall next to the door. Hurrying into Rosemary's arms, Lily inhaled her mother's familiar scent and blinked back tears. "It's been too long since I've seen you, Mama."

"Been a while," Rosemary answered, holding her daughter the full length of her arms and assessing not only Lily's advanced pregnancy but the cut of her frock and the expensive material it had been sewn from. Rosemary's approval was expressed in an admonition: "You ought not be traveling in this heat."

"I feel fine," Lily said, then turned to watch Shiloh handing Claire down.

"Afternoon, Mrs. Cassidy," Claire said, leaning on Shiloh's arm as they walked toward the porch. "My, it is hot, isn't it?"

"Come in, child," Rosemary urged. "You look right peaked."

"It's just the heat," Claire said, but she didn't let go of Shiloh's arm until she was sitting in a chair at the kitchen table.

Shiloh asked, "You mind if I water the horses, ma'am?"

"The trough's down by the mill," Rosemary answered. "We put in a well early this spring and it's a good thing we did, since the river's been gone a month now. The well water's low and none too palatable, but it's wet."

Shiloh chuckled. "It'll do, then." He tipped his hat at the women and walked out. After a minute they heard the buggy creaking away.

"Where's Theo?" Lily asked, holding her belly with both hands as she lowered herself into a chair.

"Down at the mill," Rosemary said. "Don't know what he's doing. We ain't got grain to grind and won't likely be getting much, as poor as the harvest is apt to be."

She lifted a jug out of a rope hammock hung near the door and unwrapped a damp cloth from around the jug. Leaving it on the table, she opened the cupboard for glasses, then filled them with lemonade. After she dunked the cloth in a pan of water on the counter, she rewrapped the jug and hung it in its hammock to catch any wind. From the pantry, she brought a tin of crackers, a white wedge of goat's cheese, and a jar of pickled hard-boiled eggs. "I'm ever so pleased y'all came to visit," she said, smiling as she set the food on the table.

They smiled back between sips of the sweetly tart lemonade, kept tepid by the wet cloth. Claire said, "This is the perfect drink in this heat. We go through a gallon a day at Bosque Grande, don't we, Lily?"

Lily nodded. "How you doing, Mama?"

Rosemary took a knife from a drawer and two plates from the cupboard and set them on the table. "If not for this drought, we'd be all right." She opened another drawer for napkins. "But the garden don't hardly amount to nothing. I let my flowers die, not wanting to waste water on mere beauty." She lay the yellow linen napkins beside the plates. "Jim Daniels is letting us charge staples at his store, so we got enough to eat, though the debt we're accumulating is worrisome." Finally she sat down. "I've considered selling the mill, but with no prospect of a decent harvest, I wouldn't get half what it's worth."

"The rains'll come back," Lily said, politely munching on a cracker. The cheese smelled slightly rancid. "I'll speak to Emmett about settling your account with Daniels so you won't be burdened with worry."

"Thank you, Lily. I didn't want to ask, a'course. Here, have one of these eggs. I pickled 'em just yesterday so they're fresh, but I'm afraid the cheese is past its prime."

Lily stabbed an egg out of the jar of purple vinegar and quartered the egg on her plate, then used the knife to lift a piece to her mouth. As the flavor exploded on her tongue, she winced and reached for another cracker. Observing her reaction, Claire took only a cracker.

Theo came in dragging his bum leg, a smile on his sunburned face. "Hey, Lily," he said with a grin. He gave her a quick hug, then retreated a short distance away. "Good to see you, Mrs. Daggerty."

"Thank you," Claire murmured. With a self-conscious giggle, she added, "I can't get used to being called that."

Everyone laughed as if she'd told a joke.

"You'll be staying the night," Rosemary said, half as a question.

"Reckon not," Lily said. "With Emmett gone, I don't like leaving the ranch untended."

"Ain't his brother there?" Rosemary asked.

A shroud of silence descended on the table until Claire said, "My father hasn't been well since Christmas."

Rosemary nodded. "Takes the starch out of anybody to lose a child. It's hard enough when they're babies, but when they're grown you start to figure the danger's past. Never is, a'course. I saw Mr. and Mrs. Stone in town t'other day. I don't believe they're ever gonna get over losing Jasper."

Struggling to subdue the sorrow his name evoked, Lily asked, "Did they mention Elise?"

"Said she was ailing," Rosemary answered. "Has been since their misfortune. Ain't it a pity? Mr. and Mrs. Stone brought nine children into the world and it don't seem they're gonna get to keep even one."

"I hear Mrs. Reed's expecting again," Lily said, trying to lighten the conversation.

Rosemary smiled. "We'll have three white babies in the county 'fore the new year. They'll help balance our losses some. Course the Mexicans keep popping 'em out like clockwork, and I hear the Mescaleros are on the increase, too. Least ways, Jim Daniels is claiming he feeds more on his gov'ment contract every year. He seems to be the only man in the county making any kinda financial killing." She stopped, appalled by her inadvertent choice of words.

"They're calling what happened a war," Theo said. He'd sat down and tilted his chair against the wall so his feet dangled in the air. "The county lost twenty-five men in seventy-eight, starting with the ambush of Angus Bodie back in February and ending when Whit Cantrell was s'posedly hung."

Seeing Claire bite her lip, Lily asked, "Can we have some more lemonade, Mama?"

"Surely," she said, rising to take the jug down again.

"I say s'posedly," Theo continued, ignorant of the romance that had precipitated Claire's marriage, " 'cause a fellow come through last week said he saw Whit in El Paso over the Fourth of July."

Claire stared at him, her cheeks suddenly drained of color.

"Who was it?" Lily asked sharply.

"Al Decker," Theo said, pleased with their intense interest. "You remember him, Lily? He worked at the mill the year 'fore Father died."

She nodded, then said, "Thank you, Mama." Lifting the fresh glass of lemonade, she sipped a moment before asking, "Did Mr. Decker speak to the man he thought was Whit?"

"Said he never got the chance," Theo answered. "Whit saw him and skedaddled across the Rio Grande into Mexico. Ain't that something?"

"Yes," Lily murmured. "Drink your lemonade, Claire. You need to replenish the liquids in your body."

Claire obediently lifted her glass and took a sip.

Theo said, "Al hadn't heard about Father being gone. He come looking for work. He'd heard about the war, though, and I run it down for him. How Henry Hart put Browne Carson and Johnny Riles up to killing Angus Bodie so he could get his hands on Bodie's ranch. Whit Cantrell killed Browne Carson for killing Bodie, and Bodie's ramrod, George Healy, killed Johnny Riles. William Wilson killed Father and was hung for it, then Rufus Bond killed George Healy. Whit Cantrell killed Rufus, but that came later, after Frank Cummings killed Ben Johnson. Cummings was killed by Tom Moore, Mark Peck, and Gil Lee. Whit killed Tom for his part in killing Cummings 'cause Frank had once worked for Bodie. Ned Harper killed Mark Peck, and Hank East killed Gil Lee. One of Hart's gunmen, name of Silvester, was killed by Bud Lloyd, and Whit killed another name of Cole Hardy. It was after that Whit killed Rufus Bond in Soledad. A short while later, Sammie Stone was killed, though just a child, and Jasper killed Ernie Kessel, Buck Robbins, and Jack Elkins 'cause of it, then Jasper and Whit s'posedly killed Henry Hart though there wasn't no witnesses and still ain't no proof. Jasper was killed by the posse that arrested Whit, but Whit escaped. Then Jim Daniels imported a pack of gunmen from El Paso. They killed Pat Emory, Bud Lloyd, Art White, and Joe Cales, all farmers in the valley who refused to feed into his machine, then rode into town and killed Edgar Homer, shot into his home and killed him while he was eating Sunday supper. In the meantime, Whit was tracked down and s'posedly hung." Theo smiled, proud of remembering all the names in the right order. "Now Al Decker comes along and says Whit's still alive. Ain't that something?"

The women sat in an ominous silence until Lily said, "We gotta be getting back, Mama."

"But you barely arrived," Rosemary said with astonishment. "It's a long drive from Bosque Grande just to spend half an hour here."

"A long drive home, too," Lily said. "I wanted to ask if you'd be there to hold my hand when my time comes." She smiled. "I've never done this before, you know, and I'm feeling a mite nervous."

Rosemary laughed softly. "Course I'll come, and pleased you asked. But there ain't nothing to it, Lily. Your body does what it wants and there's no stopping it."

"From my reckoning," Lily said, "I'm due toward the middle of September, and near as we can figure, Claire's due two weeks later. Can you be at Bosque Grande on the fifteenth and stay through both birthings?"

"I'll be there on the first," Rosemary said, "just in case your reckoning's long."

"Thank you," Lily said, standing up. "You ready, Claire?"

Claire stood up, too. "Thank you kindly for the lemonade, Mrs. Cassidy." She gave Theo a wan smile. "And for the pleasure of your company, Theo."

He blushed. "The pleasure was mine, Mrs. Daggerty."

Shiloh looked surprised to see them come out of the house so soon. But whatever he thought of the brevity of their visit, he expressed no opinion as he handed Claire into the buggy. When he helped Lily in, she murmured, "You're good at keeping quiet, ain't you, Shiloh?"

His blue eyes flashed up at her, wary and puzzled.

"Ain't you coming?" she asked as she lifted the reins.

"Yes, ma'am," he said, turning away to mount his horse.

Lily and Claire smiled and waved to Rosemary and Theo on

the porch as Lily slapped the reins and the buggy rolled out of the yard. As soon as they'd turned onto the road following the dry river toward the Panal, Claire whispered, "Do you think it's true, Lily?"

"Don't go getting your hopes up, Claire. A rumor ain't nothing to pin your heart to."

"I feel as if a stone has been rolled off my chest," Claire said. "If it weren't true, I don't believe I'd feel this way."

Lily didn't answer, thinking her stone would never move again.

After a while, Claire said, "Oh, Lily, Whit's alive! I can feel it."

"How come you didn't feel it yesterday?"

"Why, I guess I couldn't let myself. I mean, knowing Whit's alive, I can't ever allow Bob to touch me again."

"He's your husband, Claire. He has rights."

"I only married him because Father convinced me a child born out of wedlock has no chance of happiness. Oh, Lily, do you think Whit knows I'm carrying his child? If he heard I married Bob Daggerty, don't you think he'd guess the reason?"

Lily sighed. "You're forgetting Emmett came home with Whit's black mare that night. You think Whit lost her in a place Emmett just happened to find?"

"Whit could have let her loose. Maybe he didn't want a horse wearing Uncle Emmett's brand."

"Emmett had the bill of sale. He showed it to me, then threw it in the fire. How could he have had it if he didn't take it outta Whit's pocket?"

The confidence in her voice diminished, Claire said, "Maybe Whit left it with the horse."

Lily snorted in disbelief. "Do I have to tell you, Claire, not to mention this to anyone at Bosque Grande?"

"No, I won't," Claire promised, then added sadly, "though I wish I could tell Andy."

Lily slapped the reins to pick up the pace, hoping Claire wouldn't remember that Shiloh Pook had been with Emmett on that trip. Apparently Claire didn't remember, or if she did, the notion of questioning Shiloh didn't cross her mind because she wouldn't have waited if it had. It crossed Lily's, and she intended to get the truth out of Shiloh just as soon as they got home.

When they arrived long after dark, Claire was asleep on Lily's shoulder. Reining to a stop in front of the house, Lily asked Shiloh to carry Mrs. Daggerty inside. Claire didn't awake when Shiloh lifted her out of the buggy, and she was still deeply asleep when he laid her in bed. He stayed a moment longer than was proper, watching Lily cover her with a light blanket.

"She's the prettiest woman I've ever seen," Shiloh murmured as if to himself.

Lily looked at him sharply, knowing no man would ever say that of her. "Come into the kitchen, Shiloh," she said. "I wanta talk to you."

He preceded her out of Claire's bedroom, then followed her through the dark hall and stood in the kitchen doorway while she lit a lamp. Lily busied herself putting together a pot of coffee as she tried to formulate the best approach. "Sit down, Shiloh," she said over her shoulder as she took cups from the cupboard.

"I oughta put the horses up," he answered, obviously uncomfortable.

"They'll wait," Lily said. "What I want to know won't."

He took his hat off and dropped it on the table, then sat down, looking unhappy.

Lily stood by the stove, waiting for the coffee. When it boiled, she took the pot off the fire and set it aside to let the grounds settle. Finally she carried the pot to the table and filled their cups, the coffee's rich fragrance strong. After returning the pot to the stove, she sat down facing him and poured a generous amount of cream into her cup.

Shiloh lifted his and blew on the coffee to cool it, took a couple of sips, then set the cup back in its saucer, keeping his eyes to himself. His face was rugged, with a long narrow nose, thin lips above a lantern jaw, and cheeks stubbled with blond whiskers. His sandy brown hair was curly and perpetually in need of a trim, though looking at him as closely as she did now, Lily guessed he'd almost have to shave his head to give the curls any semblance of order.

"When we were at my mother's today," Lily began, watching his sky-blue eyes meet hers, "Theo said a man name of Al Decker came by the mill last week."

"I remember Al," Shiloh said. "He left for El Paso when the trouble in the mountains was just getting started."

"Yes," Lily agreed. "He told Theo he saw Whit Cantrell there."

"When?" Shiloh asked.

"Long after Whit was s'posed to be dead," she answered.

Shiloh looked down to sip his coffee.

"When Emmett came home last Christmas," Lily said, striving to keep her voice light and undemanding, "he told me you were with him when he hung Whit."

"Yes, ma'am," Shiloh said, setting his cup down and cautiously meeting her eyes. "After the sheriff turned back at the border, me and Emmett went on alone."

"Did you help hang Whit?"

"Now, Miz Moss," Shiloh said sternly, "you're asking me to admit I did something that's against the law."

"I won't repeat what you tell me, not even to my husband. I swear it."

Shiloh turned his cup in its saucer, watching the coffee inside.

"I know I'm asking you to disobey your boss, Shiloh. I've no doubt he told you never to discuss the very thing I'm asking about. To prove my good faith, I'll tell you something he told me never to tell." Lily hesitated, then said, "Claire's carrying Whit's child."

Shiloh's eyes flashed with surprise. "That's why she married Bob Daggerty in such a rush."

Lily nodded.

"I never could figure her choosing that perfumed milksop when she was surrounded by men craving any chance to please her."

"Her father and uncle chose Daggerty," Lily said. She took a deep breath. "Is Whit still alive?"

Shiloh looked around as if someone might be eavesdropping

in a corner of the room, then said, "He was the last time I saw him."

"So Emmett didn't hang him?"

Shiloh shook his head. "He let him go."

"Let him go?" Lily whispered.

"Yes, ma'am."

Lily felt a surge of anger for the damage Emmett's lie had done his family. To shield Shiloh from that, she stood up and brought the pot over to refill his cup. Sitting down again, she tried to calm her heart.

Shiloh lifted his cup and took a long drink, then set the cup in its saucer and asked, "You wanta hear the whole story, Miz Moss, or just the end of it?"

"The whole story," she said.

He nodded. "We caught up with Whit in Casas Grandes. Saw his horse stabled out back of a sporting house, so it wasn't hard to figure where he was. Emmett paid the barkeep to tell us which room Whit was in. The keep didn't want to do it, but Emmett's got a convincing way about him. He said he was Whit's daddy come to take him home, and the keep believed Emmett or his money won. When we went up to the room, a girl was just coming out with a tray of dirty dishes. We let her pass by and walked in on Whit pouring water into the basin to wash. His gun was on the bed, so we had him cold."

Shiloh sipped his coffee, then suddenly smiled. "When Whit saw us walk in, he laughed and said he'd offer us some supper but it just left. Then he went on with his washing like we wasn't there. He put his shirt back on and tucked in the tails, then looked at his gun on the bed. Emmett told him not to try for it, and Whit said he had no such thought in mind. Emmett asked what he did have in mind, and Whit said he'd been hoping to get some sleep, that he hadn't had much the last coupla nights. The bed was still made, so he must not've been there longer'n it took to eat supper. He kept looking at that bed while we talked. Course his gun was on it, and that might've been what he was looking at, but he seemed wore out to me, though he tried not to show it, making jokes and laughing and teasing Emmett about being so far from his bride."

Shiloh smiled at Lily, then sipped his coffee. "Whit said if he was married to either one of the women at Bosque Grande, he'd never stray far from home. 'That ain't gonna happen,' " Emmett said, and Whit said he knew it wouldn't." Shiloh chuckled. "Reckon I should've put it together about him and Claire then, but at that particular moment I was mostly concerned with the distance between Whit and his gun. Emmett was leaning against the closed door with his hands in his pockets like we was having a peaceable conversation, and Whit was acting that way, too. Me with my gun in my hand put a lie to that notion, but I wasn't about to put my gun away without Emmett telling me to. Whit's slick, you know. And despite the friendly tone in the room, I figured he knew we hadn't tracked him all that way to chat."

Shiloh sighed and leaned back in his chair. "Emmett asked Whit what his intentions were in regard to coming home. Whit said he'd gotten used to breathing, and from all the evidence there was plenty of good air in Mexico, so he didn't need none of what we have up here. Emmett told Whit if he'd promise to stay outta the territory, he'd let him be. Whit said he liked Mexico and had no intention to leave. 'Will you give me your word?' Emmett asked. Whit gave his solemn promise that Emmett would never see him again, and Emmett said, 'That's fine, but I'm gonna spread the story that you're dead so nobody'll pine for your return.' Whit said he'd just as soon it happen that way. Maybe I ain't remembering their exact words, Miz Moss, but that's the gist of what they said."

Lily nodded, her anger somewhat relieved by Emmett's mercy. "Tell me about the black mare," she petitioned.

Shiloh leaned forward again to finish his coffee, then carefully replaced the cup in its saucer. "Emmett said he'd take the mare back as proof Whit was dead. When Whit argued the horse was all he had to his name, Emmett emptied his pockets onto the bed and came up with 'bout three hundred dollars. He asked Whit if that was enough to get himself situated. Whit said he reckoned it was. "You wanta hand over that bill of sale, then?" Emmett asked. When Whit did, Emmett said, 'I'm giving you your life, Whit.' Whit said he appreciated it. Then we all just stood there staring at each other for the longest time. Finally Emmett said he was trusting Whit not to shoot us in the back. Whit said he had no such intention. So me and Emmett walked out, took the mare from the stable, and started home."

Shiloh turned his empty cup around in its saucer, then turned it back the way it had been, watching it as he said, "After we'd ridden a ways, Emmett asked if I thought he'd done the right thing." Shiloh met Lily's eyes. "That knocked me for a loop, Miz Moss, 'cause your husband ain't a man to seek advice. I told him I thought he had. Then he asked for my promise that I'd go along with whatever story he cooked up about how Whit died. I said I would, but I didn't expect him to say we hung Whit. Letting folks believe that's what happened made me guilty in their eyes of something I hope I never do, but I gave my word not to contradict his story, and I've kept that promise. Till now."

Lily gathered her wits, then said, "I appreciate your telling me, Shiloh. You've given me the gift of knowing my husband ain't as cruel as he'd have me believe."

Shiloh nodded. "You've given me something, too, Miz Moss. All I just said has been a burden to carry. Sorry if I took too many words to get it out, but my need to tell someone has been welling up inside me for a long time."

"I can understand how it would," Lily murmured.

"A lotta folks in the county were fond of Whit. After he was gone, they built him up in their minds to be more'n he was. In a way it's kinda funny."

"Funny?" Lily whispered.

"If not for Emmett, the posse would've killed Whit same as Jasper. Whit'd be dead and buried, prob'ly right next to Jasper, considering how the Stones felt about him. The general opinion held of Jasper, though, is that he cut his own life short by being too quick on the trigger. If Whit had died with him, folks would've shrugged it off as the consequence of bad company. But being taken from jail and lynched without no chance to defend himself was a situation that generated more sympathy, and Whit escaping that seemed like some kinda minor miracle. Now the word that Whit's still alive is gonna spread like wildfire, and he's gonna be resurrected into even more of a hero than when folks thought him dead. The funny part is that Emmett just wanted Whit gone, but everything he did to make that happen built Whit's legend into something so big being Cattle King of the Panal pales beside it. Don't you think that's kinda funny, Miz Moss?"

Meeting Shiloh's eyes with a new appreciation of the mind behind them, she nodded, then asked, "What did Emmett promise you for sharing the burden of creating a hero who outshadowed him?"

Shiloh shrugged. "That he'd keep me on the payroll after I'm too old to do much work."

Lily smiled. "I wonder what Beau Cairn did to earn that."

Shiloh laughed. "I know, but reckon I've said enough for one night."

Lily laughed, too. "Since I'm likely to outlive Emmett, I want you to know I'll honor his promise after he's gone." She extended her hand across the table. "I give you my word, Mr. Pook."

Shiloh looked at her hand, then clasped it in his. He didn't shake with her as he would a man, but simply held her hand in his big, rough one a moment, then let go and stood up.

"Reckon I'll see to the horses now. Thanks for the coffee."

"You're welcome," she murmured.

He picked up his hat. "There is one more thing I'd like to say, Miz Moss."

She waited.

"Emmett couldn't have chosen a more worthy woman to be his wife."

Touched beyond measure by his compliment, Lily felt tears in her eyes. "Thank you, Shiloh," she whispered.

"Yes, ma'am," he said, then he walked out the door.

Lily stayed at the table, letting all she'd learned settle into her mind. Emmett had concocted a lie to protect his family. Andy died because he believed it. Claire had survived for the same reason, but now that she suspected the truth, she'd spurn her husband and pine for the man she loved. As the news that Whit was still alive spread through the county, Emmett would be doubted everywhere he went. All Whit had to do was show up and Emmett would lose credibility forever. That fact allowed Lily to feel compassion for her husband. A feeling akin to love—pity and desire for his well-being despite his faults. He had dealt mercy, then lied to protect his family, but failed himself on both counts. Because Lily figured the only man more potent than a dead hero was one who had been resurrected.

Though she had given her word not to share what Shiloh had told her, she knew it wasn't Emmett from whom she had to hide her knowledge, it was Claire. Lily rose from the table and walked through the hall to lie in the bed of her marriage, knowing she was finally Emmett's partner.

22

*L*ily's son was born on the seventh of September. When her water broke, she was standing in the kitchen setting the kettle on the fire for tea. For a moment she stared at the pool on the floor, then looked at her mother with dismay.

"It's time," Rosemary announced, hustling her daughter to bed.

Lily's labor lasted four hours, though she'd scarcely call it work. The worst was the feeling that her bowels were moving, but when she repeatedly said she needed to visit the outhouse, her mother simply laughed and told her to stay in bed. Rosemary's prediction came true and Lily's body did what it wanted. When she first saw the tiny, blood-streaked baby in her mother's hands, Lily wept with joy. As soon as the child had been cleaned and the bedsheets changed, Emmett came in to meet his son.

"Why, ain't he a grand one, Lily!" Emmett said, beaming at his wife holding the infant to her breast. "Looks like he's got an appetite that'll put his daddy to shame."

Lily laughed. "Emmett Moss! You never touched me there while taking your pleasure."

"It wasn't 'cause I didn't want to," he answered, "but 'cause I was saving 'em for him. Ain't he fine, Lily?"

"Yes," she said, her eyes drowsing closed. "So are you, Emmett."

"You mean you've come around to liking your husband?" he teased.

"I've always loved you," she murmured. "Ever since I was a child myself."

"I know that. But seems you forgot it there for a while."

"I won't ever again," she promised.

" 'Attagirl," he said with a chuckle. "What'll we name him?"

"Emmett Moss, Junior, of course. Had you considered anything else?"

"No. I'm glad we're finally in agreement. I'll leave you now to sleep. I gotta go over the accounts with Bob, but I'll be back soon to admire the two of you again."

She smiled, watching him leave, then she slept. In the following days, she felt full to bursting with love for her son. She had never suspected she could love anyone as much. The hurt of Jasper was gone in her joy, and her love for her baby encompassed her husband. Right now she felt no hunger that her child didn't fill. Her small breasts had become fountains of milk he guzzled yet never drained dry. Even changing his diapers was fun, his tiny sex something to tickle while she had the chance. She laughed when he laughed and fretted when he cried, often walking the hall in the middle of the night to quiet him so the family could sleep.

Rosemary shared her vast knowledge of babies and took pride in her first grandchild. Those days at Bosque Grande were blessed with a bounty of love that infected Claire with a happy anticipation. Her delivery, however, was not as felicitous as Lily's had been.

For a full day and night Claire labored, drenching the sheets of her bed with sweat and shattering the peace with her screams. On the second day, not only her husband but even her father left the house, though Drew hadn't done that for months. Lily hadn't time to worry about where he went or what he was doing. Between caring for Junior, sitting with Claire, and grabbing a few hours' sleep when they could, both Lily and Rosemary had their hands full.

They sent Shiloh Pook to Rocky Arroyo for Mrs. Stone, the only midwife on the Panal, but he came back and reported that Elise was ill and Mrs. Stone wouldn't leave her. Receiving the message, Lily met Shiloh's eyes for a long moment, both of them thinking Jasper's mother might be justified in not wishing to bring another Moss into the world. Lily thanked Shiloh and returned to sit with Claire. As the hours passed filled with screams, Lily felt so cranky with exhaustion that she thought even Jasper would take pity on the suffering of this Moss. After she'd had a chance to catch a nap, however, she felt more sympathetic toward Mrs. Stone, and she allowed worry for Elise to occupy the small corner of her mind not filled with concern for Claire.

Thirty-six hours after her labor began, Claire started to hallucinate. She clamped Lily's hands with a frenzied grip and begged to see her mother. Lily couldn't convince Claire that her mother was unable to come because she was dead. A few hours later, Claire began talking to Laura Moss as if she were there. Claire even laughed with the girlish giggle of a child as she confessed to her mother that she had been naughty. The best Lily could take from the situation was that Claire had found a few moment's relief from her pain. Too soon it returned, and her next hallucination was witnessed by her husband.

Bob Daggerty was standing in the doorway, appalled at his wife's suffering, when suddenly Claire stared at the window. "Whit?" she called, her voice resonant with love. "I knew you'd come to be with me now. Oh, Whit, it hurts so much! Won't you hold me?" Then she smiled and lifted her arms to receive his comforting hug. Lily looked at Bob and whispered, "Go to her. Be who she needs."

Bob shook his head, the horror in his eyes replaced by anger. "I'd rather she die," he said, then walked out and slammed the door.

Lily hurried to Claire's side, filling the desperate arms with her own body. "Whit's alive," she whispered close to Claire's ear. Brushing the wet hair away from the beautiful face ravaged by suffering, Lily said, "He'll come back someday, Claire, but not now. Now you have to bring his child into the world by yourself."

Out of her delirium, Claire met Lily's eyes with sudden lucidity. "Whit's alive?" she whimpered.

"Yes," Lily said.

Claire fell back against the pillows, then writhed as renewed spasms racked her body. "Why is it so hard, Lily?" she begged to know. "Am I being punished for loving him?"

"No," Lily murmured, reaching into a bowl of water on the night table for a cloth and wringing it out. "I don't believe God punishes us for loving anyone."

"Is my baby dead?" Claire asked.

"No," Lily answered, wiping Claire's face. "We can feel it moving, trying to be born. You must help, Claire. Push down with all your might."

"I am!" she wailed. "But I'm afraid I don't have any might left, Lily."

"You must! Push with the power of your love for Whit."

"Yes," Claire whispered. "Where is he, Lily?"

"In Mexico," she said softly.

"Why isn't he here?"

"He wanted to stay alive so he could love you someday."

"Me and my baby?" Claire whimpered pathetically.

"Yes," Lily said. "Bring his baby into the world, Claire, so you'll both be here when he comes back for you."

"I'm trying!" Claire sobbed. "But it hurts so much, and I'm so tired."

"Yes," Lily murmured, again dunking the hot cloth into the cooling water.

Emmett opened the door. He frowned, then met Lily's eyes and said, "She won't make it if we don't intervene."

"What can we do?" Lily asked in bewilderment.

"Tie her hands to the headboard," Emmett said, crossing the room to the washstand. As he poured water from the pitcher into the basin, he looked into the mirror and saw Lily hadn't moved. "Tie her tight," he said, his voice as stern as his face.

Remembering the time he'd tied Claire to her bed, Lily did as

he had, using sashes off two of Claire's wrappers to secure her
wrists to the brass headboard. Emmett dried his hands on a towel
he dropped on the floor as he approached.

"I've done this with cows," he said. "Let's hope it works with
people." He knelt with his back pressed against the center of the
footboard and spread Claire's legs wide on the sheet sopped with
blood. "Hold her down," he muttered, pinning her legs beneath
his knees.

Claire thrashed while Lily pressed her own body on top of the
tortured one. In horrid amazement, she watched Emmett's hand
disappear inside Claire. Rosemary entered the room and closed
the door, then stood arrested by what Emmett was doing. Slowly
his hand reappeared, his fingers gripping the blue feet of a baby.
With a sucking sound barely audible under Claire's screams, the
boy's body emerged, then his face covered with blood.

"Quick, cut the cord," Emmett grunted.

Rosemary hurried to do it. Lily grabbed fresh towels off the
stack on a nearby chair and pressed them close against the torrent of blood between Claire's legs.

"Let it flow!" Emmett said.

"You'll poison her if you trap it inside," Rosemary agreed. "It's
the afterbirth, and it's gotta come out."

Holding the baby by his feet, Emmett smacked him hard on
the butt until the boy wailed with affront.

Lily gasped. "He's alive, Claire! Can you hear him cry?"

But Claire lay still and finally silent. Lily leaned close and
pressed her ear against Claire's breasts until she heard a heartbeat. Trembling, she looked up at Emmett with his bloody hands,
then at Rosemary washing the baby in the basin. "She's asleep,"
Lily whispered, as if she might wake Claire if she spoke too
loudly.

Emmett nodded. "Clean her up but don't stop the flow. Now
that the baby's out, her body'll start repairing itself better'n anything we can do."

Overwhelmed with gratitude and stunned with the wonder of
what he'd achieved, Lily whispered in awe, "You saved Whit's
baby, Emmett."

He growled in disgust, banged open the door, and stomped out, leaving a bloody handprint on the wall as he passed.

Rosemary had the child wrapped in a blanket now. She came close and showed him to Lily. "He'll be a pretty thing when he gets his color," Rosemary said.

Lily looked down at the puckered blue face, the tiny toothless mouth howling with hunger. Cradling him in her arms, she sat down in the window, opened her frock, and gave him her breast. The baby sucked hard, and Lily smiled, thinking he was a little Whit, all right, taking what wasn't his as if it were.

A month later, Claire was still in bed, and both babies had colic. Lily was at her wit's end trying to quiet and feed the two tiny boys while Claire slept in the bliss of dreams. Rosemary had gone home as soon as they knew Claire would recover. Bob Daggerty hadn't once looked at her child, and Emmett stayed out of range of the crying infants as much as he could, so Lily was alone.

Drew was no help. Though he often sat with Claire and helped her pass the few hours each day she was awake, the rest of the time he wandered the house asking if anyone had seen Laura. Emmett had quit answering his brother, Cipriano shook his head and mumbled that he didn't speak English, and Bob stared with pity. Eventually even Lily gave up trying to make Drew understand that his wife had been dead for three years.

Claire named her son Amiel after her maternal grandfather. When Lily found Bob in the parlor to tell him, he merely shrugged, then went back to reading the newspapers that had arrived with the mail from River's End. Lily disliked him even more than before. Though Bob had showered Claire with attention in the days preceding their wedding, soon after the ceremony he seemed to lose interest in his wife. Lily blamed it on Claire's pregnancy, thinking once the child was born Bob would renew his chivalrous attentions. The opposite happened, and Lily didn't credit it entirely to his having witnessed Claire's hallucination of Whit.

Bob had known all along who fathered Claire's child. Remembering how he'd fawned over Claire when she first arrived at Bosque Grande, Lily had expected him to work hard to gain Claire's affection. Instead he ignored both her and the child to such a degree that Lily suspected Bob had married Claire for the generous dowry her uncle had given her.

Emmett had also relegated his bookkeeping to Daggerty. Bob was an educated man, and his work for the Territorial Life Insurance Company had given him a thorough knowledge of the laws peculiar to the territory. By investing Claire's dowry in the company, he became a principal stockholder, which meant he often traveled to the district office in Vegas. He advised Emmett on investments and managed the cash flow between the ranch and Emmett's several bank accounts. Bob's access to the bank accounts worried Lily. She intended to speak to Emmett about it, when she had a chance to catch her breath.

Since Claire failed to produce more than a smidgeon of milk, Lily tried to keep up with the demand of both boys. They drained her dry before her body had time to replenish itself, so she began to supplement her supply with cow's milk. When the colic developed, she switched to goat's milk, but the change didn't help. Both boys regurgitated any milk but Lily's. If she favored Junior, she felt panged with pity, listening to Amiel cry from hunger. Her breasts were sore from their greedy mouths, and she dragged herself through her days feeling numb after nights spent walking first one baby then the other, soothing Junior to sleep while Amiel cried, then laying Junior down and picking up Amiel, nursing and cuddling him as she walked to and fro in the hall. By the time Amiel was asleep, Junior was awake and crying again.

Claire's ability to sleep through the crying amazed Lily. But Claire was still weak from the immense amount of blood she'd lost, so Lily forgave her. When she asked Emmett if she could hire a Mexican woman to help, Emmett replied gruffly that two babies shouldn't be more than one woman could handle, adding that Claire would soon be on her feet. Lily forgave him, too, knowing he was pressed by business commitments.

Fall roundup was in progress, and the drought had diminished

Emmett's herds to the point that he was scrambling to fill his contracts without selling his breeding stock. It was the same all over the Southwest. Cattle prices were so high, Bob Daggerty was predicting a drastic decline in another few years. Lily pushed that worry, too, from her mind, telling herself Emmett's assets were ample enough to see them through any decline in the market. All she wanted was for Claire to get well and start caring for Amiel. If that would happen, Lily could enjoy Junior without feeling so tired she could barely stay awake even in daylight.

The colic seemed to be worsening. She started rubbing a drop of laudanum on her nipples so the boys would sleep an extra hour or two. But she couldn't feed them at the same time, so couldn't administer the laudanum simultaneously, and its effect never lasted long enough for her to rest. She didn't dare give them more than a drop. Often the house was empty as she wandered from room to room with a crying child on her shoulder, the men either out on the range or staying in the bunkhouse so they could get some sleep. Lily was worn to the bone. If she chanced to catch her reflection in a mirror as she ambled by, she thought she looked like a ghost.

Though she longed for company, no one came to visit. One night as she wandered the house, it occurred to her that if a wayfarer did come to her door seeking shelter, he'd probably run in fright from the visage of a skeleton carrying a shrieking child. This thought struck her so funny, she laughed until she had to sit down. Rocking in the parlor while she erupted with hysterical amusement that competed with the baby's wails, she happened to glance up and see the repaired hole in the plaster above the viga Andy had hung himself from, and her laughter turned to grief. She smothered her face in the belly of the baby and moaned with sorrow. Then she sat up and tried to see through her tears whether she was holding Junior or Amiel. Having given up on trying to keep their clothes separate, she couldn't tell.

She blinked to clear her vision and saw the boy's hair was a shade more golden than Junior's, which meant it was Amiel in her lap. Suddenly quiet, he smiled at her. She smiled back, then whispered, "Your daddy would be proud if he could see you. So

would your Uncle Andy. If either one of 'em was here now, I
wouldn't be so alone. They were both men not too arrogant to
help a woman when she was off her oats. Your daddy helped me
care for my family when they was all down with the pox. And
your Uncle Andy could make such funny faces he'd get a person
laughing when they felt like crying. You'll never get to know him,
but maybe someday you'll get to meet your daddy."

Amiel yawned and fell asleep. Lily sat up straight, listening
hard as she tried to figure out what was different. Then she realized the house was quiet. She sat a long time, savoring the silence, afraid to move less Amiel wake up and start crying again.
When she finally decided he wouldn't for a while, she carefully
carried him down the hall to Claire's room. She was asleep. Lily
fought a jealous anger as she crossed to the cradle, then she saw
Junior sleeping there. The colic had passed in both boys at once,
as it had come. She smiled at her son, looking so peaceful in the
moonlight coming through the window. Quietly she tiptoed out
of Claire's room and into her own, where she laid Amiel in Junior's cradle. Feeling she'd found a moment of heaven, she lay
down fully dressed on top of her bed and fell deeply asleep.

In the gray light of dawn, she awoke to the sound of Drew
mumbling his crazy talk as he sat on the edge of her bed. Lily
rolled onto her back and stared at the ceiling, listening beyond
his voice to the quiet of the house. The colic had truly passed.
Neither of the babies was crying. She turned her head to look at
Drew and saw tears streaming down his cheeks. Impatiently she
sat up and asked, "What is it, Drew?"

"They killed him," he mumbled.

"Who?" she asked with a sigh, standing up and realizing she
felt stronger than she had in weeks. She walked across to the cradle and saw Amiel smiling up at her. Holding a hand down so he
could grasp one of her fingers, she faced Drew still on the bed.
"Why don't you get dressed?" she suggested kindly. "You'll feel
better after a bath and a shave."

"You're not listening," he whispered hoarsely. "They killed
him last night."

"Who killed who?" she asked, striving for patience.

He worked his mouth a moment, then licked his lips and said, "Your husband and my brother."

"They're the same person, Drew," she said. "It takes two people to make a they."

"Daggerty makes two!"

"Yes, Bob and Emmett make two," she agreed. "Are they here?"

"Not now. But they were last night."

"I didn't see 'em," she said, then added, "or you either. It must've been late."

He nodded, fresh tears rolling across his cheeks.

"What're you crying about, Drew?" she asked wearily. "Ain't there been enough tears in this house?"

"Too many," he answered. "But there's more to come."

"What're you talking about?" she asked softly, feeling Amiel's fingers hold tight to hers.

"I've been afflicted with headaches for years," he said. "Andy had 'em, too, did you know that?"

"Yes. Do you have one now?"

"No. But I did last night." He looked puzzled. "Reckon the shock drove it outta my mind. Ain't that something, Lily?"

"What shock?" she asked.

"I came up here for some laudanum. The bunkhouse is too quiet now that roundup's over." His face brightened. "I liked it when it was full of cowboys. They're so young, you know, with lots of vim and vinegar." He looked somber again. "Reckon it was the quiet let my headache take over. So I come up here for some laudanum. I don't like using opium, but my head was hurting something awful."

"It's all right if you don't take it too often," she said.

More tears rolled down his cheeks and his voice broke when he said, "I shouldn't have done it, Lily. Claire loved Whit. I shouldn't have made her marry Daggerty."

"Is that why you're crying?" she asked gently.

He shook his head. "I saw 'em go into her room, Emmett and that man I made Claire marry. I hid in the hall 'cause I had the bottle of laudanum in my hand. Emmett don't hold with opium. You know that, don't you, Lily?"

She sighed. "If Emmett had to take care of two crying babies like I've been doing these last weeks, he'd probably give 'em a lot more'n I did."

"You're not listening!" Drew accused. "I was ashamed, so I hid, don't you understand what I'm saying, Lily?"

"No, I don't, Drew."

"They planned it together, had to, 'cause I watched and they did it both at the same time."

"Did what?" she asked, shaking her hand and smiling at Amiel as he laughed and clung to her fingers.

"I seen 'em," Drew whispered. "Emmett and Daggerty went into Claire's room and smothered Amiel in his cradle."

Lily stared at Drew.

He nodded, tears dripping off his chin. "Both of 'em, Lily. Took hold of opposite sides of the pillow and pressed it down on the baby's face." He sobbed. "I kept quiet. Like when Andy died and I didn't say nothing 'cause Emmett's my brother and I owe him so much. But not my son, Lily. And now he's taken my grandson, too. I should've risen up like an avenging angel and struck 'em down when they came out of Claire's room. But I hid in the shadows 'cause I was ashamed of needing opium."

Lily shook her head. "What you're saying can't be right, Drew."

"I saw 'em! And I heard 'em, too! When they came out and closed the door, I heard Daggerty say, 'Now there's no remnant of Whit left in this house.' And Emmett, my brother and your husband, he answered, 'And no reason for him to come back.' "

Lily shook her head. "You're wrong, Drew."

"I was just in there. Amiel's dead!"

Lily tried to free her hand but Amiel wouldn't let loose.

"Come see for yourself," Drew said, standing up.

Lily didn't have to see. Claire's scream pierced the quiet with a wail of lament such as could only come from a mother discovering her child dead. Lily felt helpless, knowing it was Junior who was dead and she should be the one screaming. She wanted to right this wrong, but Amiel held her in place with his grasp on her finger.

"My baby," Drew whimpered, then hurried out the door to comfort Claire, his only baby left.

Claire's screams subsided into sobs, then were cut off as Drew closed her door. Lily lifted Amiel in her arms and held him close as she walked to the window and stared out at the willows along the river. It wasn't fair that she had worked so hard to keep both babies alive while Claire slept, yet Junior was the one who died. Amiel beat his tiny fists against Lily's breasts. She opened her dress and gave him a nipple. Watching him take her milk into his mouth, she said, "It's done."

1884

.

23

"Prick this boil on my neck, will you, Lily?" Emmett asked, sitting down at the kitchen table and unbuttoning his shirt.

Lily looked up from the pot of posole on the stove to watch Junior run in from the hall.

"Papa!" the boy squealed, laughing with delight.

Emmett picked him up and held him high in the air, laughing, too.

On the floor again, Junior climbed onto his father's knee and asked, "What'd you bring me for my birthday?"

"You got a birthday coming?" Emmett answered, bouncing his knee to give the boy a ride.

"I'm gonna be five!" Junior said. "You promised me a pony!"

"Did I?" Emmett winked at Lily. "Your birthday's not till tomorrow," he told the boy. "Reckon I should've waited till then to come home."

Junior shook his head so fiercely the ends of his blond hair flew into his blue eyes. "I'd rather have you than a pony!"

Emmett laughed. "You got both."

Junior gasped as if with surprise that his father would give him what he wanted. "What color is it?"

"Why don't you go find out," Emmett said, setting the boy on his feet. "Shiloh's putting him up in the stable."

"Won't you come, too?"

"You run along and pester Shiloh awhile. Your mama's gonna dab some medicine on my neck and it ain't apt to be a pretty sight."

"Will it hurt?" Junior asked with a frown.

"Not you," Emmett answered, "so don't worry about it. Go on now."

The boy catapulted out the door, yelling, "Hey, Shiloh! What color's my pony?"

Emmett smiled at Lily. The kitchen had been hers since Cipriano died the year before of diverticulosis, the same thing that killed Elise Stone. As well as Lily could understand it, that long word meant a sack had developed in their intestines and slowly leaked poison. She'd nursed Cipriano, so she knew it was a painful way to die. Emmett had sent for the new doctor in River's End when Cipriano took to bed. Doc Hewitt told Lily that someday doctors would be able to open the abdomen and cut the sack of poison out, but that day hadn't come yet. All he could do was prescribe strong doses of laudanum to lessen the pain. Lily had heard that Mrs. Stone refused to send for the doctor, believing her herbal remedies were as good as anything modern medicine offered. As it turned out, she was right.

Lily moved her pot of posole off the fire so it wouldn't burn, then asked, "What color *is* the pony?"

"I got him a pretty little pinto stud," Emmett said.

She frowned, coming closer to look at his neck. "Don't you think a stallion might be too much for him, Emmett?"

"I wanted to give him a challenge," he answered, "not a horse he'll be bored with in a week."

Lily studied the growth on Emmett's neck, thinking it didn't resemble any boil she'd ever seen. Boils were red and tight with pus while the lump on his neck was nearly black and felt soggy when she gingerly touched it. Seeing him wince, she said, "I don't know, Emmett. Maybe you oughta have Doc Hewitt look at this."

"I don't need no doc for a boil, Lily. If you lance it good, it'll be gone in a day or two."

She poured hot water into a bowl from the kettle steaming on the back of the stove, then set the bowl on the table beside a clean towel. From a drawer she took the needle she used to truss fowl, lifted the grate off the front burner, and sterilized the needle over the flame. Holding the towel to catch the pus before it ran down Emmett's neck, she pierced the boil. But it wasn't pus that came out. It was a black, viscous liquid so putrid she backed away, fighting the need to puke.

Emmett put a hand on his neck to stop the stuff from running into his collar. "Hell's bells, Lily! Where's that towel?"

She held it out at arm's length.

Emmett mopped his neck, then stared at the dark stain on the white cloth. "Come over here and make sure it's cleaned out," he said.

She forced herself to move closer and look at the wound again. "I ain't never seen nothing like it, Emmett," she said. She took the towel, dunked it in the bowl, and dabbed at the wound. He winced. Knowing it was unusual for him to show pain, she said again, "You oughta let Doc Hewitt look at this. Maybe he's got some medicine can clean it out."

"Just put alcohol on it, Lily. That'll clean anything in God's creation."

"It'll hurt," she warned.

"Can't hurt no worse'n it's been doing. Get to it!"

She went to the pantry for the tin of alcohol. It was way back on the top shelf, and she had to stand on the footstool to reach it. When she came out, Emmett was dabbing at the wound, bringing the towel away freshly stained each time.

"I saw Drew in Austin," he said, peering at the stain as if he could name the problem if he looked hard enough.

Lily opened the drawer for another towel. "How is he?"

"He's fixing to get married," Emmett said.

"Good for him." Lily soaked the clean towel with alcohol. "He deserves some happiness."

"Claire ain't no better," Emmett said.

Lily felt stabbed with grief and guilt whenever she thought of Claire. Softly she asked, "Did you see her?"

"No. But Drew visits her every week in that asylum. He says she cries all the time he's there and prob'ly when he ain't."

Lily slapped the alcohol-drenched towel on Emmett's neck.

"Jesus Christ!" He jerked to his feet and held the towel himself as he glared at her. "Don't ever apply to nursing school, Lily. I think they'd turn you down."

She smiled. "I've no intention of doing that, Emmett."

He took the towel away and studied the dark stain a moment, then sat down again. "How's it look?"

She peered at the wound. "It's flat," she said, "and that black stuff's stopped."

"Good," he said. "Drew told me Claire wants to come home."

Lily gathered the dirty towels, needle, and bowl of water and carried them to the counter. "Home meaning Bosque Grande?"

"Yeah. When I asked why he didn't take her to live with him, he said she wants to be here."

Lily sighed, looking out the window. Between the orchard to her right and the bunkhouse on her left she could see the rise of ground where they'd buried Andy. Beside his grave was a tiny one bearing Amiel's name. "I wouldn't mind if Claire came back."

"She's crazy, Lily," Emmett said.

She turned around and watched him button his shirt. When he looked up and met her eyes, she asked, "Who made her that way?"

"Reckon it was in her mother's blood. There's never been a Moss who lost his mind."

"Drew did."

" 'Cause he was grieving for Andy! Nothing hits a man harder'n losing his only son."

" 'Cept knowing he killed him," she murmured.

Emmett stared at her. "Nobody could've predicted what happened. Wasn't Drew's fault."

"No, it wasn't," she answered, turning to look out at the cemetery again. "Is there any chance the doctors'll let Claire come home?"

"This ain't her home," Emmett retorted.

"Her son and brother are buried here," Lily said sadly. "If that don't make someplace home, I don't know what does."

"How about folks who love and want you?"

She faced him again. "I feel that way about Claire."

Emmett started to touch his neck, reconsidered, and thrust his hands into the pockets of his trousers. "The doctors say her condition's irreversible but she ain't a danger to herself or others, and if her family can handle someone not right in her head, she'd be as well off at home as she is there. Don't sound like any kinda recommendation to me."

"But Drew asked you to take her?"

Emmett nodded.

"What answer did you give him?"

"Said I'd ask you, being as you're the one would have to handle it. Are you saying you want her here?"

"Yes," Lily said.

"You think having her around would be good for Junior?"

Lily felt a bitterness in her smile. "Can't see how having two mothers could hurt any child."

Emmett frowned. "Maybe not him, since he's already got a good start, but I've been thinking we oughta try for another while we still got the chance."

Lily took a step away. "I don't feel the inclination."

"You had an easy time birthing Junior. I don't see why you'd be opposed to doing it again."

"I'm opposed to you touching me."

He smiled. "If you're thinking I was too rough, you've forgotten how you resisted."

"I didn't resist enough. And I ain't talking only 'bout what happened 'tween me and you."

"What *are* you talking about, Lily? Just go ahead and spit it out. I've always held honesty between a man and wife is the best practice."

She snorted with scorn. "Our marriage is a bed of lies, Emmett."

"When have I ever lied to you?"

She almost threw Whit Cantrell in Emmett's face but stopped herself, remembering the lie of her silence that had claimed Amiel as Junior. Now he was, for all anyone else knew. "If you try to come to my bed, Emmett, I'll kill you, and I won't have to use more'n words to do it. So I suggest you leave me alone."

From deep within the house, a door banged shut in the wind. Emmett said, "Then there's nothing more between us, is there, Lily?"

"There's Junior," she said. "I hope we can keep our dif'rences from spoiling his childhood."

Emmett nodded. "Reckon I'll go watch him ride his pony. I feel the need of some joy after spending time with my wife."

"Joy's precious," she agreed. "If you don't mind, I'll sit at your desk to write Claire and tell her she's welcome to come."

"Suit yourself," Emmett said, walking out.

Lily avoided writing that letter for months. She often considered doing it, even attempted it several times, but the thought of Claire filled her with such melancholy that she abandoned the effort. Finally one day in March, determined to do it, she sat at the rolltop desk in Emmett's office and took out stationery, pen, and ink, positioned them in front of her, then hesitated as she stared at the letterhead. Printed in bold, black letters it read: BOSQUE GRANDE RANCH. Below that, in smaller letters: RIO PANAL, NEW MEXICO TERRITORY. And below that, again slightly smaller: EMMETT MOSS, PROP. Lily dipped the pen in ink and wrote, "March 22, 1885." Her script seemed insubstantial beneath the dark block of Emmett's name.

She dipped the pen again, then carefully printed "Mrs" in front of "Emmett" and separated the two words with a dot. Feeling pleased, she confidently wrote "Dear Claire" to the left of the date. Then she stopped and looked out the window.

Close to the house, she could see the glossy green of the rosebushes, not yet in bloom. The spikes of white pickets separated the roses from the hard-packed dirt of the yard. To her left, she could see the budding tips of the cottonwood tree that would shade the corral come summer. A well-worn path connected the corral and the bunkhouse, which was behind the main house, beyond her view. Straight ahead was the prairie, an expanse of rumpled hills gray-green with mesquite and creosote stretching to Comanche Ridge, a red slab of rock against the blue sky.

Dear Claire, Lily read in her mind, her pen poised to write. Listening to the silence around her, Lily wondered if Claire would cry all the time when she came home, if she would be capable of conversation, and if she retained any memory of the past or had lost it in the delirium of her madness. Lily remembered hearing Claire scream when she discovered her baby dead. Those screams had been almost the last sounds Claire made at Bosque Grande. Sometimes Lily thought she could still hear them echoing faintly through the hall.

The house was so huge, most of the rooms empty. Junior slept in what had once been Andy's room. Emmett occupied his bedroom and office, Lily her room and the small parlor in front of it. Otherwise they lived in the kitchen. The dining room hadn't been used since Cipriano died, but long before that Lily had felt ridiculous eating at the long table with only Emmett and Junior. Somehow word had spread that Bosque Grande was no longer a place of commodious hospitality, and the stream of travelers who had shared Emmett's table when he was a bachelor had ceased to flow.

Lily could trace the change back to Andy's death, though she hadn't noticed at the time. Right after that, she and Claire had been pregnant, and since most of the travelers on the Panal were men, Lily supposed they had considered it improper to visit women who were in the family way. Then there had been those awful weeks when both babies were crying with colic. After Amiel died and Claire lost her mind, people began saying Bosque Grande was haunted. Some even said Jasper Stone stalked the rooms with a shotgun, searching for vengeance. Lily had never seen Jasper or any other apparition in the house, but since no one repeated the stories to her face, she couldn't refute them.

Theo had told her of the house's reputation. Her brother was twenty now, eking a living off a gristmill that was often idle because of the drought. The last time Lily visited the mill, she'd been appalled at her family's poverty. When she suggested they come live at Bosque Grande, Theo said he didn't hanker to meet any ghosts. Rosemary kept quiet while he told Lily the stories. Astounded, she denied them, then implored her mother not to believe in such foolishness. Rosemary shrugged, thanked Lily for the invitation, and insisted she preferred staying where she was. "The rains'll come back and we'll be fine," she said.

Lily sent them a wagonload of food each month, but she hadn't visited again. She so seldom went anywhere these days, she was beginning to feel like a ghost herself. Occasionally Shiloh Pook brought her a turkey or deer that one of the cowboys had shot on the range. She knew these came from Emmett, and that Shiloh knew he was an emissary between them. Neither she nor Shiloh ever mentioned the conversation they'd had so long ago, but Lily suspected it was on his mind and the suspicion cramped their conversation. There were so many things left unsaid, so many desires unfulfilled. Too much sorrow and grief, too little joy and comfort. Only Junior made a glad sound in the house.

Dear Claire, Lily read, then laid down her pen and covered her face with her hands. Silence rang in her ears. Junior had gone with Emmett to River's End, proudly riding his pinto pony alongside his father's big bay, but the purpose of their visit wasn't a happy one. Emmett had finally decided to seek medical treatment for the growth on his neck. It had become so enlarged that he carried his head at a slant, and the constant pain in his eyes hurt even Lily, who had told herself she no longer cared what her husband felt.

In the darkness of her hands, Lily tried to summon a picture of Claire, thinking surely five years in an asylum would have tarnished her beauty. Lily remembered her as she'd been at Bosque Grande, not as the young girl who fell in love with Whit, or even the newly married woman carrying his child, but as she'd been when Lily tried to tell her the truth. Lily had waited too long.

One afternoon when Amiel was asleep, she had walked up the hill to Junior's grave and forced herself to concede that it was her son under Amiel's name. She sank to her knees and poured her grief into the earth between them. After a long time, she sat up and dried her face with her skirt, then looked down at Bosque Grande. The ranch would have been Junior's, but he was dead by his father's hand. Admitting that truth made Lily realize her lie not only betrayed her son, protected his killer, and denied the grievous injury inflicted on her, it also made her Emmett's accomplice in destroying Claire.

Lily had walked back down the hill and through the house to where Amiel slept in Junior's cradle. She lifted the boy and held him close a moment, then carried him into Claire's room, determined to right the wrong she had done. Crossing the threshold, however, Lily was stunned by the devastation she saw. Because she'd been unable to face the friend she'd betrayed, she had left her care to the men, and it had been poorly done. Claire lay in a fouled bed, her open eyes staring into space.

Lily laid Amiel in his cradle, then set about cleaning Claire. She combed her hair, washed her body, dressed her in a pretty nightgown, and sat her in the window seat while she changed the bed. Claire allowed Lily to do whatever she would, offering neither protest nor assistance. When Lily had the bed clean again, she led Claire to sit on its edge, then she opened the window to allow the breeze to freshen the air. Finally she took Amiel from his cradle and brought him to his mother.

"Look, Claire," she said. "Here's your baby."

Claire didn't respond.

"What happened," Lily said, fighting tears, "was a terrible mistake. *My* baby died, not yours. This is Amiel, Claire. Won't you at least look at him?"

Claire crawled back into bed and pulled the covers over her face.

Amiel beat his fists against Lily's breasts, awake now and wanting to be fed. "Claire?" Lily whispered. Then in a stronger voice, "Your baby's hungry, Claire. You have to get up and feed him."

Claire didn't move.

Holding Amiel in one arm, Lily pulled the covers away from Claire's face. "Look, Claire. Here's Amiel! He's hungry!"

Claire stared straight ahead, her eyes empty.

"Oh, Claire," Lily pleaded. "Please wake up. I didn't mean to take your baby. They were both crying that night. When they stopped, it was Amiel I had, so I laid him in Junior's cradle. Junior's the one who died. Amiel was safe 'cause I had him with me. Please understand, Claire. Please hear what I'm saying. Your baby needs you."

Amiel began to wail, and Claire pulled the covers over her face again. Lily stood holding the crying baby, crying herself. "Please, Claire."

"Stop it!" Claire shouted from beneath the covers. "Stop it stop it stop it!"

Lily quickly unbuttoned her dress and gave Amiel what he wanted. Claire cried in the quiet, then fell silent.

"Claire?" Lily whispered. She pulled the covers away.

Claire stared straight ahead, her lashes wet with tears.

"Claire?" Lily whispered again.

Claire didn't respond.

In the window seat, Lily nursed Amiel while Claire stared blindly at nothing. Amiel fell asleep. Lily sat with her breasts bare, her back to the world as the sun slowly slid from the sky. Finally she stood up and laid Amiel in his cradle, then joined Claire in bed. But all of Lily's petitions through that dark night went unheard. In the morning, men Lily had never met took Claire away. Lily lay in Claire's bed with her baby, watching them go.

That had been in November of 1879. In March of 1885, Lily lifted her pen, read *Dear Claire,* then slowly wrote:

I have been wanting to write you for a long time but have not found the courage before now. Your father told us you want to live at Bosque Grande again. I will welcome you with open arms. Your room is as you left it. I scarcely have time to keep the house, it is so large, and dust collects on the furniture. I am busy with my garden and chickens. The orchard bears lots of fruit I put up each autumn, although I don't know who will ever eat it all. Junior is hard on his clothes so I'm constantly mending and sewing more. Em-

mett is often out on the range or in Vegas at the Cattlemen's Association meetings. The drought has hit all the
ranchers hard, and the sentiment in the county is discouragement. Elise Stone died several years ago. Her mother
followed soon after. Women are as scarce as ever along
the Panal, and I would dearly love your company through
my days. If you are able to come, please let me know the
date of your expected arrival and I will ready your room. I
keep the graveyard tended, and you will be pleased to see
the roses if you come before the first freeze. Hoping for
your health, I remain as always,

Your friend,
Mrs. Lily Cassidy Moss

Lily laid down the pen and read what she'd written. Deciding
it was the gloomiest letter in God's creation, she crumpled the
page and threw it into the hearth on her way out of Emmett's office.

24

*L*ily left the empty house, saddled her horse, and rode toward the river. The cottonwoods were budding in the op-
timism of spring, the willows' long tendrils already a vibrant
green though still lacking leaves. Barely splashing her horse's
hoofs, the pathetic trickle of water made crossing the ford easy.
She urged Nugget to climb the west bank, then turned south and
let the palomino amble along the road as she studied the river
below.

In another month, snow thaw in the mountains would send a
torrent through the Panal. Once all the snow had melted, how-

ever, there would be no more water until the July rains. For the last three years, those rains hadn't come. Lily wished there was a way to save the spring rush, but dams had been tried all along the river, and the force of the thaw was so great that no dam could hold it.

Just south of the ford, a plank bridge crossed the arroyo dug by Gushing River as it met the Panal. Because it rose from an artesian spring, Gushing River was never dry. The spring was on the Beckworth ranch, but Emmett had legal rights to the flow. He drained it out of the Panal through a honeycomb of acequias that carried water to the house, orchard, and garden and made it possible for Bosque Grande to enjoy such luxuries as roses when most of their neighbors were short of drinking water.

Lily wondered if the rains would ever return. Deep River had been dry except in spring for the last three years. In her childhood, the river had been almost always difficult to cross. The summer she was eight, her father had taken the family to Union, leaving the mill early in the morning and returning in late afternoon. In the meantime, heavy rain had drenched the mountains, and when her family approached the ford, the river had breached its banks.

Close to home, with a wagon full of tired children, her father had whipped his pair of mules into the river and tried to cross anyway. Lily remembered those mules, Oscar and Abby. As they edged into the current, the mules protested, but her father urged them on until, belly deep in the swirling water, Abby laid down. Lily's father stood up to ply the whip again, then hesitated while he reconsidered. As water pushed against the side, Lily could feel the wagon starting to give way. In terror, she watched her mother reach up and touch her father's arm, a silent gesture that spoke of the harmony they shared. He turned the mules and regained the shore from which they'd started.

Gregorio Encantas was sitting his horse on the bank as they clambered up beside him. When they were safe on solid ground again, Gregorio laughed and said, *"¡Ojalá, hombre! Qué buena suerte la* Abby know best or you be swept away *con la señora y los hijos y todos!"* Everyone had laughed, knowing he was right.

As Lily ambled her palomino south along the Panal, she smiled at the memory, but mostly she felt sad, remembering how her father had heeded her mother's touch. No such harmony existed between her and Emmett. What would Junior remember of them when he was a man?

Lily reined up and stared down at the cove where she had said good-bye to Whit. She wondered if Junior would be different if he were called Amiel and was being raised by his real parents. Or even by Claire and Bob Daggerty. Wondered if Claire would have been a better mother, or if knowing his father was a famous outlaw would have given the boy a grudge against the world. For surely Claire wouldn't have let him grow up believing he was Daggerty's son.

Yet Lily was letting him believe he was Emmett's. Emmett believed it, too, though Junior resembled Whit more with each passing year. The boy also bore a strong resemblance to Claire, and Emmett probably thought the difference came from Lily's side of the family. He knew from breeding cattle that hereditary traits could be quixotic, and the boy *was* half Moss. But the half of Junior that would have been a Cassidy was a Cantrell in Amiel.

Turning toward home, Lily wondered why Whit had never written Claire. Maybe he'd died in Mexico, or maybe he'd married and was living with a wife and their brood of brown children. He may never have learned that Claire had had his child, or he may have thought, being a Moss, she had ample means to provide for it without his help. He may even have heard the child had died and Claire been committed to an asylum, news that would negate his need to write.

As her horse's hooves echoed crossing the bridge again, Lily's thoughts turned to Emmett. He was missing spring branding for the first time in anyone's memory, but Manny Tucker was a seasoned ramrod and well able to handle things himself. From what Lily had learned from Shiloh Pook, the roundup was falling short of expectations anyway. Many of the cows were fallow, their gaunt, thirsty bodies failing to conceive despite the bulls Emmett had imported to improve the stock.

He'd purchased four pedigreed shorthorn bulls in 1883 at a

cost of five thousand dollars each. It took a year for them to arrive from Kentucky, and this roundup was supposed to prove their worth. But the herd had grown by only half its rate before the drought. *The Las Vegas Stock Growers' Report,* a publication Lily had begun reading, lamented that prices for top-quality cattle in Chicago had dropped from $7.15 per hundred pounds in January of 1884 to $6.80 a year later. Though their prediction for September was bleak and the stockyards were already crowded with unsold cattle, Emmett was legally bound to fulfill his contracts at a price stipulated only as market value. The average steer required thirty-seven bushels of corn in transit. Deducting the cost of feed and shippage, he'd be lucky to break even.

Yet despite the hard economic realities that made the tally of this roundup so crucial, Emmett was in River's End because of what he continued to call the boil on his neck. Lily had known the first time she'd seen it that what he had was no boil. He'd stubbornly insisted it was and refused her advice to seek a doctor's care for months. Now when he was needed on the range, he was in River's End. Junior was, too, though he was old enough to start learning the cattle business by watching firsthand the gathering and branding of a herd that would someday be his. And since Emmett wasn't likely to take Junior to the doctor's office, the boy was probably waiting for his father in some saloon. Whatever Junior was learning in town, Lily doubted it would stand him in good stead as a rancher.

After stabling her horse, she returned to the silent house and busied herself making *gorditas* for dinner. She was at the stove frying the meat-filled turnovers when she heard horses in the yard. A moment later, Junior burst through the front door and ran the length of the long, dim hall to erupt in the kitchen like a whirlwind of energy.

"*Gorditas!*" he yelled. "You made my favorite, Mama! When'll they be ready?"

"Soon," she said. "Where's your father?"

"He's coming. I had such a good time in town!"

"What'd you do?" she asked, turning the *gorditas* so they crackled in the grease.

"We went inside a saloon and Papa let me sit on the bar while he talked to some men. They play a game in there, Mama, that's got a big wheel with red and green and black numbers painted on it. One man spins the wheel and other men bet on which number it'll stop at. Papa let me bet. I chose seven 'cause I was born on the seventh, and I won two silver dollars!" He laughed, fishing the coins from his pocket and holding them up proudly. "I wanta go back and play again tomorrow. Can I?"

She frowned down at the little gambler. "Maybe you won't win next time."

"I will! The men all said seven was a lucky number and, 'sides that, I got the luck of the innocent. I don't figure I'll ever lose."

"I hope you're right," she said, lifting the *gorditas* out of the grease to drain on a rack. "Go wash your hands."

He pulled a chair over to the sink to stand on as he primed the pump. "What I can't figure," he said, soaping his hands, "is why men ever work if money's so easy to come by in a saloon."

Lily looked at him from where she was setting the table. "After you've lost a time or two," she said, "it'll make more sense."

"I already told you I ain't ever gonna lose." He jumped off the chair as he dried his hands on a towel, then dropped it on the floor and sat down at the table.

Lily picked up the towel and put the chair back. She poured him a glass of buttermilk, then set the glass and the platter of *gorditas* on the table. He reached for a turnover and took a big bite.

"Don't eat so fast you make yourself sick," Lily said. "I'll be right back."

She found Emmett on the swing under the portal, his bay and the boy's pinto still tied to the rail. Lily sat down in a rawhide chair and asked, "What'd Doc Hewitt say?"

Emmett held his head at a slant, the growth on his neck freshly bandaged with gauze. "It's a cancer, Lily," he said, his eyes betraying no emotion. "I gotta go clear to Vegas to see a surgeon 'bout cutting it out."

Lily shuddered to hear the dreaded word. "Once it's done," she asked, "will that be the end of it?"

"Doc Hewitt couldn't say. He scolded me for letting it go so long. Said that might work against me."

Lily nodded, biting her tongue against saying she'd told him so. "Is there anything I can do?"

He shook his head, then winced at the pain.

Despite herself, she felt sorry for him. "How long will you be gone?"

"Prob'ly no more'n a coupla weeks." He looked away from her pity and studied the yard, though it was empty. "Hate to leave in the middle of branding, but Tucker can handle it. I need to see Bob Daggerty anyway, so the trip won't be a complete waste of time."

Gently, she said, "Saving your life ain't a waste of time, Emmett."

Not looking at her, he said, "I thought it was just a boil that wouldn't heal. Don't know why I thought that. I've never had a boil 'fore now." He chuckled. "Guess I still haven't. But then, I never had a cancer neither."

"The surgeon'll cut it out," she said, "and you'll heal."

He shrugged, then winced again. "I've been feeling poor lately, Lily, and I've let things slide I shouldn't have."

"Like what?" she asked.

"The Territorial Life Insurance Company's gone into receivership. I learned that in River's End this morning."

"Does Bob still work for 'em?"

Emmett started to nod, winced, and stopped. "They're being sued by the First National in Santa Fe. As a corporate officer, Bob's liable for the company's losses."

"What does that mean, Emmett?"

"One of the things it means is I gotta get to Vegas and revoke the power of attorney I gave him, otherwise he could use my assets to prop up his failed company."

"All of your assets?" she whispered.

"I ain't stupid, Lily. Just 'cause I took him into my family don't mean I gave him everything I own. He's got access to the funds here in the territory, but most of my money's in St. Louis. Still in all, there's enough in Santa Fe to get him out of his predicament, but I don't see why I should pay for his bad investments. It ain't like he's been any kinda good husband to Claire."

"No, he hasn't," Lily agreed.

Emmett glanced at her, then looked at the yard again. "I chose Bob for Claire 'cause I thought it'd be good to have an accountant in the family. But he's turned out to be such a gambler, I might as well've let her marry Whit. He won games of chance more often'n it seems Daggerty's doing."

"He also loved her and gave her a child," Lily said.

Emmett met her eyes. "I've done that for you, Lily. Do you consider me any kinda good husband?"

"You've kept food on our table and provided a home," she said.

"Is that what you call this place? It feels like a morgue to me."

"We've had more'n our share of sorrow," she murmured.

He grunted. "When I married you, Lily, I had such high hopes for our future. I thought we'd have half a dozen kids running through this house. Andy and Claire's kids, too. Folks coming to visit. A great, rollicking celebration of life making such a noise I'd be hard put to find a speck of silence. Now it seems that's all I've got."

"You have Junior," she said.

He nodded, wincing. "I bless the day you gave him to me. That was the happiest day of my life, Lily."

"Mine, too," she said.

He smiled. "Look after him good while I'm gone. But don't let him go into River's End again, nor Soledad neither. The roulette dealer tricked the wheel and let Junior win. Even though he did it on my account, I don't think it was a good idea. I've never seen a kid take to the notion of winning his living at gambling like Junior has. He talked about it all the way home." Emmett paused, then added softly, "Put me in mind of Whit Cantrell."

Lily looked down and brushed dust from the hem of her skirt.

Emmett said, "I've always liked you in that dark shade of blue."

She couldn't bring herself to look up.

"What happened to us, Lily?" Emmett asked mournfully. "I believe I made up my mind to marry you when I first noticed the child I loved was quickening into womanhood. I once believed you loved me, too. Not in the romantic way of storybooks, but I thought you had enough sense to put those notions out of your mind when you became my wife."

Sitting up straight, she said, "There's been too many lies between us, Emmett."

"I've never lied to you."

"You're doing it right now."

"When have I lied?"

"Christmas Eve, eighteen seventy-eight, when you told us you'd hung Whit."

Emmett stared at her a long time before saying, "I thought it best."

"I know you did, but Andy proved you wrong."

"I had no way to guess what he'd do, Lily."

"I know that, too," she said, looking away from the pain in his eyes. "But your lie was a mistake that killed our chance at happiness."

"My mistake was inviting Drew to bring his family here in the first place. I should've left him to make it on his own in Texas. He's doing fine since he went back. If he'd never come, Andy would still be alive and Claire would've never met Whit, let alone be seduced by him. Whit would've been hung for his part in the war and gone down in history as just another killer in a fight that had nothing to do with me."

"That's not true, Emmett. My father was one of the first men to die in that war. You promised me vengeance, but it was Jasper and Whit who delivered it."

"I paid Whit! Don't that count?"

"You mean the black mare you took back when you let him go? Did you pay him with his life, Emmett? Is that how you paid him for committing murder on my behalf?"

"It *was* on your behalf, Lily. Remember that."

"I can't forget it," she said.

"And I gave him three hundred dollars when I took the mare. I consider that fair wages."

She wanted to ask if he thought he'd been fair with Jasper, but she couldn't see any point in digging up that grave again. So she asked instead, "Do you think there's a chance Whit's still alive?"

"He was a coupla years ago," Emmett said, looking away to watch a dust devil spin across the yard.

Lily watched, too, until it disappeared as suddenly as it had been born. Staring at the place where it died, she asked, "How do you know that?"

"He wrote Claire a letter."

She turned her eyes on him.

He shrugged, then winced at the pain in his neck. "I picked it up with the rest of the mail at River's End. He didn't put his name on it, but it was from El Paso, and I couldn't figure who else would write her from there."

"What did you do with it?"

"Burned it."

"Did you read it first?"

He shook his head and winced again. "His child was dead and Claire mad. I figured silence was the best answer he could get."

Lily thought of Whit sitting down to write Claire a letter. It had probably been as hard for him as it had for her, neither of them accustomed to putting words on paper. Like hers, Whit's letter had been burned, leaving Claire in the cold. Lily hugged herself as if she could feel the chill of the asylum, though she sat in bright sun.

Emmett asked, "You think I was wrong?"

She met his eyes. "In nearly everything, Emmett."

He grunted and stood up. "Maybe you're right, though that's not the assessment I'd expected to hear at the end of my life."

She watched him untie his reins and mount his horse, then she stood up and asked, "Don't you want to pack a bag or take some food?"

"No," he answered. "If my credit's not good anywhere along the Panal, I'm already dead."

"Don't you want to say good-bye to Junior?"

"He was laughing when we got home. I'd rather remember him like that."

She watched Emmett rein his horse around and amble out of sight as if he had all day to get where he was going. Lily sank back into the chair and stared at the yard long after it was empty. There was only the pinto pony, flicking its long black tail in the sun. Finally she roused herself to go tell Junior to put up his horse. But when she found him asleep on top of his bed, she left him alone and did it herself. Then she returned to the house and sat again at Emmett's desk to write a letter to Claire. Without letting herself think too deeply, Lily quickly wrote:

> Dear Claire,
>   I would welcome having you home with me. Tell your doctors there is nothing more healing than clean air and fresh food, both of which we have plenty of, along with lots of love springing from the source of the tragedy that caused your illness. Please let me know the date of your arrival so I may ready your room. In hopeful anticipation, I remain as ever,
>
> Your aunt,
Mrs. Emmett Moss

She sealed the letter in an envelope addressed to Mrs. Robert Daggerty, care of the Asylum of Benevolent Hope, San Antonio, Texas. Feeling resolved in her decision to make amends as best she could, Lily carried the letter to the kitchen and laid it on the table, then cleaned up the mess Junior had left and washed the dishes, setting her house right in her mind.

It was ten days before Lily could send her letter to be posted in River's End. Shiloh Pook took it and came back with a bundle of mail for Bosque Grande, including the latest issues of newspapers from Santa Fe and Vegas. Lily left them in her sitting room and carried the rest of the mail into Emmett's office to await his return, then went on with her chores.

After supper, she put Junior to bed and carried a cup of coffee into her sitting room. Settling herself comfortably in front of the hearth, she soaked the fire's warmth into her skirts as she opened the Las Vegas *Optic.* She scanned the front page until her attention was impaled by a headline: CATTLE KING OF THE PANAL DEAD OF CANCER.

Lily dropped the paper on the floor and stared into the fire for

a long time. It hadn't occurred to her that Emmett wouldn't be
back. Struggling to recall their last words, she remembered she'd
told him he'd been wrong in nearly everything. She wished she
could have been kinder, but also felt glad that she'd never told
him the truth about Junior. Maybe Emmett deserved to know
he'd killed his own child instead of Whit's, but Lily took comfort
in knowing she'd spared him that. After everything, it was perhaps the only mercy she could give him.

She lifted the newspaper off the floor and read with dry eyes
the obituary of her husband:

> OUR READERS WILL BE SADDENED TO LEARN OF THE DEATH
> OF EMMETT MOSS, WHICH OCCURRED LAST NIGHT. HE WAS
> ATTENDED BY HIS DOCTOR, SAMUEL EDMONDS, WHO SAID
> THE CATTLE KING OF THE PANAL DIED PEACEFULLY IN HIS
> SLEEP, DUE TO A STRONG DOSE OF LAUDANUM THE DOCTOR
> MERCIFULLY ADMINISTERED.
>
> MR. MOSS WAS ONE OF THE PIONEERS OF UNION
> COUNTY, HAVING COME TO THIS TERRITORY IN THE EARLY
> DAYS OF ITS SETTLEMENT, AND HAS BEEN IDENTIFIED WITH ITS
> PROGRESS EVER SINCE.
>
> GRUFF IN MANNER YET ALWAYS A WARM FRIEND, HE HAD
> A COOL HEAD FOR BUSINESS AND A DESIRE TO BE A SQUARE
> SHOOTER WITH HIS FELLOW MAN. HIS ENEMIES WERE THE EN-
> EMIES OF ALL LAW-ABIDING CITIZENS, AND HE WAS A PRINCI-
> PAL AMONG THE POSSE WHO RID UNION COUNTY OF THE
> MURDEROUS JASPER STONE, AFTER WHICH MR. MOSS TOOK
> IT UPON HIMSELF TO TRACK AND HANG THE KILLER WHIT
> CANTRELL, WHO ESCAPED JAIL WHILE AWAITING EXECUTION.
> THE TERRITORY OWES MR. MOSS A GREAT DEBT FOR HIS
> CONTRIBUTION TO LAW AND ORDER, AS WELL AS THE DEVEL-
> OPMENT OF COMMERCE IN A LAND WHICH SAW FEW WHITE
> MEN BEFORE HIS ARRIVAL. NONE WERE HIS EQUAL, AND FEW
> WILL EVEN TRY TO FILL HIS BOOTS.
>
> HE IS SURVIVED BY HIS WIFE, THE FORMER MISS LILY
> CASSIDY, AND HIS SON, EMMETT MOSS, JUNIOR. OUR HEART
> GOES OUT TO THEM IN THEIR BEREAVEMENT.

Lily eyes returned to the description of Jasper. The tears she let fall were for him, that the young man she'd loved as a girl should be so remembered. Those days seemed centuries ago, not merely the seven years that had passed. Yet Jasper with his translucent cheeks and sapphire eyes was more alive in her memory than Emmett had ever been. That one night in the cave, Jasper had given her more pleasure than she'd received in all the years she'd been Emmett's wife. Now they were equally dead, and she was truly a widow.

Lily laid the paper aside, rose and lit a candle, and carried it into the hall. It seemed a cavernous space as she looked up and down its vast length, stretching fifty feet from the front door to the kitchen. For a moment, she felt afraid. Not of the house, though its walls had seen more than its share of grief, but of the future yawning before her.

She owned Bosque Grande now, yet she had only a general idea of all it entailed. A lot of cattle, but not how many. Contracts to be filled, but not with whom. Bank accounts in Santa Fe and St. Louis, but neither their numbers nor the amounts on deposit. She had twenty men in her employ, but no notion of how to pay them; a hundred horses to feed and a barnful of hay, but only a vague knowledge of how to replenish the hay when the barn was empty. The men would know, of course. Manny Tucker, the ramrod. He knew, but even he'd had a boss to tell him when to do what.

Chiding herself for balking with fear, she carried the candle to the door of Emmett's office. Slowly she opened the door, then stood on the threshold, knowing all she could see was now hers. But what she could see wasn't the problem. She'd dusted the desk and chair, the mantel and lamp, the filing cabinet and sideboard daily since Cipriano died. It was what lurked inside the drawers that frightened her. She'd never even read a contract, let alone tried to follow its stipulations. Never once had she dealt with a bank. Money came out of Emmett's pocket. That was the truth she'd always known. What she couldn't pay cash for, she'd charged on the power of Emmett's name. She still owned the name, but she doubted that many merchants would honor it now that the man was dead.

Forcing herself to enter his domain, she used her candle to

light the lamp on his desk. In its more cheerful glow, she sat down in the swivel chair and stared at the many cubbyholes and drawers, both tiny and large, in front of her. Most obvious was the stack of mail she'd left on the desk earlier. Methodically she began going through the envelopes and reading the return addresses of men and companies with whom Emmett had done business, rifling through them until she came across a letter addressed to Mrs. Emmett Moss. Its return address was the Plaza Hotel in Vegas. The handwriting wasn't Emmett's, but thinking perhaps someone else had addressed the envelope, she eagerly tore it open, hoping Emmett had written some word of farewell.

Like the envelope, the letter was on stationery from the Plaza Hotel. She looked first at the signature, but instead of Emmett's she saw his brother's. In a spidery, feminine hand, Drew had written:

March 20, 1885

Dear Lily,

Emmett wrote before he left home asking that I join him here. Though he gave no reason, the tone of his letter struck me as so urgent I hastened to this city. When I arrived, I learned of his illness and rapid decline. I was with him the days preceding his death. He could not talk, as the cancer by then had affected his vocal chords. Although I hesitated to speak of finances, I felt compelled to inquire as to the location of his will and the name of the attorney handling his affairs. He communicated by writing that he had neither, then hastily executed a will bequeathing the entirety of his estate to his son, naming you as executrix. I have the document in my possession, believing it too valuable to entrust to the mails.

Emmett extracted a promise from me that I would return his remains to the family homestead in Texas to be buried beside our parents. I leave tomorrow to fulfill my promise. From there I shall travel to Austin, as I left too hastily to leave my own affairs in good order. I hope to find a letter from you when I arrive. The doctor here witnessed Emmett's will, so have no fear that I can destroy the document to serve my own purposes, although I feel it unfair that he remembered neither me nor his niece. I feel certain you will see our side of it and act with justice. Unless I receive a letter from you stating your wishes to be otherwise, I will travel to Bosque Grande from Austin.

I regret to mention at this sad time that I saw Robert Daggerty here. He intends to divorce Claire, indeed has already started the proceedings. I am fearful his intentions include taking more than his name from my daughter. I tell you this only in the event he should contact you and represent himself as a friend and member of the family. He is neither.

I am filled with melancholy as I write these words. My brother was a good man, though often rude and rough, being a frontiersman to the core. I hope you can remember him fondly despite the grievous wrongs he committed. I am, and always will be, your friend,

Andrew Moss

Lily felt an ominous foreboding of Daggerty's intentions. Somewhat relieved that Drew had convinced Emmett to write a will, she felt angry that her husband had left no attorney familiar with his affairs. At one time he had employed Edgar Homer, but apparently when Homer was killed, Emmett hadn't replaced him. Perhaps Emmett had felt competent to handle the legalities of his business without a lawyer, but he should have known his wife wasn't.

Lily had no doubt that Daggerty had delayed divorcing Claire in the hope of controlling her inheritance. Now that he knew it was nil, Lily couldn't guess what he might do. She didn't know if Emmett had been successful in revoking the power of attorney which gave Daggerty access to the bank account in Santa Fe, but she had scant faith in Emmett's belief that Daggerty couldn't withdraw funds from the account in St. Louis.

Deciding she must act quickly to prevent that, Lily refolded Drew's letter and slid it back inside the envelope. She stared at the flame in the lamp, thinking Emmett must have known when he left for Vegas that he would die there. He must have posted his letter to Drew from River's End, then brought Junior home and left again, giving no word of advice or instruction to his wife. After all the lies, Emmett was silent in the end, not even writing her a letter.

Feeling more sorrow for the failure of their marriage than his death, she began opening the drawers of his desk. She found contracts she couldn't understand, tallies not brought up to date, lists of employees containing the names of men no longer in his employ. Cipriano was still on the last payroll Emmett had bothered to write down. For the past two years, he hadn't even opened the statements from the banks in Santa Fe and St. Louis.

The latest balance in Santa Fe was $10,385.97. In St. Louis it was $394,206.17. Including payroll, to the best of her reckoning, the outstanding bills amounted to approximately seven thousand dollars. Monies to be paid for cattle yet to be delivered would net thirty-eight thousand dollars at the current market price, if she could deliver them. Because Emmett ran his herds on open range, the only deed to land she found was for the section around the house: 160 acres including water rights from the river. She found canceled checks to the Asylum of Benevolent Hope in San Antonio in the amount of three thousand dollars for each year Claire had been confined. And for the last two years, monthly stipends of five hundred dollars to Suzanne Homer in Union. Fifteen thousand dollars to care for his niece. Twelve thousand to support the widow of his attorney. His fortune to his son. For his wife, only silence and the onerous task of sorting out his affairs.

Studying the checks endorsed by Suzanne Homer, Lily remembered Emmett saying he considered the three hundred dollars he'd paid Whit for murder to be good wages. For what service had he paid Mrs. Homer twelve thousand dollars? Was sex worth more than murder in his lexicon of values? Lily remembered when William Wilson had been hung for killing her father. Emmett had taken her to call on Mrs. Homer that day, and the lawyer's wife had treated her unkindly. She now realized Suzanne had been jealous. Emmett must have known then that he intended to propose to Lily, and he must have told his mistress of his intention, perhaps explaining his rejection of her by saying he wanted a wife who could give him children. Suzanne Homer was barren. No wonder she'd been so bitter at Lily's wedding.

Lily remembered thinking the day of the hanging that Emmett had too much honor to cuckold another man's wife. She'd learned otherwise. Now she didn't even care that he'd kept a mistress all the years of their marriage. Lily felt sorry for Suzanne because his death meant she had lost her livelihood. A livelihood she'd paid dearly for if Emmett hadn't shown any more solicitude in bedding her than he had his wife.

But perhaps he had. It was only when Lily remembered that Emmett hadn't expected her to enjoy their coupling that she felt betrayed. He had chosen to make their marriage bed a place of torture, denying his wife pleasure in the name of sanctifying the issue of his loins. Remembering how Claire had giggled and blushed when describing how she'd felt when Whit deflowered her, Lily wished she could fling in Emmett's face that it was Whit's son who had survived.

She blew out the lamp and left her husband's office feeling rage for the man he had been. She walked through the darkness of the hall to the boy's room, intending to tell him that the man he'd called his father was dead and he was better off for it. But when she saw the boy so peacefully asleep in the moonlight, she backed out and closed the door. Within the walls Jasper had built, Lily sank to the floor and pulled the memory of his love around her like a blanket, knowing what Emmett had done to her was the least of his wrongs. As so many times before, she had to put her feelings aside for the sake of the boy.

"It's all gone, Lily," Drew said. Unable to meet her eyes, he stared into the hearth of her sitting room, where a low fire burned to warm the chill of the April afternoon. "You could institute replevin of the cattle, but the court proceedings would take years and the only people who'll benefit are the lawyers."

"He's taking the cattle?" Lily asked, trying to comprehend what Drew was saying.

He nodded. "Sheriff'll be out with an attachment soon, round them up and drive them to Vegas, where they'll be sold, probably at half value given the market."

"How can this happen?" she asked, bewildered.

He shrugged. "All I know is, Daggerty emptied Emmett's bank accounts and left the country. I was told he booked passage out of New York to Europe."

"Is there nothing we can do?"

"I hired the best lawyer in Vegas to fight it, but Daggerty acted within the letter of the law. He used the power of attorney to make Emmett the principal stockholder in the life insurance company, then transferred Emmett's assets as loans to dummy companies that reneged on their debts. When the parent company went bankrupt, Daggerty absconded with the funds, leaving Emmett liable for the company's debts. They'll be settled by the sale of the cattle. The money will go into a trust to pay off the policies as they come due, so Daggerty won't see any of it but neither will we. This section of land and your house are all you have left."

"I can't believe we can't fight him in court," Lily protested.

Finally Drew met her eyes. "He's somewhere in Europe, Lily. It would cost you a fortune merely to find him."

"It's worth a try," she said.

"How are you going to pay the lawyers? They'd want a substantial retainer to begin such a complicated case."

She stared at him in numbing apprehension. "It's all gone, Drew? Everything Emmett worked his whole life for?"

"I'm sorry, Lily. I wish it were otherwise."

She looked into the fire as she murmured, "It'll take all the cash I have on hand to meet payroll."

"You could pay the men with horses from the remuda," Drew suggested. "I think they'd accept such an arrangement."

She met his eyes. "But what are we to live on, Drew?"

"You have the land," he said. "And water rights. You could farm."

She shook her head, trying to find some solid ground in the slithering quicksand of her mind. "I haven't money to buy seed."

"I'm sure the merchants will give you credit. And I've an idea, if you're willing to listen."

"I am," she said, desperately groping for any lifeline that offered itself.

"Emmett paid the year in advance for Claire. I've already spoken to the asylum and they'll return half if we take Claire out by the end of May. She'd come to you with fifteen hundred dollars to pay her keep. It would give you something to buy groceries until your first harvest. And Claire wants to come here. You already wrote saying she'd be welcome."

"That was before," Lily said. "If I'm to run a farm, I won't have time to care for an invalid."

"Bring your mother and brother here to live. She could care for Claire and Junior, too. Your brother could work in the fields. In hard times, Lily, families pull together. Bosque Grande is worth far more than the mill. Theo's already sold most of the land around it. All they have left is the mill, and it's not turning a profit."

"How do you know all this?" she asked with resentment.

"My lawyer made inquiries. I'm only thinking of you, Lily. Trying to offer possible solutions to your situation."

"Is saddling me with your crazy daughter one of 'em?"

Drew winced. "I'll keep her with me if I must, but she wants to come here. I'm sure she could do menial chores. It's just that . . ." He stopped, staring into the fire.

"Just what, Drew?" Lily demanded.

He sighed. "She lives in a world that exists only for her. It's often a good place, Lily. She's usually happy and quite childlike. Sometimes her company is delightful."

"And the other times?"

He sighed again. "She cries. She doesn't wail or carry on, she simply sits and cries. Being here might alleviate that."

"This is where she was hurt. It might make her worse."

"Benevolent Hope is the best asylum in Texas, Lily, but the fact remains, it's a prison. Claire feels punished. When she's lucid enough to understand where she is, she thinks the death of her child was her fault. That's the only way she can explain why she's tied to her bed at night and spends her days in the company of women who are truly mad." He shuddered, tears in his eyes.

"When I first put her there, I thought they would cure her melancholy, but I no longer think any cure is possible within those walls."

"Why didn't you take her out years ago?"

He raised his hands helplessly. "I could barely support myself, and if I'd kept her with me, Emmett wouldn't have contributed. Now I'm about to be married again. My fianceé doesn't want a tragedy of my former life poisoning our chance for happiness. I can't blame her. Can you?"

"Not her," Lily said.

Drew nodded with misery. "I failed my children. I don't deny it. You and Claire were friends once. Can't you take her on the strength of that?"

Lily thought of Claire tied to her bed. Emmett had done that to her as punishment for allowing Whit into her room, so it wasn't far-fetched for Claire to feel punished again. Yet her only wrong was giving herself out of love. As for the death of her baby, the guilt for Claire's burden fell on Lily as much as Emmett. Maybe by restoring the child, Lily could end Claire's punishment as well as her own. Maybe if they were all together again, they could find some semblance of happiness. To Drew, Lily said, "I won't withdraw my invitation. Will you bring her yourself?"

He shook his head. "I'll hire a nurse to make the journey with her."

"Don't use my fifteen hundred dollars to do it," Lily said.

Drew smiled weakly. "You'll be all right on your own, Lily. You have the temperament for success."

She stood up, ending the conversation. "When will Claire arrive?"

He stood, too. "I'll write from Austin and let you know. This has been a disheartening conversation, Lily. I hope our next one is more cheerful."

"It couldn't be worse," she said, leaving the room before he did.

She hurried into the family parlor and stood with her back to the place where Emmett had proposed marriage so long ago. Through a crack in the shuttered window, Lily watched Drew mount his horse and ride out of her yard.

1894

25

*L*ily sat her piebald gelding on a knoll as she watched spring branding in the meadow below. She had long ago abandoned the gentility of a sidesaddle and now sat astride, the tops of her high boots covered by the hem of her split skirt. The skirt was her only concession to modesty. Strapped around her hips was a gunbelt holding a Colt forty-one, a pistol she was as good at handling as the rifle in her saddle scabbard.

The windblown dust made it difficult to count exactly how many calves had been dragged to the fire. Bosque Grande's mark was a curlicue imprint with the *G* beginning in the middle of the *B* and dangling beneath it, a brand registered solely in her name. She'd bought Emmett's cows back, as many as Claire's fifteen hundred dollars would purchase, and bought more land with the money from the sale of the mill. The original section would one day be Junior's, and the additional land was Theo's, but the enterprise of the ranch itself was Lily's, raised from the dead with her sweat.

Now fourteen, Junior was working in the cloud of dust below, roping calves and dragging them to the fire to be branded. Theo was down there, too, working on shares he would someday bequeath to his sons. The house at Bosque Grande was full, all the rooms occupied. Rosemary was housekeeper, helped by Theo's wife, Bianca. Their children filled the hall with noise: Roberto and Julio, boisterous at six and four, and Rosamarie, only two and quiet except when she cried. Claire moved like a specter among them, always wearing white, sometimes smiling.

Shiloh Pook was ramrod at Bosque Grande, riding herd mostly by himself. Theo helped quite a bit, Junior sporadically, and extra men were hired for spring branding and fall roundup, but Shiloh did the lion's share of the work. Lily considered him her only reliable partner in keeping the ranch solvent, forget profit. Theo's bum leg provided an excuse he readily used whenever he felt lazy. Junior had developed his first taste of gambling into a habit, though his prediction that he would never lose hadn't come true. It irked Lily that the saloonkeepers allowed a child to gamble, though she'd never spoken to any of them about it. She figured they'd say it was her job to keep him home, and they'd be right, but he was already taller than Lily and difficult to discipline.

Lily watched Shiloh spur his horse up the hill toward her. Their fifteen years of friendship had seasoned into a loyalty she knew she couldn't buy at any price, and she often wondered why he stayed when she was short with his wages half the time. He'd been a top hand when they'd met, and his knowledge and skill had increased with the years, so she didn't think her promise to keep him on when he got old was what induced him to stay. He could get a job on almost any ranch anywhere for twice the wages she paid and accumulate a nest egg for his old age, if that was his concern. Unable to see that he was slowing down any, she often admired him when she thought he wouldn't notice, and sometimes her memory caressed his image when he wasn't around. Usually she did that in the middle of a sleepless night when she prowled the silent house wondering if he might be awake, too. So far, she'd never walked down to the bunkhouse to find out.

Shiloh reined his horse alongside hers, and for a while they watched the activity below in silence. Then he said without being asked, "Reckon there'll be thirty-six when we're done."

"Not bad," Lily said.

"Could sell as many as a hundred in the fall, keeping just the prime bulls and young cows." He looked at her from under the gray brim of his hat when he added, "If you've found a market."

She shook her head. "Last month the price was only three dollars and seventy-five cents in Kansas City. Ain't worth the shippage."

"No, it ain't," Shiloh agreed. "Used to be fifteen, sometimes twenty dollars per hundred pounds. With this drought getting worse every year, you'd think cattle would be in demand. I heard the other day the Canadian River's gone dry. I can't hardly imagine that."

"I read it in the *Stock Growers' Report*," Lily said, "so reckon it's true. But foreign investors are what ruint the market."

"How's that?" Shiloh asked with a teasing smile.

She knew he was amused by her reading the trade journals. Shiloh was a hands-on man, not given to wasting his eyesight on the printed word. "Investors got into the cattle business in the late seventies when it was booming," Lily explained. "As the drought increased production costs, the investors started dumping what they had, cramming the stockyards with unsold cattle, which drove prices down."

"These investors were foreigners?" Shiloh asked.

"English, a lot of 'em. Come over here to make their fortune, but what they did was ruin ours. I think we oughta have a law that a person's gotta be an American to own land in America. That way when hard times come, they're in for the long haul and can't pull out when it suits 'em."

"I'm surprised there ain't such a law," Shiloh said.

"A lotta things about the law are surprising," Lily agreed. "But what's happening now's got more to do with the banks than who owns the land. The investors borrowed money to buy cattle at interest rates that would knock your socks off. After years of drought we got hit with the Big Freeze. Blizzards up north killed half the herds on the Great Plains."

Shiloh nodded. "The winters of eigthy-eight and eighty-nine were the coldest I've seen even down here."

"When the investors' loans came due," Lily said, her gaze on her pitifully small herd, "they sold whatever cattle they had to keep from going under, pulling the bottom outta the market and leaving us with what we got now." She shrugged. "They couldn't do nothing else, being as most of 'em didn't have no other way to raise capital."

"What's capital?" Shiloh asked.

"Cash," Lily said, looking at him.

Shiloh's gaze had wandered to the front of her shirt, damp with sweat between her breasts.

Lily looked away. "But the worst part of this whole situation is there ain't hardly any forage on the range for those of us who wanta stick with ranching till the market comes back. Look at all that dust down there! That meadow should be thick with grass 'stead of dirt."

Shiloh studied the meadow. "Nothing grows without rain."

"It's more'n that! Emmett overgrazed this range, running eighty thousand head of cattle up and down the Panal. Land that fed buffalo, deer, and antelope for centuries was wore out in the twenty years he was here! I'd spit on his grave if I didn't have to ride clear to Texas to do it."

Shiloh laughed. "I'm glad you do, then, 'cause I'd sure hate to have *him* haunting us."

"It ain't funny! He ruint this land for future generations, his own son included."

"Maybe so," Shiloh said, chastened by her anger. "But I don't think he intended to do that, Lily. Folks just never thought the land would wear out."

"Everything else in God's creation wears out. Why not land?"

"I don't know," Shiloh said. "We was just wrong, is all."

Lily sighed. "Well, we're in for a tough haul now. The truly hard times are just starting. I read in the newspaper last night that the stock market crashed. Banks are closing back East. Thousands of folks lost their life savings 'cause some highfalutin bankers couldn't see nothing but their own greed. Makes me mad enough to spit."

Shiloh chuckled. "If it'll make you feel better, Lily, go ahead and do it. I won't tell nobody."

Meeting his blue eyes, warm with affection, she laughed, too. Then she looked back at the scene below. "How long you figure to keep the extra men on?"

"I'd planned on paying 'em off at the end of the day."

"Will they be staying the night in the bunkhouse, then?"

"Reckon they might and leave in the morning. What'd you have in mind, Lily?"

She studied his teasing smile, wondering what he thought she had in mind. "My mother needs to know how many men'll be wanting breakfast, is all."

Shiloh nodded, then looked back at the meadow. The branding was over, the cowboys whistling at the cattle as they drove the herd toward the river and a well-deserved quenching of thirst. When the dust settled, she saw Junior and Theo talking by the dying fire. Her son stood straight and proud next to her brother, who leaned on his horse, his bad leg cocked at an odd angle. Softly she murmured, "Junior's growing up right quick, ain't he?"

Shiloh nodded. "Sometimes I have trouble believing he's your son."

She looked at him sharply. "What makes you say that?"

"Oh, the way he's so wild and rambunctious, while you keep yourself under such a tight rein it makes a man ponder what you got to curb so hard."

"Maybe the same thing he lets loose," she answered defensively.

Shiloh smiled. "If you ever let your reins fall slack, I think you'd discover the stampede you fear ain't gonna happen. But I'm pretty sure if Junior lost your rein, everybody'd fear what he'd let loose. The two don't add up in my mind."

Lily looked down at her son and brother still talking by the fire.

In a tone of idle speculation, Shiloh said, "Junior puts me in mind of Whit Cantrell and Claire, too, the way both of 'em lost what mattered when the chips were down. Whit stayed calm when he got mad. That helped his effectiveness, but he still did what men do when they're mad, and that lost him his future. Claire, being a woman, lost her mind. It remains to be seen what

Junior's gonna lose when nip comes to tuck, but I s'pect it might be his name."

Slowly Lily met Shiloh's eyes. "Quit beating around the bush, Shiloh, and say it."

"Now, Lily," he answered with a smile, "you know I'm good at keeping my mouth shut."

"That'd be hard to prove by the way you've been flapping it these last five minutes."

He chuckled. "Reckon I've said enough, then. See you after supper when we go over the tally?"

She nodded, and he rode back down the hill. Lily sat a few minutes longer, watching him talk to Junior and Theo, then she reined her horse toward Bosque Grande, thinking if Shiloh had noticed all he'd just said about Junior, other people probably saw it, too. She wondered what she'd say to Claire when the truth was told. For surely that day was coming. Junior would top out taller than Whit, but the resemblance between them was so striking that Lily couldn't understand why Claire hadn't already seen it. Maybe she'd forgotten what Whit looked like, confusing him in her madness with the heroes in all the novels she'd read growing up.

Though Lily had meant to tell Claire the truth, somehow the moment never presented itself. She thought it had one day when she'd seen Claire laying roses on Amiel's grave. Lily had ridden up to the cemetery intending finally to lay the right child to rest. But Claire had smiled so happily, looking up at Lily on her horse, that Lily lost her resolve to disturb the peace of that grave.

"Will you give me a ride back down the hill?" Claire had asked with an impish grin.

Lily nodded and slid behind the saddle, then stared as Claire climbed onto Amiel's tombstone and stood waiting. Lily didn't move until Claire laughed and said, "He doesn't mind giving me a hand up." Lily edged her horse closer so Claire could settle herself sideways in the saddle. Smiling at Lily, she said, "This is how we first met. Do you remember, Lily, that day you brought me home from the river?"

Lily nodded again, sliding one arm around Claire's waist as she turned her horse back down the hill.

Claire sighed and leaned her head on Lily's shoulder. "When I remember that day, I see you as you are now, riding astride and wearing a gun. You've always been ferocious, Lily, even when you were trying so hard to act girlish."

"Is that what you think of me?" Lily asked.

Claire kissed her cheek. "If I was a man, you'd scare me to death. Since I'm not, I thank God every day for our friendship. Your love keeps me alive, Lily. Don't ever take it away."

Hearing that, how could Lily tell Claire the truth? It was so sordid, so full of tragic betrayal, and Claire had found respite from tragedy in the way she'd arranged her memories. To disturb them would risk destroying her. Lily couldn't bring herself to do it, though she admitted that sparing Claire was also letting herself off the hook. But to clear her conscience at the price of Claire's happiness wasn't any kind of honorable solution, so Lily kept quiet, dreading the day of reckoning she knew was coming. Now Shiloh's comments had made her suspect that day was near.

As Lily rode into the yard, Claire waved from where she sat under the portal. Lily swung down and tied her horse to the rail, then joined Claire on the swing. The years in the asylum had deepened her smile lines and creased her brow into furrows she hid with a flounce of hair, darker blond than when she was young, though her figure, in the white dresses she wore, was as willowy as a girl's. Lily figured Claire wore white in an attempt to reclaim her stolen youth, but then again, Claire had always liked white. She'd been wearing it the day she and Lily met. Then as now, Lily felt like a country bumpkin next to the girl who'd grown up rich and beautiful, though Claire was neither anymore.

"How was the branding?" Claire asked.

"Dusty," Lily answered, stretching her legs to rest her bespurred boots on the rail.

From inside the house, they heard Rosamarie cry. Then the child burst through the door and ran to the swing, lifting her arms to Claire, who picked her up and nestled her close. "What's the matter, Rosamarie?"

"Toof's hurt," the child pouted. She was a pretty girl, with long black ringlets and lush olive skin.

"Let me see," Claire said.

The child opened her mouth.

"Oh, yes," Claire said. "Three of them now. They must be sore."

Closing her mouth, Rosamarie nodded. Claire cradled the child against her breasts. "This is a hard time, Rosie, but there's nothing to be done about it. You just have to wait till they all come in, then they won't hurt anymore."

Lily remembered comforting Junior when he was getting his first teeth. She wondered if she'd been as kind as Claire, or if her unhappiness had made her impatient with the child's seemingly insignificant pain. Hearing the rolling cadence of hoofbeats, she looked up and watched Junior gallop his big buckskin into the yard.

The pinto pony he'd been so proud of had been given to Roberto with no sense of loss. As far as Lily could see, Junior wasn't sentimental. The buckskin was only green-broke when he'd chosen it from the remuda, and he'd trained it with fear to obey his every command. Now as he reined sharply to a stop in front of the house, the horse half reared, then stood quivering in place. "I'm going to River's End," Junior announced. "Is there anything you'd like me to bring back?"

"Yourself in one piece," Lily said.

Junior laughed. "I'm gonna do some gambling. If I win, ain't there some pretty you'd like?"

Lily shook her head. "Where'd you get the money?"

"From gambling," he said. "Guess I'm just naturally lucky."

"Or foolish," Lily muttered.

Junior laughed again. "How about you, Claire? Is there something you'd like from town?"

"No, thank you kindly, Junior. I've everything I need right here."

"I can't hardly believe that," he said, his smile seductive beyond his years. "A woman as pretty as you are, wouldn't you like a ribbon to tie your hair away from your face and show it off?"

"Why, Junior Moss," she said in the honeyed tone of genteel repartee, "are you flirting with me?"

"What would you think if I was?" he asked with a grin.

"That you'd outgrown your britches," she answered. "I'm old enough to be your mother."

Lily winced. "You could bring your cousins some candy if that ain't beneath the dignity of a gambler."

"It ain't," he said, reining his horse to rear as it spun around. "Don't wait up," he called, then dug in his spurs and galloped out of the yard as quickly as he'd come.

Watching the dust settle behind him, Lily said, "He's only half grown. When he's a man, ain't nobody gonna be able to tell him nothing."

"He's cocky, that's for sure," Claire said with a girlish giggle. "But I kinda admire his style."

"Ain't surprising," Lily said. She stood up, untied her reins, and swung onto her horse.

"What's that supposed to mean, Lily?" Claire asked, still holding Rosamarie.

Lily looked down at the two of them and managed to smile when she said, "Just that you've always favored desperadoes." Turning her horse, she heard Claire say, "Run along back to your mama, Rosie. I have a bone to pick with your aunt."

Lily didn't wait but kicked her horse into a trot across the yard toward the stable. She was hefting the saddle onto the rack when Claire came in, her white dress luminous in the dim light. Lily led the horse into a stall and came out carrying the bridle. She eyed Claire standing just inside the door but kept quiet as she hung the bridle on a nail, scooped oats out of a bin, dumped them in the manger, and replaced the scoop. Finally she faced Claire and asked, "You got something needs saying?"

Claire nodded. "I'm tired of you throwing Whit Cantrell in my face every time I turn around."

"Do I do that?" Lily asked as gently as she could.

"Yes, you do," Claire answered, her voice shaking. "I loved Whit. I'm sorry you didn't feel that way about Emmett. I'm sorry he killed Jasper and broke your heart. I'm sorry Andy hung himself, and I'm sorry I lost my mind. I'm sorry for everything except loving Whit Cantrell. He was the one shining moment in my life, and I won't ever be sorry I loved him."

"Do you think that's what I want?" Lily asked.

"I don't know. Are you sorry you loved Jasper?"

Lily shrugged. "We were children."

Stridently Claire asked, "Are you sorry you loved him?"

Lily stared at the waif dressed in white, the flush of her cheeks testifying to the effort this conversation was costing her. Softly, Lily said, "I still do."

Claire's posture relaxed. "Then why can't you understand that I still love Whit?"

"I understand it," Lily said, watching her closely. "I'm worried about Junior, is all."

"What's he got to do with Whit?"

The moment was there, but Lily let it pass. "Junior thinks the world of you, Claire. What do you reckon it's doing to him to hear you praise an outlaw?"

Claire closed her eyes, then opened them again and blinked back tears. "Whit was hung. Isn't that enough evidence of the error of his ways?"

Lily hesitated, then said, "Emmett lied."

Claire paled, turned away and stomped her foot as if in anger, then turned back and wiped the tears from her cheeks before she whispered, "Whit's still alive?"

Lily shrugged. "Coupla years 'fore Emmett died, Whit wrote you a letter."

"What happened to it?" Claire wailed, not bothering to wipe away her fresh tears.

"Emmett burned it."

"Where was it from?"

"El Paso."

Claire sank to the floor, sitting in a pool of white linen and lace as she cried.

Lily let her go on for a while, then said sternly, "Pull yourself together, Claire. I can't handle you going crazy."

She raised her eyes and shook her head. "I won't ever let that happen again."

"Good," Lily said.

"More than anything, I don't want to be a burden to you, Lily.

You took me in when even my father didn't want me, and I'll be beholden forever. I love you, Lily, almost as much as I love Whit."

Lily managed a smile. "I'm glad it's not as much or I might find it necessary to high-tail it to Mexico."

Claire laughed, wiping her tears with her hem. "Do you think he'll ever come back?"

Lily nodded. "There's no telling when that'll be, though."

Claire stood up and brushed the straw from her skirts, then met Lily's eyes. "I hope it's before I'm old."

"You'll always be the same age he is, Claire."

She smiled. "And you'll always be younger than both of us."

"I feel ten times older," Lily said.

"That's because you have a child. It's children that date a person. If Whit were here now, I'd feel like the girl who fell in love with him, though I know that's not who he'd see. If Amiel were still alive, I'd have that compensation for my years."

Lily looked down.

"To my eyes," Claire said, "you're the same girl I met at the river so long ago." She laughed lightly. "Except that girl didn't wear a gun."

"Lotta water under the bridge since then," Lily mumbled.

"You *are* the bridge, Lily," Claire said. "I owe you my life. Come give me a hug."

Lily took the few steps into Claire's arms. As they held each other close, Lily thought if she was the bridge, then Claire was the water flowing free over the rocks. Stifling her tears, Lily said, "Let's go up to the house and find out what's for supper."

Claire laughed. "Your hunger proves your vitality, Lily. I so seldom want to eat, you'd think I was a ghost." With her arm around Lily's waist as they crossed the yard, Claire snuggled close. She broke away when they entered the house. "I think I'll take a nap before supper. Wake me when it's ready, won't you, Lily?"

She promised she would and watched Claire disappear into the room that had always been hers at Bosque Grande. Lily continued on down the long hall, the timbre of her spurs announcing her approach to the women in the kitchen. Rosemary and

Bianca were cooking, Rosamarie already in her high chair, chewing on a wooden spoon.

"Hi, Mom," Lily said, snitching a tidbit of the smoked ham Rosemary was slicing.

She playfully slapped Lily's hand with the flat of the knife. "Wash before you do that," she said, her smile teasing.

Lily popped the ham into her mouth and smiled, then looked at Theo's wife. She wasn't yet twenty, a voluptuous woman who'd gained weight with each of her three pregnancies. Her black hair fell in a single braid down the middle of her back, and her cheeks were flushed from the heat of the oven, where potatoes and biscuits were baking. "Hi, Bianca," Lily said.

Bianca glanced up with a nervous smile. "*Buenas tardes*, Lily," she answered.

Lily gave her a smile back, but she was already concentrating on chopping an onion to be fried with the ham. Knowing Bianca was afraid of her, Lily could neither understand why nor break through the fear with kindness. She suspected Bianca would have preferred that Theo had kept the mill, or at least that he worked for a man rather than a woman. But since he was half crippled and mentally weak, Lily thought his wife should be glad he worked for his sister rather than a stranger. Feeling impatient with the Mexican notion of machismo, Lily walked out the back door and saw Roberto and Julio playing marbles in the dust.

She let the boys continue their game as she herded the chickens into the coop for the night. That was supposed to be their job, but like their father, they seemed to understand responsibility as something to shirk. Part of Lily's campaign to win Bianca's friendship, however, was to never criticize her children. Since Junior, too, worked only when he felt like it, Lily had no example to offer of her own maternal guidance toward productive manhood, so she often found herself biting her tongue.

Shooing the last of the recalcitrant birds through the gate, Lily latched it, then laughed as the rooster crowed his dominion over his hens. "Cock of the walk don't count for much around here," Lily told him. The rooster eyed her with his beady gaze, then opened his yellow beak and crowed again.

Lily walked past the newly green grape arbor into the orchard. The peach, apple, and pear trees were ablaze with blossoms, the abundant pink and white petals predicting a good harvest. She inhaled their delicate perfume carried on the breeze as she left the orchard and walked beneath the willows along the river. Like the roses around the house, the willows bore no fruit, proving a romantic side to Emmett's nature she hadn't seen expressed in any other way.

Lily snapped off a dead twig and beat it against her leather skirt as she wondered if Emmett had been tender with his mistress. Life was a series of quirks, as far as Lily could see. If her father hadn't been murdered, she wouldn't have married for vengeance. If Suzanne Homer hadn't been barren, *she* might have married Emmett. If Claire hadn't been seduced by Whit, she would be a mother and wife instead of an abandoned divorcée. If Theo hadn't been kicked in the head by a horse, he wouldn't be crippled. If Junior had been crying that night, both babies would have been in the right cradles and Amiel would have died instead of Junior. Lily wouldn't have carried the weight of her lie all these years, Claire wouldn't have gone mad with grief, and Junior née Amiel would not now be the spoiled brat Lily's guilt had made him.

Beating the switch against her skirt, Lily came out of the willows below the bunkhouse, then stopped dead still at the sight of Shiloh Pook stripped to the waist. She watched the muscles in his back as he washed dust from his face, his butt in his trousers pulled taut as he bent low over the basin set on a plank, his thighs long and lean, his boots sporting spurs shiny red in the sunset.

He reached to the plank for a small towel he held over his face as he stood up and turned around. While he scrubbed his face dry, his chest muscles rippled, covered by a thick mat of brown hair that funneled into a narrow line on his flat belly and disappeared beneath the buckle of his belt. When he took the towel away, he met Lily's eyes. She beat the switch against her skirt as he slowly smiled.

"What cha doing down here, Lily?" he teased.

"Just walking," she said.

He nodded, glancing at the stick she continued to whack against the leather of her skirt. "The boys're gone," he said. "You wanta come in?"

Lily had never been inside the bunkhouse; it was where Shiloh lived and she'd always respected his privacy. "Supper's nearly ready," she said.

He dropped the towel on the plank and reached for his shirt. She watched him button it, then turn his back to open his trousers and tuck in the tails. He turned around again and gave her another smile. "You look pretty," he said, "in the red light falling from the sky."

Embarrassed, she answered curtly, "Red light ain't none for a lady."

He shook his head in a charade of chastisement. "You got a knack for killing a compliment, Lily."

"Maybe I don't believe any compliments coming from a man," she retorted.

He winced. "I'm sorry your memories are so bitter."

"I'm a lady. What'd you expect 'em to be?"

He studied her a moment, then asked sadly, "Is that what Emmett taught you?" When she didn't answer, he said, "I wish you'd let someone show you otherwise. If you don't want it to be me," he shrugged, "I can understand that. But you're young yet, and it'd be a shame to go your whole life without knowing what sweetness a man's touch can give."

She felt badly, knowing she'd caused the hurt in his eyes. "It ain't nothing against you, Shiloh. I just don't have the need of a man's touch."

He looked at the switch in her hand when he said, "I don't believe that, Lily."

"You think you know my mind?" she mocked.

He smiled, coming closer. "I wouldn't dare say it if I did." Towering over her now, he asked, "Would you use that switch on me if I kissed you?"

"I might," she whispered, her hand limp at her side.

He took hold of her arms and bestowed a long, familiar kiss that gave credence to his knowledge. She felt her loins contract with pain in the same way her stomach twisted when she'd gone too long without food. Then she remembered Emmett pinning her beneath him, and she yanked herself free of Shiloh's hands and struck him across the chest with her switch.

He stepped away from her. "If it wasn't still daylight," he said, "I'd drag you down right here and make you take that back."

She yearned for him to do it, to let her beat against him until he subdued her anger in the coupling he claimed would be so sweet and which she wanted so badly. But the supper bell rang, calling her back to her senses. She threw the switch far into the chaparral, then gave him a tentative smile of truce. "Let's go to supper."

He shook his head. "I'll ride into River's End and eat there. The tallies are on my table, if you can't wait till morning."

"I can wait," she said.

"So can I," he answered.

They stared at each other across the deepening shadows of dusk. Then he returned to the plank holding the washbasin, lifted his gunbelt, and buckled it on as he met her eyes.

In the gentleness of his mercy, she asked, "Will you look after Junior in town?"

"Yes, ma'am," he said. He took his hat off the plank and settled the brim low above his eyes before he turned and walked toward the stable.

She watched him go, listening to the song of his spurs fade in the distance. After a while he rode out on the black stallion bred from the mare that had once belonged to Whit. She wondered if Shiloh was making a statement in his choice of mounts; if he was saying he offered the same depth of love Claire had received, or if he thought it appropriate to ride the descendant of Whit's horse while looking after his son.

Suspecting all the lies were about to fall on her head, Lily walked toward the house alone.

26

*A*fter supper, Lily settled herself at her desk, opened the latest issue of the *Stock Growers' Report,* and read an article on the effects of overgrazing. The writer recommended fencing the range and rotating livestock among pastures to allow some to recover while others were in use. Lily thought this approach was sensible, but she didn't know where she'd get the money.

The first expense would be to hire a surveyor to locate the property lines, then she'd have to buy fencing. Barbed wire was the cheapest. A hundred-pound spool containing 550 yards cost $4.10 plus seventy cents per hundred pounds of freight. If she divided her two sections into four pastures each, by her quick calculations, she'd need 1,034 spools to string a fence of four strands at a cost of $4,963. Setting posts every forty feet with three stays on each panel would require 10,656 posts and 15,984 stays. Stays she could have cut off the range and pay only for labor; mesquite posts cost ten cents each plus freight. Cedar posts, however, cost two dollars plus freight; she'd need them for the corners and gates. So over five hundred dollars for posts. Aside from the surveyor's fee, she was looking at a cost of over six thousand dollars.

Once the materials were purchased, the work could be completed inside of a month if she let everything else slide for a while. Branding was over so that schedule was feasible, if she could get Junior to work every day for a full month. Theo would complain, but he'd do it. She couldn't predict Shiloh's reaction. The new idea of fencing didn't sit well with men accustomed to the open range. And then what had happened just before supper might change things between her and Shiloh all the way around.

She herself didn't much like the notion of fencing. An aspect of freedom would be lost with the vast vistas of wide-open spaces a rider could cross without hindrance. Caught in a pasture, a person could spend a great deal of time searching for a gate that led only to another enclosure. Precious manpower would be spent maintaining the structure of confinement, and barbed wire was called devil's wire because it was difficult to see in the dark or during a storm and horses had died after running full speed into the strands. Another consideration was that fencing controlled not only the movement of livestock but also wild game, so the face of the land would change. No longer a paradise of free forage and equal access to water, the range would become a cattle farm, every acre controlled for production.

Control was the pertinent word. Without it, the land had already changed. Instead of cultivating its bounty so future generations could thrive, Emmett had raped the land he'd found virginally intact, subdued it beneath his ambition, and ravished it with greed, leaving only a bed of dust as his legacy. Now Lily was master of that domain. To save what was left and resurrect what had been destroyed, she had to be excruciatingly careful with every decision she made. One wrong move could put her in a bed no better than Emmett's.

The house had fallen silent around her. Lily extinguished her lamp and sat in the dark, thinking of Emmett's legacy. She'd heard the gossip that said she'd married him for his money, then poisoned him to make the cancer grow on his neck. Before hearing that story, she'd known her reputation wasn't a pleasant one but she hadn't suspected it was so bad. Folks didn't cotton to a woman riding and wearing a gun like a man, let alone running a ranch. She could slough that off; being considered a murderess wasn't so easy. Although she was innocent, truth carried little credence in the realm of gossip, and she knew no matter what she did from here on out, the story that she'd killed her husband would be whispered long after she was dead. Eventually even Junior would hear it.

She had tried to paint Emmett in glowing colors so the boy would grow up loving his father, but there were so many lies in her praise she often doubted that Junior believed what she said.

In truth she hated Emmett Moss, and in truth he wasn't Junior's father. Though it had seemed best to keep the boy from knowing that, he wasn't turning out well, perhaps because he sensed her dishonesty.

She stood up and watched the moon rise over the distant ledge of mountains, thinking she'd spent the years since her marriage propping up lies. Maybe she should sweep them out like dust with a broom, knock all the cobwebs from the corners, and open the shutters the lies had erected. Maybe with the wind of truth blowing through the house, Junior would stay home more often. Except he wouldn't be Junior anymore. He would be Amiel. Claire would be his mother, and Lily would be a childless widow.

Feeling weary, she went to her bedroom. Like the office, it had once been Emmett's. Usually she slept well in the massive black walnut bed, knowing he'd always slept on the floor. But tonight she lay awake, thinking of her family. The room next to hers had once been Andy's, then Junior's. Now Theo's sons, Roberto and Julio, slept there, apparently not bothered by ghosts. The room behind theirs, which had once been Drew's, was now Rosemary's, and the room behind that belonged to Junior. Claire slept in the room that had always been hers. The baby, Rosamarie, slept in what had once been Lily's small parlor. And the bedroom she'd been given as a bride now belonged to Theo and Bianca.

Except for Junior, they were all home, probably asleep. Certainly the children. Claire, perhaps, was reading one of the novels she mail-ordered from Boston. Rosemary might be awake, either planning her work for the next day or reflecting back on her life, maybe remembering when she hadn't slept alone. Only Theo and Bianca shared a bed in this house. They, too, might be awake, maybe making love, perhaps conceiving another child in the bed of Junior's conception. The Junior who was buried in Amiel's grave. When the truth came out, Lily would have nothing left unless she acted now to find something of her own.

When she heard horses in the yard, she sat up, waiting for Junior to come into the house. Finally she heard the kitchen door open, then his spurs as he passed through the pantry and entered his room. She waited until she thought he'd had time to undress and fall asleep. Slowly she threw the covers out of her way and fumbled in the moonlight to take off her nightgown and pull a shimmy and her dark blue dress over her head. She buttoned the dress quickly and put on her stockings and shoes, striving to be quiet. As she stood in front of the mirror to brush her hair, she lost courage.

She was homely and skinny and thirty years old. Shiloh didn't want her. He'd merely been titillated that afternoon because she'd seen him without his shirt on. Probably his kiss had been only a tease, for himself as much as her. He may even have bought a whore in town and was now already asleep, perfectly satisfied. Her visit would be a bother to him, one more duty to get out of the way before he could rest.

She met her eyes in the mirror. Earlier she'd been telling herself it was time for the truth. The truth in this case was that the only man she'd ever loved was dead and someday she would be, too. In her grave she would be alone forever. Now she was alive, and Shiloh *had* kissed her. That wasn't a tease but an invitation. And even if not, she didn't have to throw herself at him. She could scout out her reception, talk business first, and leave with nothing lost if she decided that was best.

As silently as she could, she crept through her office and went out the front door rather than passing by everyone's bedroom. The moon lit the yard with a milky light as she circled wide to approach the bunkhouse. Shiloh's door was open, a small fire in the hearth throwing flickers across the threshold. She edged closer until she saw him sitting on the edge of his bed. He was still dressed, leaning his elbows on his knees as he stared into the fire. When she stopped in the doorway, he looked up, then he smiled.

She glanced around the room, seeing the whitewashed adobe walls barren of decoration other than his jacket, hat, and gunbelt on hooks, a round table with one chair in the middle of the floor, the tally sheet weighed down with a rock on the table, the narrow bed he sat on pushed against the wall opposite the hearth.

"Since you've come this far," he said softly, "you may as well come in."

She stepped across the threshold and closed the door.

"Afraid we'll be seen?" he teased.

"Don't reckon there's anybody else awake," she answered, her eyes on the tally sheet.

"Is that what you came for?" he asked.

She shook her head, then remembered her intention to talk business first. "I've decided to fence the range," she said.

He chuckled. "Have you?"

"I came to ask what you thought of the idea."

"Why ask, if you've already made up your mind?"

She moved to stand in front of the fire as if she were cold. With her back to him, she said, "Thought maybe you'd have an opinion to offer."

"I like your hair loose like that," he said.

She turned around and met his eyes.

"Why don't you sit down, Lily?"

She moved to the chair and pulled it out from beneath the table.

"I meant over here by me," he said.

She looked at him again.

He smiled. "It's where it's usually done."

"Maybe I didn't come here for that," she said.

"You still want to talk about fences?"

"I think it's important."

"All right. What do you want to say?"

She took a deep breath, still standing by the table. "I don't ever want to get married again."

He laughed. "Usually the man says that, Lily. If he's honest with the girl, which most of 'em ain't."

"I'm not a girl," she said.

"And I'm not looking for a wife. I would marry you, but I'd just as soon we give each other secret comfort and leave the rest as it is."

"Then we're in agreement," she said.

He nodded. "Now we got that settled, why don't you come sit down?"

Hesitantly she approached and settled herself with a foot of empty space between them. Shiloh reached under the bed and brought out a bottle of whiskey. He uncorked it and took a sip, then offered it to her. Cautiously she swallowed a tiny taste and gave the bottle back, feeling the whiskey warm her stomach. Shiloh took another sip and set the bottle on the floor.

Nervously she sorted through her mind for a topic of conversation, then asked, "Where'd you find Junior?"

Shiloh turned to lean against his pillow, one foot flat on the floor and the other knee bent so that foot hung over the edge of the bed to keep his spur off the covers. "Hannigan's Saloon."

"Was he gambling?"

Shiloh nodded.

"How'd he do?"

"Won thirty bucks, all told. He's a natural-born gambler, Lily. I watched him take ten off Woody Wheeler, who wasn't none too happy about the loss."

"Serves Woody right for playing with a child," Lily said. "He prob'ly thought Junior'd be easy pickings."

"Nobody who's ever played with him thinks that. He's got a knack for cards like I ain't seen 'cept when Whit Cantrell was at the table."

She dropped her gaze to the bottle of whiskey. Shiloh handed it to her, and she took a bigger sip this time, then gave the bottle back. He took another sip, too, set the bottle down, and said, "Whit once told me he had a power over cards, that it's a magical ability to communicate with fate. Said it was a gift he got from his daddy, and being as it's a manly ability, it's fairly reliable, the problem being another name for fate is Lady Luck, and everyone knows women are fickle."

"I didn't realize you knew Whit so well."

"Reckon there's a lot about me you don't know, Lily."

She wet her lips, which were suddenly dry.

Shiloh watched her tongue, then smiled.

"Do you believe that," she asked, "about women being fickle?"

"I ain't known enough women to say."

"I can't hardly believe that, Shiloh."

"Why not?"

She shrugged. "A man as handsome as you must've had a lotta women in his life."

"Most every one I've had was bought and paid for."

She frowned.

He laughed. "I'm forty years old and never been married, Lily. That oughta tell you something."

"What do you think it should tell me?"

"That I'm prob'ly as scared right now as you are."

She met his eyes.

He smiled.

"If we're both scared," she said, "maybe we shouldn't do it."

"Maybe not," he said. "But the things in my life I've been most glad I did were things that scared me 'fore I did 'em."

She nodded. "Know what I was thinking just 'fore I came down here?"

"What?"

"That I didn't want to go my whole life without sharing love."

"I've loved you for years, Lily. Maybe since that day you chewed me out for leaving the garden gate open." He smiled. "You remember that?"

She nodded.

"I thought to myself at the time that Emmett found himself a worthy bride for Bosque Grande. Even though I still have a lotta respect for Emmett, from the day I saw you looking so forlorn in your wedding dress I knew he wasn't doing right by you. I wanted to say something to him many times but it just ain't the kinda thing a man says to his boss. So I'll say it to you now, Lily: You deserved better. I've never been a husband, but I've shared love in plenty of beds that didn't have no legal sanction. If you'll allow me, I'll show you what that kinda love's about."

"I'd like that very much, Shiloh."

"Come over here then and lie down beside me," he said, guiding her to do it. "We've both waited too long for this."

Lily lolled through the summer in the pleasures of love. Each night after everyone in the house was asleep, she walked down to Shiloh's room and joined him in bed. The few sips of whiskey they shared, while his conversation circled her like a coyote circles his prey, lulled her into an acquiescence she wouldn't have believed possible, as his words mesmerized her into following his lead into a country she had only imagined. The sensations he elicited from her body were such marvels that she often felt she had become a new creature fashioned from his desire. Yet the desire was also hers, and before long she rose to his challenge and forged new trails in the wilderness of their union. Leading him to precipices she dared him to leap from, he held her close as they tumbled together. Diving into waters too deep to be fathomed, she beckoned him to follow, then found him waiting in the depths with welcoming arms. When she surfaced to breathe in the open air again, he was there with her, shuddering as violently and clinging as desperately in the passing of their passion.

Sometimes he caught her alone on the prairie, where his caresses dappled her skin like sunlight falling through the trees overhead. She listened to the meadowlarks and the horses grazing nearby as he coaxed her into a lazy rhythm that soon drove the world into retreat. Though their lust was a visceral downpour after her lifetime of drought, he nestled it in words as if it were a water jug suspended in the breeze of their friendship between the times they took it down to quench their thirst. Its effect was liberating to Lily. The stone that had sealed her heart so long ago gave way beneath Shiloh's power of persuasion.

She laughed with exuberance, often turning heads at home, the eyes of her family puzzled and wary at the change that had come over her as quickly as a summer storm. Blind to its beauty, they feared the storm's potential destruction. If they knew it had been born in Shiloh's bed, they never said so; and in their company she tried so hard to shelter the source of her joy that she often pelted him with the cold hail of indifference. He suffered it with grace, and when they were next alone she strove to compensate for the stings she'd delivered, making the balm of their coupling all that much sweeter.

Among her family, Junior was the most troubled. Though not yet fifteen, he was no novice in carnal pleasure, and he smelled sex on his mother even when she was fresh from a bath. It was a vital, animal scent replacing the stale odor of dormancy that had permeated the air around her all his life. Now she was quick, and he felt angry that she'd been revived from the lethargy that had given him free rein. She cared about everything with an energy that displeased her son, who suddenly had become the focus of her attention. His table manners were crude, his hygiene lacking, his carefree attitude a remnant of childhood he should have outgrown.

He bridled under the quirt of her criticism, at first astonished, then resentful, then quivering with a rage he didn't dare let loose. When she decided to divide the range into pastures and ordered him to work alongside Shiloh to build the fences, Junior's sullen wrath stretched as taut as the barbed wire strung between them. Shiloh watched him warily. Theo, setting the posts in holes they dug, stayed neutral as he nailed the wire separating Junior's suppressed fury and the well-worn path of Shiloh's devotion to duty.

Shiloh understood the problem but didn't figure it would behoove anyone to hurry it to a head. Once the romance was common knowledge, his guess was that Lily would feel so ashamed she'd break it off or make it legal. If she broke it off, he'd sorely miss the pleasure they shared, and he also severely doubted they could resume their former relations as if the sex had never happened. On the other hand, though he wouldn't mind being married to Lily, he was a cowpoke with no assets and she was the widow of the Cattle King of the Panal, a title that carried prestige if not wealth. In truth she was a hardscrabble rancher, but in legend she was the black widow who'd hoodwinked the wiliest man in the territory. Being her second husband would be no easy row to hoe. So Shiloh bided his time, waiting for Junior to force Lily's hand.

In July, the rains returned. Lily kept her cattle out of one pasture entirely all summer, and the grass was replenished. After fall roundup, when the herd had been diminished to her breeding stock, she let them loose in that pasture and left the other land to recover. With the scant profit from selling the cattle, she bought forage for supplemental feed through the winter.

All those months she kept Junior working hard, he simmered with resentment while growing taller and stronger. The former friendship he'd shared with Shiloh was now an uneasy truce, each of them waiting for the explosion that would shatter their peace. That seemingly inevitable confrontation was averted by Claire on Junior's fifteenth birthday.

Rosemary was in the kitchen frosting his cake, with the younger children an avid audience, while Bianca finished up supper. Lily was in her office wrapping his present, a fancy shirt she'd ordered from the best seamstress in River's End. Idle, Claire walked out of the house and beneath the willows to enjoy the rustling music of the wind in their leaves. The afternoon was hot and she plied a fan on her face beneath the wide brim of her straw bonnet. When she came out from under the trees, she was beyond the bunkhouse, and she saw Shiloh and Junior washing together behind the building. They both had their shirts off, and she tarried longer than was proper to admire them.

Junior's young, lithe body knelled a memory from deep in her past. Several times recently she had felt jarred by a particular smile that sometimes played on his mouth, or by the possessive way his gaze often slid over her figure. The reminiscence of Whit he stirred couldn't be denied, yet she credited it to Junior's youth and the special closeness they shared. As his mother, Lily controlled him. His subsequent resentment seemed natural to Claire, merely the fledgling's attempt to free himself of maternal apron strings. As his older cousin, she offered an unconditional love that she hoped balanced the onerous demands of his mother.

That those demands cut against his grain was obvious. So little did he cherish the virtues of work and duty that Claire often wondered how he could be a Moss. She supposed he was like Andy in that regard, a dreamer without her brother's artistic bent, which had distinguished him from being a run-of-the-mill bum. Andy hadn't done a day's work in his life, but while he read books and studied music, Junior's interests were more worldly.

He could spend hours practicing picking a handkerchief off

the ground from the back of a galloping horse, or standing in the saddle while his horse circled the corral at a lope. Sometimes he did handstands on his saddle, coming down to sit astride backward on the horse's rump, then raising himself on his hands again and somersaulting through the air to land standing straight on the ground, his arms outstretched with pride. It was Claire who applauded these feats, watching from under the shade of the portal. Lily scoffed at them as useless.

Claire supposed they were, yet recognizing that they demonstrated an unusual agility and balance, she prevailed upon Lily to order a Victrola from Philadelphia so the boy could be given dancing lessons. He was already taller than Claire, and he made a good partner in the intricate steps of the cotillions and waltzes she remembered from her youth. He laughed easily, and fell with a natural grace into the playful banter of her stylized flirting. Once when they were alone in the parlor, he boldly kissed her mouth, stirring a desire only one other man had ever aroused in her body. After that, she discontinued their dancing, belatedly realizing she had been teasing the man out of the boy in an unfair way.

The afternoon she stood beneath the willows to watch Junior and Shiloh washing together, Claire was so struck with the boy's resemblance to Whit that she felt dizzy. The men were talking as they scrubbed dust from their faces and splashed water on their torsos, then dried themselves with towels, but she was too far away to catch more than the nuances of their voices on the wind. She closed her eyes and listened to Junior, hearing Whit. Tears filled her eyes at the familiar cadence and textures from so long ago. When she opened her eyes again, the men were buttoning their shirts and staring at each other, Junior with hostility, Shiloh with a wariness that spoke of impending violence.

Impulsively she walked out from under the trees, plying her fan with vigor. "Mercy, it's hot," she said with a laugh.

"Yes, ma'am," Shiloh mumbled.

Junior kept quiet though his eyes were ferocious on the man they all knew had found his way into Lily's heart. No one had said anything, but they all knew.

Holding out her hand, Claire asked, "Will you walk with me, Junior, up to the graves?"

"It'll be hotter'n blazes on that hill," he argued, his eyes still on Shiloh.

"No more so than here," she answered softly. "Perhaps we'll catch a cooling breeze on top."

Junior shook his head. "Go away, Claire. I got a bone to pick with Shiloh."

"I need a gentleman's arm," she insisted, still holding out her hand as he angrily met her eyes. "Surely that's not something you'll refuse me."

"Go on, Junior," Shiloh said. "I'll be here when you get back."

Junior swept his hat off the plank and settled the brim low above his eyes, then roughly took Claire's hand and tucked it into the crook of his elbow as he led her in a fast walk toward the hill.

"Slow down, sweetheart," she protested gently. "I can't climb at this pace."

He shortened his stride, scowling as he looked straight ahead.

"What was it," she asked, plying her fan, "that you felt you needed to speak to Shiloh about so urgently?"

"Nothing for your ears," he muttered.

She laughed lightly. "Do you think they're so delicate?"

"Yeah, I do," he retorted. "You're a lady, which is something I wish I could say about my mother."

"Do you think a lady," Claire asked, watching her footing as she struggled to breathe within the constriction of her corset, "doesn't feel the need for physical affection?"

"Do you?" Junior scoffed, obviously expecting her denial.

"Yes," she said without raising her eyes, though she felt him look at her sharply.

They stopped on top of the hill and she plied her fan as she looked down at Amiel's grave and Andy's close beside it. When she'd caught her breath, she said, "There are a great many things you don't know, Junior."

"Why don't you tell me?" he mocked with sarcasm. Yet when she leaned against him, his arm encircled her waist with a tenderness negating his anger.

Her cheek was against the front of his shirt so she could hear his heartbeat as she kept her eyes on the tiny grave. "I was carrying another man's child when I married Robert Daggerty. I never loved Robert, and I regret that the name on my son's tombstone is a lie."

After a moment, Junior asked, "What name should be there?"

"Cantrell," she whispered. "The father of my son was Whit Cantrell."

"The outlaw?"

Claire met his eyes, feeling something unnameable stir within her. "Have you heard of him?"

"Sure." He looked down at the tombstone. "Amiel Cantrell. That's quite a name."

She smiled sadly. "I have another one to tell you."

He looked back at her.

"Jasper Stone," she said. "Have you heard of him?"

Junior nodded.

"He and Whit were best friends. Though fate didn't decree for either of us to find happiness with them, I was in love with Whit, and your mother was in love with Jasper."

"My mother was in love with Jasper Stone?" Junior asked incredulously.

"Yes," Claire answered with a smile.

"But my father led the posse that killed him."

"Yes," she said again, this time with a sigh. "Lily's lived with that all these years. If now she's able to find comfort in Shiloh's bed, don't spoil it for her, Junior. She's waited so long for love."

The perplexity on the boy's face was painful. "But it ain't right, Claire."

She smiled her forgiveness of his masculine arrogance. "It wasn't right for me to lay with Whit, but he gave me the most pleasure I've known, and I wouldn't take a moment of it back despite all the tragedy that followed."

"What tragedy?" he asked.

"Oh, my," she said, laughing a sigh. "It started with your cousin's death. Andrew Moss, Junior, your cousin and my brother, hung himself in grief for Whit. He did it because Emmett, your father and my uncle, came home one Christmas Eve and told us he'd hung Whit for loving me. Andy, who loved Whit as much I did, hung himself. Then I married Bob Daggerty, and after your father's death, Bob stole the family fortune and left Lily with only this land. In the meantime, Amiel died, and I lost my mind in grief. But I never knew that baby. It's Whit I mourn and always will. Lily's finally been freed from her mourning. Don't take that away from her, Junior."

He stared down at the tombstones catching the red light of dusk. "I'm sorry for all that," he finally said. "But if what my mother's doing ain't wrong, why do I feel so angry about it?"

Claire touched his cheek. "Because you love your mother, and being a man, you're jealous at the notion of sharing her with another. What you feel is natural, Junior. But for the sake of her happiness, you must rein it back."

He studied her face a long moment before he leaned low and kissed her mouth. She let him do it, then shook her head in mock dismay. "That's something else you must rein back. It isn't natural, and I can't allow it."

"Seems all I get to do is rein things back," he muttered.

She laughed. "I'm sure there are plenty of young girls who would welcome your kisses. I probably shouldn't say that, but since it seems you're bound to dally, almost anyone would be a better partner than I, who stands in the place of your aunt."

He pulled her close and kissed the top of her head. "I can't imagine feeling for any girl what I feel for you."

"I love you, too, Junior," she answered, "but when you're older, you'll put me away with all the other childish things of your heart."

"Then I hope I never grow up," he said.

She looked down at the graves as the wind whipped her skirts against his legs. "You will. You must. You're our last hope to keep the name Moss alive on the Panal." She met his eyes. "Promise me, Junior, you won't shirk your duty."

He laughed. "If making babies is a duty, I won't shirk it."

"You've already started, haven't you?"

"I ain't made any babies that I know of. But I've dallied with a few girls, as you so genteelly put it."

"I should chastise you," she teased, "but Whit started at your age, and by the time I met him, he was a wonder to behold."

"What was he like?"

"Oh, I think we'll save that conversation for another time. Shall we go to supper?"

He offered his arm. "Will you allow me, Miss Claire?"

"Why, I'd be honored, Mr. Moss."

27

For five years, Lily cracked the whip and kept Junior jumping, as if deliberately pushing him toward the point of no return. He grew as tall as Emmett had been, and as lean as the range under the drought. Gradually he and Shiloh were able to resume their friendship without ever mentioning what had fractured it. They worked comfortably alongside each other, sharing banter and jokes but nothing more personal than their preference in whiskey.

Theo shied away from his nephew's company, expecting Junior to explode at any moment. Junior often did explode, but only in town. On Friday nights he'd ride north to Soledad to drink in Foxy Strop's Saloon. Since Foxy's attracted drifters, Junior usually found someone to tangle with, a man down on his luck and ready to take it out on the world, a newcomer to the Panal who neither knew Junior's name nor the reputation he'd built with his fists. Often bruised and bleeding but invariably victorious, Junior finished the evening at Celia's bordello, taking the madam herself for his pleasure. Though his poker winnings could have bought the youngest and prettiest girl in the house, he preferred Celia, never guessing that her acceptance of him stemmed from his resemblance to a man she'd once loved, just as he never suspected the wide swath he cut was due less to his talent for tackling strangers than to the fact that the local rowdies backed him up because of his name.

Hungover when he left Celia's bed in the early hours of Saturday afternoon, he'd mosey down to River's End and hit the poker tables. After that, he usually spent the night with a Mexican girl he'd set up in a shack on the edge of town. On Sundays he'd ride farther south to Siete Rios to gamble and brawl with the punks. After enjoying another whore, never the same one twice in a row, he'd buy a bottle and drink all the way home, arriving in the wee hours before dawn to fall asleep in a drunken stupor that challenged Lily to put him to work.

She always did it. By noon on Monday, he was in the saddle, finding Shiloh and Theo wherever they were and joining their labor with his sullen company. They moved the cattle from pasture to pasture, drove wagons of hay out to the herd when the forage was scant, opened and closed gates a thousand times a week now that the range was fenced, branded the new calves in spring, kept the acequias flowing into the orchard and garden all summer, harvested the fruit in the fall, then gathered the cattle for market.

As the years passed, it got so that Junior rarely spent even a weeknight at home. Usually he left for town at sunset and returned at dawn. One morning when he didn't return, Lily went looking. Having watched him ride out the afternoon before, she'd noted he took the south trail across the river, so she knew he hadn't gone to Soledad. It was a blustery October morning, the sky crystal blue, the wind icy cold, so Lily intended to make the trip into River's End alone. At the last minute, however, Claire joined her in the stable and asked to ride along. Since Claire hadn't been off the ranch since she'd come home from Texas, Lily didn't have the heart to refuse. She unsaddled her horse and hitched a team to the buckboard, thinking if they found Junior drunk somewhere, at least they could throw him in the bed and cart him home.

Claire settled on the seat in a pale gray frock enveloped inside a long, hooded black cloak. Lily handled the reins, her face shadowed by the brim of her Stetson, her dark leather skirt covering the tops of her scuffed boots still adorned with spurs, and her short suede jacket granting easy access to the pistol on her hip.

As she kept the team moving at a quick trot on the road, she decided to visit the girl Junior had ruined. If he happened to be there, maybe his two mothers could shame him into bringing his illicit family home.

"Reckon we'll pay a call on Alma Labrado," Lily said, " 'fore going into town."

"All right," Claire answered with a smile. "Who is she?"

"Junior's mistress," Lily said. "I hear tell she's raising his bastard."

Claire's smile froze, then thawed with forgiveness. "He's twenty years old now. Guess nobody should be surprised that he's sown a few wild oats."

"He's sown more'n a few," Lily said. "But this is the only one I know of that sprouted."

They rode on another mile, the jingle of the harness, the hoofbeats, and the rumble of the empty wagon the only sounds between them. Then Lily said softly, "I'm lucky I ain't been caught by Shiloh."

Claire's smile was mischievous. "I've been wondering when you'd get around to talking about him, Lily Moss."

She laughed. "Reckon I figured it was one of them things that're better left unsaid."

"We've all seen you blossom under his love, and I, for one, feel happy for you."

"Who's for two?"

Claire looked at her quizzically.

"You don't have to say it, Claire. I can tell the others don't approve."

"It's not their place to approve or disapprove," Claire said. "They're all dependent on you for the food on their table, so they've kept their mouths shut except to eat." She laughed at her own joke.

Lily laughed, too, but said, "I'm as dependent as they are. I couldn't run the ranch by myself."

"You do, though," Claire said. "All the rest of us do are chores you could as easily hire done and get a better deal. Well, except for Shiloh. He's a prize."

"He's that," Lily agreed.

"Me and the children," Claire continued, "certainly don't earn our keep. Bianca does, doing most of the housework, and Rosemary runs the kitchen. Theo, bless his heart, does the best he can, but sometimes I wonder about Junior. Is he much help to you, Lily?"

"He can turn out a day's work when he has a mind to. It's his play that's so expensive."

"His gambling, you mean?"

"I don't pay for that, though he generally comes out ahead at the tables. But he's killed five prime mounts these last few years, running 'em too hard. Boils my brains to see an animal misused. And you know he won't ride none but the best. He's spent more'n one night in jail, too, on account of his brawling. I won't pay his fines. Figure he can do that himself out of his gambling winnings, and he does, but I'm fixing to start charging him room and board since he seems to think money's something to be thrown away. I don't foresee any decent future ahead of him."

"He's young yet, Lily. He'll settle down and make you proud."

"I ain't holding my breath. Reckon I spoiled him as a child. Never could bring myself to strike him. Emmett did plenty of times, but after he died, I just didn't have the heart to discipline Junior. By the time I realized the error of my ways, he was too big to turn over my knee. The one time I tried, he laughed at me. The situation was so ridiculous, I laughed, too, and that took all the spite outta my anger." She shook her head. "That boy can charm the pants off anybody when he puts his mind to it. Just ask Alma Labrado."

Claire laughed. "I don't think she'd appreciate the question."

"No, prob'ly not," Lily said.

"There's something about Junior," Claire said wistfully, "that so often reminds me of Whit."

Lily kept her eyes on the team as if they suddenly needed more attention.

"Do you think he'll ever come back, Lily?"

"It's been twenty years," she answered, "but he always was unpredictable."

"I've thought of going to El Paso and searching for him."

Lily looked at her sharply. "Don't you think if Whit Cantrell was living in El Paso we would've heard about it?"

"He might've changed his name," Claire suggested.

"He's in Mexico," Lily stated, "if he's still alive. He only posted that letter in El Paso 'cause the mails in Mexico ain't real reliable. Whit speaks Spanish better'n I do. He's prob'ly got himself a comfy life down there, maybe even a wife and children. I don't say that to hurt you, Claire, but I can't see Whit living alone all these years, can you?"

She shook her head, biting her lip.

"You can't blame him," Lily argued.

"I don't blame him for anything," Claire said. "If he does have a family in Mexico, I hope he's happy."

Lily couldn't resist asking, "So happy he leaves it to come back to you?"

"Twenty years," Claire answered, "is a long enough time for a family to grow up and not need him anymore."

"That may be true. But I never heard of children who didn't have a mother."

"You're a perfect example of the disadvantages of not reading novels," Claire replied. "You don't know how to enjoy a fantasy, Lily. One must let her mind run with the possibilities, not forever be mired in the bogs of reality."

Lily laughed. "Why don't we ask Alma Labrado about the pay-off of fantasies?"

On the western edge of town, Lily turned the team down an alley that meandered through the hovels of the *pobres*. Ramshackle adobes, the houses of the poor were pitiful habitats, their yards teeming with children half naked despite the cold. They all watched the two women ride by in the sturdy buckboard pulled by a team of matched bays. At the end of the alley, set off by itself, was a tiny shack with a thin wisp of smoke spiraling out of the chimney into the wind.

Lily reined to a stop in the bare dirt of the yard, surveying the bleak home she'd been told sheltered Alma Labrado. No porch graced the front, and the one window was sealed with a wooden shutter. From inside she and Claire could hear a baby crying, which probably explained why Alma hadn't heard her visitors arrive. As Lily stepped down and tethered the team to a hitching post, she saw no stable or corral and no other horse, so guessed Junior wasn't there. After she helped Claire down, they approached the door together. Lily knocked.

It was opened by a pretty Mexican girl who couldn't have been more than sixteen. She held a wailing infant as she gave her visitors a tentative smile of welcome.

"Buenos días," Lily said kindly. *"Soy Señora Moss, y ella es Señora Daggerty. Usted es Señorita Labrado, ¿verdad?"*

The girl nodded, looking at each of them shyly, then she stepped back and opened the door wider. *"Pasa, señoras,"* she whispered.

They stepped down into the house and looked around as Alma closed the door. There was barely enough room for them all to stand inside. A wooden bed with a cornhusk mattress took most of the space. Beside it was a small, scarred table with two chairs. A black cookstove was the only other furniture, though Lily saw a crucifix on the wall above the bed. It was a gory rendition typical of those favored by Mexicans: Christ's face twisted in agony, the blood from His wounds bright red against the dark wood of His body.

"Siéntese, por favor," Alma murmured, nodding at the table.

As Lily and Claire sat down in the chairs, Alma sat on the edge of the bed, rocking the baby and crooning to quiet it.

"Let me," Claire said, holding out her arms.

Alma looked doubtful, then surrendered the baby. In a moment it was quiet beneath Claire's smile. Alma breathed a deep sigh of relief. "Es good," she said. "You are a good mother, no?"

Claire shook her head, still watching the baby's face. "What's its name?" she asked.

"Josefa Sofia," Alma answered, then added boldly, "de Moss y Labrado."

Lily met the girl's defiant eyes and nodded to let her know the child's paternity was not in dispute. Alma's shoulders dropped a notch, then she stood up and crossed to the stove, opened the lid, and began lifting cow chips from a basket on the floor. As she dropped the dried dung onto the fire, the downdraft blew ashes out to float through the air before they settled on the women, the table, the baby, and the bed.

"*¿No tiene madera?*" Lily asked.

The girl quickly closed the stove and stood in front of the basket so her skirts hid her fuel as she shook her head. "I no see Junior for two weeks now. I gather this on the prairie. It makes a hot heat. When he comes, I will have wood again." She leaned the scant distance to brush the ashes off the table with her hand.

Lily looked above the stove at the shelf holding one limp bag of cornmeal for tortillas, nothing more. She thought of her own pantry, larger than this room, its shelves crowded with preserves that had sat unopened for years. Every night Junior was home he walked through that pantry on his way to bed. How many times, Lily wondered, had she sat in her office and listened to him come in while this girl lay here with her baby, cold and hungry? Lily knew the child was six months old, though small for her age, her mother worn thin with nursing while having only cornmeal to eat. "Have you any money?" Lily asked.

"Not now," Alma said. "Junior gives me five dollars each week, but I no see him for two weeks now, so my money is gone."

Lily looked at Claire cuddling the baby, then she looked back at Alma. "Would you like to come live at Bosque Grande?"

Alma's eyes flared with surprise. "Junior no like."

"I ain't asking him," Lily said. "I'm asking you."

"I hear you have big orchard with many fruit. I love the fruit, to pick it from the tree when it is juicy as you bite it. Do you have such an orchard?"

Lily nodded.

Alma laughed. "Such a thing is like a dream to me. I like very much to live with such an orchard. But Junior no like me there. It bring you trouble, señora. I no want this."

"I can handle my son," Lily said. "Ain't Josefa his daughter?"

"*Sí, ella es,*" Alma answered proudly.

"Then she's my granddaughter," Lily said. "*Soy la abuela de la chica. ¿Verdad?*"

"*Sí, es verdad,*" Alma said.

Lily forced herself to smile though she was seething with anger. In Spanish she said, "If you come, Junior might be mean. Maybe he won't give you as much as he does now, but I will. So will Señora Daggerty. Also my mother lives with us, and my brother and his wife, who have children for Josefa to play with when she's older. We will all welcome you, Alma, if you'll trade us for Junior's high regard. If you'd rather have him, I'll give you money. Which do you want?"

Alma's gaze dropped to Lily's gun, then met her eyes. "If you will protect me from Junior's anger, I will come gladly to live at Bosque Grande and serve you with the work of my hands and the love of my heart."

"All right," Lily said, standing up. "Pack what you want. I've got a wagon outside to take you home."

"*Muchas gracias, abuela de mi hija,*" the girl said with tears in her eyes.

"*Somos familia, Alma,*" Lily said. "*Hay no necesidad por gracias.*"

"*Sí,*" the girl whispered.

Lily looked at Claire, holding the baby.

"Isn't she lovely, Lily?" Claire asked.

Lily glanced at the child. She was brown, like her mother, but kin just the same. "I'd like to take a buggy whip to Junior," Lily muttered.

"I think that's what you're doing," Claire answered with a smile.

Alma's quilt had been given to her by her mother when her father drove her from their house in shame, so she used it to wrap the crucifix, her clothes, and the baby's few things into a bundle the women laid in the bed of the wagon. The rest of the house they

left intact for some poor drifter to stumble upon. With the three
women on the seat of the buckboard, the mother and child in the
middle, Lily hupped the team toward home.

Alma didn't even have a coat, only a thin rebozo she wore
around her shoulders and tied in front to cradle the baby. Halfway
home, Josefa began crying with hunger. Alma opened her dress
to nurse the baby while Claire watched with fascination. Lily had
to bite back her anger that Claire would find all this so charming.
It was Claire's grandchild they were taking home, and her son
Lily had worked so hard to raise to a decent manhood, which evidently wasn't in him. He was the offspring of an outlaw and a
foolish girl who thought life was a romantic novel. Neither of
them lay awake at night worrying about the trouble Junior
caused. They had both gotten off scot-free while Lily struggled to
raise their ne'er-do-well son. Amiel Cantrell! She wanted to
scream the name loud enough to rattle the heavens. Junior and
Whit were two peas from the same pod, that's for sure. Feeling
so mad she could spit, Lily slapped the reins so the horses picked
up their feet.

When they crossed over Gushing River, she glanced down,
then yanked the team to a stop in the middle of the bridge. The
riverbed was nothing but mud. She looked west toward the
spring and saw a dam had been built, backing the water into a
huge lake on Beckworth land. Why hadn't she seen it this morning? Because of Claire. Lily had been so concerned that their banter about Whit would upset the delicate balance of the girl he'd
left behind that she hadn't even noticed the river was gone.
Damn Whit!

"What's wrong, Lily?" Claire asked.

Lily stared at her, incredulous that anyone could be so stupid.
But you couldn't talk to an idiot. If you told Claire the truth you
risked driving her crazy. So all Lily said was, "Get that baby off
your tit, Alma, or you might lose it." When Alma quickly obeyed,
Lily lashed the team to a gallop and kept that pace all the way
home.

She pulled up the team, dripping sweat, in front of the house,
jumped down, and yelled over her shoulder as she ran for the stable, "If there's any men around, tell 'em I need 'em pronto."

She had just finished saddling her horse when Theo dragged his bum leg into the barn. "What's going on, Lily?" he asked.

She swung into the saddle. "Ride to River's End and buy a crate of dynamite and whatever else we need to set it off."

"Dynamite?" Theo asked worriedly.

"Yeah, dynamite," she said, looking down at him as she gathered her reins. "Where's Shiloh?"

"Riding the north fence. You want me to go get him?"

"I told you what I want you to do. Ain't no time to fetch Shiloh, and God only knows where Junior is. Take a good horse and ride hard, Theo. Meet me at Gushing River fast as you can." She spurred out of the stable, then reined back around just beyond the door. "Theo," she asked, "you think you can carry dynamite without blowing yourself up?"

"Reckon I can," he answered with wounded pride. "You gotta set the fuses 'fore it explodes, way I understand it."

She nodded. "Don't forget the fuses, then." Yanking her horse around, she galloped out of the yard, through the trees, and across the Panal, its lazy curl of water barely making a splash. The rains had returned this summer, but the drought was far from over. Even if they came back with a vengeance, it would take years for the range to recover. The flow from Gushing River belonged to Bosque Grande. It was in the deed of title. Though the Beckworths owned the spring, they had no right to dam the flow, and Lily was sure as hell going to tell them that. If they didn't open the dam themselves, she'd blow it sky high along with anyone who got in her way.

After she crossed the bridge over the arroyo of mud, she turned her horse up the trail to the Beckworth spread. Soon she lost the trail beneath the lake backed up from the dam. She had to circle way around, eyeing the water all the time, an immense amount of life's blood stolen from Bosque Grande. When she rode into the Beckworths' yard, she felt ready to explode with righteous wrath.

Clarissa Reed opened the door and came out on the porch with a gaggle of children hanging on to her skirts. Mrs. Stone had been wrong to think Clarissa wasn't built for birthing babies. To help with the first one, the Stones had left their own children alone that fateful day. Clarissa's birthing had been easy, but Sammie had been murdered and Elise raped while Mr. and Mrs. Stone were gone. Jasper, too, had been lost in the aftermath, while Clarissa went on popping out babies who'd popped out the babies now clinging to her skirts, so Lily felt no sympathy for the Beckworths and their thirsty brood.

"Where's your husband?" she asked without getting off her horse.

Clarissa looked toward the barn, then back at Lily when she said, "Wouldn't you like to come in for coffee, Miz Moss?"

"I ain't after coffee but water," Lily retorted. "Fetch your menfolk from wherever they're hiding, for surely they knew I'd be coming."

Adam Beckworth, Clarissa's brother, came out of the barn carrying a rifle. He scowled as he walked across the yard, then forced a smile as he looked at Lily, not failing to notice the gun she wore. "Won't you come in and sit a spell, Miz Moss? Clarissa made a pineapple upside-down cake just this morning. It'll taste mighty good with a cup of coffee."

"I don't want any cake," Lily said. "I wanta know why you dammed up my water."

Adam smiled. "Funny thing about that. I don't see your brand on a single drop of it."

"Bosque Grande's got rights to that water! It's writ in the deed."

"Is it now?" he drawled. "Our deed says we got rights to all the water on our land, which is where the spring is."

"We been using that water for twenty-five years, Beckworth. Not only do we have legal title but the law of precedent's in our favor."

"My daddy settled on our land 'fore Emmett ever come to this terr'tory. So if it's precedence you're claiming, Miz Moss, we got more'n you."

"Your daddy sold that water to Emmett back in seventy-five. I got the document that proves it."

"I ain't got any such writing," Beckworth answered with a humoring smile. "Whyn't you step down, Miz Moss, so we can talk about this like civilized folk?"

"Any cayoot'd steal water ain't civilized in my estimation. He's a low-down outlaw, reneging on a contract that's been honored for a quarter of a century."

Again Beckworth gave her a maddening smile. "Now what do you know about the law, Miz Moss? You was just a child when that contract was writ. Maybe it ain't legal."

"It sure as hell is!" she shouted. "My husband wasn't no fool when it came to contracts."

Beckworth glanced at his sister, who hurried into the house, taking the children with her. "Now see what you done," he drawled. "You've offended the ears of a gentlewoman. I'm just as glad you didn't accept our invitation to sit at our table, if that's how you're gonna talk. Anyhow, I ain't accustomed to dealing with females in business. Where's your brother," he paused, then added, "or your illustrious son?"

"They're coming along. But they won't tell you nothing I ain't. We got a legal right to that water, and we'll take it with or without your say-so. I'll dynamite the dam if you don't tear it down. You got my word on that."

"You must be addled to make such a threat," Beckworth said. "I want you off my land."

Lily looked behind him and saw Paul Beckworth, Ben Reed, and his passel of sons come out of the barn, every one of them carrying a gun. She tried to calm her voice when she said, "This drought's pinching us all, Adam. But the fact remains Bosque Grande's got a legal right to that water. Surely you get enough just by running acequias off the spring without damming it up."

"We did," he answered, "till we decided to increase our herd. The market's coming back, you know, and we figure to make a killing in the next coupla years. But we can't raise more cattle'n we have been without more water."

"It's too bad your daddy didn't look to the future! Emmett did, and I ain't letting you steal what he had the good sense to buy when the likes of you couldn't see its worth."

"How you gonna stop us?" Beckworth asked, arrogant with half a dozen guns backing him up.

"I told you my intention. In case you've already forgotten, I'll say it again: Break that dam or I'll do it for you."

He snickered. "Go ahead'n try, Miz Moss. We ain't afraid of no woman, even if she does wear a gun. Takes balls to use one, and no matter how high on the hog you consider yourself, they're something you ain't got."

"I ain't alone," she said.

He laughed snidely again. "We ain't afraid of your crippled brother, your gambling son, nor nobody else on Bosque Grande. Come next spring, we figure you'll all be tired of coughing up dust and go back to Texas, where you belong. The whole length of the Panal, folks'll celebrate to see the last Moss in these parts."

"That ain't never gonna happen," Lily said. "Do I have your final word on the dam?"

"You bet'cha."

"Just remember I gave you fair warning," she said, wheeling her horse and galloping away.

Once out of the yard, she reined back to a lope, then stared with malevolent eyes at the lake, which had grown even since she'd last skirted around it. "Look at all that water!" she shouted to her horse. "It's mine, and they're stealing it!"

The horse nickered nervously, comprehending only her anger.

When Lily reached the dam, she was in sight of the road and the bridge crossing the arroyo of mud. The dam was built of mortar and rocks, the gentle lap of the lake not strong enough to break through it. Once released, however, the torrent would probably take out the bridge along with any remnant of the dam. The acequias at Bosque Grande would flood with the sudden deluge. The orchard could take it but the garden couldn't, so she'd lose food. Probably have to replace the bridge, too, to keep the road open to River's End. It was doubtful the county would compensate her expense since destroying the bridge was an illegal act. She could sue the Beckworths for compensation, but in her experience all that would get was a couple of fat paychecks for the lawyers.

Lily dismounted and let her horse graze while she paced up and down the south bank of the muddy arroyo, cursing and stewing as she waited for Theo. Finally he came ambling up the road through the lengthening shadows of dusk, walking his horse to keep from jarring the box he carried in his lap. Lily took the box and set it on the ground, then squatted beside it as she read the printed label.

Theo swung down and said, "Maybe we oughta get a lawyer, Lily."

Still reading, she asked, "What do you think a lawyer would do?"

"File an injunction that'll force the Beckworths to open the dam till the issue is settled in court."

"And who do you think'll serve that injunction?"

"The sheriff, I guess."

She stood up. "He's fifty miles away, Theo. I ain't waiting for lawyers to scribble words on a paper they gotta present to a judge who'll take his time making a decision 'fore that paper's even sent to the sheriff. We could all die of thirst waiting on the law. Did you get caps and fuses?"

Theo opened his saddlebags and took out two separate parcels tied with string. Unhappily he handed them to her. "Butch Simon at the store said the most important thing is to cut the fuses long so we got time to get away 'fore they hit the 'mite. That's what he called the dynamite."

Lily nodded, unwrapping the parcels.

"He said we're s'posed to have a permit 'fore we set it off, Lily."

She squatted beside the box, laying the parcels down and taking her knife from its sheath on her gunbelt to pry the lid off. "Where we s'posed to get this permit, Theo?"

"From the county clerk in Union."

"I s'pose it's gotta be approved by somebody."

"The territorial surveyor's office in Santa Fe," he answered.

Lily turned her head and spat in the dust. "There's my permit," she said.

She studied the score of dynamite sticks wrapped in orange paper and nestled like eggs inside the box, looked at the fuses and caps again, then reread the instructions, trying to figure out how to put them together.

"Don't you think maybe this is dang'rous, Lily?" Theo asked.
She resheathed her knife and stood up with the fuses and caps
in her hands. "Bring that 'mite over here," she said.

Theo followed her with the box, looking miserable as they
stood on the edge of the arroyo peering at the muddy side of the
dam. Lily jumped down, crammed the caps and fuses into separate pockets of her jacket, and reached up for the box. Theo carefully knelt to hand it to her, then slid down himself and stood
with his bum leg at a crooked angle as she read the instructions
again.

She studied the dam, thinking she could probably pick at the
mortar with her knife and break it open enough that the water
would seep through, eventually gouging holes. But Beckworth
would simply repair them. She had to blow the dam to
smithereens and widen the channel, too, so if he tried this again,
he'd not only have to start from scratch but would have considerably more work to do.

For the fourth time, she read the instructions. With her hands,
she dug a hole at the base of the dam. She took the dynamite out
of the box, set the sticks upright like a bunch of candles, tied
them together with string, attached a cap to each stick, and a fuse
to the one in the middle, then placed them in the hole. Unwind-
ing the fuse off its spool as she went, she walked through the
mud to the arroyo's bank. "Get up there, Theo," she said.

Awkwardly he climbed the five-foot cliff. She tossed him the
spool, then climbed up after him, took the spool back, and unwound the fuse all the way to her horse. "Get mounted, Theo,"
she said, straining for patience that she had to tell him every little
thing to do.

He held the horn while he jumped for the stirrup and swung
his bad leg over the saddle. She waited for him to get settled, then
handed him the spool, swung onto her own horse, and knotted
the reins to ride its neck before she took the spool back. "You got
a match?" she asked.

He reached into the breast pocket of his jacket and fished one
out.

Lily cut the fuse with her knife, put the knife back and the
spool in her pocket, then met Theo's eyes. She could see he was

scared, but she was too mad to be wary. She took the match from
his fingers, struck it against her saddlehorn and lit the fuse, then
realized they should have crossed the bridge first. It was too late
now. When she dropped the sizzling fuse, they galloped south
until the ground rolled under their horses' hooves in the same in-
stant the explosion nearly broke their eardrums.

Lily yanked her horse around to watch rocks and mud fly
high, then catapult back down into the roaring torrent of water.
She yelled a war whoop of victory. "Goddamn, we did it, Theo!"

"I've never heard you swear before," he said quietly.

She reached across and slapped him on the back. "Let's go
look at the destruction of a woman's wrath."

It was a sight to behold. True to her prediction, not only had
the dam blown, but the arroyo had a huge hole gouged out of it.
Tearing between the banks, the water took the edges with it,
carving a channel twice as wide as before. As they watched, the
bridge creaked, then fell and broke into pieces that were swept
into the Panal. Lily grinned at Theo. "Reckon we'll have to ride
clear to River's End to get home."

"Goddamn, Lily," he whispered.

They stared with rapt fascination at the water swirling fast
and free. But they stayed too long admiring her handiwork. Lily
realized it the minute she heard galloping hoofbeats coming
closer. As she and Theo turned their horses to face Adam Beckworth, Lily slipped the keeper strap off her pistol.

"Goddamn you, Lily Moss!" Beckworth shouted, swinging off
his horse and letting it go, so angry he didn't even care that it was
still running and would probably be halfway home before he
thought to catch it. "You goddamn bitch from hell!" he
screamed, stalking closer. "I should've known you wouldn't be
civilized and do by the law!"

"You're the one broke the law!" she yelled back. "Keep your
distance, Beckworth."

"The hell I will!" But he stopped, spreading his legs to strad-
dle more ground. "This is Beckworth land. You're trespassing."

"Let's go, Lily," Theo murmured worriedly.

"That's right!" Beckworth bellowed. "Hide behind your crippled brother, who ain't even wearing a gun!"

"I got a gun," Lily said, nudging her horse away from Theo.

"As befits a black widow who poisoned her husband!"

"I didn't do that," Lily said coldly. "But I'll defend what he left me and protect my family any way I can."

"Your family's nothing but dirt-eating Mexicans and a card-sharp son!"

"All you got is a sister who pops out kids by the litter!"

Beckworth growled and reached for his gun.

Lily beat him. She drew her pistol and pulled the trigger before he'd leveled his barrel. The shock wave reverberated up her arm to her shoulder like a quicker version of the dynamite charge rolling underground. Through the delicate wisp of smoke she watched Beckworth stagger backward as a blotch of blood appeared on the front of his shirt. He stared at her in disbelief, dropped his gun, then fell as if someone had kicked his knees out from under him. His hand groped in the dust for the gun, then he shuddered in a spasm and lay still, his eyes blind in death.

Suddenly she heard the river again, then more horses galloping closer, then Theo saying, "Give me your gun. Let 'em think I did it."

She looked at him, too stunned to comprehend.

"You'll go to jail," he argued desperately. "What'll become of us if you're in jail, Lily?"

"I shot him," she said.

"Think of Bianca and my children," he pleaded. "Our mother! Your son! And Claire! Junior's baby that's just come with his mother to live with us. Think of them, Lily! I ain't no good. I ain't never been no good at providing for nobody! Let me go to jail if somebody's got to, and somebody's got to, Lily. Beckworth's dead!"

She stared at her brother, not moving.

He reached across and yanked the gun from her hand. "Don't make me out a liar. For once in your life keep quiet and let me handle this."

She turned to see three of the Beckworths riding toward them through the falling dark of evening. Then she looked down at Adam, who was definitely dead. "I did it, Theo," she mumbled.

"Keep your mouth shut!" he muttered harshly, adding in a softer tone, "Please."

The Beckworths reined up in a cloud of dust, their horses snorting and heaving as Old Man Hugh, his son, Paul, and his son-in-law, Ben Reed, all stared down at Adam dead on the ground. One by one they raised their eyes to Lily, then shifted their gaze to Theo with the gun. They looked at the blown-up dam, then at Adam again, then Theo again. Ben Reed said softly, "Give me your gun, Theo."

He handed it over, butt first.

Hugh reached for the rifle in his scabbard.

"No!" Reed shouted. "Adam was wrong! We knew it and argued against it. He paid. Now Theo's gonna pay by the law. We'll deliver him to the sheriff, Hugh."

Hugh had his hand on the stock of his rifle, but he didn't pull it from his scabbard. He looked at Lily, at the empty gunbelt she wore, then at Theo.

"I killed him," Theo said.

"With her gun?" Hugh mocked.

"When Adam came galloping up madder'n hell, I took her gun to defend myself."

"Makes sense," Reed said.

"Mad or not," Hugh said, "Adam wouldn't shoot an unarmed man."

"I wasn't unarmed," Theo said.

"If what you're saying's true," Hugh said, "you had a gun in your hand when Adam rode up. That makes what you did murder straight out."

"He drew on me," Theo said. "His gun on the ground proves that."

They all looked at Adam's gun an inch from his hand.

"Let the sheriff figure it out," Reed said sternly. "Hugh, tote Adam back to the house. Me and Paul'll take Theo to Union."

"I'm coming, too," Lily said.

Reed shrugged, then jerked his head at Theo. "Get going. We'll skirt the ranch and catch the Deep River Road."

Theo nudged his horse west, toward the remnants of the sunset crimson above the mountains. Reed and Paul Beckworth fell in behind, and Lily followed, leaving Hugh to tend Adam's corpse.

All traces of sun had been lost behind the Sacramentos when the solemn party hit the Deep River Road. In only the metallic light of the stars, the hooves of the horses beat a measured cadence as they climbed toward the mountains. Lily's initial shock at what she'd done had given way to concern for Theo, her joy of victory at blowing the dam swamped with regret for having caused what lay ahead.

She considered all the angles of letting Theo take the blame. It didn't sit well, but she saw the logic of his reasoning: No one else could run Bosque Grande. If she and Shiloh were married, he'd have the legal right to act in her absence; since they weren't, he could make decisions but sign neither contracts nor checks. Neither could Theo. She could give him power of attorney, but her experience with such documents made her distrust them. If Theo and Shiloh had a falling out, there was nothing to keep Shiloh from leaving, and Theo himself admitted he couldn't run the ranch alone. Junior wasn't of age but soon would be. If she was still gone when he turned twenty-one, he'd claim his inheritance and run the ranch into the ground, maybe even lose it in a poker game. All that added up to Theo's plan being best.

She couldn't bring herself around to believing she'd been wrong to blow the dam, but she'd been wrong in nearly everything else. If she'd lived according to what folks expected of a woman, Adam Beckworth would never have drawn down on her. Even if by some quirk of circumstance she'd killed him anyway, she could have left Bosque Grande in good hands because she would have married Shiloh years ago rather than thinking she could get away with living in sin. For all she knew, maybe only relatives were allowed to visit women in prison, and according to the law, Shiloh was no more to her than a stranger. And though he might have married her at any time during the last few years, she doubted he'd risk it now. Shiloh was brave, but a man would have to be downright foolhardy to marry a woman who had confessed to killing one man and was reputed to have killed another.

She rode through the dark, watching her brother's back: her crippled kid brother now carrying her burden. The moon rose, throwing a white light through the Deep River Valley. When they passed Cassidy's Mill, the buildings were hollow shells of what had been her life as a child. In the distance she could see her father's grave surrounded by a stone wall that was already tumbled down here and there. Around him were the smaller graves of her brothers and sister, who had died in childhood. Her horse kept plodding on, carrying her beyond the mill until it was behind her. The night was cold and she felt alone.

The forest thickened and darkened, the road winding through the trees as the wind soughed in the branches. Shivering, she realized she hadn't eaten since breakfast. She thought of Bosque Grande, of the mother and child she'd brought home, then left to their own defenses. Junior was probably back by now, angry that she'd interfered in what he considered his private business. No doubt Alma was crying, maybe the baby, too. Bianca would be worried about Theo, trying to convince herself he'd be home soon. No one would worry about Lily. Everyone knew she could take care of herself. And she could, most of the time. Right now she longed for Shiloh's shoulder to lean on.

They ambled past the first house in the pink light of dawn, around the graceful curve of the road and into the village. Union hadn't grown since the war. There was talk of moving the county seat, even of splitting the county in half so people on the Panal wouldn't have to travel a whole day to see the sheriff or the court clerk. If that had already happened, Theo would be in River's End now and Lily might be home. Instead he faced trial where the name Moss carried no prestige, and Lily faced finding hospitality in a town where she had no friends. She realized she didn't even have money for a room or a meal. Her credit was good along the Panal, but in the mountains she was just another traveler.

Dismounting with the men in front of the sheriff's office, she tied her horse with theirs, and walked in behind them to hear what was said. Red Bond stood up from behind his desk, looking disgruntled to be needed so early in the morning. Ben Reed ran down the facts. Theo glanced at her, then looked at the sheriff and said he'd killed Adam Beckworth in self-defense. Lily kept quiet until Reed gave the sheriff her gun.

"It's mine," she said. "Can I have it back?"

Everyone looked at her, Theo's face pained.

"Are you saying," Sheriff Bond asked, "that the killing was done with your gun?"

"I took it from her," Theo said before she could open her mouth. "Beckworth was in a rage, and I was unarmed."

The sheriff opened the cylinder, checked the rounds, and smelled the barrel, though no one disputed it was the weapon used in the killing. He closed the cylinder with a sharp click, then tossed her the gun. She caught it and dropped it back in her holster. Meeting Theo's eyes, the sheriff asked sternly, "Are you confessing that you, and you alone, shot Adam Beckworth?"

"Yes, sir," Theo said.

The sheriff reached for a big ring of keys hanging on the wall behind him. "I'll have to lock you up and hold you till the inquest."

"Go home," Theo told Lily. "Bianca must be worried sick."

"That's right, Miz Moss," Sheriff Bond said, swinging the door of the front cell open. Theo walked in. The sheriff closed and locked the door, then faced her with the keys in his hand. "Nothing'll happen to your brother now he's safe in jail. You go on home and look after your fam'ly. I'll notify you in plenty of time to come back if you wanta be here for the inquest."

"I do," Lily said.

"The circuit judge won't be in town for a coupla weeks," Sheriff Bond said. He studied the calendar on the wall. "We're looking at the first week in November." He met her eyes. "I suggest you get your brother a lawyer."

"Is there one here in Union?" she asked.

He nodded. "Franklin Blackerby. Married the Widow Homer last year and got her first husband's law books, if nothing else." He smiled at Ben Reed and Paul Beckworth.

"Where can I find him?" Lily asked.

"They're living in the Homer place. You know where that is?"

She nodded, then looked at Theo. "I'll be back."

"Go home, Lily," he pleaded. "There's nothing more you can do here."

She looked at the sheriff. "You gonna feed my brother?"

"Sure. I'll have meals sent in from the hotel. Is that where you'll be staying?"

"I ain't decided," she said. "See you later."

She walked out and swung onto her horse, then turned toward the Homer house. Thick smoke billowed from the chimney, telling her someone inside was awake. Lily didn't relish knocking on the door of her dead husband's mistress, but she did it, steeling herself for the onerous chore of asking for help.

28

$\mathcal{T}$olliver opened the door, an aged man now with stooped shoulders. "Why, Miz Moss!" he said in surprise. "Come in outta the col', chile."

"Thank you," Lily murmured, stepping into the vestibule. She glanced toward the parlor, tempted by its warmth though she felt an aversion to the woman she could see standing up to greet her. To Tolliver, Lily quickly said, "I've come to see Mr. Blackerby on business."

"He ain't home jus' now," Tolliver said.

The lawyer's wife hovered on the threshold. In an elegant wrapper of forest-green silk, Suzanne Homer Blackerby was still handsome at forty-five but not the beauty she had been. "Hello, Lily," she said, assessing her from the scuffed bespurred boots to the crown of the man's hat, not missing the gunbelt in between. "Please come in and have some coffee. It's frightfully cold out, and you look like an apparition adrift in the dawn."

"I need to hire Mr. Blackerby," Lily said again.

"You can do that in the warmth of the parlor," Suzanne coaxed, "better than here on the doorstep."

Lily looked at Tolliver. When he nodded, the kindness in his eyes encouraged her, so she followed the lawyer's wife deeper into the house.

The hearth drew Lily toward its fire. She stood for a long moment staring into the flames as she listened to the door close behind her and the slither of Suzanne's silk skirt.

"Coffee's on its way," Suzanne said. "Won't you sit down, Lily?"

She turned around and studied the woman's crimped curls above the golden hazel of her eyes; her smooth, pale complexion obviously never exposed to sunlight; the pleated bodice, slim waist, and graceful drape of her elegant wrapper; the tiny toes of velvet slippers poking out from under the hem. Suzanne smiled, obviously making her own study of Lily's attire, the only concession to femininity being her skirt, though it was split so she could ride astride.

"Two more different women God couldn't have created," Suzanne teased gently. "Yet I've always felt we're friends. Are we, Lily?"

Lily shook her head.

"No? But we were once. In the beginning."

"Before I married Emmett, you mean?"

"Yes," Suzanne murmured.

Tolliver came in with a silver coffee service and two cups on a tray. Bending his long fence post of a body as he set the tray on a low, mahogany table, he asked, "Shall I pour, ma'am?"

"I'll do it, thank you, Tolliver," she said, dismissing him.

"Pleasure to have seen you, Miz Moss," he said.

She nodded and regretfully watched him leave. Smelling the rich fragrance of hot coffee, Lily turned back to watch Suzanne fill the cups from where she sat in a gold brocade wing chair. The ornate furniture was ostentatious in the tiny parlor, and Lily realized how keenly Suzanne must have yearned to be mistress of Bosque Grande. She had been denied that privilege not because she hadn't earned its master's affection, but because she was barren.

Extending a delicate china cup, Suzanne said, "Please sit down, Lily."

She accepted the cup and sat on a stool close to the hearth. As the fire warmed her back, Lily felt the coffee hit her stomach with a renewal of energy. Remembering her purpose, she asked, "When do you reckon Mr. Blackerby'll come home?"

"He's gone to Vegas, but should return late tomorrow."

"I can't stay that long." Lily emptied her cup and set it in its saucer on the floor. "Can I contract with you to hire him?"

"Certainly. What is it you wish him to do?"

"Defend my brother, Theo."

"What crime is he charged with?" Suzanne asked, placing her cup and saucer on the tray.

"Murder, but it was self-defense."

Suzanne's eyebrows rose in surprise. "Whom did he kill?"

"Adam Beckworth."

"What was the cause of the altercation?"

"The Beckworths dammed up our water. I blew the dam with dynamite. The quarrel happened after that."

"*You* blew the dam?"

Lily nodded.

Suzanne smiled. "I can well imagine the heat of that argument. Were you there when the shooting occurred?"

Lily nodded again.

"Did anyone else witness it?"

"No."

"Who first resorted to weapons—Beckworth or your brother?"

"Beckworth," Lily said. She hesitated, then added, "Theo acted in my defense."

"Beckworth aimed his weapon at you?"

"I was the one he was arguing with."

Again Suzanne smiled. "You're quite the wildcat, Lily. I admire you immensely."

"You admire me?" Lily asked in disbelief.

"Indeed. I wouldn't be surprised if you were the one to shoot Beckworth." She glanced at Lily's gun. "The purpose of wearing a weapon is to use it, is it not?"

"They're handy against rattlers," Lily said.

Suzanne laughed softly. "Unfortunately, many snakes in this country walk on two legs."

"So you think I shot Beckworth, is that what you're saying?"

"Did you?"

"My brother confessed."

"He has more wisdom than I would have suspected. If the facts are as you've told me, I feel certain Mr. Blackerby can win a reduced sentence if not an outright acquittal for Theo. Water, after all, is life in this country, and I think the jury will be sympathetic to a plea of self-defense. A woman, however, who has the audacity to kill a man would be given no mercy. She would be perceived as an aberration that must be stopped at all costs. You, in particular, would elicit a harsh punishment."

"Why me in particular?" Lily asked, though she knew.

"Because of the gossip concerning your husband's untimely demise," Suzanne answered smoothly.

"Do you believe the gossip?"

"No. But since my knowledge of Emmett's illness was given to me in confidence, I can't repeat it in your defense."

"Given to you in bed, you mean," Lily said.

Suzanne's eyes flashed with surprise. "I wasn't aware you knew about me and Emmett."

"I saw the checks after he died."

"Of course," Suzanne said. "I loved him, Lily, long before his marriage. What I did was not a strike against you."

"Since it kept him out of my bed, I don't much care."

"Did it?"

"Soon as I was pregnant."

"He told me that, but I didn't believe him." Suzanne smiled sadly, then asked, "So you never learned to enjoy his passion?"

Lily shook her head.

Suzanne *tch*ed and looked away as she murmured, "What a fool he was." She looked back at Lily. "Men can be such obstinate creatures. It's why women are so practiced at accommodation."

"I ain't," Lily said.

"No, indeed. But it's an art you could benefit from learning.

The case in point, for instance. You could have found a more peaceful solution than blowing up the Beckworths' dam."

"File an injunction, you mean, and take 'em to court? In my experience, all that accommodates is lawyers."

Suzanne laughed lightly. "You could have married one of the Beckworth boys and joined your ranch to theirs. That would have been a woman's solution."

"I like owning Bosque Grande free of a man's control."

"Yes," Suzanne said. "It's unfortunate more women don't have your courage to assume command, Lily. The world would be a far different place if we did."

"All you gotta do is take it," she said.

"But at such a cost, my dear. I'm afraid most of us are confined within our petticoats because we thrive on being admired. Your course doesn't gain many compliments, does it?"

"Can't eat compliments," Lily said.

"Oh, I don't know," Suzanne teased. "I've redeemed them for bread and butter more than once."

Resisting the impulse to say that made Suzanne a whore, Lily stood up. "I gotta get home. Are you certain Mr. Blackerby will take my brother's case?"

With a slither of her silk skirt, Suzanne stood, too. "I shall insist upon it. He'll call at Bosque Grande in a few days and inform you of his progress."

"I'll pay him a retainer. Whatever he wants."

"That's fine, Lily. I'm so glad we had this chat, though I'm sorry for the unfortunate circumstance from which it arose. Please call on me again when you're next in town."

"Thank you," Lily forced herself to say.

Outside, the morning was still cold despite the thin sunlight now filtering through a congestion of clouds. Lily swung onto her horse and trotted back to the sheriff's office. Only Theo was there. He stood up from the bunk as Lily walked in, and they met each other's eyes through the bars. Finally she asked, "Where's the sheriff?"

"Gone to fetch my breakfast," Theo said.

Lily nodded. "I've hired Franklin Blackerby to defend you."

"Ain't no defense, Lily. I've confessed."

"There's no need to throw yourself on the mercy of the court, Theo. A jury'll see our side of it better'n a judge."

"But if I go through a trial, we might trip ourselves up." He shook his head. "I'm sticking with my confession. Whatever happens to me, least I'll know you're taking care of my family. Now go home, Lily. Bianca's prob'ly worried sick."

"I'm going. But I ain't throwing you to the dogs, Theo, for something I did."

"I'll deny you did it with my last breath. They'll think you're lying to protect me, so don't even try, Lily. For once in our lives I got the upper hand, and I'm gonna keep it."

She sighed. "I wish I could say I appreciate what you're doing, Theo, but I'm not sure I do."

"I ain't doing it for you. Promise me you won't contradict my confession and make me look like a fool."

"All right. I promise."

"Good. Now, *please,* go home, Lily."

"I'll be back for the inquest," she said, then turned and left him alone.

She walked along the one street of the village until she found a gunsmith's shop that was open. Knowing she would never use it again, she went inside and sold her pistol, then used part of the money to pay a hostler to feed her horse. Granting it a short rest, she fed herself, too, in the dining room of the hotel, before they began their long trek home.

At what had once been Cassidy's Mill, she let the horse graze on the stubby brown grass growing in front of the delapidated house. She didn't go near the graveyard but looked at it only from a distance, afraid of encountering her father's displeasure if she got any closer. Certainly he couldn't have imagined a more pitiful fate for his children than what Lily was feeling just then. Impatient with her melancholy, she continued her journey home.

Because of their slow pace, the night was well gone when Lily arrived at Bosque Grande. Bone-tired, she stabled her horse, then stood for a moment enjoying watching it eat. Animals were easy, their needs fundamental, their companionship and service reliable. None of that could be said about people.

Suspecting the sound of the door would wake at least Bianca and begin Lily's part in perpetuating Theo's lie, she delayed that moment and approached the bunkhouse, craving Shiloh's love more than food. Quietly she opened and closed his door, then crossed the dark to sit on the edge of his bed. As she gathered her courage to wake him with news of her trouble, she listened to his breathing. It was different, more shallow, less sonorous. In a sweep of suspicion, she moved to the table and struck a match, seeing Junior in the brief flare before she lit the candle. She kicked the leg of the bed until he opened his eyes and stared at her in the feeble light.

"What are you doing here?" she demanded.

He sat up so the blankets fell into his lap, revealing his bare chest sculpted with the taut curves of youth. "Good thing you didn't crawl under the covers and wake me with a kiss."

"What are you doing here?" she repeated through clenched teeth.

"It's called pecking order. Starts with the chief hen and gets passed on down the flock." He snickered with sarcasm. "When I came home and found my bed occupied, I moved Shiloh outta this one. He's in a bunk next door, as befits a hired hand."

"You had no right to do that. He earns his keep around here more'n you do."

"He didn't seem to mind. I believe one bed's the same as another to him."

Lily resisted an impulse to slap Junior. "I found Alma and your child with only cornmeal to eat and cow chips to burn in that pitiful shack you put 'em in."

"Why didn't you leave 'em there?"

"I acted outta simple human compassion. That child's your blood, Junior, but she ain't none of mine."

The sneer slid from his face. "What're you saying?"

She sank into the chair and hid her face in her arms, folded on the table. It would be easy to tell the truth now when she was so exhausted and weary of lies. But she had a new one to promote, and needed the scar tissue intact to buffer the blows. She raised her head and met his eyes. "I don't know what I'm saying. I'm tired and near starved."

"Where've you been?" he asked, his voice subdued.

"Union," she said. "Theo's in jail."

"In jail? What for?"

She took a deep breath. "Killing Adam Beckworth."

Junior snorted in disbelief. "Theo can't swat a fly."

She built the story, chink by chink: "Beckworth dammed up Gushing River. Theo and I blew the dam with dynamite. Adam heard the explosion and came running. He and Theo had words. One thing led to another."

Junior ruminated on that, then asked, "Why didn't you get me to help you blow the dam?"

" 'Cause you were gambling in a saloon, like you always are when I need you."

"You don't need anybody," he retorted. "You prob'ly killed Beckworth and Theo took the blame."

Lily stared at him, wondering if everyone would guess that's how it happened.

"Goddamn," Junior whispered, seeing the truth in her eyes. "Are they gonna hang Theo?"

"No! Beckworth drew first. It was self-defense." She took another deep breath to calm herself. "But there's a chance, depending on the jury, that Theo'll go to prison."

"Are you gonna let him do that for you?" Junior taunted.

"Everything I do is for Bosque Grande," she answered.

His expression quivered between defiance and a need for reassurance. "They call you a black widow for poisoning my father. Tell me you didn't do it."

"I shouldn't have to deny something like that."

"If you could kill Beckworth, why not my father?"

"Theo confessed to killing Beckworth. I promised I'd never contradict his confession, and I won't, not even to you, Junior. As for Emmett, I did everything in my power to be a good wife."

"You've been a lousy mother," he muttered.

She blinked back tears. "That you'd say such a thing proves

you right. But you're a man now, or should be. I'll need your help
to keep Bosque Grande solvent till Theo comes back. Since someday it'll be yours, seems to me you'd be interested in doing that."

"You've never acted like any part of it was mine. Not one cow
on this land wears my brand, though a third of 'em wear Theo's."

"He did the work to earn 'em."

"I've done plenty of work around here. All I ever got was
wages, same as Shiloh."

"Less than Shiloh, for less work."

"Before or after you started paying him in bed?"

She stared at him a long moment before saying, "I don't barter
with love, Junior. Evidently you do, so I'll make a deal. If you've
proved yourself responsible by the time you're twenty-five, I'll
turn over title of Bosque Grande to you."

"And if I don't?"

"You'll have to wait till I die."

"That's how it'll be, then, 'cause there's no way I'll ever prove
myself to you."

"Why not?"

"How the hell should I know! Something happened when I
was a baby or maybe even before I was born that set you against
me. Maybe it was my father having a hand in killing Jasper Stone.
Whatever it was, I think the fault's yours for wanting what's
gone."

Surprised he knew about her and Jasper, Lily carefully laid her
hands flat on the table and pushed herself up, fighting dizziness.
"Maybe you're right," she said. "I loved Jasper in a way I never
loved Emmett. If that's what you've felt is wrong all these years,
I'm sorry for it. But it is gone, Junior. Can't we at least act like
we're friends?"

"I won't live a lie," he said.

She almost laughed in his face. Sorely tempted to say his very
name was a lie, she kept quiet out of fear she'd destroy what little virtue he had. She walked out and closed the door. The house
loomed ahead, the repetition of Theo's lie, which she knew
would evoke tears and accusations, yet to be endured. She felt so
weak, so tired. Turning to the door of the bunkhouse, she walked

into the long, dark room where only one bed was occupied. "Shiloh?" she whispered.

"Over here," he said.

She followed his voice to the wall closest to the room she'd just left. "I'm sorry," she murmured, sitting on the edge of his bed. "I love you more than any man alive."

He chuckled as he pulled her into his warmth. "I've never been one to compete with the dead."

Her face against his bare chest, she sighed. "Oh Lord, how many times am I gonna have to say this?"

"You don't have to tell me what happened," he said, kissing her gently. "I heard you and Junior through the wall."

"I'm glad," she answered, then met his eyes in the dark. "I killed Adam Beckworth, Shiloh. His blood's on my hands, though Theo's taking the blame."

"Shhh," Shiloh said. "Junior can hear as well as I did. Let's give him something worth listening to."

She laughed. "You're sinful."

"It's good to hear you laugh," he said. "But there's one thing I wanta know: How'd you use that dynamite without blowing yourself to kingdom come?"

"I read the directions on the box," she said.

This time he laughed. "What'd you think you were doing, Lily? Following a recipe in a cookbook?"

She giggled. "I hope to shout none of my cake's ever rise that high."

29

That winter, heavy snow fell on the mountains, and the next summer, the July rains returned. The drought had finally broken but August was still dry and hot, stirring the dust in the

yard of Bosque Grande. Claire sat under the portal cooling her
face with a wooden fan as she watched Lily work a new horse in
the corral. The gelding was two years old and such a bright sorrel that it looked like a new penny shining in the sun.

Lily was training the horse to stand still on command, a lesson
that involved tying its head close to a stirrup when the sorrel dis-
obeyed. Lily stood with her booted feet spread wide and her
hands on the smooth hips of her skirt as she watched the horse
with a righteous enjoyment of its discomfort. She hadn't worn a
gun since Theo was sent to prison for shooting Adam Beckworth.
Although Lily never discussed her decision, Claire had decided
the ease of taking a life when a gun was so handy persuaded Lily
the risk wasn't worth it.

Theo had been convicted of voluntary manslaughter and sentenced to ten years. He'd started serving his sentence in the pen-
itentiary in Santa Fe before his lawyer could file an appeal with
the territorial court. Pending the outcome of the appeal, Theo
was released. When he came home, however, he announced he
wouldn't go back for any reason. He was so gaunt after only three
months in prison, his eyes dark with an unspoken horror, that no
one argued with his decision to move to Texas.

Lily mortgaged Bosque Grande to give him a stake, borrowing
enough money for Theo to buy a small spread in the Davis Mountains. Rosemary chose to go with him, saying Bianca needed help
with the children. In April, Alma ran off with a cowboy hired for
spring roundup, taking her baby with her. So Claire and Lily lived
in the house alone now. Despite the five empty bedrooms, Junior
continued to sleep in the foreman's quarters, when he came
home at all. Shiloh took his meals with the women and sat on the
portal making conversation after supper, but he, too, slept in the
bunkhouse, though he'd partitioned one end of the dormitory
into a private room. From what Claire could gather from Lily's
oblique comments, Shiloh preferred his independence.

In Claire's opinion, she and Lily were more like sisters than
aunt and niece, the remnants of the respectable Mosses along the
Panal, even though one of them had a lover. Since her father had
died of a heart attack in January, bequeathing his small estate to

his second wife, Claire had no hope of ever having her own money, but she was comfortable on the ranch. The orchard provided more fruit than they could eat, and the sale of the surplus brought in a few dollars each autumn. The market had revived and Lily earned decent money for her cattle. Her herd was so small, however, that she had to sell her stock to other ranchers who shipped larger herds, so her profit was diminished. What she gained made the yearly mortgage payment and satisfied the taxes, a new innovation that everyone complained about.

Still in all, little cash was needed. They kept a goat for milk, and chickens for eggs and meat. A butchered steer lasted them the better part of a year. Claire cultivated the garden and aged a sweet red wine from the grapes Emmett had planted so long ago. Everything that had happened back then seemed of another lifetime to her, as if she were two people: the girl who had fallen in love with Whit Cantrell, and the woman who had come home from the asylum. The years in between were gone from her mind, as if she had died, then been reborn in the same body, owning the same memories but having no future other than this somnolent existence she lived in Lily's shadow.

From the shade of the portal, Claire saw that Lily was unsaddling the sorrel, so she guessed the day's lessons were over. Knowing Lily would be parched after her work in the dusty corral, Claire left her fan behind and went into the house for a pitcher of apple cider. She had a pot of posole simmering on the stove. Last winter they'd bought a pig from Old Man Stone. Shiloh had butchered and salted it down, so they'd had a barrel of pork to pull from when they wanted something other than beef or chicken. This morning Claire had to reach deep into the barrel and search through the rock salt for any tidbit to throw into the posole. Except for chicken, they'd go without meat until roundup next month, when Shiloh would butcher a steer.

She took a pitcher of apple cider from the new icebox, a modern miracle that not only kept food from spoiling so quickly but allowed the supreme luxury of a cold drink. She set the pitcher and three glasses on a tray. The third was for Shiloh, who would ride in from the range hot and dusty. Usually he sat with them awhile before going to the bunkhouse to wash up before supper. In those interludes, the pure masculinity of his person sometimes took Claire's breath away, and she envied Lily's trysts in his bed. Though Claire was now thirty-nine, she still longed for a man's touch and guessed she always would.

When she returned to the portal with her tray of cider, she saw a man sitting his horse as he talked to Lily outside the corral. Claire set the tray on the small stump planed smooth for a table, then sat in the swing and moved it with her foot to stir a breeze as she studied the man. Visitors were rare at Bosque Grande, but beyond that, there was something intriguing about him that Claire couldn't quite put her finger on. Lily's hat shadowed her face, so Claire couldn't read her expression, but her posture was taut, as if she expected the man to be unpredictable.

Claire picked up her fan and toyed with it nervously. She could feel a hum inside her body, as if something important was about to happen. When Lily glanced at her, then said something to the man, he, too, looked toward the house. He was dressed like a Mexican charro, with a short black jacket and silver medallions along the seams of his black trousers, but under his flat-topped black hat, his hair was a tawny blond, as was his full beard, and his eyes meeting Claire's were honey brown.

She knew those eyes—they knelled inside her, stirring memories long buried. He turned his horse to amble toward her, and slowly she stood up. When her fan fell forgotten from her hand, the noise startled his horse so it skittered a few steps to the right. She heard him speak to calm the animal, and she recognized his voice, though her mind denied it while her heart clamored the truth. Still she waited until he'd dismounted and tied his reins to the rail. When he looked at her, they both smiled as if they'd last seen each other only yesterday and it had been too long.

"You're as beautiful as ever," he said.

"Whit," she whispered.

He chuckled. "Name's Caleb Thorn now."

She came out from under the portal and extended her hand in the sunlight. "I'm so very pleased to meet you, Mr. Thorn."

"Mrs. Daggerty, I understand," he said, clasping her hand.

"In name only," she said. "Never more than that."

He smiled with forgiveness. "It's been more'n twenty years, Claire. I didn't expect you to wait."

"I've waited in my heart."

"Me, too," he said. "I would've come sooner, but things happened."

Suddenly Lily was there, though Claire hadn't heard her coming.

"Mr. Thorn's staying the night," Lily said, her voice crisp and sharp. "We got enough for supper, Claire?"

"Only the night?" she asked, unable to look away from his eyes.

He laughed softly, the gentle sound she'd heard in her dreams. "We'll look at everything again in the morning," he said, "and take it from there."

"Why don't you offer him some cider?" Lily asked. "He's ridden a ways and I reckon he's thirsty."

"Forgive me," Claire said. "Please, sit down, Mr. Thorn."

"I'll put your horse up," Lily said.

"I can do that," Caleb said, dragging his eyes off Claire.

Lily looked at the two of them still holding hands. "So can I," she said, then untied his reins and led his horse toward the stable. She felt them watching her halfway across the yard. At the door of the stable, she glanced over her shoulder and saw they were kissing, their arms around each other, melding them into one silhouette against the setting sun.

Lily walked on into the stable and unsaddled his horse. The trappings were high quality, the horse itself a prize, and she wondered if Whit had done well in Mexico or if he'd scrimped for years to come home in style. He'd told her next to nothing when they'd spoken by the corral, and she realized he'd asked her questions so he could keep his history a secret. She knew only that his spirit was undamaged, as his love for Claire apparently was. Certainly hers for him.

Lily gave them time to say whatever they needed in private, though she doubted if Claire would be wily enough to get more than kisses out of him. Alone in the stable, she sat on the wooden box that held old bridle bits and buckles, metal pieces salvaged from tack as the leather wore out. When polished they could be added to another piece of harness and shine like new. Whit had come home shining like a mint, but Lily suspected it was more than love that drew him back to Bosque Grande.

She considered the ramifications of extending a welcome. He'd been sentenced to execution, and as far as she knew, there was no statute of limitation on death warrants. But his beard camouflaged his face enough that she hadn't recognized him until he spoke, and not too many people were left from the old days who'd likely remember the sound of his voice. Half a dozen, maybe. Chief among them the sheriff, though Red Bond hadn't been to Bosque Grande since shortly after Emmett died. If Whit stayed close to home, the odds were good his identity wouldn't be discovered. If it was, Lily would be guilty of harboring a convicted killer. On the other hand, if she denied him sanctuary, she'd lose Claire. He may not take her with him when he left— that would depend on his reason for coming—but she would be irrevocably turned against Lily. Then there was Junior.

Lily thought it would be at least interesting to see if father and son, both ignorant of their connection, would feel any affinity for each other. Claire and Junior shared a bond, but even under the guise of Lily's lie, they were cousins, the children of brothers. Whit would think Junior was the son of a man who had caused him a lot of grief. What would Junior think when he met this stranger whose name he'd never heard but who obviously had an intimate knowledge of his family? It was almost worth keeping Whit around just to find out.

Hearing hoofbeats, Lily looked up as Shiloh rode in with the last light of sunset. He sat his horse and studied her a moment, then said to explain his being late, "Found a stretch of fence down on the east range. Took me all afternoon to get it up again."

She nodded, keeping quiet.

"Who's that on the porch with Claire?"

Lily smiled. "Says his name's Caleb Thorn."

"Never heard of him," Shiloh said.

"You've met him, though," she answered with another smile.

Shiloh swung down and put his horse up, eyeing the new one in the adjacent stall. "That his?"

Lily nodded.

"Damn fine horse," Shiloh said, coming out. "Don't recognize the brand."

"Ain't from hereabouts," she said.

"Where's it from?"

"Mexico."

Shiloh looked toward the open door, then back at her. "Goddamn," he whispered. Then with a laugh, "That ain't Whit Cantrell with Claire, is it?"

"Come see for yourself," Lily said, standing up.

Claire and Caleb sat close together on the swing, watching Lily and Shiloh approach across the yard. Lily sauntered under the portal and turned so she could see Shiloh's face when she said, "Mr. Thorn, this here's my foreman, Shiloh Pook. Shiloh, this is Caleb Thorn."

Caleb stood up and offered his hand. "Pleased to meet cha."

"Been a while," Shiloh said softly, shaking with him.

Caleb nodded, still standing up as if waiting judgment.

Lily sat down and poured Shiloh a glass of cider. When she gave it to him, he settled himself on the railing in front of her and leaned against a pillar as he emptied the glass. "Have you had some of this cider, Mr. Thorn?" he asked. "Mrs. Daggerty makes the best on the Panal."

Caleb chuckled and resumed his seat next to Claire. "No argument," he answered, displaying his half-full glass. "Might be the best in the territory or maybe even the whole Southwest."

Shiloh handed his empty glass to Lily, who refilled it as he asked, "What line of work are you in, Mr. Thorn?"

"Oh," Caleb drawled, "I've just now mosied up from south of the border hoping to find me a situation."

Lily caught a teasing tone in their conversation that made her suspect they'd seen each other more recently than twenty years ago. She thought back over the times Shiloh had left the ranch since Emmett died. Almost always he'd gone north driving cattle to Vegas to be shipped to market, but he could've caught a train from there to El Paso and back without her knowing it. His honesty had been the one solid ground she could count on in the quicksand of lies she lived within, and she felt hurt. Standing abruptly, she said, "I'll finish up supper."

She was lighting the lamp on the kitchen table when she heard him in the hall. He came up behind her, slid his arms around her waist, and leaned to kiss her cheek. She stood rigid and unyielding.

"You mad at me, Lily?" he asked.

"Is there a reason I should be?"

"Reckon you could see it that way." He turned her around to face him.

Reading his teasing smile as ridicule, she broke free and moved to the stove, stirred the posole, then banged the spoon on the edge of the pot and turned to face him again. "How long've you been visiting Whit?"

"Almost since he first left."

"Why didn't you tell me?"

"He asked me not to."

"Why?"

"That's his to tell."

She nodded, trying to swallow her anger. "Reckon that's right. But tell me this: Why'd he come back?"

"He's looking for the same thing you and me've shared all these years."

"What we shared was trust. Now Whit sashays in and it's gone."

"No, it ain't. You're a smart woman but you don't understand that things happen 'tween men a woman can't touch. That's the way it is, Lily. If we didn't keep something for ourselves, you women would have us hog-tied and branded without us having no say in anything that mattered. I follow your orders year in and year out, and every night when you come to my bed, what we share is sweeter'n anything I've known. But there's a part of me I share only with men, and another part I keep just for myself. If that weren't so, you wouldn't want me in bed or on your ranch either one, so for once in your life, Lily, let it lie."

He wasn't known for long speeches. Since the night he'd told her Emmett had let Whit go, she hadn't heard such a string of words come out of Shiloh's mouth. Though it cost her a lot, Lily smiled and said, "Why don't you go wash up for supper? You've done a man's work today. What happens in a kitchen is woman's work."

He laughed. "Think I'll put on a clean shirt to celebrate the occasion."

Lily watched him walk out the door, trying to feel reassured. But she couldn't help noting that the first effect Whit had on her home was to disrupt the harmony she'd always shared with Shiloh. Striving to be fair, she wondered if it really had to do with Whit or with the fact that Shiloh had been the only grown man at Bosque Grande and Whit changed that, giving Shiloh a friend in his corner. Then she wondered if Shiloh had chosen not to move into the house because he felt overpowered working for a woman he also slept with yet had no right of dominion over.

She had been the one to deny their love the legitimacy of marriage, stating from the first that she felt no need of a husband. Yet if they were married, the ranch would be as much his as hers, in the same way she'd told Emmett the ranch was as much hers as his. Emmett hadn't liked that notion any more than she did now, but she realized that by denying it to Shiloh, she'd kept him in almost the same way Emmett had kept Suzanne Homer. If Lily allowed Whit to move into Claire's bedroom, she might as well start calling Bosque Grande a bordello. Certainly she had no right to criticize Junior for spending so much time with Celia. At least he had the decency not to bring her home.

Lily set about mixing corn bread, thinking it had been a long time since she'd done any cooking. When she remembered the girl she'd been, she wondered if Jasper had shied away from marrying her because he didn't want to fight a woman every step of his life. She remembered how submissive his sister had been, and how his mother never challenged her menfolks' right to rule. Lily realized if she had married Jasper, she would have turned that family upside down. Despite all the love she felt for him, she'd taken great pleasure in pointing out the error of his ways. She guessed she'd been looking for someone to subdue, and a wild boy with an uncontrollable temper had been an irresistible challenge to a girl who felt she had no power over the people around her.

After supper, Lily went to her office as usual and sat at her desk, listening through the open door to the quiet sounds of Whit and Claire in the kitchen. When Claire began washing the dishes, Whit came down the hall. Lily looked up and saw him watching her from the threshold.

"Come in," she said, "and close the door."

As he did, she studied the buckle of his gunbelt, its metal dull so it wouldn't reflect light, telling her Whit Cantrell still possessed the wariness of a man with enemies.

He gave her a smile. "Claire said you'd most likely want to get some things settled tonight."

Lily nodded. "Sit down."

He sat on the edge of the black leather settee Emmett had chosen for this room, then leaned forward with his elbows on his knees as he looked around. Finally he gave her a smile and said, "Texas Lily. I could always picture you sitting behind a desk in a room like this."

She frowned, thinking he was trying to finagle her with a compliment. "What'd you come here for?"

He smiled. "The same thing I came for last time."

"Don't play games with me," she warned. "I ain't gonna guess and let you ride my mistakes."

He chuckled. "No, I can see you're not one for games, Lily."

"Not when I stand to lose," she said.

"That's the nature of a game, though. Someone always does."

"I don't want it to be Claire."

"Me, neither."

She watched him, thinking if he'd had a hard life in Mexico it didn't show on his face. "I want to know where you were," she said, "what you've been doing, and what you want now."

He leaned back with a sigh. "I've been living in a village in Chihuahua called Bachoachi. Ever hear of it?"

Lily shook her head.

"I had me a wife. We were married in the Catholic Church, so it was as legal as it gets. Five daughters, pretty as they come. We had a son but he died when he was only three. I grieved for him, then decided maybe it was best, that what I had to teach a boy wouldn't do him much good. My wife died last year." He shrugged. "Wasn't no doctor in our village so I don't have a name for what she died of. My daughters are all grown and married now. They love me but," he paused to laugh with self-deprecation, "their husbands didn't mind seeing me leave. I was in the way. You understand what I mean, Lily?"

She nodded.

"So I came home. Home meaning Claire, this county, the place I was 'fore I spent the better part of my life living a lie. I loved my wife. I don't want you to think I didn't. But with the money Emmett gave me I set myself up as something I wasn't. Married a pretty girl who never knew the truth about her husband. The money didn't last long, but we did all right. I raised sheep. Can you believe that?" He laughed again. "Had thousands of the little white buggers. They're peaceful critters, and I did my best to match 'em. When I decided to come home, I split the flock among my daughters and outfitted myself as a charro. That flashy horse out there in your stable is all I got to my name."

"He's a fine horse," she said, unable to imagine Whit Cantrell herding sheep.

"I know what you're thinking," he said. "I kept myself alive by traveling up to El Paso. First thing I'd do is buy myself a bath, then I'd hit the tables. I ain't lost my knack at cards, and I'd go home with enough money that my wife never gave me a hard time 'bout being gone. She prob'ly wouldn't've anyway. Mexican women understand that a man's gotta get away sometimes, that he can't always be a husband and father but has to be just a man once in a while."

Thinking of what Shiloh had said, she nodded. "I think all women can understand that if it's put to 'em in the proper light."

"Maybe so," Whit said. "I'm sorry for what Claire went through. Feel like it was my fault. But by the time I learned what had happened, the baby was already dead. I wrote her a letter but didn't get no answer. She told me just now Emmett burned it. I never suspected that. When I heard Claire was in that asylum, I went to San Antonio and tried to visit her but they wouldn't let me in. So I went back to my wife. She was so happy to see me, I figured I oughta count my blessings. But all those years with her I was living a lie, Lily. My name now's a lie. I know that, and I don't intend to flaunt who I am. But I can be him without the name. That's all I want. That and a chance to love Claire 'fore it's too late. Can you see your way clear to letting me stay?"

Lily looked into the empty hearth. Feeling like a hypocrite, she asked, "Do you intend to marry her?"

Whit laughed softly. "I'll do it if she'll have me, but I sure don't hanker to stand in front of any judge."

Lily met his eyes. "There's that to consider, too, Whit."

He nodded. "Would help if you'd get in the habit of calling me Caleb."

"How'd you come up with that name?"

"Caleb was one of the two men allowed to enter the Promised Land."

"Who was the other one?"

"I don't rightly recall, but I wouldn't be surprised if his name was Shiloh."

Lily smiled, thinking Whit hadn't lost any of his winning ways. "He told me he's been visiting you all these years."

Whit nodded. "Don't hold it against him, Lily. I made him promise not to tell."

"Why?"

He shrugged. "Couldn't bring myself to abandon my wife, and couldn't see any reason to get Claire's hopes up."

Lily looked out the window at a red rose pressed against the pane. "What did Shiloh tell you about the baby who died?"

"Under the circumstances," Whit answered softly, "we both think you did the right thing."

Lily felt tears sting her eyes. Still staring at the red rose distorted against the glass, she said, "The boy's seeing Celia Broussard now. He spends more time with her than here at home."

"She was always good company," Whit said.

Lily met his eyes. "What do you think'll happen when he meets you?"

"I'm hoping we can be friends."

"No more'n that?"

"I didn't come to take anything away from you, Lily. And I sure don't wanta open any wounds in Claire that're healed and scarred over. I'm looking forward to meeting him, that's all."

She looked out the window again and asked in a near whisper, "Do you believe in justice, Caleb?"

"I don't believe it's human," he said. " 'Cept once in a while, a person gets a chance to deliver it."

"Do you think Emmett did that when he let you go?"

"I think that's what he was aiming for, but Andy was worth more'n me."

She looked at him. "Everyone else seems to have forgotten Andy."

"I'll never forget the beauty he coaxed outta Celia's piano. Only two other things in this world made me cry: when my mother died, and then again when Jasper did. But those were tears of grief and self-pity 'cause I was alone. What Andy made me feel was the pure joy of being alive."

"Junior needs to learn that. Do you think you can help him?"

"I'll do my best, Lily, if you'll let me stay."

"All right," she said. "In the name of Andy and Jasper, I'll take my due when it comes."

"I hope that day never arrives," he said, standing up. "But if it does, try'n remember the due the world gives ain't the one that counts."

She watched him walk out and close the door, then she looked through the window at the roses, knowing Emmett had planted them because he wanted beauty in his life. Whatever Whit did for Junior, and whatever happiness he brought Claire, the miracle of his return for Lily was that it finally allowed her to forgive Emmett. She blew out the lamp and walked through the quiet house toward Shiloh's love, thinking that maybe, in this new light, peace could settle on Bosque Grande.

Once outside, she looked up at the stars. Their multitude always impressed her with a keen appreciation of nature's splendor, and she usually enjoyed her walks through the night to and from Shiloh's room. It wasn't as pleasant to run through rain, and when it was cold she found it difficult to force herself to get up before dawn and scurry across the icy yard to shiver in her own bed alone. Tonight, though it was warm and clear, she thought it was time for a change.

His room had a small potbelly stove that gave better heat than a hearth though it wasn't lit now. Besides the brass featherbed, he'd brought in a rawhide settee she'd made more comfortable with a Navajo blanket woven in a red and black lightning pattern. Sometimes they sat there and talked when the weather kept them inside, and sometimes when he was gone she wrapped herself in that blanket and remembered the pleasure they shared.

Tonight he was waiting for her on the settee. She never knocked. He'd told her she was always welcome and a knock might wake Junior in the other end of the building, if he happened to be home, so she always walked into Shiloh's room as if it were hers. She closed the door, then sat down beside him and snuggled close.

"You still mad at me?" he asked, his arm around her and his hand resting lightly on her hip.

She shook her head, her face against his shirt. "I've been thinking," she said, then stopped, surprised that she felt afraid he might turn her down.

"About what?" he prodded gently.

"That maybe I'll stay the night," she continued bravely, "and not get up till we're ready to go to breakfast in the morning."

"That's fine, Lily. I like a little sugar 'fore I start my day."

She sat up and met his eyes, realizing there was a lot she didn't know about this man she'd thought she knew so well. "You could've been getting that all along," she said, "if you'd moved up to the house."

"Or if you'd move down here," he answered with a smile.

"I didn't 'cause of Claire," she said. "I don't like to leave her alone all night."

He nodded, but kept quiet.

Lily sighed, leaning against his chest again. "Do you think Caleb will stay?"

Shiloh thought for a minute. "Reckon that depends on how him and Claire hit it off after all these years."

"And on Junior," Lily said.

"Yeah, there's that," Shiloh agreed.

30

He's been at the ranch five months now," Junior told Celia, "and you'd hardly know it's the same place."

"How is it dif'rent?" she asked, rolling away under the goose-down comforter to reach for the bottle on the table.

He watched her refilling her glass, the wine sparkling ruby red in the gray light of the stormy day outside the window. "My mother's moved into Shiloh's room. 'Stead of bringing him up to the house to be an owner with her, she's lowered herself to the level of a ranch hand. Which means Caleb and Claire are living in the house like cattle kings when neither one of 'em owns a speck in it."

Celia punched the pillows against the headboard, then leaned back against them and picked up her glass. She gave him a sad smile before taking a sip.

He lay on his side, his elbow bent and his head resting in the palm of his hand. They were both naked, the covers tangled around them. Snow buffeted the window, stinging the pane like a thousand tiny whips. "To listen to 'em laugh," Junior went on, "you'd think they'd died and gone to heaven. I hadn't realized how few times I'd heard anybody laugh at Bosque Grande before Caleb showed up. Reckon it's why I was always jabbing, just trying to get some kinda rise out of 'em."

"A joke's a better way to make folks laugh than jabbing 'em," Celia answered dryly.

"Christmas is tomorrow," he said. "We'll see if they're so chipper then. Always before it's been the most melancholy time of year 'cause Andy hung himself on Christmas Eve."

"That made us all sad, Junior. That and getting the news about Whit Cantrell."

"I've heard rumors he ain't dead."

She shrugged. "You always hear stories like that about outlaws, 'specially ones that died someplace else."

"You knew him better'n most," Junior said, watching her carefully. "Think you'd recognize him if he showed up again?"

"Yes," she said into her glass. She emptied it, then watched the snow pelt against the windowpane.

"Why don't you come out to the house for Christmas dinner?" he asked with what he thought was a sly intention.

She snorted with scorn, reaching for the bottle again. "Lily'd love that."

He watched Celia's breasts as she settled back with another full glass, then met her eyes when he said, "I think Caleb's Whit."

She stared at him so long he smiled, pleased with the intensity of her reaction. Throwing the covers aside, she carried her glass over to stand by the window. Though she was close to forty, he admired the lean line of her figure topped off with breasts still full and ripe. The thick braid of her mahogany hair fell down the middle of her back to tickle her butt, though almost as much hair was out of the braid as in it after their tryst in bed. Crimson in the light filtered through the frosted pane, the glass of wine she sipped added a voluptuous touch to the portrait of a whore thinking of the man who'd deflowered her. Junior had ruined a few girls himself, but he'd found the experience wasn't as savory as imagining Celia losing her innocence to Whit Cantrell. Softly Junior asked, "What'd he look like?"

She jerked her head around as if she'd forgotten Junior was there. "Who?"

"Whit Cantrell," he answered, enjoying the sorrow in her eyes, which she was trying hard to hide.

"He looked a lot like you, Junior," she said with sarcasm.

He laughed. "You mean he was handsome?"

She stared out the window again. "Not in a pretty-boy way, but he had the most charming smile I've ever seen."

"Caleb's quick with a smile, and I can't fail to notice how Claire melts into pudding just to see it."

Celia came back to stand by the bed and set her glass on the table. "You oughta leave 'em alone, Junior. Claire's had more'n her share of torment. Ain't no reason why she shouldn't take a lover in the sunset of her years."

"She ain't any older'n you, Celia, and you're a long way from sunset."

She lifted the bottle to pour herself more wine.

"Come to Christmas dinner with me," he coaxed, "so you can see if Caleb's Whit or not."

"Why don't you bring him here if you want me to see him so bad?" She set the bottle down and walked across the room to take a wrapper from her chiffonier. The robe was satin, robin's egg blue.

"I've asked but he won't come," Junior said, watching her tie the sash tight. "Not here to Soledad nor River's End either. Says he's had his fill of towns and all they got to offer. But you know what I think?"

She didn't answer, sitting in front of her vanity to unbraid her hair.

"I asked you a question, Celia."

She met his eyes in the mirror. "No, I don't know what you think, Junior."

"I think he's hiding out. If anybody shows up, Caleb goes inside the house or any other building close enough to hide him. Leastways, that's how it looks to me. One time I saw him go into the chicken coop and stay there the entire time Lash Cooper was visiting. I was in my room with the door open, so I could see the coop plain, and I sat there the whole time thinking of Caleb communing with the hens."

"If you were in your room," she said, pulling the last twist out of her braid, "how'd you know who was visiting?"

"Lash came down to say hello. I was mighty tempted to show him around our chicken coop just for the hell of it."

She picked up her brush. "You're a devil, nobody doubts that."

Watching the highlights shimmer through her hair in the wake of her brush, he asked, "Why don't we get married, Celia?"

Her hand stopped in midstroke, then she laughed and said, "Don't tempt me, Junior."

"Are you tempted?" he teased.

She finished the stroke and laid down her brush. "If I was looking to be abused by a man half my age, I might be."

"I've never hurt you," he argued.

She picked up a comb and pinned one side of her hair away from her face as she said, "No, you're good to your whores, but I don't think you'd be good to your wife."

"Why not?"

" 'Cause you'd own her. As it is now, all you own is the time you pay for, and if you misbehave, a whore doesn't have to let you back in."

"You're not just another whore, Celia. You've always been my favorite."

"That's good enough for me," she said, pinning the other side of her hair.

"You wouldn't like to be Mrs. Emmett Moss? It'd put you on an even keel with Lily."

"It'd take more'n changing my name to do that." She turned her face back and forth in front of the mirror, touching her cheek as if assessing its texture.

"I don't see why," he said.

"No, you don't see much when you look at her. But I do."

"What do you see?" When she didn't answer, he said, "Tell me, I'm curious."

Celia came back to sip from her glass. "Your mother has backbone every inch of her spine. I've always been quick to fold under a man, but I admire women who walk through life with their heads held high."

"My mother folds herself under Shiloh Pook."

Celia shrugged, carrying her wine to the window again.

"I've been under him a few times myself. It's a nice place to be."

"So what's the dif'rence 'tween you and her?"

"She's had two men and both of 'em gave her good service. I've had hundreds, and I was the one doing the serving."

"Maybe she's had three," Junior said. "I've heard she was in love with Jasper Stone."

"Yeah, she was," Celia said, staring through the icy pane. "But she didn't give herself to him."

"How do you know?"

She laughed, meeting his eyes. " 'Cause unlike you, your father wouldn't have accepted less than a virgin bride."

Junior frowned. "You knew Jasper, too, didn't you."

She nodded, watching out the window again. "He was something to behold. I thought Whit was handsome, but I never saw a more beautiful man than Jasper Stone. Many times I had both of 'em in the bed you're in now, and I felt like the sky 'tween heaven and earth, feeling their love for each other slide through me like a healing rain."

"They loved each other?" Junior asked with scorn.

"Um-hm." Her eyes mocked him. "You ever feel love for anybody, Junior?"

He laughed with sarcasm. "I ain't ever loved a man. How were they in bed?"

"Not as good as you," she said dryly.

He laughed again. "Do you remember any marks on Whit that could identify him no matter how old he got?"

She emptied her glass and came back to set it on the night table. Pulling the covers off Junior, she studied his sex as if she'd never seen it before, then reached down and touched her fingertip to the inside of his left thigh. "He had a scar from a bullet right there." She smiled. "I used to tickle it with my tongue. He got a kick outta that." When Junior frowned, she grinned. "Not the kinda thing a man likes to hear from his wife, is it, Junior?"

"Do it to me," he said.

"You ain't been shot."

"Do to me what you'd do to him if he was here right now."

She laughed. "I'd run out screaming bloody murder that I'd seen a ghost."

He caught hold of her hand and pulled her down beneath him. "Come to Bosque Grande and see one for real."

She shook her head. "If Caleb Thorn *is* Whit Cantrell, the last thing I'd do is betray him."

"I gotta know, Celia. You gotta help me find out."

"I already told you about his scar. All you gotta do is catch him in the bath. If you'd stay home more often, that wouldn't be too hard."

"Come home with me now. I wanta see their faces when you walk in on my arm."

"I ain't gonna do it, Junior."

"I could make you."

"No, you couldn't."

"What if I said I'd never come see you again?"

"I'd miss you."

He smiled. "Let's get married, Celia. I'm twenty-one. I don't need anybody's permission."

"Except mine."

"As my wife, you'd inherit Bosque Grande. Think of that."

"I'd have to share it with Lily."

"Maybe you'll like each other."

"Maybe we won't."

"Why don't you come meet her and find out?"

"It ain't her you want me to meet."

"So we kill two birds with one stone."

She laughed. "I ain't trading your someday title to Bosque Grande for betraying Whit."

He stared at her. "So you do think it's him."

She sighed. "Have you ever just come out and asked him?"

Junior shook his head.

"Why not?"

"I've meant to a coupla times, but when the moment came I couldn't say the words."

"Go home and ask him. If you can be man enough to do that, I'll never call you Junior again."

"Will you marry me?"

She shook her head. "Someday you're gonna want children. I can't give 'em to you."

"I don't care about that."

"Emmett Moss did. He married Lily and killed Jasper and ran Whit outta the country in the int'rest of keeping the Moss name alive on the Panal. If you don't have a son, all that suf'ring will come to naught."

"Maybe it should."

She studied him. "Do you really believe Emmett was wrong?"

Junior closed his eyes, trying to see clearly through the shadows of a legend he'd grown up under. In all his mental meanderings through the intricacies of that legend, not only of Emmett Moss but also Whit Cantrell and Jasper Stone, in all the times both drunk and sober when he'd pondered why he felt so out of sorts with who he was, in the moments he'd been stabbed with a fierce love for Claire that offended propriety, and a resentment of Lily that bore no resemblance to what a son should feel for his mother, through all the anger he'd fought to control, the love that fell where it shouldn't, the quicksand of confusion that sucked at his stride, he'd found only one truth: His life was a lie. He looked at the woman he loved because she'd witnessed his past before it began. Having no explanation for the hell of his life other than that his father was wrong, he answered, "Yes."

Slowly she blinked, her long dark lashes throwing shadows across her cheeks, then rising again to reveal the clear brown of her eyes. "Go home and tell that to the man you think is Whit Cantrell."

"If I do, will you marry me?"

"Come back after and ask me again."

She watched him spring from the bed and dress quickly. The last thing he put on was his gunbelt, buckling the strap around his middle as if it held him together. Taking his hat off the hook by her door, he turned back with a grin and said, "See you tomorrow."

She didn't answer until he was gone, then she said to the empty room, "I doubt it."

He found them all in the formal parlor, a room that hadn't been used in the years between Andy's death and Caleb Thorn's arrival at Bosque Grande. They were drinking eggnog. A punch bowl of the stuff sat on the sideboard, globs of whipped cream floating on top. Junior crossed the room, ignoring their curiosity as he emptied a dipper into a cup. He turned and faced them, noting a sprig of mistletoe had been tacked to the belly of the viga underneath where Andy had hung himself.

Caleb was wearing the charro outfit he'd arrived in, the short black jacket and snug black trousers with silver medallions gleaming in the firelight. He stood in front of the window, and Junior smiled, knowing Caleb had gone there to see who had arrived. Caleb smiled back, but it was a tentative smile, testing the waters.

Claire, as usual, was dressed in white, her frock an ivory-hued wool. Her jewelry was gold and abundant—dangling earrings, a mesh choker, a starburst brooch—and she'd brushed her cheeks with rouge and left her hair down. The blond curls cascading to her waist were only slightly streaked with silver, as if the gray were a dramatic effect she'd deliberately achieved to match the sterling combs above her temples. She was the only woman Junior knew who wore gold and silver at the same time, and he admired the effect. Sitting on the settee facing the window, she was alone, though the two cups on the table in front of her told Junior that Caleb had been there before they'd heard a horse crossing the snow in the yard. Claire had smiled warmly when Junior first came in, but now she kept her gaze on the wide gold bracelet she was nervously twisting on her wrist.

Lily sat on the facing settee, the one between the window where Caleb stood and the blazing fire in the hearth. She wore a dark blue frock that closed high at her throat. Junior's eye was educated enough to see that she wasn't wearing a corset, but then she never had practiced the art of feminine wiles. As always, her hair was wound into a bun at the nape of her neck, and her face was unadorned except for tiny sapphire earrings that caught light. Whenever he saw her wearing a dress instead of her usual leather skirt and bespurred boots, Junior felt surprised at how delicate she was. She watched him now, her expression hovering between pleasure and a wary suspicion of the reason he'd chosen to join them.

Shiloh wore a gray swallowtail coat that Junior knew had

come out of Emmett's closet. Standing in front of the hearth watching the eggnog he swirled in his cup, Shiloh would have cut a patriarchal chord even without the coat. From his earliest memories, Junior had admired his father's top hand, who'd taught him everything he knew about horses and cattle. The lessons hadn't gone beyond those skills to broach what it meant to be a man only because Shiloh had been careful not to overstep his bounds. By the time Junior felt the need of that knowledge, Shiloh's relations with Lily had stopped her son from asking.

Junior glanced down at his own body covered with the rough clothes he habitually wore on the range, then he grinned, remembering he was unbathed from sex. "Sorry I didn't dress up," he said in a mocking tone. "Hope I don't offend the celebration."

"We're glad to have you," Lily said with a smile.

"Soon as I remembered it was Christmas Eve," he answered, "I decided to get outta Celia's bed and come home." When Lily's smile faded to a frown, he looked at Claire and said, "Your beauty puts the stars to shame, Claire."

She looked up in surprise. "Why, thank you, Junior. That's an uncommonly poetic compliment coming from you."

"I ain't Junior anymore," he announced, scanning the eyes suddenly focused on him more intently. "I came of age in September, though no one around here seems to have noticed."

"I baked you a special cake," Lily said. "When you didn't come home, I threw it away."

"If I'd known, I would've come home, but somehow I didn't expect nothing special to happen."

"I always bake a cake on your birthday," she said.

"So what was special about this one?"

She shrugged. "It had a whipped cream frosting."

He chuckled. "I ain't a kid no more who can be satisfied with a bunch of pretty frosting covering up a lotta lies."

Only the snapping of the fire broke the silence until Junior looked at Caleb and said, "Celia asked me to tell you hello."

Caleb glanced at Claire, then looked back at Junior. "Don't think I know the lady."

"I think you do," Junior said, feeling his heart pound. "No, that was a lie. Not what I just said, but what I said before that. Celia didn't ask me to tell you nothing." He shook his head. "I came home to put an end to the lies and here I am spinning more. Reckon it runs in the family."

Caleb smiled in a way that struck at Junior's heart.

"Actually," Junior said, "it was a question she wanted me to ask for her sake." He laughed, feeling himself sweat. "No, that ain't right either." He met Shiloh's eyes. "Damn, this truth business is hard, ain't it?"

Shiloh's smile was forgiving. "Just say it. You're among friends here."

Junior finished his eggnog and set the cup aside, then looked up at the mistletoe. "Is that for Andy? The boy who hung himself outta grief and guilt for what happened to Whit Cantrell?"

"It's for him," Claire said sadly, "but not for that reason."

" 'Cause Whit ain't dead?" Junior asked.

Claire looked at Lily, so he did, too.

"Let's talk about this another time," Lily said. "This is Christmas Eve. Let's enjoy it in peace."

"That ain't our family tradition," he said. "How many years ago was it that my father, in this very room, on this very night, first spoke the lie that started us all down the road to this hell we've been living ever since?" No one answered him. "Or maybe that wasn't the beginning. Maybe it was when you married him though you loved Jasper. Or maybe it started when your father was killed, leaving you without a man to provide for your family, and Emmett Moss fit the bill when Jasper Stone didn't. Or maybe it started even before that, when Whit Cantrell killed Browne Carson for killing Angus Bodie, or maybe when Browne killed Angus, or maybe when Cain killed Abel. How far back do you want to go?" He took a deep breath. "If you take it all the way back, it was a woman's lie that exiled us from the Garden. Ain't that right, Caleb?" Junior finally garnered the courage to look at him.

Caleb shook his head, his eyes warm with an emotion Junior couldn't name.

"Ain't that what you told me your Bible-reading wife in Mexico said about man's fall from grace, that it all started when

Eve lied about what apple she was serving for supper that night?"

"It started with the snake in the grass," Caleb said.

"Oh, yeah, the snake," Junior said. "Wonder if it was a lady or a gentleman snake. What does the Bible say about that?"

"It calls it a he," Caleb said.

Junior nodded and looked at Lily. "Emmett lied, didn't he?"

"Yes," she said.

Junior felt a weight lift off his chest. "Okay. We're getting closer here. Another hundred years and we may get to the truth that matters."

"Which truth?" Lily whispered.

Junior waved his hand in the air. "I didn't really come home tonight to talk about all this. I came to bring glad tidings of joy. Leastways, they would be in any other family. In ours," he shrugged, "I ain't so sure."

"What'd you come home to tell us?" Lily asked.

"You're eager for good news," he said. "There's been a dearth of it, that's for sure." He turned to face the punch bowl, feeling like a coward. "Anyone else want some more holiday cheer?"

"I'll have another cup," Claire answered meekly.

"Well, step right up, darling," he said, scooping the dipper deep in the bowl.

She came close and offered her cup to be filled. He held her eyes while he did it, then asked softly, "Do you know the truth I'm looking for, Claire?"

She shook her head and took a step back, then sipped at the eggnog. "I brought this recipe from Texas. It's part of your heritage, Junior." She stopped herself and gave him a shy smile. "I'm sorry, I meant to say Emmett. You're a man now and deserve that name. This eggnog is one of the genteel customs of the Old South, from which your heritage springs. I'm so glad you're here to share it with us."

"I know you are," he said gently. "Sit down, Claire. I'm afraid what I'm about to say will take your breath inside that corset you're wearing."

She blushed at his mention of her undergarment, but she obeyed him. He watched her do it, feeling tender toward her because she was from the old school, a school Lily couldn't have gained admission to if she'd tried, a school Celia couldn't have applied to because of Whit Cantrell. Junior raised his fresh cup of eggnog high and said, "I'd like to propose a toast to the next Mrs. Emmett Moss."

His words were met with silence. He emptied his cup and set it aside, then grinned. "Her maiden name's Miss Celia Broussard. I'm sure you're all acquainted with her reputation."

"You can't," Lily whispered.

"I'm twenty-one," he said. "There's only one lady who can stop me." He met Caleb's eyes. "She put a condition on her acceptance, though."

"What was it?" Caleb asked lightly.

"She wanted me to ask you a question. If I get satisfaction, she said she'd never call me Junior again." He hesitated, then asked, "What do you think she's gonna call me, Caleb?"

"Being as I don't know the lady," he answered, "I can't guess what she'd call you, but a man's name doesn't change who he is."

Junior looked around at all the faces watching him. "Something happened here a long time ago," he said, striving to keep his voice soft. "I want to know what it was."

Everyone was silent.

Junior met Caleb's eyes and said, "I've tried several times to ask you a question. When I told Celia that, she laughed at me for losing my courage."

"What's the question?" Caleb asked.

Junior opened his mouth but his tongue wouldn't work. He looked at Shiloh. "I can't say it."

"Sure you can," Shiloh coaxed.

Junior looked at Lily. "Maybe I'm trying to ask the wrong person. Maybe you're the only one who can answer me. So I'm asking you: Who was my father?"

"My husband was Emmett Moss," she said. "I knew no other man until long after you were born."

"Oh, you're sneaky," Junior accused. "Why won't you tell me the truth?"

"I can't," she whispered.

"Why not?"

"It concerns more than you," she answered, glancing at

Claire, who sat spinning her gold bracelet, lost in her own private reverie.

Junior watched her, the truth flickering in and out of his mind like the shine fluttering off her bracelet. The baby whose death preceded Claire being committed to an asylum, and the baby buried on the hill whose mother wasn't the same woman. The son conceived within a marriage without love, and the son conceived in a love without marriage. The boy called Junior long after his father had died because his name had never been Emmett. His name was the one etched on the tombstone on the hill. That boy looked at his father and said, "In a way, Celia answered my question a long time ago, but I didn't put it together till now."

"What'd she say?" Caleb asked.

"She said my father made her a whore. Is that the truth?"

Caleb nodded.

Junior's legs folded beneath him. He sat on the floor and held his head in his hands as the world whirled around him, the faces he couldn't see in the darkness of his confusion, the hurt and the glory that sucked at his breath while he felt himself sink in the quicksand shifting beneath him every time he tried to find solid ground.

Into that bog Claire threw a rope when she asked in a baffled voice, "Why are you sitting on the floor, Emmett? You'll soil your trousers."

He raised his head and met her eyes. She nodded, encouraging him to get up. He laughed, gaining his feet. "I'm sorry, Claire. You're right. It was unseemly of me and inconsiderate of my mother," he paused to smile at Lily, "who's worked so hard to make me respectable." Lily smiled back. "I want you all," he said, meeting Caleb's eyes, "to disregard any impropriety I've mentioned. Reckon I had too much holiday cheer."

Caleb grinned. "We've all been there."

Junior scarcely had time to share the naughty innuendo before Lily came over and gave him a hug. He held her close with gratitude when she murmured, "Thank you, Emmett, for coming home tonight."